GALLANT KNIGHT

Geoffrey swooped low to claim Juliette's lips with his.

He'd kissed her once before, that first night, with the starved desperation of one human being reaching out to another, as if to validate that he lived. This kiss, so demanding, so assured, indicated to her that something about the man had changed.

Or had something about herself changed?

Could this really be the Widow Walburn, tough and independent, determined to never again indulge in sinful passions, clutching tightly to a man's shirtfront on the open prairie, drinking in his kiss?

"Juliette, lovely Juliette," Geoffrey murmured, banishing all worries straight from her mind.

He bent her backwards, shaping her body against his while his lips and tongue ravished her with gentle thoroughness. Then, quite literally, he swept her off her feet.

"A remarkably delightful tale of love, brimming with warm, appealing characters, daring adventure, and sexual tension."

—*Rendezvous*

Books by Donna Valentino

Conquered by His Kiss
Mirage
Prairie Knight

Available from HarperPaperbacks

Prairie Knight

✧ DONNA VALENTINO ✧

HarperPaperbacks
A Division of HarperCollins Publishers

For my agent, Cherry Weiner, whose support
and encouragement never waver

And for Sir Joseph,
who has never failed his lady

HarperPaperbacks   *A Division of* HarperCollins*Publishers*
10 East 53rd Street, New York, N.Y. 10022

Cover illustration by Bob Berran

First printing: May 1995

Printed in the United States of America

HarperPaperbacks, HarperMonogram, and colophon are
trademarks of HarperCollins*Publishers*

❖ 10 9 8 7 6 5 4 3 2 1

Prologue

Northwest England, 1283

    Geoffrey d'Arbanville bent low over Arion's surging neck, shouting encouragement that he doubted the stallion could hear over its own labored breathing and thundering hooves. Geoffrey knew that no steed possessed a greater heart; no knight could boast a stronger sword arm. But one man and one horse, no matter how valiant, could not stand against the murderous horde chasing them to the ground, and so they must run.

He risked a quick backward glance and cursed. Drogo FitzBaldric and his men had gained a full hundred yards on the tiring Arion. The barren countryside offered no shelter, no possibility for hiding, save for the cluster of ancient mist-shrouded oaks Geoffrey had hoped to avoid. It was said no man could pass beneath that leafy canopy and live. It was said no beast, save God's twittering birds, dared enter that sacred grove. It was said that the oaks rimmed a yawning chasm, a precipice so steep that any man who stumbled into it would spend all eternity falling, falling, neither living nor dead.

Superstitious nonsense. Geoffrey urged his warhorse toward the oak trees. The crude Celtic pendant he wore bumped against his throat in time to Arion's pounding strides. It was the symbol of Angus Ōg, an obscure Celtic god said to restore life to those who relinquished their last breath in the cause of love. King Edward, his own liege lord, had assured him that the pendant would keep him safe. It would permit Geoffrey to take shelter in places such as this sacred oak grove; it would lend him the aura of Celtic magic should one of the king's enemies threaten him while Geoffrey was engaged in delivering the pendant.

It would condemn him to excommunication and eternal hellfire should a churchman chance to see the pagan deity dangling round his neck. Geoffrey knew the rest was naught but legends and fancies.

Arion's stride faltered at the grove's first overhanging branches, and nearly came to a standstill. Reluctance to enter the haunted copse? Or good horse sense, considering that the gnarled roots protruding from the ground posed hazardous footing? Geoffrey could not credit a horse with subscribing to superstition, and indeed the well-trained destrier continued on in response to the pressure of Geoffrey's leg. Two enormous age-twisted trees guarded the entrance to the grove like branched sentinels whose bark and leaves seemed to conspire to shut out all sound as Geoffrey passed between, almost as though two huge invisible doors had swung shut behind him. He could hear nothing save Arion's nervous snorting, his own pulsating heartbeat. Not the twittering birds he had been told populated the grove. Not even the sound of the traitor Drogo's pursuit.

Could there be any truth to the pagan lore surrounding this grove, this pendant? The Celtic relic lay hot against his skin, tempting him for a moment to cast aside his true Christian beliefs. Only for a moment. For no sooner had Arion's ears pricked with interest over the strange surroundings, and Geoffrey's own attention swung to the cool dark sanctuary, than the trees shivered with the force of Drogo's violation of the quiet.

So much for the vague hope that the pendant would indeed bestow upon its wearer some aura of Celtic magic.

Arion sprang into a full run, as full as the confining horse armor permitted. Once again Geoffrey crouched close over the steed's neck. It seemed they traveled no distance at all when Arion skidded to a rearing halt, his frightened scream echoing to the heavens. The horse's forelegs pawed at nothing, for the destrier had barely halted in time to keep them both from plunging into an obscene gash marring the earth.

The Eternal Chasm. Geoffrey soothed Arion as they backed away, hoping the horse would not sense his dismay over the steep walls carved through earthbound rock that seemed to plunge straight toward hell.

He drew his sword as he spun Arion around, sensing that they hadn't enough time to seek another path for escape, and, indeed, found his way already blocked. Drogo and a score of his men formed a loose semicircle, their pinched eager faces, their white-knuckled grips upon their tightly clasped weapons, telling Geoffrey without words that he would not leave this oak grove alive. Geoffrey's breath rasped harsh against his ears, seeming to scour iron filings from his inner helm, as if desperate to make these last few earthly breaths heard.

Drogo heard; his cruel thin lips curved into a malicious sneer. "So, good fellows, we have trapped ourselves a *knight*."

"Trapping me will not convey the title to you," Geoffrey said, knowing Drogo's festering resentment that King Edward continually refused to honor him with knighthood.

Drogo's sneer vanished as his lips compressed into a thin line. "You and your precious king will pay for your insults."

Drogo's eyes—one brown, one blue—marked him as the son of a whore who had lain with two men. Geoffrey had always found meeting Drogo's gaze disconcerting, since his own hazel-colored gaze seemed unable to decide whether to settle on Drogo's light or dark eye. There was no such difficulty now. Triumph dyed both of Drogo's eyes with the same feverish intensity.

"Give over the relic," Drogo ordered, holding out his hand.

Geoffrey wrenched off his helm and balanced it over his saddle horn. He cupped a hand over his ear. "Say again?"

"The relic. I will have it now."

"Aha. I wanted to make certain I heard you correctly." Aiming carefully, Geoffrey spat into Drogo's outstretched palm.

Drogo's men roared their outrage over this insult to their leader. One flung a rock which found its target against Geoffrey's now-unprotected forehead, drawing blood which trickled annoyingly from Geoffrey's skull, blurring the vision in his left eye. It did not stop him from seeing, though, that when the horde pressed close, it forced Arion to yield a precious step back toward the Chasm.

"Give over the relic," Drogo repeated. "*I* will be the one to carry it to Demeter at Rowanwood Castle."

Geoffrey touched his glove against his throat, feeling the pendant pressing against his skin.

The ancient relic belonged to the rebellious border lord John of Rowanwood, husband to Demeter. One of Geoffrey's fellow mercenary knights had kidnapped Rowanwood during a hunt and turned him over to Edward for ransom. A stint spent moldering in King Edward's dungeons had mellowed Rowanwood's rebellious nature, particularly after the king threatened to lay siege to Rowanwood Castle, starving out his lady wife and devastating the surrounding lands.

"I could not bear for my beloved wife Demeter to suffer," Rowanwood had begged the king, pleading to surrender. "Take this pendant to her. This symbol of Angus Ōg will convince her I am willing to sacrifice everything for the sake of our great love. She will recognize it as my sign to cease holding the castle against you, and we will accept you as our liege in exchange for your mercy."

The king, amused to think that marriage-lust would eradicate one of his nagging border problems, had charged Geoffrey with delivering the pendant and accepting Demeter's homage. Should Demeter fail to submit as her husband had sworn, Edward himself would behead her husband and then besiege Rowanwood Castle, laying waste to the surrounding countryside.

Drogo FitzBaldric's treacherous intervention could destroy the delicate negotiations before they had even begun.

"Plague me another time, FitzBaldric. There is too much at stake just now to waste time disposing of the likes of you."

"Aye, the stakes boggle my very wits, d'Arbanville. Once you yield that pendant to me, Demeter will throw open the doors to welcome me into her stronghold, thinking I bring news from her husband. She might

resent it a bit when I enslave her, but I will do my best
to see she grows accustomed to my attentions. You see,
once her husband dies at Edward's hand, I will force her
into marriage and claim all of Rowanwood as my own."

Drogo's loathsome leer lent an added stench to his
treason. Geoffrey shifted his grip to throw his sword
like a dagger, but stilled his hand with a growl of frustration when Drogo's men advanced an ominous step.

"You care nothing for the devastation this would
spawn."

"I care only that the mighty Geoffrey d'Arbanville
will have personally relinquished to me the means to
place Rowanwood Castle under my control. And this
countryside has never witnessed devastation such as I
will wreak from my border stronghold. Edward will
regret every insult, every slur against me, until he begs
for the mercy of death to relieve him of his humiliation."

"I will die myself ere I lose the relic to one whose
baseborn belly crawls lower than that of worms."

"A wasted sacrifice. Lacking the pendant I will
merely besiege the lady's castle. Soon enough she will
grow thirst-maddened and starving." Drogo made a
lewd gesture toward his privates. "She will beg for the
release only I can give her."

The knave's lecherous intent sickened Geoffrey. He
dashed the trickling blood from his forehead and spat-
tered it in Drogo's direction. He jammed his helm back
in place, knowing the motion would signify his intention to fight to the death.

"Edward will grow tired of waiting for my return.
He will suspect Demeter has not honored her husband's wishes. He will march against Rowanwood and
catch you at your traitor's work."

Drogo brightened. "Why, thank you for explaining
the king's strategy to me, d'Arbanville. I would not

have thought to keep close watch on my rear flanks and devise a trap for him. Since his royal arrogance will not be expecting to encounter me along the way, he should make easy prey."

"You know how the king stages his battles as well as I, FitzBaldric. Leave off accusing me of spilling strategy."

"But you see how simple it could be, d'Arbanville, to join forces with me and save yourself? You would find me a generous liege—far more generous, I daresay, than stingy Edward. Or mayhap he has finally granted you that title and estate you have always pined for, hmm?"

Geoffrey did not even try to conceal his loathing. "Edward was right to deny you your spurs. A howling jackal boasts more honor than you."

"Ah yes, I never could manage to acquire your most proper knightly attitude." Drogo's contemptuous glance shifted to Geoffrey's back, reminding him how uncomfortably close Arion stood to the Chasm's edge. Drogo's gaze shifted again, drawing Geoffrey's along in an examination of the twenty fully armed men who stared at him with hate and a lust for violence. "I suppose we should all be cringing in our boots, now that we are faced with your knightly determination." A muffled sound accompanied a quick hitching motion of Drogo's shoulder, and then the knave's lips parted with full-throated laughter.

One by one, the armed men took up the merriment until the sacred grove rang with their mocking glee. Drogo wheezed when his shoulder-shaking mirth subsided enough to permit him to speak. "Your bold posturing matters naught, d'Arbanville. Nor should you harbor any hope that my siege might fail. So much effort will not be necessary. Demeter shall fling her gates open for me. You cannot best us all. Already you bleed. Take your stand against me knowing this, d'Arbanville: I will have the relic once you are dead. I myself will pry it from your cold dead fingers."

He motioned to one of his men, evidently tiring of his sport now that victory seemed assured. "Run him through."

Geoffrey had fought against five men and prevailed, against ten men and hacked his way to a draw. Against twenty plus Drogo he stood no chance. Nonetheless he could wreak considerable carnage before falling to the superior force. He set his sword and Arion quivered beneath him, sensing the battle to come, when Drogo's words echoed in Geoffrey's mind.

I will have the relic once you are dead.

Depressing enough, to realize that he faced humiliating defeat at the hands of outlaw scum hooting with laughter. It seemed a cruel jest that the relic signifying eternal love would instead lead to rape, execution, widowhood, and widespread slaughter, even though Geoffrey fully intended to perform the ultimate sacrifice a knight could make for his liege.

He had always known he would die young. But perhaps . . . perhaps he could spare the lady.

Bellowing a war cry last uttered in the Holy Land, Geoffrey twirled his sword above his head in a whistling circle before sheathing it snugly in its scabbard. He dug through his chain-mail cowl to his gambeson and ripped the Celtic relic free. He raised it high in benediction.

And then, before Drogo's incredulous disbelieving eyes, Geoffrey swung Arion around and plunged them both into the Eternal Chasm.

He held the relic aloft, hoping the sunlight would glint off its dull pewter surface, mocking Drogo's ambitions as the relic forevermore fell beyond his reach. Drogo could yet besiege Rowanwood Castle, but with luck the lady could hold out long enough to spare herself the indignities Drogo meant to inflict. With luck Edward would not fall into Drogo's trap and some of the devastation could be averted.

Luck. No knight worth his spurs entrusted important matters to luck. It was unfortunate that the Celtic pendant did not confer the promised magic.

"I swear this," Geoffrey bellowed, wishing with all his heart that it could be more than a hollow vow, "I will find some means to return and claim vengeance upon you, Drogo FitzBaldric!"

Geoffrey's solemn oath echoed off the endless walls of stone as he soared with his stallion toward certain death.

Strange that at such a moment he would wonder what Angus Ōg thought of one insignificant knight's sacrifice on behalf of a doomed couple's love.

1

Juliette Walburn's first glimpse of the buffalo herd came framed between her gee mule's bobbing ears.

She doubted the close-packed passengers sitting behind her in the wagon bed could see, so she urged the straining mules on for another few hundred feet before setting the brake. "There they are, Alma," Juliette called quietly to the schoolteacher who'd helped organize the excursion.

"Look sharp, children," Alma urged. "It's like Miss Jay said—someday you'll be able to tell your grandchildren that you saw buffalo near Walburn Ford."

"I see 'em! I see 'em!" piped a young girl, struggling to escape Alma Harkins's restraining arms.

"Keep your voices down and stay in the wagon," Juliette cautioned. The women and children she had hauled to this spot sat packed like poorly stacked cordwood, and she feared that removing even one of them would send them all tumbling to the ground.

"We can't scarcely see them old buffaloes from way back here, Miss Jay," Robbie Wilcox protested.

"Don't you sass Miss Jay," his mother admonished.

"We promised your pa we wouldn't ride too close if we found buffalo. Now, all of you stay in the wagon. We have to sneak up on them kind of quietlike, a little at a time." Juliette secured the reins and then stood and shaded her eyes, the wagon lending her height as she peered across the undulating prairie.

Dozens of buffalo bent huge shaggy heads toward the sun-dried grass. Even from this distance their bulk cast ominous shadows; their muffled snorts and low bawls vibrated the air.

"My son Herman will be mighty put out with me," Mrs. Abbott fussed. "He's always after me to visit him out West. Wait until he hears a wagonload of us women and children rode out here by ourselves to see buffalo. I just know he'll say to me, 'Mama, why did you risk your life? If only you'd come out here to live with me I could offer you the protection of the entire Army Corps of Topographical Engineers.'"

Juliette stifled a sigh, but she might as well have let it out, considering the rousing chorus of groans that rose from her passengers. Alma must have concurred, for she didn't bother chastising the children. Mrs. Abbott's continual references to her illustrious son wore down a body's tolerance sooner or later. Since they'd all spent the best part of a hot sun-baked morning riding out to see this herd, everyone's patience with Mrs. Abbott's boasting was even more quickly exhausted.

"I'll take us a little closer." Juliette decided they all deserved a little reward, and though one old bull had issued a warning snort in their direction, the herd grazed on peacefully, not objecting to their presence.

But before she had completely lowered herself back onto the seat, the sky suddenly roiled black and then exploded in a dazzling burst of lightning.

A child whimpered. Low rumblings shook the air, increasing in volume until it sounded as though the very heavens were ripping apart along invisible seams. The child's whimper escalated into terrified shrieks, but when she turned to comfort the crying babe, Juliette found herself thrown off balance; jarred from her perch, she landed hard on her bottom alongside the wagon. The impact knocked the breath from her, sent her bonnet flying off, loosened her hair from its lightly pinned chignon.

Through a dim haze she saw her well-trained mules lay back their ears and heard them bray in fright. Juliette had endured a hundred Kansas prairie storms, but never one of such sudden and short-lived violence. The wagon quaked; children screamed and clutched at one another, the women adding their shrieking terror to the din.

Robbie shouted to Juliette. "It's Injuns, Miss Jay! And they spooked the buffaloes!"

A few dozen buffalo couldn't possibly shake the earth and darken the sky—but their sharp hooves, their gouging horns, could maim and kill. She couldn't permit such disaster to strike these young members of the Walburn Ford community. Juliette shook off her pain-clouded confusion and scrambled to her feet, working her way to the heads of the plunging kicking mules, knowing only that she must somehow guide the terrified women and children to safety.

A quick desperate glance toward the buffalo herd nearly sent her swooning with relief. The bellowing animals were racing on a westerly trajectory that would carry them well away from the wagon. What a strange cloudburst! No rain had fallen, and yet the thunder-clouds that had startled the buffalo had dissipated like morning mist, leaving a benevolent sun shining down as if nothing had interrupted the day.

Rubbing her aching posterior, Juliette had no time to ponder the wildly fluctuating weather. Robbie's keen eyesight had indeed spotted the cause of the stampede: five mounted Indian men rode alongside the raging beasts, their skillful mastery of their ponies enabling them to cut a few buffalo away from the main bulk of the herd. Excitement coursed through her, replacing the trembling that had set in after her hard fall.

"Watch, everyone!" Alma ordered. "You might never have the chance to see anything like this ever again."

Some of the children continued crying. Mrs. Abbott appeared to have fallen into a dead faint, leaving Alma Harkins and two other women to soothe the young ones and describe what was happening. Juliette knew she should help calm the children but found herself incapable of joining them. No matter how hard or how often she'd tried to curb her frivolous impulses, her impetuous inclinations, they kept springing up at times like this to hold her spellbound, urging her to abandon common sense for the excitement of the unknown.

She should have been well accustomed by now to watching man conquer beast, should have felt noth-ing but relief witnessing nature prove its mastery over humanity only to relent and allow benevolent sunlight to drive away the cloudburst. No woman could lose her parents, her husband, and still possess an all-but-unquenchable expectation that something magical would happen to her someday. A child, or a half-grown girl, might be excused for flights of fancy. Not a respectable widow.

She welcomed the flickering motion at the corner of her eye that drew her attention away from the Indians and her wistful thoughts. For a moment the sight that greeted her looked so improbable that she thought her brain might have been jarred by her fall. She shook her head, and then gathered her hair away from her eyes, but the fantasy image remained.

A man sat on the prairie. He gleamed as if molten silver had been poured over his arms and legs. He bent low, hunched over his knees, clutching his metal head between his hands. Next to him swayed a four-legged creature; the way the tail streamed down behind and the ears stood up on its head marked it as a horse, but it was clad in an outlandish *skirt,* a match to the loose tunic the man wore over his shiny parts. It all had to be a trick of the light reflected from the sun, which seemed determined to shine even brighter now that the miniature cloudburst had ended.

She might have turned back to watch the Indians, might have ignored such an outrageous hallucination entirely, except for the enraged buffalo cow that bellowed mournfully over the still body of a calf. The beast suddenly cut away from the herd; it appeared to have caught sight of Juliette's impossible vision and raced toward it with lowered head as if it meant to wreak vengeance for the attack upon its young.

The metal man and skirted horse seemed oblivious to the danger. The buffalo would be upon them in moments. Its powerful hooves tore clods of turf from the prairie as it ran; it seemed to Juliette that the beast's mean eyes glowed with malevolent delight, that it cocked its horns from side to side in anticipation of burying them in the apparition's soft unwary flesh.

Whether they were dream-conjured phantoms or not, Juliette couldn't allow the horse and man to be destroyed.

"Get on back, you stupid cow!" she found herself hollering. Heedless of her neighbors' protesting cries, she ran straight at the bereaved bison, her hair and arms and Bloomer skirt all flapping wildly, wishing she'd brought her shotgun along and praying buffalo were as easy to spook off course as cattle.

Geoffrey longed to remove his helm. Surely such pain could not stem from the cut inflicted by the rock Drogo's man had flung at him. And yet he hesitated to inspect the source of pain, half afraid that removing the confining metal would permit his skull to burst open spilling out all his brains, so poundingly did his head ache. He eased his helm off and his head stayed whole, so he tempted fate a bit more by pushing his metal coif back and tearing the thin leather helm cap away from his hair. He groaned, and then had to clench his throat to keep from retching; his gullet had turned so sour that his belly complained as if he'd last feasted upon rotted flesh rather than King Edward's sumptuous banquet fare.

Arion wheezed beside him, spraddle-legged and more exhausted than if Geoffrey had ridden him throughout an entire day of tourney. "'Twas a fearsome leap, old friend, well made," Geoffrey meant to say, but his stiff lips wouldn't bend around the words. It took an uncommon amount of effort to lift his arm and place a comforting hand against his steed's trembling foreleg. His throat tightened with silent gratitude.

They had lived. They'd braved the Eternal Chasm and lived. Good solid earth provided a seat for his backside; God's own sun beat hot upon his sweaty bleeding head. Only then did Geoffrey realize he clutched the relic of Angus Ōg so tightly it had all but imbedded itself in his palm.

It seemed beyond his abilities to loosen his grip from around the relic, but he forced his fingers to obey, forced his lips to curve. No smile had ever been harder to fashion, or struck sweeter, than the one quirking his lips now at the memory of Drogo FitzBaldric's impotent outrage at seeing the relic fall beyond his reach. Despite this happy vision, Geoffrey winced at the jolting pain that greeted his slightest movements, at the thundering sensation that seemed to shake the very earth he sat upon. He grimaced, screwing his eyes shut tight against the sun's overbright glare, but the thundering intensified.

He risked opening one eye the narrowest measure, and then found himself powerless to prevent both eyes from boggling wide. It was no leap-induced shaking that drummed the ground—he and Arion must have landed deep in the bowels of hell, for demons were besetting them from three sides.

From the front surged Satan's own creature, a bearded cloven-hoofed humpbacked beast crowned with its master's curving horns.

From his right raced a mounted bowman—a Mongol, to judge by the shape of his eyes and set of his nose, though the color of his skin was wrong, its yellow cast burned red-brown from its exposure to hellfire. The Mongol's skull was very nearly hairless, save for a fist-sized clump springing from the back of his head and streaming down like the tail of a horse, and caked with a thin mud the most vibrant shade of scarlet. Thin streaks of the same scarlet mud patterned his skin; otherwise he rode all but naked, mastering his barebacked steed with unearthly skill.

Most frightening of all, a wild-haired witch flew at them from the left. Clothed in outrageous garb none but a devil-sent sorceress would dare wear, she sped toward him, her hands clawing at the air as if she meant to bend the sun's strength to the incomprehensible spells she shrieked as she ran.

If he *were* dead and in hell, the demons could do him no greater harm than welcome him to their infernal abode. But something within Geoffrey d'Arbanville scorned sitting complacently while demons, harmful or otherwise, raged unchecked. Cursing the weakness that turned his bones as treacherous as worm-riddled roof planks, he managed to clutch Arion's horse armor and haul himself to unsteady feet. He tried to don his helm but couldn't manage to lift it, so he kept it tucked under his arm where it clanged against the shield strapped to his back. It took him three tries to force Angus Ōg's relic past the neckline of his cowl to lay safe against his breast—he'd be damned if he'd lose it now! He grasped at his sword hilt a dozen times without mustering enough strength to draw it free.

Satan's beast was nearly upon him, so close Geoffrey could smell its quite ordinary bovine scent, not at all the charred brimstone odor he expected. Arion's eyes rolled with fear and he issued a weak terror-stricken whinny unlike the steed's usual sharp challenge. The Mongol drew forth a primitive bow and sent an arrow sizzling straight across the devil-beast's leathery nose. It came to a plunging snorting halt, and then fixed its reddened eyes upon Geoffrey before pawing the earth, obviously intending to run him through. And then it caught sight of the shrieking witch, casting her spells while her gown billowed about her waist like a miniature thundercloud. Tucking its supple, serpent-headed tail between its legs, the satanic creature wheeled about and ran for its life.

As should I, Geoffrey thought when the witch raised a tentative hand to salute the Mongol. The warrior hefted his bow in response and its horse carried them after the departing beast with no apparent instruction from the Mongol—leaving Geoffrey alone to face the Medusa-haired witch while the ground shivered and shook beneath him. Truth to tell, Drogo FitzBaldric suddenly seemed a less-daunting foe.

"Who are you?"

Geoffrey blinked, certain his senses had gone awry. The witch's words, indecipherable, nonetheless soothed his aching head with their gentle tones. Up close, her hair seemed less wild than . . . streaming, a thick wealth of silken brown curls lifting gently in the breeze.

"Your forehead's bleeding. Are you all right?"

Her lips curved sweetly as she spoke. A tiny pucker of concern formed between her brows, which arched over wide lustrous eyes. Blue eyes, reflecting excitement and curiosity. Geoffrey had always heard that witch's eyes were black and dull as lava rock, murky pits meant to swallow men's souls. They would indeed do better to lay claim to blue eyes, like this one's, for he felt an uncommon urge to let himself drown in their azure depths. He let go his sword hilt just long enough to cross himself against the unholy thought.

"Are you all right?" she said again, reaching toward his injury. He backed away, unwilling to accept a witch's touch. She stuffed her hand into the folds of her gown. "What's your name? You might have been killed."

He memorized her words and tested them against the dozens of tongues he'd learned over a lifetime of knighting for hire. He'd always possessed a ready wit for tongues, much as others showed talent for plucking a once-heard tune upon lute strings, or for spouting a bard's complicated tale word for word. It was a handy skill for one in his profession, considering the variety of masters he'd hired out his skills to over the years. This witch certainly didn't speak his native French. Nor Italian nor Greek.

Though harsh, her words lacked the guttural German inflection. There was something about the rhythm and cadence that struck him as familiar. English? Of course. The Eternal Chasm rent apart English lands, after all.

"Your poor horse." She slanted a glance toward Arion.

Hors. He mouthed the word, feeling it roll over his tongue. English—an exceptionally crude version of that barbaric peasant tongue, to be sure, but a simple enough variation to master for one who had spent years in service to the English king. He should have recognized the tongue sooner, considering how many years he'd spent hankering after his father's English estates.

A horde of children scampered toward her and arrayed themselves about her, using her as a sort of living shield, clutching the folds of her ridiculous gown with dirty fingers. Had she mothered the lot of them? Her unlined face revealed nothing of a mother's strain. Of her form he could make out only the proud curve of her breasts—unlikely that they would thrust so had they suckled such a litter—and the narrow curve of her waist. From there down her gown belled to her knees in such a strange fashion over a set of baggy chausses that he couldn't tell whether the rest of her lived up to the slim promise of her upper reaches. He'd never seen any female, witch or woman, dressed in such a foolish fashion.

The children's prattling intruded upon his thoughts, and although their words sounded little better than a crow's cackle, he concentrated, confident of his ability to comprehend as soon as he sorted out their rude pronunciations. "Who is he, Miss Jay? What's he doing here? Why's he dressed so funny? What's that dress doing on his horse?"

"*Ho . . . hors,*" Geoffrey whispered, the word striking harsh against a throat that felt so dry and disused an eternity might have passed since last he'd spoken.

"You children get back and stay with Miss Harkins. Robbie, fetch our water bottle from the wagon bed." At the witch's command, a youth disengaged himself from the reluctantly dispersing crowd and hurtled back toward an oversized cart.

The witch cast an assessing eye over Arion and Geoffrey, and he suddenly remembered that he stood clutching his sword hilt with his battle helm tucked under his arm. Most *men* would hesitate to accost a fully armed knight. Yet this witch, not knowing that his muscles had gone limp as bread dough, took a deep breath and boldly approached him. Her head came no higher than the pit of his arm, her slender width was less than half his own, and yet she faced him with the courage of a fellow knight.

She reached toward him, entrancingly hesitant yet determined. "Your horse needs some water," she said. She set her heels and tugged at his helm. "Give me that bucket."

Concern for the horse held Juliette rooted in place when all of her instincts urged her to load the women and children back into the wagon and run. Good Lord, the stranger could be a border ruffian, and here she'd gone and saved him!

The stranger towered over her. Perhaps the odd garments he wore contributed to the sensation of overwhelming power held tightly checked. Tiny metal rings, all intertwined and riveted together, formed a clinking suit of clothes garbing him from neck to ankle. A light woolen sleeveless tunic of pale blue hung over the metal suit and was belted in darker blue around his waist. Lustrous silk embroidery across his chest depicted a fierce midnight blue hawk attacking a snarling golden lion; the skirt his horse wore sported the same colors and fanciful design. He had some sort of wooden shield slung over his back, and little squares of metal tied atop his shoulders, all embellished with matching hawk-and-lion pattern.

His shoulder-length chestnut-colored hair hung damp against his skull, darker where it had absorbed blood from a nasty gash at his hairline. Except for the blood, he looked as if he'd spent the day doing his plowing in that ridiculous getup. His blood-soaked hair clung against a sort of cowl that he'd pushed off his head, drawing her attention to the taut-muscled column of his neck and a few dark brown curls peeping over the edge of his neckline.

He relaxed his arm to permit her to remove the bucket, and she could see the metal links bulge where his muscles flexed. She should run, she knew, before he turned those metal-bending muscles toward the sword tucked in his waist belt, but concern for the horse held her still. Concern for the horse, and nothing whatsoever to do with the pain-wracked bewilderment clouding the stranger's hazel eyes.

"Horse." He repeated the single word as if he knew no other.

"I'll water the horse. And we'll pull up some grass for him if he's too tired to graze," Juliette promised, but none of the confusion faded from his eyes.

"Here's the water, Miss Jay!" Robbie puffed to a halt next to her. Juliette held the stranger's bucket by its cumbersome handles and lifted the hinged covering, wondering why anyone would have bothered to make a lid that didn't close all the way. Robbie tilted the water bottle toward it, when the stranger took an ominous step toward them.

"Nay!"

His deep voice sounded the unmistakable note of command. Robbie reacted to the sound of authority and righted the bottle before any water spilled into the bucket.

"Neigh?" Juliette repeated. It seemed the man knew only horse-related words.

His face lit up with a smile. Tiny crinkles formed around his deep-set eyes, and the taut wary planes of his face relaxed. Even the dark shadow of his incipient beard seemed to lighten, and something within Juliette's breast quivered in response.

She watched, spellbound, clutching the bucket to her chest, while he dropped to one knee and sketched an elaborate pantomime. He touched his head, wincing when he accidentally grazed his wound. He pointed to the bucket, mimicked the act of pouring water into it, and shook his head violently from side to side. He made loud groaning scrubbing motions, twisting and rubbing an imaginary rag with great force, before holding an invisible bucket to the sky, peering into it, and then clapping both hands to the top of his head.

Juliette stared uncomprehending but nonetheless intrigued, absurdly wishing he'd continue the pantomime so she could watch his compelling movements a little longer.

"I think he wants to use the water to wash the blood out of his hair, Miss Jay," Robbie interpreted, drawing Juliette's attention back from the whimsical place it had gone.

"Well, that's just plain silly. Water's not so scarce we can't spare enough for man and horse both." She held the bucket back toward Robbie. "Pour the water."

The stranger's broad shoulders sagged and he shook his head in defeat.

And well he might. The durned bucket leaked at every seam, and if that was what he'd been trying to warn her about, he'd done a poor job of it. Juliette had to lope a few steps in a rather unladylike fashion to reach the horse before all the water was lost. The exhausted beast gave a surprised-sounding sniff, but eagerly plunged its nose into the liquid.

She felt a cool shadow step between her and the burning sun at her back and knew the stranger had come to stand behind her. Her skin prickled, but not with fear—it was as though a sudden sense of anticipation leaped to life within her. He reached for the bucket, his metal-gloved hand brushing against hers as he took over the watering of his horse.

Except for that accidental feather-light touch, he made no effort to touch her or restrain her, but she found herself powerless to step away, felt tendrils of heat waft from his body to wrap themselves around her like the silken threads of embroidery adorning his costume.

Once the horse slurped up the last bit of water, the stranger tipped the bucket over and wiped the inside with the edge of his tunic, shaking his head ruefully at the light smears of rust staining the soft blue cloth.

"Miss Jay! Miss Jay! The buffaloes are all gone!"

Buffaloes? Gracious, she'd forgotten all about the purely educational purpose of this excursion. Mortified at how easily she'd forgotten her responsibilities, Juliette glanced toward the wagon and saw that Alma had turned the children over to one of the mothers and was striding toward them now.

Robbie stared up at her with a woebegone expression, and she tousled his hair. "Another herd might come someday."

"It's *his* fault." Robbie bent an accusing glare at the stranger.

"Robbie," Juliette chided. "Anything could have spooked those buffalo. We might have done it ourselves, or the Indians, or that cloudburst. . . ."

Her voice trailed off, the cloudless sky, the glaring sun showing no trace of the roiling blackness and sudden thunderous flash of light that had knocked her from the wagon onto her backside just before the stranger appeared.

"Where'd he come from anyway?" Robbie demanded, and then his belligerent tone softened into hopefulness. "Maybe he's the one my pa's been waitin' for. He promised Ma that someday someone from the Vegetarian Settlement Company would come to make up for the money folks lost."

The Wilcoxes, like many others, had journeyed to Kansas as members of the Vegetarian Settlement Company. These vegetarian settlers had pooled all their worldly resources with the goal of creating a paradise on Earth; instead, the Company's officials ran off with all the money.

Nothing had been built in Octagon City, as their town was called, except for a drafty meeting hall. Many of the disillusioned settlers returned East. But some, like the Wilcoxes, refused to admit total defeat and took up homesteading in nearby Kansas communities. All had grown bitter, and some, it was whispered, had gone mad at the realization that they'd lost everything. Maybe this bewildered-looking stranger did have something to do with the vegetarian community . . .

"He's not a vegetarian," Alma called out, dousing Juliette's hopes that the man might be something other than a border ruffian. The teacher sounded nearly breathless from crossing the prairie. "Men don't grow that big without being meat-fed. Oh my, look at his head bleed."

"He wouldn't let me examine it."

Alma didn't seem overly concerned. "Miss Jay, I do think he's dressed up like a knight!" The schoolteacher turned her attention to Robbie. "You remember what we learned in class about silent k's, don't you young man?"

"Yeah. I mean, yes, Miss Harkins. Knight. K-n-i-g-h-t—sounds like 'night' but looks like 'kuh-nigget.'"

The stranger's head swiveled abruptly at Robbie's dutiful response. His deep voice boomed an interruption. "K-n-i-g-h-t?" His lips moved, silently testing each letter again, and then understanding dawned over his expression. "Kuh-nigget. *Kneht?* Knight?" Upon Alma's tentative nod, delight radiated from him as he pounded his gloved fist against his breast, the metal rings clinking, his chest thumping like a kettledrum. His voice reverberated, as if speaking a new word gave it new life. "Kneht . . . knight!"

"Oh, Miss Jay, just look at him!" Alma sighed and all but swooned as the stranger flexed powerful biceps and clapped a hand over his animal's neck.

"*Hors* . . . horse!" He kicked at the prairie turf. "*Gras* . . . grass!" He copied Juliette's earlier motion and rubbed his metal-gloved hand over Robbie's hair. "*Boi cild!*"

"Boy child," Alma corrected his oddly inflected accent in her schoolmarmish tone. He echoed the words perfectly, and she beamed upon the stranger, looking as proud as any teacher upon witnessing her most backward student parse his first difficult sentence.

"Alma, I've never heard anything so ridiculous," Juliette protested. "There aren't such things as knights anymore. And even if there were, what would one be doing in Kansas Territory?"

"Well, I'm not saying he's a real knight."

"Then what kind of knight could he be?"

"I know—I'll bet he's an actor," Robbie offered.

"An actor?"

Alma gave the boy a delighted smile. "Why, you children do pay attention when I read the newspaper out loud." She explained to Juliette, "A couple of months ago I read the class a story from the *Kansas Tribune* about a troupe of Shakespearean actors who traveled all the way from England to play at that new theater in Lawrence. Maybe he's one of them."

"Alma, Lawrence is two days' ride from here."

"Maybe he got lost. Or maybe he got waylaid by border ruffians while traveling to another town. An actor probably wouldn't know much about defending himself."

"That would explain the wound on his head," Juliette admitted. "But what about those outlandish things he's wearing?"

"Costume." Alma nodded confidently. "Actor."

"Cos . . . tume. Ac . . . tor," said the stranger, nodding in an uncanny imitation of Alma's movement.

"I guessed right, didn't I, Miss Harkins?" said Robbie.

"Yes!" Alma clapped her hands.

"Yesss." The stranger clapped his hands, too.

Juliette knew that Robbie received precious few compliments, so she didn't voice her concern that the stranger's words, his actions, too closely mimicked those of Alma for them to ring quite true. He would bear watching.

"Well, I'm glad that mystery's solved, Miss Jay. I don't see any other way of explaining the way he's dressed. I'll have to admit I never expected playactors would strive for such detail in their costuming. Look at his shield, and the chain mail, and the coat of arms. That's no ordinary horse—that's a, whatchamacallit, a destrier. He's dressed like a knight, like the ones from Camelot."

"Knight," the stranger agreed in a low rumble. He slanted a lazy cocky grin toward Alma before devoting the full force of his attention to Juliette, daring her without words to deny his status.

"But maybe not Camelot," Alma said. "I don't think Shakespeare wrote any plays about Camelot. You know the lines from *Romeo and Juliet,* Miss Jay. Why don't you quote him a few, see if it jogs his memory?"

"Don't be ridiculous, Alma. Why on earth would I stand out on the middle of the prairie quoting Shakespeare to a stranger?"

Destriers, Camelot, coats of arms and chain mail . . . Juliette shook her head, wishing she could as easily shake away this whole episode. Alma seemed determined to spout nonsense, and the stranger was flirting with Alma in an open manner that made Juliette want to kick him right on his chain-mail shin, except she was afraid of stubbing her toe. Most likely the man was an armed-to-the-teeth border ruffian sent out by his proslavery cohorts to cause trouble for Walburn Ford, and here she was, with a wagonload of women and children to protect, and no shotgun. Then again, he'd fashioned that elaborate pantomime to discourage her from filling his helmet with water. Maybe he was an actor, just not a very good one.

"We'd better get the children back home," she said, her voice as stiff as her backbone as she gripped both Alma and Robbie above the elbows and started marching them back to the wagon.

"But what about him? What about the knight, er, actor?" Alma asked, craning her neck back toward the stranger.

"You know it's not safe to trust strangers, Alma. Whoever—and *what*ever—he is, he got himself out on the prairie, and he can just get himself back to wherever he came from."

They hadn't quite reached the wagon when Robbie tugged at her sleeve. "He's following us, Miss Jay. His horse looks about ready to keel over."

Concern for the horse—that's all it was, Juliette told herself—caused her to take a reluctant glance behind her.

The stranger—she would *not* call him a knight—met her gaze over the distance. He stood tall and straight, his long legs taking one short step and then another, carefully timing his pace to that of his ailing horse, asking no sympathy for his own physical woes. Guilt stabbed at her.

Her mind turned traitor, replaying the image of him pounding his chest and proudly calling himself knight. For one wild, insane moment, she imagined the prairie disappeared and she found herself on a well-manicured field, a fairground. She imagined she heard trumpets heralding the stranger as he sat astride his spirited prancing destrier, shield drawn, sword raised high, the bucket clapped over the top of his head while unseen crowds of people roared their approval and pelted him with fresh-plucked roses. Stalwart, commanding, imbued with an inner confidence only repeated success could grant, he accepted every accolade.

A knight. He could be nothing less.

And then the image faded, the phantom cheering receded into the familiar sound of the incessant prairie wind. Juliette thinned her lips. Her fancies were growing as far-fetched as Alma's.

"It don't seem right to just leave him here, Miss Jay," Robbie whispered.

"You did save his life," said Alma. "That sort of obligates you to help him, doesn't it?"

"I tried to look at his wound and he stepped away like I meant to kill him." She found she was still inwardly smarting from the peculiar expression that had crossed his face, the furtive way his hand had moved, as if he'd sketched a quick sign of the cross for protection against her.

"He's just hurt and confused," Alma said, patting Juliette's hand as if she were a pouting child. "Besides, you're the only one in town with space to lodge him while he regains his bearings. And since I'm rooming with Robbie's folks this month, I'll be close enough to pop in every now and then and . . . and lend you a hand with him."

A furious blush marked Alma's offer, and Juliette knew what it meant. Alma's interest had been caught by a metal-clad, horse-obsessed actor calling himself a knight.

If only Juliette could claim her boarding house was full up, but only the aged Captain Chaney, her sole regular boarder, shared her quarters just now. Her two best rooms sat empty and everyone in town knew it. Frontier hospitality, complicated by her own intervention in the stranger's affairs, decreed that she offer room and board to a man who probably couldn't pay, to a sickly horse that possessed a better wardrobe than she did.

She glanced back. The rust-stained hem of the stranger's tunic flapped in the wind, reminding her of how he'd tried to stop her from pouring water into the bucket. Not a bucket, but his helmet. A stage prop, if Alma could be believed.

"Maybe he's interested in settling around here and got wounded while making his way toward Walburn Ford," Alma speculated. "You're always eager to welcome newcomers, Miss Jay. Goodness, maybe we could talk him into giving a performance. Folks in town might even get to play parts. Everyone would surely relish a little entertainment."

Juliette could feel her objections ebbing away. If

there was the chance that he might settle hereabouts, she couldn't afford to discourage an able-bodied, if not quite able-minded, man. Especially one who could offer some entertaining diversions—nobody knew better than she that the townsfolk were desperate for anything to break up their monotonous late-summer routine. Besides, his memory was bound to return. And if it was all an elaborate sham . . . well, no one could fool her for long, not even an actor.

"Two days."

"A month," Alma countered.

"A week," Juliette compromised. "And you answer all Mrs. Abbott's nosy questions yourself."

"You have a generous heart," Alma said with a sincere smile. She turned toward the self-proclaimed knight and waved furiously, beckoning him to follow.

"I do not." Juliette spoke brusquely, to cover her surprise at Alma's comment. She knew she'd had no choice in the matter. She glanced back at the stranger and felt an inappropriate impulse to smile, which she quelled. "I'm just doing what's best for the town, like always."

2

Geoffrey's strength surged anew with each step he took in the wagon's wake. His scattered wits resumed their normal course with each breath. He wished he could shuck his armor, but though Arion too seemed to regain strength with motion, he didn't want to burden the steed with the chain mail's weight. Besides, he didn't know whose keep Mizjay's wagon approached. Or what manner of defenses he would find set against him once they got there. Perhaps he'd soon appreciate the weighty armor's protection.

An unexpected knight did not always receive a warm welcome. But the man who ruled these flat grassy acres seemed singularly unconcerned over protecting his manor. No sentinel towers loomed, no mounted knights rode out to challenge their presence. The peasants had constructed their hovels in such far-flung indefensible positions that no lord could hope to save them all in the face of a surprise attack.

Geoffrey, with no prospects whatever of inheriting

any of his father's lands, had nonetheless learned better husbandry. His long-suppressed craving for land taunted him now. He forced it aside, much as he'd ceased thinking upon the witless notion that he'd somehow landed in hell, that Mizjay was a witch rather than a comely peasant lass possessed of a most unmelodic name.

The overladen wagon she drove disgorged a pair of children next to a hut constructed of what looked like huge bricks made of turf, topped with a hay thatch. Though the land should have been burgeoning with preharvest bounty, only a few cultivated acres interrupted the swaying grass stretching behind the hut, with one lone peasant hoeing the crops.

Geoffrey's tactician's mind, and aching legs, objected when they traveled at least a half mile more before coming up alongside another dwelling. This one looked formed of thin slabs of wood overlapping one another from roof to floor, its fields lying near fallow with the same scant amount of cultivation, the same shocking lack of labor. Several more passengers disembarked after casting curious glances toward him and Arion.

There was room enough now should Mizjay ask him to ride in the wagon, but she sat rigid in her seat, looking straight ahead as though she'd been harnessed in place as securely as her mules. And she'd donned a cloth helm much like that worn by the other women. It hid her glorious hair from view, and shielded her face at the sides, not unlike head coverings worn by nuns.

He wondered if, in his muddleheadedness following the leap, he'd cried the word "witch" aloud, which might explain her wariness of him. He'd done naught else to warrant her stiff-backed distrust. Surely, no woman feared a knight, not even a woman so unworldly that her set task looked to be nothing more than the hauling about of women and children.

Mizjay drove the mules with exceptional skill, considering she had no road to guide her, only narrow wheel tracks snaking through the grass. Geoffrey would have liked to gain a bit of ground on the wagon. The wagon wheels interested him; he'd never seen their like, what with a dozen or more spokes encircled by a thin metal band. It seemed impossible that such wheels could support such a heavy conveyance.

The wagon's driver interested him even more. He strained his ears to hear more of her tongue, though Mizjay seemed closemouthed in comparison to the other passengers. He began to sort out the odd pronunciations. He would have no trouble understanding these people, though speaking their unusual dialect might take a bit of practice.

Where am I? He would ask that straight off. Everything about this place struck him askew. Vast lands not turned to cultivation. Broad pasture without grazing beasts, while demon cattle snorted and shook the earth. Peasants roaming about with no purpose, speaking English—and yet not quite English—wearing outrageous garments, exchanging salutes with Mongol warriors.

He straightened his shoulders, dismayed by the frightening possibility that suddenly occurred to him. God's blood, had he leaped straight off the edge of the Earth to land in heathen China?

On the wagon traveled, with Geoffrey and Arion following, shedding children as it went. Each poorly constructed hut they approached sat in isolation, receding completely well before they came across another, until the wagon held only Mizjay, the one she'd called Alma, and an obviously mean-tempered old crone intent upon frowning at him.

Geoffrey considered grimacing back at her, but they

came to a pitiful gathering of huts, and he eagerly craned his neck, certain they approached the village at last. Soon he would count herds of grazing sheep and cattle, spot pigs rooting amidst the oak leaves, measure broad well-tended acres planted with sufficient foodstuffs, with peasants aplenty to tend the life-sustaining beasts and crops. The keep would soon loom tall, with banners flying proudly in the brisk wind, bearing the crest of the lord who ruled these rich lands in such careless fashion.

Nothing greeted his questing glance save for the collection of crude huts, and more grass rippling in the wind, stretching onward until it merged with the sky.

Mizjay halted the mules and the three women deserted their seats in favor of clustering together, arms folded, watching him approach. Quite a bold stance for women of their position when facing one of his rank.

Though he could see little of their features because of the unattractive helms they wore, Geoffrey thought they were as unalike as three women could be. The frowning crone stood tallest, and stoutest, with her downturned lips pressed into a grim line. The one called Alma boasted a fine full figure as well, but lacked the height which would have lent her grace. They both wore gowns that clung tight from shoulder to waist and then burst into fullness over their hips to trail near the ground. Not peasant garb, and not what women in King Edward's court favored, but not so outrageous as Mizjay's garb.

As if she'd sensed he'd settled his attention upon her, Mizjay pulled the covering from her head and freed her hair to tumble in the breeze. A few tendrils curled over her breast, falling shorter than hip length, but lifting with the light springiness that hinted at recent washing. Rare, to find a peasant woman careful of her hair. In face and courage she was truly exceptional, and it was a wonder she'd escaped her lord's attentions, that she roamed this treeless plain without men besetting her at every turn.

"I don't know if this is such a good idea." The old crone frowned more fiercely as she spoke, but managed to look affrighted nonetheless. "Why, look at the size of him! You'd stand no chance at all against him if he took it into his head to—well, you know. If only my son were here, instead of off with the Army Corps of Topographical Engineers—"

"Don't be silly, Mrs. Abbott," Alma interrupted. Her face bloomed an unbecoming shade of scarlet. "Captain Chaney wouldn't let anything happen to Miss Jay."

"That old fraud," Mrs. Abbott muttered, turning her own shade of red. She gathered her breath for another outburst. "He's probably out riding around on one of his mysterious errands just when Miss Jay needs him most. You should lock this stranger in the barn until the men get back from the fields. Let them find out who he is and what his business might be."

And then Mizjay met his gaze, holding it for no more than the space of a heartbeat before her blue eyes skipped past his, and a delicate pink suffused her golden skin as well.

Blushing women, all atremble in the presence of a knight—some things were not so different about this keep after all. The smile he gave them held less of practiced courtly skill than relief.

Mizjay blinked, her proud chin tilted high as if something in his smile had smote her a fearsome blow.

"Mrs. Abbott's right, Alma, we don't know enough about this man to trust him." Her voice struck cold, but was still somehow silken and pleasantly pitched when compared to the others. "I'll keep him in the barn with his horse."

*   *   *

The stranger's forehead had stopped bleeding, which was for the best, since he paid the wound no attention and Juliette didn't intend to repeat her abortive attempt to look at it.

After setting aside his helmet, shield, and sword, he tended his stallion with meticulous care, although anyone with two eyes in her head could see his limbs virtually quaked with weariness. She'd never seen anyone so devoted to a horse. The chain mail he wore looked heavy, very heavy. Juliette imagined that even an actor accustomed to wearing such ridiculous gear on stage might find its weight oppressive. She felt a stab of guilt for having forced him to walk behind the wagon all afternoon, wounded as he was, and just as quickly shook it away, reminding herself she still knew nothing about this man.

Where had all her good sense gone? What foolishness compelled her to stand there, watching him, when there wasn't a soul around to help her if he turned against her? At least she'd left the door open, so sunlight could brighten the interior. Someone could hear her scream if he turned on her.

But he paid her no mind, his attention bent upon removing the massive saddle and then peeling away the draping skirt covering the horse from ears to tail. Some structure which looked quite like a hoopskirt fashioned of hay twisted through wooden staves covered the horse's breast. Juliette must have gasped aloud at the surprising sight, because the stranger paused in his work to stare at her over the animal's back.

Her barn, built to house a couple of ordinary-sized mules and a milk cow or two, had never held such an imposing stallion, but that didn't explain why Juliette suddenly felt a constriction all about her, as if the compact space were closing in even more, as if she dared not take another breath while the stranger's gaze locked with her own.

"Who are you?" she whispered.

He tilted his head, a quizzical expression creasing his brow.

Juliette gestured toward the animal, striving for some manner of communicating with him. "Horse?"

The stranger smiled, instantly grasping her purpose, and rested his forearms on the horse's back. "Horse. Arion."

"Arion," Juliette repeated, not quite mastering the musical flow of his pronunciation. She put a hand to her breast. "Juliette. Juliette Walburn."

His eyes clouded with confusion. "Mizjay?"

The title of respect, which she'd so diligently cultivated, sounded suddenly crude and harsh. "Well, yes, I like folks to call me Miss Jay. But my real name's Juliette." Now, why had she gone and told him such a thing when she'd spent the best part of the past four years trying to erase that frivolous name from everyone's memories?

"Juliette," he repeated, drawing a shiver from her at the way his deep husky voice gentled the syllables. Spoken with traces of the old world, like the man in her father's beloved Shakespeare play might have said it, calling from his hiding place beneath his lady's window. "Juliette." The stranger said her name again, as if quite pleased that her father had saddled her with such a trial.

He rested his metal-clad hand against his own breast.

"D'Arbanville."

Juliette. D'Arbanville. Hearing both names spoken so closely together sent a completely unwarranted flush to heat Juliette's cheeks. The musical ebb and flow of his voice called to mind the vegetarian woman she'd met in Octagon City, Mamselle Dupree, who'd come to Kansas from France by way of Montreal, only to lose all her money and worldly possessions like the other ill-fated vegetarian settlers. Might this d'Arbanville person have followed a similar route?

"Geoffrey," he added.

"D'Arbanville Geoffrey?" Juliette winced at how coarse she sounded in comparison.

He seemed not to notice, but sent her another dazzling smile and flipped his hand back and forth.

"Geoffrey d'Arbanville?"

He inclined his head toward her, seeming to bow from his shoulders down, keeping his eyes upon her all the while. And there, in her dusty old barn, with horseflies buzzing all around and soiled mule bedding heaped in the corner, the Widow Walburn absurdly felt like a pampered young Italian noblewoman accepting homage from her forbidden Romeo.

She didn't like it, not one single bit, the self-consciousness that flooded her, leading one hand to smooth the bedraggled folds of her Bloomer dress while the other pushed at the mass of windblown hair tumbling wantonly over her shoulders.

She took refuge in issuing orders. "There's feed for the horse in those barrels over there, but make sure you refasten the lid so the mice can't get in. You can draw a bucket of water from the pump outside. You'll have to muck out, er, Arion's stall every day yourself, and I'll expect you to put him out to pasture once he's regained his strength."

Geoffrey watched her lips carefully, his head cocked to the side.

"Oh, you're not acting. That blow to the head must have robbed you of your ability to speak. You don't understand a single word I say, do you?" she ended in frustration.

He nodded slowly. "Understand. And me . . . *speken* ye English . . . soonly." He gave Arion a final, reassuring pat. He drew a great deep breath and then walked toward her touching his breast, his face gone solemn. "*Helpan* me . . . Juliette?"

She meant to tell him she'd already offered all the help she intended to give, meant to correct him, to tell him she preferred being addressed as Miss Jay. But he stopped no more than two feet in front of her, and his broad chest filled her vision, crowding every thought from her mind.

His arms began a slow ascent, curving upward, where beams of sunlight struck against the metal links, creating the sensation of a guardian angel's wings unfurling to surround her within their sheltering embrace. Her knight, come to protect and defend her from harm.

"*Helpan* me, Juliette," he whispered again, drawing a quivering response from low within her.

And then she saw that he'd awkwardly bent one arm back to tug at the edge of his tunic, which had gotten caught in the relaxed links of his chain-mail cowl.

Mortification held her still for a moment. She'd swayed before him like her love-struck namesake, caught up in the sound of his voice, imagining *angel's wings,* for heaven's sake, when all he wanted was a helping hand to tug his tunic free. He was an actor, all right—skilled at holding an audience in thrall. How everyone in Walburn Ford would laugh if they knew that she'd actually savored the sound of her frivolous name coming from his lips!

Angry at herself, she pulled at the soft blue cloth, not even caring when it tore at the seam. It would serve her right to have to mend it. She hated sewing, and it would be a fit punishment to stitch away while her mind considered how she'd come to this pass.

Geoffrey stepped away from her, leaving her to fold the tunic as if he didn't know how to take care of his own garments. He bent at the waist and made several hitching motions with his shoulders, accompanied by deep grunts, and the chain-mail shirt fell into a silvery heap at his feet. He staggered a little as the weight fell away, but crouched close and poked through the chain mail until he'd withdrawn a length of leather cord with a primitive pewterlike pendant dangling from it. He straightened with a sigh of relief, holding the pendant against his heart. After a moment he fastened the leather cord around and stood, and Juliette found she had taken leave of her senses yet again.

He wore an unusual shirt of thin supple leather, a shirt with no sleeves and with a V neckline. His bare arms bulged like none she'd ever seen on a man, with strong well-defined muscles banding him from wrist to shoulder. The pendant he'd tied on lay nestled amidst the riot of chestnut-colored curls darkening his chest above the leather V. Strands of his hair fell over his shoulders, the same chestnut, and yet sun-gilded to a barely perceptible lighter shade.

His chest rose and fell quickly, as if shedding the metal clothing had taxed his strength. The leather shirt stretched with each indrawn breath, pulling taut over sculpted planes that promised great strength. Without the mail he looked younger, and even stronger; every supple, well-honed inch of him declared his status as a man who relished each moment of his prime.

And marring his clean perfect lines were silvery-white scars. Thin marks, triangular-shaped nicks, long snaking trails, as if the sharp points of knives and swords had repeatedly hacked their way through his

chain-mail protection. She wouldn't have expected a
soldier's body to be so scarred, let alone someone who
practiced the acting profession.

He noticed where her attention lingered, for he held
out his arms and turned them for her, showing her that
he'd been marked front and back.

"Knight," he said, offering only a single enigmatic
word of explanation.

Although a tiny, distressed line creased her smooth
forehead when Geoffrey bared the badges of his trade for
Juliette, she displayed none of the weak-stomached revulsion that sometimes sent women stumbling backward
with hands pressed tight over their mouths. Nor did she
show the avid grasping pleasure yet another sort of female
took in rubbing her fingers over his scars as if delighting
to think of the pain he'd suffered in acquiring them.

Her troubled gaze met his. In the azure depths of
her eyes he fancied he read concern for him, the man
called Geoffrey d'Arbanville. Not the knight who'd
been well paid for the blood he'd lost, but an ordinary
man who'd endured blows beyond counting.

A warm balm seemed to flow from her, promising a
calm quiet haven for a questing soul. Geoffrey suddenly
understood why noblemen risked the king's wrath to lie
with women such as this, why landless louts like himself
dared to dream of foregoing the knighthood and trading
their silver spurs for the simple pleasures of a wife, a
country cottage, a score of arable acres.

Perhaps, once he'd fulfilled his king's task, once
he'd wreaked his vengeance and rid the earth of Drogo
FitzBaldric's putrid presence, he might explore such
dreams. For now, thoughts of pleasure must be set
aside. The Celtic pendant hung heavy round his neck,
reminding him of his oath, his obligations, the people
depending upon his return.

This night, when his old friends the stars coursed the sky, he would take his leave of this unfamiliar place. It did not matter where his leap into the Eternal Chasm had led him. One such as he, who'd tourneyed and bartered his sword for masters everywhere from Italy to the Holy Land to England's far northern reaches, would have no trouble guiding himself back home by those same stars, even if he'd leaped straight into some English-speaking settlement of the Orient.

He had leaped into the Chasm to arrive in this place; it would seem he must needs then climb out to return. So he would hunt for mountains.

A scuffling sound near the stable door drew his attention. It was a male peasant, possessed of great years judging by the stoop to his shoulders and the grizzled state of his hair and beard. Geoffrey could tell the man had once stood tall and sturdy, although it looked as if the wasting sickness might hold him in its grip now.

God's blood, but these people shrouded their bodies in the strangest garments! This old one had his tunic stuffed into loose-fitting chausses, and both tunic and chausses were bedecked straight down the front with tiny disks the color of a gnawed beef bone. A tough-looking leather strap encircled the peasant's waist, and dangling from it lay a matching leather pouch, from which protruded a bone-colored handle. The peasant grasped this handle and pulled it free with a quick motion, one it seemed he had often practiced, revealing a long round snout of dark metal attached to the bone. He waved the object in Geoffrey's direction in a some-what menacing fashion, much like an enemy would brandish a weapon.

But it was not a knife, nor had Geoffrey's many travels acquainted him with any weapon such as this. And yet the peasant's approach did not herald a welcoming gift.

"Make one move toward her and I'll plug you where you stand," the peasant stated. "Ought to be ashamed of yourself, takin' advantage of a widow woman."

"Juliette? Widow?" Geoffrey found the notion most interesting.

But Juliette seemed disinclined to explain her status. "Captain Chaney, no! Put your gun away!" She whirled, placing herself between Geoffrey and the belligerent peasant.

She raised her hands as if to ward off a blow, although the peasant stood a good ten strides away. Intolerable, that a woman should so doubt his ability to react to a threat, no matter that she'd come upon him while he sat weak as a starveling lamb. There was nothing to do but grasp her round her slim delicate ribs, lift her with no more effort than it took to swing Arion's saddle in place, and set her safely behind him.

The peasant made a growling sound, lifted the bone and metal object, and squinted over it at him. Geoffrey lowered his head and squinted back, uncertain of the peasant's intent. Juliette gave a cry of alarm and made to move around him, but Geoffrey could sense her warmth, could smell her sun-kissed hair, could feel the air stir with her every movement, and so easily blocked her, shifting from hip to hip and bracing his outstretched arms against her weight as she tried to forge past him.

"Captain Chaney, don't shoot!" she cried.

"Can't shoot, long's you keep hopping around him like a rabbit. Run to the back of the barn, Miss Jay, and get out of the way. I'll plug him sure if he tries to go after you."

"He's not going to go after me, and you're not going to plug him."

Geoffrey felt Juliette's fingers warm against the flesh of his arm, tentative and then certain as she pushed

down to enable herself to peer over at the irate peasant.
Geoffrey hid a grin; she'd not been able to overcome
his arm's strength despite his weary state. She sighed as
if realizing it herself, and then with a devious motion
ducked beneath Geoffrey's arm. She slanted him a triumphant smile before turning toward Captain Chaney.
Geoffrey tightened his lips, certain this unpleasant
interlude achieved only one good purpose, that of helping him further master her tongue, for he fully intended
to serve her the sharp side of it.

Juliette cast a furtive, almost embarrassed glance at
him "We found him wandering out on the prairie. He's
been hit in the head. Alma thinks he's an actor." She
tapped her temple with her finger.

"*I* think he might be a border ruffian."

"Well, you can't just walk into this barn and shoot
him without finding out for sure, Captain Chaney."

"What's to stop me?"

"Civilization. This isn't the wild West anymore."
She scolded the man. "Gracious, this is the year of our
Lord 1859!"

It seemed to Geoffrey that Juliette's senseless utterance echoed from the walls, or perhaps it only seemed
so because of the roaring buffeting his ears. He cursed
himself for his false pride, for imagining that he'd
already acquired a command of her tongue, for surely
he could not have heard her aright.

"This is the year of our Lord 1283." The words
wrenched free of Geoffrey's throat, all hoarse and
uncertain, accompanied by a sudden racing of his heart
when he saw how his words caused Juliette and the
peasant to stare at him, she with sympathy clouding her
expression, the man with his mouth agape.

Long moments passed before Juliette asked him, "You
really don't know where you are, do you, Geoffrey?"

He hated the wariness that had sprung into her eyes, the soothing yet tremulous voice she used, as if she thought she confronted a lunatic . . . or perhaps she feared that despite all her precautions to hide the land's treasures, to keep him away from personages of importance, he had nonetheless divined the location of this place. He straightened his stance and spoke with as much conviction as he could muster.

"China. The year of our Lord 1283."

Pity crossed the male peasant's face as he lowered his horn-handled object to his side. "I see what you mean, Miss Jay."

"Oh, Geoffrey," Juliette whispered.

3

Juliette clutched Captain Chaney's spare clothing to her breast as she watched Geoffrey prowl her best guest room like a boxed cat set free in strange surroundings.

No detail escaped his attention, from the construction of the bedstead to the stitching on her quilt. With the lift of an arrogant brow, he silently demanded she tell him the name of every object. Glass, admittedly in short supply here on the Kansas frontier, seemed to fascinate him. He ran callused fingertips over the windowpane, smearing the sparkle she'd achieved with a vinegar rinse, and grunted grudging admiration when she showed him how the window frame could be lifted to admit the evening breeze. He disengaged the chimney from the lamp and peered through it as if it were a spyglass. She feared for her treasured mirror when he caught sight of himself in it and sprang into a threatening stance, his hand flying to where his sword would have hung had she not insisted he leave it in the barn.

Some knight, ready to attack his own reflection!

"The captain says you might want to borrow these clothes," she said, with a meaningful look at his chain-link trousers, careful to avoid staring at his leather-clad torso. "He's about your height. He'll want them back, of course, as soon as you get some of your own. Or maybe you'll remember where you put your, um, regular clothes?"

He ignored the question in favor of picking up the homespun shirt and shaking it free of its careful folding. His nose wrinkled at the scent of camphor wafting through the room.

"They've been packed away and protected against moths," Juliette explained. "You should wash your wound—I have salve and clean cloth bandages. There's water enough for a shower, too, if you'd like one, and we could hang the clothes out for airing while you get cleaned up."

He treated her to a brooding glance which darkened into confusion. He stared back at the shirt with growing dismay, rubbing one huge thumb over each button in turn, and then swung his gaze toward Juliette's front. Before she realized what he meant to do, his hand brushed the skin at her neck and his long supple fingers caught the edge of her neckline and worked her top button free.

"Geoffrey! My button!" She leaped back quickly, but not before he'd slipped another button through its hole. He leaned forward, closing the slight gap she'd made between them with a mere shift of his body, making it clear without words that she could not outrun him. Her pulse raced while her limbs refused to move. Her breath quickened when his head bent close to her bosom, when his warm breath caressed her throat and the tender skin of her breasts peeping over the edge of her camisole. He slapped the borrowed shirt over his shoulder and brought both his hands to work upon her. But not, as she feared, to take liberties. Frowning with concentration, Geoffrey d'Arbanville trained all of his attention on refastening her two top buttons.

And then setting them loose again. Only those two.

And refastening them.

Juliette thought she might grow as mad as he if it didn't stop, the subtle brush of his fingers against cloth that might as well have evaporated into mist for all the protection it offered her now. His heat, his scent, his very breathing rhythm permeated every fluttering breath she managed to gulp.

He fastened the buttons one last time, and his thumb lingered upon the top disk, pressing it lightly against her throat. He drew the shirt from his shoulder and flicked one of the buttons. He smiled, although a bleakness remained in the depths of his hazel eyes.

"Understand, Juliette. Understand."

Now her own fingers trembled with a wanton urge to help him dress so she could toy with the buttons on his shirt. She backed away before giving in to such a ridiculous impulse, coming up hard against the edge of the door. "Captain Chaney will stop by to show you where to find things. We eat supper at five. I'm starving, and I'll bet you are, too."

His hand passed lightly against his taut abdomen, and seemed to linger briefly against his heart. "Empty," he agreed.

Geoffrey followed Captain Chaney toward Juliette's kitchen, feeling clean and fit despite the too-tight garb binding his limbs. He sorely missed his squire, Hugo. Hugo would despair over the rust Juliette's careless handling of his helm had raised, but how he would marvel at the exceptional weave of these chausses. How the two of them might together shake their heads over the foolishness of closing a man's essential frontal gap with yet another row of buttons. And Hugo might have made a better job of fastening the buttons, for Geoffrey had not managed on his own to achieve the neatly aligned row Captain Chaney's shirt sported.

He had accepted Captain Chaney's offer of the thing called a shower bath and reveled in the spray of water cascading over his head. Warm from sitting near the roof all day in the sun, the water had roused wondrously clear thoughts from his all but benumbed mind. If King Edward had known of this contrivance, he would certainly have ordered every keep in the land equipped with a water cask connected to a rusted hole-punched bucket so that all knights might stand beneath it and refresh themselves before battle.

But Geoffrey had traveled in the royal presence often enough to know that King Edward could never have heard of this shower bath. Nor the disks called buttons. Nor the implement with the familiar name of razor; unlike his own shaving tool, this razor's steel carried such a finely honed edge a man must needs take the utmost care lest he slit his own beard-bristled throat. And nowhere in his travels had he encountered multichambered peasant huts boasting movable glass windows and smooth walls. Unsettling, to witness common folk enjoying luxuries unknown to members of the ruling class.

Unsettling, everything that had happened since leaping into the Eternal Chasm—from the curved-horned beasts that first greeted him to the delicate perfume of Juliette's hair, matching the scent of the fine soap he'd used in the shower bath.

But he would not let these people lure him into believing their outrageous contention that it was the year of our Lord 1859. Their purpose in doing so he could not fathom, save that they feared his presence and sought to disarm him by casting self-doubt upon his wits. It was not beyond belief that word of his prowess had spread this far, and that they had devised this novel method to thwart him.

At the threshold of Juliette's hut, Geoffrey toyed with the notion of first bolting toward the stable for a glimpse of Arion, so desperate was he of a sudden to restore his spirits with the sight of something familiar.

Juliette glanced up as he bent his head to enter the kitchen, causing him to pause a moment in appreciation. She'd donned a different, less outrageous, gown, of a blue not unlike the background to his own colors. Her eyes sparkled a deeper hue of blue, her skin shone pink and golden, her well-brushed hair lay exposed in a loose knot at the back of her neck. He caught an elusive whiff of flowery scent. It struck him suddenly that she must have been the last one before him to use the soap in the shower bath. His skin tingled, his loins reacted to the thought, and he took a deep steadying breath lest she and Captain Chaney sense his susceptibility to her and seek to turn it to their advantage.

A knight must ever be on guard against such sexual ploys.

He fixed his gaze instead on the squat metal crypt-like thing she rested her water pot upon, and wondered at the heat all but shimmering from it, at the long pipe snaking from its back into the wall.

Feminine tittering from a corner of the chamber drew his regard to a knot of whispering peasant folk. From their covert glances he knew he'd been the subject of much debate amongst them. Some of them he recognized as passengers from Juliette's wagon, but their numbers were reinforced by several hard-eyed men whose cross-armed stance bespoke challenge.

"Sit, Geoffrey." Juliette waved a graceful hand toward a stool so spindly legged that Geoffrey would have never entrusted his fully armed weight to it. As it was, he lowered himself onto it with great caution, gripping the edge of the table for support should the chair collapse. Had these folk collected to watch a knight take a tumble, want would be their master.

Juliette bustled around the metal crypt. "I'll have coffee and something for you to eat in a moment." She yelped when her hand grazed the water pot; from the way she stuffed her fingertips into her mouth, one might have thought she'd gotten burned even though any fool could see there was no fire nearby.

One of the men stepped forward, holding tight to the shirt collar of the boy-child Robbie, who darted him a surreptitious smile.

The man shot him a challenging look. "State yer business, sir."

The man had called him sir! At last, someone who accorded him his proper title. Geoffrey relaxed none of his caution, but strove to gather the right words for a response.

Before he could reply, though, young Robbie piped up. "I told you, Pa. He's a knight." And he earned a bone-jarring shake from his father for speaking the truth.

"Ain't no knight, and I done told you so." He shook the child again for good measure.

"Mr. Wilcox, please," Juliette whispered. Although the others murmured disapproval, none other than she dared chastise the man over his churlish behavior.

It was a father's right to handle his offspring as he wished, but a spark of rage kindled in Geoffrey's breast.

The shaking might have been deserved, had not the father first addressed Geoffrey as sir. By jostling the boy, Wilcox made a mockery of apparent courtesy; worse, he brought distress to Juliette. It could not pass unremarked.

Geoffrey sprung at once from his seat, which confirmed his poor opinion of it by toppling backward. Ignoring the clatter, he fixed his sternest glare upon Wilcox. "Had I my sword at my side, I would run you through for this insult."

He knew not whether he spoke all their words correctly, but the peasants seemed to have no trouble understanding the threat. The women and children gasped as one and clung to one another, shivering back against the wall. Each man scrabbled at his waist for a bone-handled snout similar to the one so prized by Captain Chaney, and to a man pointed them, nose holes first, straight at Geoffrey's heart.

Juliette became alarmed. "Will you stop it, all of you? Can't you see he's taken a blow to the head and it's left him crazy as a bedbug?"

Several self-conscious giggles and a wavering of the snouts greeted her words. Juliette settled the stool back in place and rested a gentling hand upon Geoffrey's arm. The warmth of her touch passed through the shirtsleeve, and he acceded to her mild pressure by lowering himself once more onto the seat, glowering at Wilcox all the while.

"He's not crazy, Miss Jay. Just confused." Alma bustled to the forefront of the small crowd, clutching a rustling packet to her bosom. "I ran home for that issue of the *Kansas Tribune* I told you about, the one with the story about the acting troupe that visited the new theater in Lawrence."

She set her packet down on the table, pushing it toward him. "Look here, Geoffrey. There's the story about the acting troupe, and the date, plain as day: June 2, 1859, Lawrence, Kansas. Do you remember everything now?"

Sweat sprung to Geoffrey's brow as he stared with incomprehension at the flat, ink-tracked object sitting before him. Perhaps the crowding of so many people into this one chamber had turned the air so suddenly heavy and explained why, with no hearth in evidence, it felt as though a crackling fire blazed somewhere nearby.

Alma tapped a tapered fingernail against one collection of markings no more legible than any of the others. "Here, Geoffrey. Read the newspaper."

Read. As if the flat fragile substance might be parchment worked upon by churchly scribes. As if any monk would content himself with such closely spaced unadorned lettering. As if any knight would have wasted his time mastering a task suited to weak-bodied men!

He caught the edge of the newspaper between his thumb and forefinger, rolling the corner, marveling at its pliability. He'd never seen its like, and that knowledge smote him with a sense of desolation. How many other strange objects would be thrust before him? How many strange faces would gape at him, all bent on convincing him he'd taken leave of his senses?

His hand commenced a violent trembling, causing Alma's newspaper to tear with a harsh crackling sound. He sprang to his feet, the spindly legged chair again clattering to the floor from the force of his movement. He brought his fist down upon the table with all his strength.

"Enough!" he bellowed, relishing the sound of his strong sane voice vibrating from the hut's walls. "If you long for someone to read to you, hire yourselves a priest. Torment me no more, lest you draw down the full wrath of d'Arbanville upon your baseborn heads."

With that he strode boldly from the room, taking

particular pleasure at sneering upon the womanish cowering exhibited by the child-mauling Wilcox. Aiming for the chamber Juliette had assigned him, he prayed Arion was resting well and would be ready to ride in the morning, for he could not bear staying in this accursed place a heartbeat longer than necessary.

"Well, I never!" Mrs. Abbott sniffed audibly, breaking the silence that followed Geoffrey's outburst. "Baseborn? Why, I don't think I care for the sound of that at all. If my son Herman were here—"

"I'm sure no officer of the Army Corps of Topographical Engineers would tolerate anyone making such a spectacle," Juliette said, once again returning Geoffrey's stool to an upright position. "Now, if you folks would just go on home, I mean to have a word with my guest before I send him on his way."

"You cain't go in there yourself, Miss Jay," said Captain Chaney, to a chorus of murmured agreement.

"He won't hurt me." Juliette spoke in Geoffrey's defense, curiously certain of what she said. She had no firm evidence to prove her belief, only his gentle handling of his ailing horse, the brave but foolish attempt he'd made to shield her from Captain Chaney's pistol, the burning anger flaring in his eyes at Josiah Wilcox's rough treatment of young Robbie.

She wished all these people would leave the two of them alone, and guilt struck her at the thought. She'd promised her dying husband that she'd devote herself to building on this sense of community, this evidence of neighbors who cared about one another. She'd vowed aloud over his death rattle that she would spend the rest of her days nurturing Walburn Ford into a town worthy of bearing Daniel's name.

It had seemed the least she could do, considering how in her heart she'd never quite lived up to her promise to love and cherish Daniel while he lived. His grateful smile had eased his way into death, and the sight had stilled her silent scream of denial when she realized that she'd tied herself to Walburn Ford for the rest of her days. It was a good trade, she'd firmly assured herself then. She reassured herself of the same now.

She shooed the townsfolk away, placating Captain Chaney by posting him at the end of the hall and promising to scream as loud as she could if Geoffrey even dared look at her threateningly. And then she gave Geoffrey's door one sharp rap before smoothing her skirt and letting herself into the room.

Excitement coursed through her, excitement that had to spring from fear, because surely no respectable woman would thrill to the thought of being alone with him once more.

Geoffrey seemed uninterested in her arrival. He stood next to the window, his arms raised and braced against the frame, staring out, the barest hint of a dejected slump rounding his mighty shoulders.

"Geoffrey? Everyone's gone. Would you like to come back to the kitchen for something to eat?"

A full minute passed before he acknowledged her presence with a sigh. He heaved himself away from the window and turned to face her, standing so self-assured and forbidding that she questioned her earlier impression of vulnerability.

"I might have known they would sense my weakness and send you."

"I don't understand," she said. Wounded animosity radiated from him, as if she'd betrayed his trust in some manner. Well, she supposed she had, in a way. His outburst proved he suffered no lingering effects from his injury. Despite her eagerness to see Walburn Ford flourish with new settlers, she fully intended to berate Geoffrey for his rude behavior and ask him and his oat-guzzling horse to leave at first light.

"The words sound clear to mine own ears. Is my mastery of your tongue so incomplete you cannot fathom what I say?"

"I can pretty much figure out what you mean, but some of the words you use do sound strange," she admitted.

"Some of my words?" He uttered a disgusted snort. "Would that words were the only oddities heaped upon my head by the lot of you."

"Well, clothes aren't oddities, mister, but look at what you've done with a perfectly normal shirt and britches."

With so many people clustered in the kitchen, she hadn't noticed how badly he'd dressed himself. He'd buttoned his shirt with less skill than a four-year-old. The shirt gapped wide at his neck, since the top button had been fastened to the buttonhole midway down the shirt, leaving the left shirttail four or five inches shorter than the right. And instead of tucking the ends neatly into his britches, he'd left the shirt hanging out, and had belted his waist around the outside of the shirt, where the strong leather strap wouldn't do a bit of good in holding up britches sewn for a fleshier waist. Why, one would think he'd never before threaded a belt through britch loops! He'd drawn his long woolen socks up over the outsides of his pant legs, and the long laces on his boots crisscrossed up his socks all the way to his knees.

Her gaze settled at his neckline. The improperly buttoned shirt sagged at the collar, exposing where his smoothly muscled breast joined the strong column of his neck. His primitive pendant cast off a dull gleam, like pewter, or poorly polished silver, against his golden skin.

"I have done nothing harmful to the shirt and britches," Geoffrey said, jolting her attention back to their conversation. He scowled down at her. "Since you sent no squire to help me dress, I did the best I could with such strange garb."

He crossed his arms and stared at her with the affronted look of a man insulted by a deliberate slight, as if he expected an apology for her failure to provide someone to help him button up Captain Chaney's old clothes. She remembered his fingers quick and light against her own buttons and felt an odd fluttering start somewhere low within her at the thought of reworking his shirt, of standing close to him and breathing in his scent and heat while she arranged the buttons until they lay flat against his muscled torso. The wayward thought lent an unfamiliar hoarseness to her voice.

"We're fresh out of squires here on the Kansas frontier. Around here we dress ourselves, and we speak politely to people who are trying to help us, and we don't go around spreading nonsense about what year it might be."

He paled, his stance growing rigid. "Rest assured I shall not trouble you over that matter again. I have worked it out in my mind and understand what has happened."

Relief washed over her. He wasn't crazy. And although that shouldn't have mattered at all, somehow it did, and she fought down the giddiness the thought created. "It was the buffalo, wasn't it? Somehow you hurt your head, and when you saw that cow running at you it addled your mind a bit, right?"

"I know naught of buffalo." He took two quick strides and stood directly in front of her. "There are but two possible explanations for my confusion. Either I am dreaming, or I am dead."

His comment doused her spirits, leaving her frustrated and angry in turn. "Well, then, if you're asleep that means I'm part of a nightmare. And if you're dead, what does that make me?"

"An angel?" he offered at once, with the conviction of a man who'd given the matter much thought, his voice as gentle as a spring breeze.

She could do nothing but stand there, struck speechless, while his finger traced a light circle over the spot where her hair crowned her head. "But I see no halo here, Juliette." His hand stroked lower, touching her back where her shoulder bones jutted out. "Nor do I find wings sprouting here." She felt his fingers at the back of her neck, and then her hair was released from its obedient chignon to fall in a loose wanton tumble around her shoulders. "But what have we here—a flower-scented cloud? I thought you a witch, but where is the clinging scent of potions, the snaggle-toothed, ear-splitting cackle? 'Tis clear to me you are no dream, so you must be an angel."

"Geoffrey." She knew she must protest his behavior but wasn't exactly certain what it was she found so objectionable about it. "Geoffrey, believe me, I'm no angel."

"Excellent," he said, "for angels may consort only with saints, and I am no saint."

He cupped her head with both hands, tilting her face up. He traced light circles over her cheeks, against the soft skin below her eyes.

"No pockmarks," he murmured. "And your breath is as sweet as that of a child who has never known a rotted tooth."

Any frontier farmer could summon more ardent

endearments; Juliette had heard her share during her
flightier days, before she'd become wife and widow in
the space of a year and learned how a woman's romantic inclinations could doom her to a lifetime of disappointment.

"Prove to me, Juliette, that you are neither dream
nor witch."

She'd received her share of kisses, too—maybe more
than her share, if the truth were told—but none had
prepared her for the sensations prompted by the touch
of Geoffrey d'Arbanville's lips against hers.

Despite his flirtatious banter, his voice had carried
the edge of desperation; he touched her now not with a
lover's caress, but as if to reassure himself that her
hair, her skin, her lips were real and not figments of his
imagination. Her bones seemed to desert her, so that
she swayed in his embrace, leading him to clamp strong
supportive arms around her. And then her arms turned
traitor, ignoring her firm wish to push herself free of
his embrace in favor of creeping up around his shoulders, until she clung to him as tightly as he held her.

He calmed when she pressed against him, and a
thoroughly masculine tremor reminded her of his great
size, his obvious strength. His lips, firm and supple and
experienced, teased and tantalized, sending wild nameless cravings shuddering through her.

She felt his tongue touch hers, and that hot intimacy
roused warnings within her mind. Gasping, partly to
fill her heaving lungs and partly at the startled realization of how unseemly she'd behaved, Juliette pushed
herself free of Geoffrey's embrace.

His breathing rasped as harshly as her own. Juliette
cursed her own weakness, for as she stared at the heaving rise and fall of his chest, her entire body tingled
with the remembered feel of his muscled frame hard

against hers. Surely there was something in this bedroom she could stare at besides that portion of Geoffrey's anatomy below his misplaced belt. She felt suddenly grateful that he hadn't tucked in his shirt, that it belled loosely over his lower body after being nipped in snugly around his waist.

"I came to tell you that you must leave here tomorrow, at first light," she said, avoiding his smoldering gaze.

He nodded, a quick, accepting motion that seemed to restore his control to him. "Mayhap 'tis for the best, Juliette, for you have proven to me you are neither dream nor witch. And parts of me are clamoring even now to convince me I am most definitely neither asleep nor dead."

4

Geoffrey bestirred himself when the eastern horizon developed a thin layer of gray outlining the black, heralding the imminent arrival of dawn. Lest he waken Juliette and Captain Chaney by fumbling about in these unfamiliar surroundings, he lifted the wondrously movable glass and squeezed himself through the small window.

He doubted that anything could induce him to remain in this place. Even so, it would be best not to test his determination to leave by drawing Juliette, fresh from her bed, warm and disheveled and slumberous-eyed, to tempt him to stay. Witch, wanton, or woman, it mattered not at all; she roused in him all manner of appalling weaknesses, and his very soul might depend on showing this place the back of Arion's racing heels. He crouched low as he ran to the stable, his boots soundless against the thick springy turf.

Arion nickered a greeting, and Geoffrey thought he'd never heard so welcome a sound.

He groped the length of each stable wall without finding a single candle or torch, or the flint for lighting them, and then cursed his dim-wittedness. Of course, Juliette would fasten such necessities at a level she could reach. He commenced patting the walls again, lower, seeking some manner of lighting the darkened stable. Naught but a metal and glass contrivance reeking of smoldering coal could be found; in shape it felt like the object in his chamber that Juliette had called a lamp. It made splashing sounds when his hand struck it, and coated his fingers with an odorous oily liquid.

He continued patting, adding a wiping cloth to his list of wants, when his questing fingers encountered living human flesh.

He uttered an unearthly howl to cover his shock, employing the knightly strategy of loud noise to disconcert his enemy if a surprise attack was intended, and flung himself facefirst onto the hay-littered floor. No zinging arrow, no twanging bowstring, no slash of sword rending air greeted his ears, only a decidedly childlike shriek of terror, followed by the thud of a small body joining his in the dirt.

"Geoff . . . Geoffrey?" a voice whimpered.

"Robbie?" Geoffrey scrambled upright, peering through the predawn gloom at the pale blur of Robbie's woeful young face. "God's blood—had I been wearing my sword at my belt, you would be headless now!"

"I'm sorry. I stayed with your horse, to keep him company. I ain't never seen a horse like him before."

Bad enough, to realize that the presence of a stripling had prompted one of Geoffrey's most fearsome battle cries and sent him flopping to the ground like a speared salmon. The lad's concern for Arion reminded Geoffrey of the strangeness of this place, where no well-trained squires stood by to coddle a knight's steed, or help a knight dress, or light a knight's way in the dark.

"How fares Arion?" Geoffrey asked, rising and brushing the dirt and bits of hay away from the shirt and britches Juliette seemed so concerned over.

"Oh, he's grand! I'll light the lantern so you can see for yourself." Geoffrey heard a metallic squeaking and then his nose inhaled a dose of the same sulfurous scent clinging to his fingers. There was a rasping sound, and then fire sprang to life at Robbie's fingertips.

"God's blood! 'Tis unholy sorcery!" Geoffrey moved to knock the hellfire from Robbie's hand, but the boy shielded the flame.

"Gosh, Geoffrey, my pa told me folks used to trick Injuns by lighting matches, but I didn't believe him. Maybe . . . maybe I ought to believe him about you, too. You ain't no knight, you're some kind o' Injun."

The lad and his father thought him a siege-engine? While Robbie applied the fire to the lamp and cast him reproachful glances, Geoffrey mulled over the various types of siege-engines he'd fought alongside, always in battle, never during a match. Ballistas, petraries, mangonels, and bombards, all unwieldy, heavy wooden contrivances that no person possessing a whit of intelligence could mistake for a man.

Then again, Geoffrey had seen a finely wrought Genoese mangonel hurl its projectile with such force that it had killed twelve men with one stone. His shoulders straightened. Perhaps Robbie's comment indicated a keen, if childlike, perception of Geoffrey's battle prowess. He found that thought quite cheering.

"There." Robbie transferred most of the fire he held to the wick protruding from the lamp and then shook the excess flame away. He settled a hollow glass tube

over the burning wick and hung the lamp from a nail.
A pleasant steady glow illuminated the stable.

"What feeds yon flame?" Geoffrey demanded, keeping a suspicious eye on the lamp.

Robbie favored him with a blank stare. "Oil, o' course.
Kerosene. I think Miss Alma says it's made from coal."

"Aha!" Geoffrey's triumphant cry reverberated from
the walls. He pointed an accusatory finger at the suddenly cringing boy. "At last I have caught someone in
an outright lie. I know all there is to know about coal,
and I see not one single lump of it in your lamp. Any
fool knows coal does not burn so briskly; it smolders
red. Explain your purpose in trying to deceive me."

Robbie's face took on a sickly pallor replacing his
normal sunburnt countenance. Before Geoffrey could
remark on it, the boy emitted a frightened yelp and
bolted from the stable.

Unaccountably regretful at speaking so harshly to
the boy, Geoffrey kicked at some straw as he crossed
the aisle to Arion's stall. "The boy lacks the makings of
a squire," he muttered.

"The boy lacks a loving father."

The soft voice spun Geoffrey around. Juliette leaned
against the door frame, looking every bit as delectably
sleep-warmed and tousled as he'd feared. Her hair fell all
atumble over her shoulders. She wore some sort of volu-
minous white gown that managed, despite its wide folds,
to hint at the soft supple form it hid. She clutched a shawl
over her shoulders, her long slender fingers gripping it
closed at her neck. Geoffrey gave Arion a pat, glad that
the stallion's broad frame kept Juliette from seeing how
his lower reaches reacted to the sight of her. He straightened his shoulders, conscious of the ground-in dust and
hay bits clinging to his borrowed clothes.

"You seem bent on following me," he said. A practiced

seductress would react to such a comment with a coy smile, a teasing remark. The unruly part of his nature hoped her appearance bespoke an attempt at seduction, while something within him grieved to think of her carrying out such a role.

Juliette responded with a careless shrug of her slim shoulders. "I own this place. I have a right to know what's going on in my own barn." She followed up her outrageous statement by flinging his own words back at him. "You seem bent on' bellowing insults at everyone you see."

As if he would have wasted his very best battle cry upon these peasants! "You have not heard my true bellow."

"Roar?"

"Lions roar, Juliette." Like that noble beast, he found himself instinctively stalking her. With each spoken word, she moved a tiny step farther into the stable; he moved a longer step away from Arion, toward her.

"Shout? Howl? Yell?" She challenged him as they approached one another.

"Do you look upon me and see naught but a shrieking wild beast, Juliette?"

By this time they stood so close that his breath stirred her hair and, God's blood, but he did feel a sudden envy for every wild thing that could scent and claim a mate with none to stop him.

"What I see standing before me is a wolf in sheep's clothing. An *actor*." She dashed his primitive passions with a contemptuous sniff. "Pretending you don't know how to dress properly, pretending you don't know how to speak English. Now look at you—all buttoned up and talking so fast a runaway train couldn't keep up, and picking on a little boy to boot. You're good, I'll admit that much. You almost had me feeling sorry for you."

"You almost felt sorry," asked Geoffrey d'Arbanville, squaring his shoulders to their full mighty width, "for *me?*"

His entire demeanor conveyed incredulity, his stance, swaggering self-assurance. For a moment the dusty barn receded and she imagined a hushed crowd encircling a sun-drenched tournament field and Geoffrey standing fully armed and triumphant over a fallen warrior.

She shook the fancy away, but it still didn't seem possible that this cocksure individual standing before her was the lost bewildered stranger who'd embraced her the night before. For a moment . . . for a moment, he seemed exactly like the sort of man who might be dubbed a knight.

It wasn't possible. She stole a covert glance at his waist. A leather belt, slipped through each and every loop, encircled his neatly tucked-in shirt, bringing to mind the tight leather sleeveless shirt hugging those same muscled curves. The same man. She swept her gaze over the brawny arms straining the fit of Captain Chaney's borrowed shirt. The same man.

She could see only the crest of his ever-present pendant gleaming at his neck; her attention shifted higher, to the full curve of his lips, lips that had possessed hers with a desperate need that had shifted into something more compelling, something more demanding. The same lips. The same man. And yet not the same.

"So I inspire your sympathy, Juliette?" he asked, the low huskiness in his voice vibrating against an answering chord within her.

She shook her head. "I thought you might need a friend."

She would just die if he laughed. She should have held herself distant from him like the dried-up disapproving widow everyone thought she was. She should have stayed true to the aloof nature she'd so assiduously cultivated and bid him good riddance as he mounted his horse and rode away. Nobody knew better than she the consequences of indulging casual attraction, or legitimizing it until it locked you tight within vows you couldn't break.

Unfortunately, some frivolous sprite had lodged itself in her breast after Geoffrey had kissed her last night. Never before had the presence of a boarder rendered her sleepless. Never before had she found herself lying awake shivering at the curiously intimate realization that her home's rough walls closed out the rest of the world. Within those walls, she breathed the air Geoffrey breathed, she heard the sounds he heard; both of their rooms held the soothing scent of the beeswax she'd used to polish the furniture, the lingering scent of dinner stew, the potpourri she'd mixed with her own hands.

"You would be my friend, Juliette?" Geoffrey cocked his head at her. The lantern's glow scattered golden highlights across his face, softening his chiseled features. A wistful smile tugged at his lips. "My profession discourages most such overtures."

She felt a stab of sympathy. Naturally a traveling actor would find it difficult to make friends. "Perhaps you should pursue another profession."

At once, all notions of softness or wistfulness vanished from his face. He inhaled sharply and stiffened as if she'd dealt him a mortal insult. "Knighthood is a sacred charge. It cannot be cast aside for the sake of surrounding oneself with pleasant company."

Knights, always knights! Well, one thing she could say for Geoffrey, he stuck to his guns—unlike herself. Ever since meeting him she'd wavered in her purpose like a wind-whipped willow. Though she stood firmly rooted, his smile could bend her one way, his words yet another, making a mockery of her determination to remain unaffected by him.

"You promised to stop talking about living in the past." Her reminder served to recall her earlier accusations against him. "Besides, even if you are an actor, you're not a very good liar. If you wanted us to believe your story —"

" 'Tis no mere story."

"—you shouldn't have dressed yourself this morning as if you knew exactly how a normal person wears his clothes."

"A keen observant eye is one of the first skills a knight must develop." He treated her to a triumphant glare. "I studied those men clustered about your kitchen and restyled my dress after their fashion."

Juliette gave him silent grudging credit for coming up with a quick explanation. And then she smiled, certain he wouldn't be able so easily to explain away her other observation. "What about the way you speak? You throw in a funny word now and then, and fool around with the pronunciation, but you seemed to learn our language right quick."

"Of course I did." He crossed his arms and stared down the length of his nose at her, managing to convey both arrogance and proud dignity. " 'Tis a gift I possess, handed straight from God."

"Ha!"

"Ha?" He leaned down until scant inches separated his nose from hers. He quirked one brow, and the hint of a smile tilted his lips. "Well might you question my mastery of your tongue, given your own humorous rejoinder."

"It's not humorous when someone says 'ha' like that," she said.

"An insult, then?"

"If you want to call it that."

"Ha! Put me to the test, Juliette. Summon that Mongol warrior you saluted yesterday. I give you my knightly oath that I have never spoken a word of his heathen tongue. I need hear only a little to grasp any language in full. I will prove my gift to you by conversing in Mongol ere the day is out."

Juliette took an involuntary step back. His teasing so flummoxed her mind that she couldn't understand what he was talking about. *Mongol warrior?* Putting a bit of breathing space between them helped, for once away from him she realized he might be talking about the buffalo hunter who had helped save his life.

"I've never heard of Mongol Indians in these parts." Juliette tried to explain. "Around here we usually see Osages, Potawatomies, Kansas Indians —"

"Now who finds herself telling stories, hmm?" Geoffrey wagged a reproving finger before her face. "That warrior was no Indian."

"Well, of course he was!"

"Juliette." He gave his head a stern shake and uttered a humorless laugh, one which sounded as though he recalled an unpleasant memory. "I once spent a full month in India's wretched clime. Likening that warrior to an Indian is akin to calling a Chinaman an Egyptian."

The more time she spent talking to him, the crazier he sounded. Though the morning sun now beat hot through the barn door, she clutched the wrap tighter at her neck, wishing she'd never followed him out to the barn, wishing she'd let him mount his horse and leave without being reminded once more of his lunacy. It might have been nice to treasure his memory in her mind, to call it back now and again when the nights seemed endless and only loneliness pressed close. To remember the feel of his lips warm and demanding against hers, the brush of his fingers against her skin as he'd toyed with her buttons, without having the memories stained by the knowledge that she'd thrilled to the touch of a madman.

"I don't mean to sound inhospitable, but if you and your horse have recovered from your ordeal, I'd suggest you be on your way. A contingent of soldiers heading for Fort Scott is due to arrive here any day, and they'll require every one of my rooms." Her stiff, clipped words seemed to carry an unusually harsh edge. But maybe not. She'd sounded all too breathless and fluttery lately, her voice a whispery shadow of its normal, no-nonsense self. Maybe that's why her return to brisk businesslike behavior struck her ears with snooty nasal discordance, like a prudish spinster scolding an errant child.

Surely she didn't sound so stuffy all the time. She couldn't. Why, not so long ago, before she'd learned to curb her impulsive behavior, she'd been told her voice chimed like tiny golden bells. Funny how she'd forgotten.

"I must admit to being surprised that you would allow me to leave if your liege lord has dispatched soldiers to take me prisoner."

She felt suddenly weary, her sleepless night, her witless knight, all conspiring to rob her strength. Had he really wanted her to summon soldiers to investigate him? Without coming right out and saying it, he'd convinced her he was an actor. A person wasn't drawn to acting unless he loved being the center of attention at all times. "Geoffrey, the soldiers are coming because it's a convenient place for them to stop and rest. They have no interest in you. They don't even know you're here."

"You did not notify your lord that a knight swearing allegiance to another had entered this outlying village?"

He seemed astonished that she hadn't reported his arrival to someone in authority.

"What lord? Walburn Ford doesn't even have a mayor, for heaven's sake."

He puzzled over her statement for a moment, and then squared his shoulders. "'Tis not a trap, then? I can ride away without fearing to expose my back?"

"Yes." The whispery softness was back in her voice, coupled with an embarrassing tremulousness brought on by the image of Geoffrey's broad back disappearing over the horizon.

She knew then that she *would* savor those memories of their brief moments together, no matter that his behavior made the antics of a catnip-sated kitten seem sensible. With so much insanity crowding his mind, would he ever spare a stray thought for her?

"Just be sure to watch out for the border ruffians. They probably won't bother you once you ride away from town. They're all a bunch of cowardly blatherskites, so if they make any threats, just point your gun at them as if you mean business."

"Border disputes I understand well. But *blatherskites,* Juliette? *Gun?*"

Funny, that although he spoke so low she could barely hear him, his voice nonetheless echoed inside her like a gong, bringing her gloriously aware of him in a way no man's normal speaking tone ever did.

"Your God-given gift doesn't help you understand those words?" she asked to cover her trembling reaction.

"The hand of God never turns aside a bit of help."

She hid her amusement. "A *blatherskite* is . . . well, it's sort of a cussword, but not blasphemous. And everyone knows what a *gun* is, Geoffrey."

"Everyone save me." A rueful smile, accompanied by a bleak shadow, darkened his face. "I regret being charged with a quest that does not permit me the time to comprehend the many strange things about this place."

Men and their precious quests—she understood them well. Wasn't she even now working to bring Daniel's dream to fruition? She'd heard tell of all kinds of men heading West without the first bit of knowledge of how to take care of themselves. Even so, it twisted her heart to think of Geoffrey riding out in pursuit of his mysterious quest with Indians and border ruffians roaming all over if he really didn't know anything about firearms.

She had to press her lips together to keep from blurting out that he should stay, at least until he familiarized himself with the use of a gun. She shook off the impulse. What if he were lying? Geoffrey d'Arbanville might be a little muddleheaded just now, but he didn't strike her as a helpless tenderfoot fresh from the eastern train. He seemed so supremely confident of himself, it was hard to believe he'd never learned about guns.

Very well—she would put him to the test. Daniel's sole legacy had been a good hunting pistol. It lay dusty and unused in her bureau drawer. A tiny voice inside warned her that only a madwoman would arm a madman, even if providing him with the gift of a gun was one sure way to make him think about her once in a while. She quelled the doubt.

"I'll fix your breakfast before you leave," she said. "And then I'll fetch my husband's Colt. We'll see how well you can handle it, and whether God gave you any gifts for hitting targets."

He seemed to brighten at the idea of taking target practice. He flexed one arm, as if balancing something in his fist, and sent her a confident smile that all but melted her bones.

"He blessed me with many formidable talents, Juliette. I daresay I shall amaze you."

5

Geoffrey said nothing complimentary about the sumptuous fare Juliette offered to break his fast, considering how she seemed determined to convince him it was scarcely worth eating. No others joined them, though he knew peasants abounded hereabouts. It seemed passing strange to sit quietly at such a table, without grimy hands filching tasty tidbits from his plate, without dogs slinking through the rushes—without rushes, as she kept her wooden floor clean-swept.

Forks—she held a fistful of the rare implements and counted out one for him, one for the sour-tempered Captain Chaney who'd arrived at table before them, and one for herself. Bacon rashers, neatly sliced and fried to perfection, lay atop that cryptlike box she called a stove. There were eggs—a veritable feast's worth, all to himself; bread—whiter and finer than that turned out by King Edward's best bakers; an interesting yellowish gruel, cornmeal she called it, that would have in itself served to fill his belly.

Salt, not in a bowl but contained within an odd contrivance that managed to shake an even portion over the top of the food.

Tea, as well as that Saracen drink, coffee, for which he had developed a fondness while squiring during crusade, and which he had not tasted since earning his spurs.

And sugar.

And a confection called lazy-day cake, redolent of cinnamon and nutmeg and spices unfamiliar to his nose.

All served upon delicately wrought plates that resembled fine porcelain but lacked the proper glaze.

Geoffrey quaffed some coffee and then studied the mug. Only one country boasted such an opulent wealth of luxuries.

"China," he muttered.

"Naw, they're just Miss Jay's ever' day dishes," Captain Chaney said, chewing his rasher.

Geoffrey's appetite abruptly deserted him. It rankled, knowing this aged peasant felt comfortable and confident uttering witless statements whilst Geoffrey d'Arbanville fretted with confusion and a sense of inadequacy. He would put an end to this once and for all.

"Fetch your colt, if you think an untried steed can stand against Arion. 'Tis time to confront the tourney field targets," he announced. He clapped his hands against the tabletop and leaped to his feet, once again sending his stool clattering to the floor.

"You oughta push yourself back from the table afore you stand up," Captain Chaney commented with a smirk.

"Ha!" Geoffrey flung the insult in his face and stormed to the stable to fetch Arion.

*   *   *

Rebecca Wilcox stood near the window, using her hip to brace a dishpan of water against the sill so she could keep both her hands submerged. With her fingertips reddened and shriveled, Josiah wouldn't suspect that she'd spent parts of the past hour peering through the tiny gap between the flour-sack curtains.

He'd never exactly forbidden her to stare through the window, never ordered her to confine herself within the cabin while he was away from the homestead. But she'd learned over the years that things went easier for her and Robbie if she holed herself up like a broody hen, if she pretended complete disinterest in the outside world. With her wrinkled hands and a huge stack of freshly washed dishes as evidence of her feverish industriousness, Josiah might not demand a minute-by-minute accounting of her time, or waste the remaining daylight studying the dusty yard for evidence of another man's footprints.

Then again, he might. It was a hard thing, loving a man who didn't trust you.

She stared across the prairie toward Walburn Ford, watching, waiting, until a smudge developed at the horizon. She risked watching a few moments more, until the smudge defined itself into a small group of people, all men except for Alma Harkins, who had the misfortune to be boarding with the Wilcoxes through the end of the month. Their mouths moved in silent clamor, arms waving with impassioned fervor as they approached the cabin.

She didn't see Robbie among the crowd; he must have stayed behind to help Miss Jay, which would infuriate Josiah, but Rebecca could always better endure Josiah's furies when the boy wasn't around to bear the immediate brunt of his stepfather's anger. She darted toward the drainboard before anyone could catch sight of her, and when she heard the hum of raised voices and the scuffle of footsteps in the yard, she drenched the clean, dry dishes with her dishpan water to make it seem that she'd just finished the chore.

"Coffee, missus." Josiah stepped through the door and placed his order much like any man would upon entering a restaurant, without a shred of happiness at greeting his wife after an hour-long absence.

"Yes, mister." There had been no warmth in his greeting; neither had there been antagonism. Rebecca dared relax the slightest bit.

"Evenin', Miz Wilcox. Howdy do. Coffee smells good." The neighbors crowding behind Josiah offered the greetings Josiah never bothered with. Rebecca fashioned her well-practiced smile—not overly welcoming, even though she felt all but numb with relief that they were there to deflect Josiah's attention—and turned to face them. They all looked upon her husband with the apprehensive expression one might bestow upon a doctor about to prescribe an unpleasant, albeit lifesaving, dose of quinine. It always astonished her that people who wouldn't dream of calling Josiah Wilcox friend would nonetheless turn to him for all manner of advice.

"We're settled on it, then." Josiah stared from neighbor to neighbor, daring each to voice a difference of opinion, before his gaze settled on Alma Harkins.

While the balance of the group muttered agreement, Alma commenced flushing an unbecoming shade of red from the neck on up. "I can't say I'm happy about this."

Curiosity gripped Rebecca, but she knew better than to show any interest in Josiah's affairs. She kept her false smile in place while she poured overboiled coffee into their three tin mugs and passed them out: Josiah first, and then to the most senior of Walburn Ford's men. The others would have to wait their turn; but for all the attention the fortunate few paid their mugs, the others might be better off heading home for a cup.

"I just don't see why I have to be the one to do it,"
Alma said. "I'm the schoolteacher, and it's only natural
for people to turn to me for . . . well, for all sorts of things.
Why, if word got out that I spied on that poor Geoffrey
d'Arbanville, nobody would ever trust me again."

"If word got out to who?" queried Bertie Walters.
"Someone from just about ever' family in Walburn
Ford's here in this room. We all know what yer up to."

"It's for the good of the town," added Bean Tyler. "It's
like Josiah said—that Geoffrey could be a border ruffian
sent in to learn all our secrets about the town's defenses."

Rebecca polished a nonexistent spill from the table,
hiding her fascination from the others. She'd have given
anything to have gone last night with Josiah and the
other Walburn Ford settlers to meet the newcomer. She
felt sure most of the other wives had been there, but
then they wouldn't have to spend the next month listening to their jealous husbands wondering aloud whether
the stranger had been summoned by secret letter, or if
he'd come to complete a tryst arranged ten years earlier.

"It doesn't seem right," Alma continued with
dogged persistence. "He seems to like m . . . I mean,
there are other single women in this town, you know.
Miss Jay, for one. Why can't she and I both take him on
a picnic? I'd certainly feel better about it that way."

"Miss Jay doesn't hold with frivolous outings like
picnics," Bertie said.

"And she's boarding him, ain't she? For all we
know, she could be in on his plans," said Josiah.

Rebecca listened admiringly while Alma braved
Josiah's wrath to come to Miss Jay's defense. "How
dare you say such a thing, Josiah Wilcox! Miss Jay
wouldn't fall in with a border ruffian, not after what
happened to her husband and folks."

"Maybe not." Rebecca could have sworn that she

heard a note of grudging apology come from her husband, but then he turned belligerent again, with an edge to his voice that would have sliced apart any further interference. "Anyway, you're the only single woman living off the town's generosity. It wouldn't look right for a married woman to take him on a picnic. Seems to me you'd want to jump at this chance to make yourself useful now that school's out for the summer."

Alma's mouth closed with an audible snap, and Rebecca wished she dared reach out to lend the schoolteacher's hand a reassuring squeeze, wished she dared whisper for Alma to give in and do whatever Josiah wanted. Alma need only live beneath Josiah's roof for another few weeks at most, and then she could snap her fingers beneath his nose if he ever asked for another favor. The thought both cheered Rebecca and filled her with dread, for her own sentence stretched into eternity.

"It's only a picnic, Alma," coaxed Bertie.

"And you certainly like to eat," added Bean Tyler.

"Oh!" Indignation over Bean's comment seemed to wipe out Alma's objections. Josiah, ever one to notice an advantage, pressed in.

"A pleasant afternoon in the sun, Alma. You can help yourself to anything you like from the pantry. Ask him what he's looking for and how long he plans to stay around. That's all."

"You know I wouldn't fall in with any plan that could place you in danger, don't you, Miss Alma?" Bean cleared his throat after speaking, as if the words had come hard.

"Oh, all right. But I'm telling you that you're all going to feel mighty foolish when it turns out he's nothing more than an actor who hurt his head and lost his memory for a little while." Alma's blush deepened as she gave in with ill-concealed disgust. "I had high hopes, very high hopes, I don't mind telling you, that he'd treat us to a performance."

"A performance?" Bertie's face creased with excitement. "I don't know, Josiah, it's been awful dull here. Maybe we are being a bit hasty here."

"He can do his playacting after he proves he's no danger to the town," Josiah insisted. The other men murmured reluctant agreement.

"Very well. Now, if you'll excuse me, I have next session's lessons to prepare." With an inelegant sniff and toss of her head as she passed Bean Tyler, Alma moved toward her room at the rear of the cabin.

With their business accomplished, the Walburn Ford men seemed disinclined to linger in Josiah's company. Rebecca scarcely had time to stammer good-bye before she found herself alone with Josiah, only the table and three cooling mugs of coffee between them.

As always, when she found herself alone before her husband's silent inexplicable anger, his whip-thin body seemed somehow more powerful, like a prime thoroughbred waiting for the starter's pistol. It was hard, now, to remember that there had been a time when she'd been unaware of his frightening aspects, that once she'd been completely mesmerized by his thick shock of midnight-black hair, and by his eyes, always looking so dark in his thin face, that weren't black, but a deep dark blue. But in those days, Josiah Wilcox had smiled and held her within the protective curve of his arms. How eagerly she'd fallen in with his plan to invest all his savings in the Vegetarian Settlement Company and journey to the wilds of Kansas.

"Your past won't mean a thing there, Becky. And I'll love the boy just like he was my own." He'd repeated the phrases so often Rebecca couldn't help but believe him; indeed, she'd taken comfort from them, certain all her dreams for herself, for her son, would come true through her love for Josiah Wilcox.

"What do you think about this Geoffrey d'Arbanville, missus?" Josiah asked, the harshness in his voice so violently contrasting with her tender memory that she couldn't suppress a shiver.

She couldn't look at her husband, knowing his sharp eyes would be watching for any shred of interest she might express over the mysterious newcomer. No matter how innocent her curiosity, he would read sinister meaning into it. During the years since their marriage, things had turned inexplicably sour; Josiah's promises to forget her past indiscretions had hardened instead into an implacable unforgiving jealousy. She sought some innocuous phrase to placate him.

"I can hardly give an opinion about a man I've never met."

The words had sounded innocent enough to her own ears; they roused Josiah Wilcox into a towering fury. "Oh, so now you're interested in meeting him?" he sneered, completely twisting the meaning of her remark. "Maybe this smooth-talkin' newcomer is all dressed up and playacting to disguise who he really is. Maybe he's someone my wife might recognize from the past."

"Oh Josiah." She whispered his name, consumed by equal measures of anger and despair. When would she ever cease hoping that one day he'd realize there were no grounds for his sick jealousy? When would she ever cease caring? How long before her love, weakened by this constant undermining, simply caved in and disappeared?

"Well, just look at that curtain," Josiah marveled with heavy sarcasm. "Looks like someone must have wasted some time looking out that window, missus."

A leaden heaviness settled around Rebecca's heart

when she realized her thumb had left a faint bulge along the side seam; her damp fingers had puckered the edge of the flour sack.

"I . . . I was watching for you. So I could have the coffee ready."

"Is that so?" Three words, an innocuous phrase—but Rebecca knew what three words he really meant to speak: *Liar. Faithless slut.* Sometimes . . . sometimes she just wanted to curl up and die from the unfairness of it all. But then Robbie would be at his stepfather's mercy. And Josiah would never ever realize how much she truly loved him.

"Supper's ready whenever you want it," she managed to say around the ache in her throat.

"I'll be expecting something real special, since you had all day to prepare it." He headed for the door and called over his back, "I'm going outside to have a look around the yard. Have everything ready in fifteen minutes."

"Yes, mister."

Fifteen minutes was no time at all to set the table and dish out the supper food, all vegetarian dishes painstakingly prepared to soothe Josiah's balky constitution. She hadn't a minute to waste, but she felt as helpless to move as a prairie hen paralyzed by snake venom, until Alma ventured tentatively back into the kitchen, her face creased with such commiserative pity that Rebecca wished she could flout convention and give up on her marriage, just pack up Robbie's things and run away.

Alma gave Rebecca's hand a reassuring pat. "Border ruffian or actor or whatever he is, it looks like that Geoffrey fellow's going to stir things up around here."

"Oh Alma, I sure don't want to stir things up." Rebecca stared at the pots lining the stove top, fighting the uncommon urge to fling them all outside into the dirt to give Josiah something to discover. "You've seen what my husband's like when he's crossed. You're only going to be boarding with us for a little while longer. I don't know what I'll do when you're not here anymore to stand between us."

"You could invite Miss Jay over for a cup of coffee."

"What?"

Alma busied herself with gathering utensils. "You and Miss Jay are a lot alike, you know."

"We are not." Rebecca plopped into a chair, completely startled by Alma's comment. "Miss Jay's responsible and independent. She wouldn't put up with Josiah's jealous fits for a single minute."

"Miss Jay has a lot of inner strength, just like you. And just like you, she's been put into a difficult position by her husband. She endures, just like you."

"Goodness, I've always admired Miss Jay." Rebecca groped for a folded napkin and began fanning herself. After so many years of accepting Josiah's poor opinion of herself, it seemed so impossible to believe she could share any of the admirable qualities possessed by Miss Jay Walburn. It made her feel funny, and kind of hopeful. "Now, if only you could tell me that Josiah's just like Geoffrey."

"Well, since you noticed the resemblance yourself . . ." Alma cast her a mischievous grin, ignoring Rebecca's gasp of protest. "I never did see two men who walked around with so many crazy ideas in their heads without a shred of proof for anything. Peas in a pod, Becky. Peas in a pod."

"I wouldn't have thought of it, but I do believe you're right, Alma. Though what good it will do me to know this, I can't imagine."

Alma cocked her head and sent Rebecca a fond smile. "If I'm inviting Geoffrey on a picnic, I'm going to bake a cake. Should I just set all the ingredients in separate pans in the oven, or do you think it would be better if I broke a few eggs and stirred them into the sugar and water until it all looks like mud?"

Rebecca managed a shaky smile at Alma's silliness. "You've got to stir it all up, of course."

"Well maybe that's your problem, Becky. You've spent too many years trying to walk on your eggs and keep the sugar from melting in the water. Maybe it's time you started doing things a little different."

"You always manage to sound like a teacher." Rebecca sniffed back tears. "Cakes don't turn out right every time, you know."

"No, but they always taste sweet, even if they're lumpy and pitiful." With that, Alma glanced down at her bosom and rolled her eyes heavenward.

Rebecca couldn't stifle a giggle. Lord, but it felt good to laugh. It felt good to think that she carried strength within herself. Maybe there was something to Alma's stirring-up theory. "It can't get any worse, can it?" She asked the question with the same deceptive lightness she always used with Josiah and, like Josiah, Alma wasn't fooled one bit.

"Things can always get worse, Rebecca. But every so often—often enough to keep us hoping—something sort of magical happens to make things better for those who are willing to take a chance."

6

Geoffrey walked beside Juliette, leading Arion. The steed, obviously recovered from their fearsome leap, tossed his head and snorted his confusion as they neared the tourney field. Well might Arion wonder what was going on, for even Geoffrey felt baffled. Despite promising to do so, Juliette had brought no untrained colt to test his horsemanship. No practice field greeted his eyes. Not one single quintain, no cache of rings awaited his well-aimed lance. There was naught to mark this stretch of pasture as being any different from the endless acres of waving grass save for a single tree stump poking its crumbling head above the turf.

"There's one!" Juliette sounded inordinately pleased to see the stump. She rushed over to it and crouched down, patting through the grass until she found a small rock, which she balanced atop one of the stump's jagged edges.

She returned to Geoffrey's side and cast a critical glance toward Arion. "I still think you should have left your horse back in the stable. If you're telling the truth, if he's never been around gunfire, he might spook."

Geoffrey bristled. He knew nothing of gunfire, but he and Arion had fought through showers of the Greek fire many times. Throughout this walk Juliette had been badgering him to return Arion to his stall, as if a knight could prove his prowess at striking targets without being mounted upon a horse capable of anticipating his movements. Perhaps, lacking a well-trained horse of her own, she sought to put him at an equal disadvantage. But to cast slurs upon Arion's bravery!

"Think you Arion lacks battle courage?"

"I'm sure he's very courageous. Still, I'd hang on tight to his bridle if I were you." She appeared worried as she withdrew one of the bone-handled metal snouts from her pocket. Everyone in this place seemed possessed of such an object; he would be glad to learn its function. She held it up before his face and flipped it to and fro. "Daniel, my husband, taught me how to protect myself, but I haven't used it much. I cleaned it while you saddled the horse. Do you want to take the first shot? Daniel got this gun straight from the colonel who designed it. He always said that once folks discovered what a fine pistol it is, everyone would be carrying Colts."

Truly, he could not fathom her purpose. Carrying colts? And did she mean for him to fling the gun at the rock? "You show me, Juliette," he said.

With a nod, she raised the gun to nose level and peered over it at the rock, squinting much like Captain Chaney had squinted at Geoffrey during their first meeting in the stable. Perhaps she meant to draw her arm back and whirl it like a discus—Geoffrey never knew, for she had time only to make the slightest motion of her finger before a thunderous roar shattered the calm, accompanied by a cloud of smoke so acrid it seemed that the very Earth had rifted apart to permit the stench of hellfire to desecrate the air.

"God's blood!" Geoffrey's oath could scarcely be heard above Arion's frightened scream, but he had no attention left for the bolting horse. He must at all costs protect Juliette from their unseen attackers. He flung himself against her and bore her to ground, bracing his arms as they landed, hoping to spare her the worst of his weight. Nonetheless, their nether reaches were pressed close, and he could feel her firm uptilting breasts brush against his chest as she wiggled beneath him. She thrashed about, her hair loosening from its infernal coil, calling his name, begging him to let her rise.

"Hold still, I know not whence they attacked," he cautioned, more breathless than his actions warranted. Inappropriate, that lustful thoughts should intrude whilst a lady was subjected to unknown danger. He must needs confess this unknightly behavior when next he visited a priest.

"Nobody attacked us, Geoffrey."

"God's blood, woman, hold your tongue lest you draw their attention to us. Never have I encountered enemies with such fearsome weapons."

"Geoffrey, listen to me! *Nobody attacked us.* I made the noise. I shot the gun. Look." She wriggled a hand free and stuck the gun beneath his nose. A fine wisp of smoke trailed from the open end of the snout, where he smelled the same acrid stench that had filled the air following the eruption of noise.

"You caused that unearthly sound, Juliette, with the gun?"

She nodded eagerly; he could feel the silken slide of her hair drift over his hands. It was her lack of fear that convinced him she spoke the truth. The roar Juliette claimed she made would have sent most women he knew into a shrieking hair-tearing cowering frenzy. Knowing that no superior enemy lurked should have suffused him with relief; instead, he felt the fool, ever plowing nose-first into the dirt when confronted with tricks mastered by these people.

How she must be laughing at him!

He meant to heave himself away from her, but found himself disinclined to abandon his soft sprawl. When she'd moved her arm to wave the gun at him, his belly had come to rest against hers, and although layers of clothes separated their skins, he could feel the fluttering rise and fall of her flesh beneath his. A faint flowery scent redolent of the soap they shared drifted from her dispelling all else, so that for the moment he forgot all thoughts of humiliation and confusion.

Juliette sensed the rapid shifts in his emotions, from selfless protector to confused madman to aroused male. She knew she should push the big oaf away so she could stand up. Gracious! What if someone should happen by and see the Widow Walburn wallowing around on the prairie with her lunatic boarder?

Unfortunately for her reputation, her body ignored her urgent commands. Instead of pushing in a firm manner, her hand found itself sort of resting against Geoffrey's shoulder. Instead of forming strong words, her tongue traced a delicate path around her lips, which had gone suddenly dry. There were any number of reasons why a sensible, down-to-earth woman like herself could take offense at the high-handed way he'd pushed her to the ground and now held her captive.

Instead, something within her thrilled to realize his first thought upon hearing gunfire had been to protect her. Even now he sheltered her within his embrace, covering her thoroughly with his huge muscular frame, baring his own vulnerable back to attack—never mind that the danger was all in his muddled head—like a real knight protecting his lady.

She heard a soft whooshing sound, and then felt a velvety muzzle near her shoulder nudging Geoffrey away from her.

"Arion! Your leg!"

Geoffrey let loose with a string of foreign-sounding words uttered with such explosive venom she figured them to be curses. She felt like muttering a few herself, though she wasn't sure why, when he abandoned her to crouch next to his blasted horse.

"I fear he has turned a foreleg." Solemn-faced, Geoffrey pressed his fingers against a swollen area above Arion's hoof.

"I told you to leave him back in the barn."

"Aye, you did." He shook his head and sighed. "For what purpose did you make such a noise, Juliette?"

She rose to her feet as gracefully as she could, considering her legs had gone shaky while Geoffrey d'Arbanville had lain stretched out on top of her. "You said you didn't know anything about guns, so I wanted you to see what you'd be up against if you came across a gun-toting border ruffian."

"Do these border ruffians not understand the value of a stealthy approach?" Geoffrey shook his head. "'Twill be a simple matter to catch them by surprise if they go about announcing their presence with these noisy guns."

"The noise comes after the damage is done, Geoffrey. By the time you heard a border ruffian's gun, you'd be dead." She pointed toward the stump. "Look, I shot the rock right off it. My husband always claimed I had excellent aim for a woman."

He squinted toward the now-empty stump and nodded. "Aye. The noise jostled the rock from its unsteady perch. I assure you I am not so easily toppled, even though I have had occasion of late to fling myself to ground."

Though he held his chin at a proud tilt, an air of embarrassment hung about him. He must have realized how unlikely she found it that any man could so deliberately misunderstand the purpose of a pistol, but he seemed determined to bluff it out regardless.

Very well. She would go along with his actor's antics. She found the soft pouch that hung at her waist and fished out a bullet. "The noise didn't move the rock. A bullet like this one did, and if you find yourself getting hit with one, you'll most likely end up dead."

He rose to his full height and stared down at the bullet nestled in her palm. He touched it with his forefinger. When the bullet rolled away from the pressure, his fingertip lightly, accidentally, brushed her tender flesh. Never before had another's touch sent such shivery sensations coursing straight to her heart. And her a widow, who had known the way of a man with a woman. It seemed somehow disloyal to Daniel, that Geoffrey should affect her so.

"This cannot hurt me," Geoffrey scoffed, capturing the bullet between his fingers. Oblivious to the way his movements added to her distracted state, he pulled at his shirt until the right end came free of his belt. A rough knot of scar tissue marred his abdomen's muscled flesh; another jagged dead-white streak commenced at his waist and disappeared amid the soft brown curls covering his chest. He pressed the bullet against the scar. "You see, such blunt metal cannot dent my tough hide."

He dropped the bullet and caught her hand, pressing her fingers against his warm skin, firm and smooth, adding pressure until she felt an alien hardness beneath it.

"Therein, Juliette, lies my mortal enemy Drogo FitzBaldric's finest sword tip. Though that one time he had me near gutted, my superior battle maneuvers snapped it off like the burnt end of a twig. Bled like a stuck pig for two days and then thrashed with fever a sennight longer. If such a proud weapon failed to slay me, I doubt your little bullet can succeed, no matter how heartily a border ruffian might throw it at me."

Her fingers moved in accord with the rise and fall of his ribs; his steady heartbeat pulsed against hers. Bleeding for two days, thrashing with fever, and smiling down at her now with complete confidence that he was impervious to gunshot wounds.

"You're just like Daniel." She hated the choking sound that thickened her words. "You think nothing can hurt you."

Juliette snatched her hand away from Geoffrey and whirled away from him. If only she could whirl away from her thoughts as well! And she had, for years now, until this . . . this demented *knight* came barging into her life, reminding her of another battle-scarred fighting man.

"I am not Daniel, Juliette." He spoke with a gentle reassurance not unlike the tone he'd used to calm his gun-shy horse.

Nonetheless, he spoke the truth. Daniel Walburn had been a mere boy compared to Geoffrey d'Arbanville, but there were other similarities.

"Daniel was fascinated with fighting," Juliette found herself explaining, "for the glory of the town bearing his name, he would say, and my mother would always tell me it was an understandable obsession of a lad scarcely past his youth. All I knew was that he was my first friend, maybe my only friend. We'd both grown up with fathers constantly searching out new frontiers. Our paths crossed here, and when Daniel's pa moved on, Daniel dug in and named the town after himself, said he'd never leave it dead or alive."

She held silent for a moment, not caring to tell Geoffrey that Daniel's kisses, innocently bestowed, had roused decidedly noninnocent responses from her, and proven to her that a wanton lay hidden beneath her respectable exterior. Daniel's marriage proposal had coincided with her father's stated intention of settling permanently in Walburn Ford. Even as she'd given herself to Daniel, she'd suspected it was a craving for affection more than love that ruled her body, but she'd promised God she would devote herself to loving Daniel more and more as time passed. The time had been denied her, and so she'd had to make up for it in other ways.

"When the border ruffian attacks started, I begged him and begged him to move away. I even prayed that my father would pull up stakes and move the family away, so I could make the excuse that we had to go along with them. Instead, my pa and Daniel both thrived beneath the constant threat of danger."

She'd taken refuge in Daniel's promises that her love would keep him safe, that their efforts would help Kansas earn the right to enter the Union as a free state. He didn't know that her love wasn't strong and true enough for the task.

Daniel had been whispering that very promise in her ear one starlit night, a night redolent with sweet springtime scents carried by the incessant breeze. At first, nothing more than the swishing sound of windblown grass had provided a background for their lovemaking. Her passions, not as deeply engaged as Daniel's, never deafened her ears to outside noises. She easily heard the gunfire over her quite ordinary heartbeat; in his aroused state, Daniel had ignored her pleas to investigate the commotion. By the time she convinced him that Walburn Ford was under border ruffian attack, a half-dozen innocent settlers had been murdered—Juliette's parents among them.

"Your husband died during one of these battle skirmishes?" Geoffrey asked.

She bit her lip and nodded, certain that embarrassment flooded her face. "We'd been drinking dandelion wine. Daniel was a little muzzy. I didn't realize he'd left without arming himself."

"He died a noble death, defending his lands," Geoffrey said.

If only that were true! Juliette shook her head. "Gut-shot," she said. "It took him three long months to die from his wounds. I promised God I'd do anything to ease Daniel's suffering."

Geoffrey blanched. "One must take great care when bargaining with the Almighty."

Juliette gave a little laugh. "Oh, my task was easy enough. All Daniel ever wanted was my promise to stay on here in Walburn Ford, to finish building up our boarding house business and help the town grow and prosper. It wasn't easy, but I did it. I'm Walburn Ford's most solid citizen. My boarding house business keeps food on the table. And I have plenty of spare time to tend the graves." Her laugh degenerated into something embarrassingly like a sob.

"Do you no longer fear living here with violence so close to hand?"

She leaped at the question, eager to turn their conversation in another direction. "At first I felt frightened every single moment. But so many deaths shocked even the ruffians and they haven't bothered us here in Walburn Ford. But not long after they attacked here, there was a near-massacre in the town of Ossawatomie, and the ruffians lost quite a few of their supporters. Just this past May, a proslaver shot five innocent men in Marais des Cygnes. That's when the soldiers started coming back. Since then, the ruffians' attacks have been more mischief making than anything else. The way we hear it, there's more trouble now in the States than there is here."

"So you have taken root here, never to be dislodged?" Geoffrey asked.

"Like a well sunk into the ground," Juliette said. She'd become Miss Jay, the Widow Walburn, property owner and respectable town citizen, devoted to the town's welfare. She had turned a proud face to the town, staring down those who dared whisper she'd never finish the boarding house or develop enough business to keep herself alive. She'd buried her sinful nature and pain beneath layers of respectability; she'd stifled her emotions and buried every last trace of the joyous free-spirited girl she'd once been right alongside her dead, and had sworn never to let her emerge again.

A vow she seemed to have forgotten ever since Geoffrey d'Arbanville had begun toying with her buttons.

Realization of how far she'd slipped from her self-imposed aloofness struck with an almost physical ache, like walking into harsh sunshine after spending the day in a cool quiet cave. One could become reaccustomed to sunshine, but it was less painful to return to the cave and wait for blessed darkness to obliterate all danger. How could she have forgotten?

A rabbit hopped from its burrow, intent upon nibbling at a wildflower. Miss Jay turned back to Geoffrey, confident once again in her ability to act as the teacher—and nothing more—for this actor-man who'd already proclaimed his intention to leave in pursuit of some sort of quest.

"Hold tight to Arion's bridle, and watch that rabbit. I'll show you what a gun and bullet can do."

She aimed. She fired. She looked away, the smoke still clouding her vision, and pressed her face against Arion's trembling neck while Geoffrey swore and pounded away toward the rabbit. Silence stretched over the prairie, turning the air heavy and still, until not even a blade of grass shimmied. Her head might have weighed five tons, so difficult did she find it to turn her face toward Geoffrey, and she caught her breath at the air of utter desolation that held him in thrall as he crouched staring at the rabbit's shattered body stretched over his hands.

Desolate. Shattered. She'd been wise to resurrect her invisible walls because, unlike Geoffrey, she felt none of those painful emotions. She didn't.

A thin shimmering liquid streak marked Arion's glossy neck, commencing right below the spot where her forehead had rested, right where tears would leave a trace if some soft-hearted woman had decided to cry. She rubbed the wetness away with her thumb.

7

Generations of noble blood coursed through Geoffrey's veins, a legacy of inborn pride and self-assurance envied by lesser men. Stern taskmasters had sharpened his keen intellect; a lifetime of hard practice tempered by occasional pleasure had honed every powerful inch of his body. Order of birth had denied him a title and possession of ancestral lands, but by virtue of his battlefield valor and fierce integrity, Geoffrey had forged a life marked by accolades and admiration.

All brought low by a nub of metal and a dead rabbit. And a malicious Celtic god.

Geoffrey lifted his head to the sky, closing his eyes against the sun's powerful glare. The movement sent Angus Ōg's pendant slapping against the base of his neck.

Since arriving in this godforsaken place, Geoffrey's instincts, his intelligence, had been warning him something was amiss. He'd ignored his suspicions—nay, squelched the belief—that such wondrous contrivances, such unfamiliar behavior, could not be found in an insignificant village tucked away in an obscure corner of England. The rabbit lying heavy in his hands, slain by a chunk of lead no bigger than an Italian olive, whispered the truth of what everyone had been telling him all along. Not even the Chinese boasted such fearsome weapons capable of killing with but the slightest movement of a frail woman's finger.

The strangers surrounding him had spoken the truth.

It was no longer the year of our lord 1283.

He and Arion had somehow hurtled nigh unto six hundred years into the future.

Edward, King of England, by now a moldering mass of dusty bones, had handed him into the care of Angus Ōg, restorer of life to those who died for the cause of love. By proving his willingness to die for the pendant representing the love between John and Demeter of Rowanwood, Geoffrey had entered the Eternal Chasm, that endless plunge dooming those who dared leap to an eternity of falling, falling, neither living nor dead.

And though he breathed, though he felt the sun hot against his skin, though his heart ached with a sudden constriction, it seemed that the Chasm had proven all the superstitions true. What life could one such as he now claim, a knight sworn to complete a quest commenced more than half a millennium before? What life, with his family, his friends, his hopes and dreams vanished like embers doused by rain?

He'd failed his king. The Celtic pendant hung round his neck, its weight suddenly oppressive. His mind tormented him with the fates that might have befallen those who'd depended upon his skill. Well could he imagine Edward's impatient fury as the king counted the passing days, waiting for Demeter of Rowanwood to acknowledge him as her liege. When her acknowledgment did not come, Edward would surely have ordered the death of her husband John and marched forthwith upon Rowanwood Castle.

And Drogo FitzBaldric—Geoffrey held no doubt but that the knave would have made good on his threat to besiege the lady Demeter. Had he succeeded? If so, he would have used her gentle person in violent ways, and taken control of the strong castle crouching at England's far northern border. Whilst Edward and Drogo clashed, such devastation would have been wrought that the royal line of Plantagenet blood could have been interrupted, the sovereignty of the nation rent irreparably apart.

It was a chilling thought, to consider that the very course of history might have been altered by Geoffrey d'Arbanville's unanticipated venture into the future.

Better he had died than endure this wrenching agonizing pain of knowing everything familiar, everything beloved, had gone from the earth. Better dead than to admit failing his knightly duty, despite making the ultimate sacrifice. Dead, he need not read wariness in Juliette's eyes, need not sense ridicule in place of the admiration he'd once accepted as his due.

Dead, he'd be consigned to eternal hellfire, courtesy of a centuries-long ride as the guest of a pagan god.

God's blood, it was a winless position he found himself occupying. What, then? Ask Juliette to dispatch one of her lead bullets into his six-hundred-year-old head?

The rabbit's skull, shattered like a kicked melon, hinted at the sweet oblivion he might thus find. A shuddering commenced from deep within, and he sought to master it while a gusting breeze flattened the rabbit's brownish gray fur against its cooling flesh, set its long ears quivering with false liveliness. The gun had rid the rabbit of its earthly woes, but had done nothing to change the fact that it was a rabbit he held.

Six hundred years old might he be, but still a knight. Succumbing to despair because his predicament seemed particularly daunting would not change the essence of Geoffrey d'Arbanville. No true knight would bow to the bullet whilst his quest remained unfulfilled. He could well imagine God's disdain should Geoffrey face his maker with his brains leaking from his head and seek to blame a pagan relic for his earthly failures.

He must needs find his way back. That was all there was to it. He had jumped into a chasm to get here; knightly logic dictated that he must find the base of the chasm, a mountain range, and climb his way back out.

Mountains. He must find mountains rising far above this discouragingly flat place.

"Ha!" He swore the 1859 oath and leaped to his feet, reaching for his dagger that he might gut this 1859 rabbit so cleanly delivered into his hands by an 1859 gun. "Ha! Ha! Ha!"

"Geoffrey? Is something funny? Should I be laughing?" Juliette approached, tentative as a curious doe, as well she should be.

"I cannot vouch for your safety should you laugh at me at this moment," Geoffrey warned, not yet as comfortable with his new situation as he would like to be.

"You wouldn't hurt me!" she exclaimed, and then a bewildered expression clouded her azure eyes, as if she'd startled herself by her pronouncement.

She spoke true; he'd sooner disjoint his hands at the wrists than cause her a moment's pain. And yet *he* hurt, a nameless aching no person on this 1859 Earth could share. Would that his hands weren't bloodied by the rabbit, for then he'd catch Juliette against him and bury his face against her soft sun-scented hair, revel in the feel of tender woman-flesh against his own harsh lines. How reassuring it would be to clutch a living breathing person until his swirling thoughts settled back into place and he could devise a plan for putting things to rights.

But embracing Juliette would not settle his thoughts; more likely, it would rouse all manner of inappropriate urges within him. Small wonder, considering six hundred years had passed since last he'd bedded a woman, surely a stint of celibacy unmatched by the most pious of priests. There was a depressing thought. His father, were he watching Geoffrey now from heaven, must be rubbing his hands together with glee to see centuries of abstinence foisted upon the son he'd dreamed might follow the path of the Holy Church rather than the knighthood.

Then again, bemoaning the lack of exercise for his lusty nature had never before overruled Geoffrey's battle sense, not even in his youth when, excruciatingly conscious of the length between dalliances, it had sometimes seemed that nigh unto six centuries had passed.

He'd thought Juliette a witch at first sight, running and shrieking and striking fear into satanic cattle and Mongol alike. Perhaps she did possess witchly skills! Since meeting her, he'd scarcely passed an hour without giving in to the urge to touch her in some manner. None of the other women he'd seen since arriving had aroused similar desires. A spell had been cast upon him. Naught else could explain why thoughts of dallying with Juliette stood foremost in his mind at this moment, eclipsing even his determination to resolve the dire predicament he found himself facing.

"What do you know of hurt, Juliette?" he asked, his voice grating roughly against the outdoor quiet as he shook away his thoughts. "Can you fathom the pain a man might feel to know he might never again look upon a familiar beloved face, to realize everything he valued matters naught, that he is powerless against the whims of fate?"

She flinched, and he fancied he read a bleakness in her eyes that he would have sworn none but he could know.

"Fate toys with us all, Geoffrey." She tilted her chin upward. "You can wallow in your misery, or you can beat it down and live as best you can. That's what I did."

"At what cost, Juliette?"

"It cost everything I had," she said. "Everything."

Spoken so simply, her words conveyed all the more the magnitude of her inner pain that made Geoffrey's loss of six hundred years seem a trifling inconvenience. Caring naught for the waste of good meat, he flung the rabbit into the grass. He wiped his hands as clean as he could against his borrowed chausses and brought Juliette into his embrace as he'd longed to do, but with a different purpose, an uncommon urge to soothe, to ask her to explain the agony he sensed she felt.

She spurned his embrace. She shrank away from his touch, as if accosted by some leprous baseborn lout. Women the world over had turned all agog at receiving his attention, when naught but lust ruled him. Another cruel trick of fate, that purity of purpose should now meet such sound rejection.

"If you want to stay at my place while your horse's leg heals, you'd better learn to keep your hands to yourself. You can't go around grabbing any woman who catches your fancy!" she shouted. "This isn't the Dark Ages, it's 1859—"

"I know what year it is." Seldom had any utterance of his sounded so devoid of feeling.

She made a noncommittal sound in response and cast him a suspicious glance, doubt writ plain upon her delicate features. Geoffrey bit his tongue against the urge to explain everything to her. It would merely serve further to exacerbate her poor opinion of him, were he to explain that he and his horse had ventured through time for no good purpose. Then, too, he must needs consider how that townsfolk would greet such a pronouncement.

Nay, best to keep the truth to himself. He had thought her a witch; how would she react if she knew the truth? Might she resume her witchly shrieking and run through the town, divulging a secret he scarcely dared believe himself? He repressed the shudder that arose at the thought of how the people he knew would treat any person claiming such time-traveling sorcery: burning, trial by ordeal, drowning.

He dared not confide the truth to anyone. So, then, it was a blessing that she'd scorned his touch. One gentle touch of Juliette's hand, one freely bestowed kiss from her soft lips, and he'd find himself rivaling a monkey in his eagerness to chatter his innermost thoughts. And if he convinced her, if he gained her affections, what of it? No true knight would meekly accept being shifted through time, not with a quest left unfinished. Nor could he ask her to cast her lot with him and accept this gut-wrenching sense of dislocation should he be successful in fighting his way back to his own time.

Knighting, always a friendless profession, had nonetheless done a poor job of preparing him for this solitary stance against the world, for he'd never felt so alone.

And so it was that he welcomed the trilling "Yoo hoo!" that drifted over the prairie, coupled with the sight of the buxom Miss Alma Harkins and the ever-dour Captain Chaney heading their way. Juliette, too, seemed relieved that she need no longer endure his undiluted presence, for she smiled and sent her friends a hearty wave.

Geoffrey turned back to Arion's injured foreleg. Ha!

Let them deflect each other's attentions, for he had serious matters to ponder. What had hurtled into the future must somehow find its way back, lame horse and all. He meant to find mountains and climb his way back to his own time, or die trying, even if it meant hardening his heart against the one person who roused its softest inclinations.

Juliette noticed with relief that the long walk over the sun-struck prairie had left Alma looking as red-faced and out of breath as she felt herself, which meant explanations over her agitated state might not be necessary. Events of the past few moments had made a muddle of her mind. Her only clear thought taunted her with the inconsiderate way she'd rejected Geoffrey's gesture of comfort, the shrewish way she'd shrieked at him, when every ounce of her being recognized that here was a man who understood some of the pain and hurt she tried so hard to bury. She doubted she'd ever forget the way an unreadable mask had slipped over his wonderfully expressive features. It shouldn't matter. It didn't matter. It didn't. It didn't.

Try as she might to convince herself that she'd acted in a manner befitting the respectable Widow Walburn, she stared at Geoffrey's rigid back and couldn't shake off the feeling that she'd made a terrible mistake.

She wished he'd turn away from his stupid horse and make one of his incomprehensible remarks . . . and smile at her.

But when he rose and turned in response to Alma's continued hailing, he didn't even spare her a glance. He stood ramrod straight, as if the ridiculous metal outfit he'd worn when she'd found him had been melted down and forged into a back brace worn beneath his borrowed homespun. The wind teased his hair away from his face, revealing the firm set of his jaw, the steady deep-set stare that judged Alma and Captain Chaney's approach.

He might have been one of Fort Scott's best scouts, calling no attention to himself and yet vibrantly alert. An ever-vigilant knight, aware of everything around him. Except her.

"That rabbit you shot will be just the thing." Alma's broad face glowed with the light sheen of perspiration. "I came out here to invite Geoffrey on a picnic tomorrow. I can't ask you to join us, Miss Jay—I mean, I know you don't bother with that sort of thing. Doesn't a picnic sound like fun, Geoffrey?"

"Nay." He seemed completely baffled. "'A picnic' sounds nothing whatsoever like 'fun.'"

Captain Chaney chuckled. "Can't blame you there, Geoff. Sittin' on a blanket with sticky young uns and stingin' ants crawlin' all over me ain't my idea of fun, neither."

"Geoff?" Geoffrey cocked a disbelieving brow toward Captain Chaney; Juliette felt like doing the same. The diminutive suited Geoffrey not at all, but even more surprising was hearing the warmth in Captain Chaney's voice.

"You're sounding awfully friendly all of a sudden, Captain," Juliette said.

"Well, sure, after I saw him knock you down when you took that first shot." Captain Chaney cast Geoffrey an appraising glance.

"He didn't mean anything by it." Juliette rushed to Geoffrey's defense, fearing Captain Chaney's prickly protectiveness might cause him to challenge the younger man. "He's not familiar with guns—"

"Good reflexes, son." The captain interrupted and nodded approvingly. "You reacted as if you'd had some military training. I especially liked the way you used yourself as a shield when you thought there might be trouble."

Geoffrey commenced nodding as well, the two of them beaming at one another as if they'd each found a kindred spirit in the other. "Protection of the gentler sex with quick reflexes forms the basis of the knightly code. . . ." Geoffrey's voice trailed away, and he jerked his attention back to his horse.

"Well, do you have a particular reason for avoiding a picnic?" Alma stared from one man to the other with puzzlement.

"Oh, Alma, can't you see Geoffrey doesn't know anything about picnics?" Juliette said. Truth to tell, after his crazy talk about knightly codes, she wasn't certain she believed his assertion that he realized what year it was.

"Nonsense! Everyone knows what a picnic involves, isn't that right, Geoffrey?"

Geoffrey cast Captain Chaney a sidelong glance. "Sticky young un and stingin' ants," he said after a pause, the rough-spun words sounding bizarre when spoken in his musical cultured voice.

"*Uns,*" corrected Captain Chaney. "Sticky young *uns.*"

Alma giggled, and then shot Juliette a nervous defiant look. "Actually, Geoffrey, I was told . . . er, hoping that we needn't share our picnic with any young uns, sticky or otherwise. Or anyone else, for that matter. Maybe you'd be interested in a personal guided tour of the territory around Walburn Ford."

Juliette nearly echoed Captain Chaney's surprised grunt at Alma's boldness. Social conventions practiced back East had little bearing on frontier life. Alma had every right to invite Geoffrey to share a picnic basket with her. Juliette certainly had no intention of preparing quiet private meals for two, of consuming them far away from prying eyes. And yet the thought of Geoffrey lounging upon Alma's picnic blanket, of having any of his appetites slaked by Alma's offerings, suffused her with a sudden raging jealousy so inappropriate and unexpected that she didn't know how to deal with it—especially when interest sparkled in his hazel eyes, and he bent his tall length toward Alma, granting her the smile Juliette longed to see.

"You would serve as my guide?"

Alma's answering yes was little more than a breathless frightened whisper.

"I am most interested in finding mountains so high it would take a man twelve full lifetimes to climb them." Geoffrey's voice betrayed a shocking amount of excitement.

"There aren't any mountains in this part of Kansas, Geoffrey," Juliette couldn't resist saying.

Geoffrey's lip curled with disdain. "A man of my recent experiences finds that impossible to believe. What say you, fair Alma?"

Juliette watched in disbelief as Alma stared down at her own breasts and blushed to the roots of her hair.

Oh, she'd been wise to retreat rather than give in to the urge to cling close to him! His touch had kindled fires she'd thought buried; his voice, his smile, had lured her into thinking that she alone might be special enough, important enough, to make a difference to this man. His blatant flirtation with Alma, his eagerness to be alone and spend the rest of his life climbing Alma's blasted *mountains,* proved exactly how special and important Geoffrey d'Arbanville considered Juliette Walburn.

"We might run into border ruffians," Alma cautioned with a coquettish batting of her eyelashes. "What would you think about that, hmm?"

"I would relish the chance to test my lance against any who dare challenge me," Geoffrey said softly.

Juliette snorted with disgust. She left them ogling one another and strode purposefully home. She had a bit of trouble seeing, no doubt because the relentless prairie wind pricked at her eyes, but it didn't matter. Nothing mattered. Nothing.

Alma called after her. "Miss Jay! Do you mind if I fry up your rabbit for our picnic?"

Juliette made a tunnel of her hands to make certain her voice would project, stopping long enough to holler in response, "Take it, Alma. Do whatever you like. I don't want anything to do with it."

8

Geoffrey came to Juliette's kitchen door an hour later, dusty and disheveled, the scent of horse liniment wafting from his clothes.

"I am to make myself presentable." He scowled fiercely. "And then I am to call for Miss Alma Harkins at the Wilcox cabin so that we might eat rabbits and explore the local terrain."

"Ah, yes, your picnic." Juliette congratulated herself, certain that with her light tone she'd managed to convey an utter lack of interest, and betrayed none of the simmering smoldering tension that had gripped her for the past hour. And then she had to go spoil the impression of her detachment by muttering the phrase that had weighed so on her mind. "Your mountain-climbing expedition."

He perked up visibly, and a nameless gnawing sensation stirred within her at his blatant eagerness. "Incomparable mountains, I hope."

"Bigger than most, I'd wager."

He braced one arm against the doorjamb, stretching his borrowed shirt taut against arms bulging with muscled strength. The movement sent a puff of dust drifting off the coarse fiber. Juliette wondered how much of the dust he'd acquired while tending his injured horse, or if it had gotten ground into the homespun during his attempt to protect her when he'd heard the Colt fire. It seemed impossible, looking up at his tall solid length, that he'd pressed her to the ground without squashing her flat. It seemed impossible that her body could so clearly remember the imprint of his weight against her, that merely thinking about it roused the most inappropriate tinglings and shivery sensations.

He ran his free hand over his head and smoothed his hair behind his neck, shaking off more dust and tiny specks of dried grass. He performed the small tidying motions without once lifting his gaze from her, as if he were well accustomed to attending to his toilette under a woman's scrutiny.

"Would you consider coming with us, Juliette?"

No hint of lechery marked his expression, which Juliette knew she should find reassuring. Embarrassment held her tongue-tied for a moment, mocking her with the knowledge that while she'd been reading all manner of lusty significance into his innocent comments, Geoffrey appeared to be genuinely interested in nothing more than finding a very tall mountain range to scale. Like any man, he'd decided he wanted to do something, in this case climb a mountain, and that thought occupied his mind to the exclusion of all else.

At once her embarrassment deserted her, replaced by euphoria, which just as quickly crashed into the same weighty gnawing that had been plaguing her since leaving Alma alone with Geoffrey on the prairie. Gracious, what ailed her? After years of keeping her impulses under control, they seemed determined to batter her all at once every time Geoffrey d'Arbanville came near.

"I can't go with you, Geoffrey. I have a business to operate. I'm busier than ever now that the soldiers are reopening Fort Scott. Walburn Ford's the perfect spot for them to stop for the night, and they always bring in supplies and our mail from the States. There's another party due to arrive tomorrow." She ignored the inner clamoring that protested her announcement. "You and Alma go off and enjoy yourselves."

He studied her with hooded eyes, betraying nothing that would tell her whether her refusal had disappointed him or whether it pleased him, or whether she'd declined an offer made only from courtesy.

"Very well," he said at length, just when her self-imposed silence was making her uncomfortable. "There is still the matter of making myself presentable."

There went her impulses again, yipping with silent delight that she could offer so little to aid him in primping for Alma. "Captain Chaney had only that one spare set of clothes to lend you. What about your own things?"

"Aye, my armor requires attention ere it rusts past pliability. And yet look as I might, I could find no armor polish in your stable."

"Darn, out of armor polish again." Juliette clucked with not completely false sympathy as she shook her head. He still acted as if the armor were the only garment he owned in this world; she wondered how long she should continue pretending to understand Geoffrey's bouts of incoherency.

"Fear not, Juliette. All is not lost. Have you great quantities of fine sand and vinegar? And a large sack? I assure you I have not forgotten my squirely lessons."

Great quantities of vinegar? At this time of year?

"I'm afraid vinegar's in short supply until the apples ripen. You might find sand down by the river."

"Sand alone will hardly do." His scoffing tone told her he thought a babe scarcely out of diapers wouldn't have made such a senseless suggestion.

"Then I guess you'll have to make the best of what you're wearing," she said. "Stand away from the house and brush the hay from your hair and dust off your clothes."

"Performing these manservant's tasks will render me presentable?" He cocked a dubious brow toward her.

Actually, Juliette doubted Alma cared one whit whether Geoffrey made himself presentable or not. Juliette herself couldn't imagine a man looking more appealing than Geoffrey did at that moment. She could just imagine Alma, frying that rabbit in a frenzy, counting the minutes until Geoffrey came calling. Juliette wished suddenly that she did possess a huge sack along with great quantities of fine sand and vinegar, that she could spend the rest of the afternoon taking squirely lessons from Geoffrey, to see if an amnesia-stricken actor really could use such commonplace ingredients to polish his armor costume.

"You'll do." For some reason, her throat had gone dry and hoarse.

"I cannot do, lest you help me, Juliette." He gave a self-deprecating shrug of his shoulders. "I have no brushes."

She fetched hers, knowing there was no good reason to deny him the request, but she didn't actually have to perform the intimate tasks for him. She presented the brushes to him and then watched from the stoop while he placed himself downwind. He managed well enough, raising veritable clouds of dust from his clothing, taming his hair with vigorous strokes.

"Have you a thong?" he asked when his self-made dust storm subsided. "'Twould make sense to tie my hair back," he said, and paused, sending her a meaningful stare, "should the afternoon prove physically demanding."

So much for her notion that his plans involved nothing more than innocent hiking. Wordlessly, she rummaged through her catch-all drawer and found a soft leather strand, which she handed to him. He gathered his hair in a loose queue, pulling the dark chestnut mass back to reveal the pleasing angles of his face in clearer detail. His eyes appeared deeper set than ever, smoldering with anticipation for whatever awaited him.

"I have done," he announced with a satisfied sigh.

Yes, he would do.

"I can call now for Alma?"

At her reluctant nod, he inclined his head toward her, and then swiveled with fluid grace. He tilted his head skyward, and then slanted a glance toward Juliette. "I am presentable and I may call?"

She knew she should find his concern over his appearance cheering. She supposed actors worried quite a bit about looking their best. Maybe his interest boded a return of this awareness, and not simple male vanity.

He apparently trusted her to tell him the truth, so she really should make some effort. She made a twirling motion with her finger, and he obediently turned full circle, giving her an unimpeded view of taut-stretched homespun molding his wide shoulders. A smudge marred the broad expanse of his back. "There's a spot between your shoulders that you've missed."

Murmuring a thank you, he swiped ineffectually at what he obviously couldn't see.

"I'll do it." Juliette accepted the brush from him, her fingers closing around the handle and finding it still warm from his grip. She gave the offending smudge a tentative swipe, but it stayed stubbornly lodged. Nothing less than a brisk scrubbing motion would do; without giving much thought to how touching him would affect her, she rested her free hand against his upper arm for support and leaned close. He tensed beneath her touch, and she blindly dealt with the smudge, wondering how blood could course, how flesh could flex, through muscles that felt like sun-warmed solid rock.

"I am presentable?" he queried once her brushing ceased.

"Yes, Geoffrey." She sighed and stepped well away, wishing he'd get going now that he'd gotten himself all fixed up, and yet absurdly unable to stifle the tiny hope that he would stay. She would have to take herself sternly in hand the minute he left her property. It shouldn't matter a fig to the Widow Walburn that one of her boarders had gussied himself up with brushes she'd provided and was taking himself off with another woman on a picnic where the Widow Walburn had provided the main course. Maybe permitting him to call her Juliette instead of Miss Jay was part of the problem. When he got back from his stupid picnic, she would insist Geoffrey accord her the same respect as all the other villagers.

"Alllllmmmmaaaa!"

Juliette's ears were still ringing from Geoffrey's startling resounding bellow when he drew in a huge breath and let loose again.

"Alllllmmmmaaaa!"

He stood with his feet planted apart, his arms crossed at his waist, breathing easily despite issuing such a frightful noise and looking as if he meant to stand there and roar Alma's name all day long. Juliette dashed back across the intervening space and reached up, clamping her hand none too gently over his mouth just in time to prevent another outburst.

His eyes widened. And then his lips fashioned a kiss upon her open palm.

Muffled childish laughter drifted from near the stable. Robbie! Knowing the child watched them released Juliette from the inexplicable paralysis that made it seem that only the warm pulsating contact of Geoffrey's lips upon her skin held her upright. She snatched her hand away and whipped her head from Geoffrey to the stable and back again, uncertain which boisterous male more deserved a tongue-lashing.

Geoffrey's eyes glittered with roguish good humor, and those lips that had all but scorched her palm tipped with masculine satisfaction. She didn't feel capable of chastising him just then, though he certainly had it coming. She turned her attention to the male more easily mastered.

"Robbie Wilcox, you get away from behind my woodpile!" Juliette smoothed her skirt tight against her thighs to hide the way her well-kissed hand trembled. That only made things worse, for she imagined she felt the brand of Geoffrey's lips pass straight through the folds of cotton to burn against her leg.

Robbie emerged slowly, his head hanging so low that his chin nearly rested on his chest, and his dusty toes kicked at tufts of turf as he approached.

"You stopped my calling for Alma." Geoffrey's low voice roused a trembling within her that made a mockery of her feigned interest in Robbie's progress. She turned to face him and found herself confronted with a look of such handsome supreme complacency that her inner trembling solidified into firm resolve. Men! She'd caught that look before, when they sensed a conquest was at hand. Geoffrey must have interpreted her stopping him as a jealous attempt to prevent him from meeting with Alma. Well, she would soon set him straight on that matter.

"You can't stand there hollering a woman's name like you're calling hogs to the trough. Whatever were you thinking of?" Embarrassment lifted Geoffrey's jaw by a good two inches. His obvious discomfiture, along with the silly image of Alma hiking her skirts and running down the street, oinking in response to such a summons, cheered Juliette inordinately.

"I sought but to carry out Alma's instructions, though it seemed a witless, discourteous custom to me," Geoffrey muttered, sending her a dark scowl. "Someone might have explained it properly, knowing no true knight would attempt to summon a lady thus unless he *assumed* he were enacting a local, if heathenish, custom."

"Well, I doubt many of us in Walburn Ford know much about the way true knights behave," Juliette retorted. His return to delusions of knighthood killed her faint hope that he might be regaining his memory, and made it easier to ignore the effect he had on her senses. She shifted her attention to Robbie, who had dragged his way to her side. "As for you, young man, you know you shouldn't be spending so much time tending to chores around my place."

She felt obligated to reprimand the youth, although her heart ached to think of the alternatives awaiting him. The whole town whispered over the way Josiah Wilcox ruled his small family with iron-fisted intolerance. He seemed peculiarly set against Robbie, missing no opportunity to correct the child's real or imagined mistakes with remarks so cruel they would make a grown man cringe. There wasn't a soul in Walburn Ford who would grieve if Josiah Wilcox met the sharp tip of an arrow or a border ruffian's bullet. Unless some tragic accident ended his tyrannical control, Josiah's nervous wife and sad-eyed child could expect no lessening of their earthly suffering.

"I was keepin' watch on Geoffrey's horse," Robbie explained. "Arion's awful nice for a stallion."

Geoffrey's chest swelled with pride. "The finest destrier in all Christendom. One could search to the very edge of the Earth without finding Arion's equal."

Juliette rested a forgiving hand on Robbie's tangled hair and shook her head. Geoffrey fit so well the fairy-tale image she held of a knight. His complete immersion in his fantasy made the impossible seem plausible. She could understand Robbie's fascination; her own impulses urged her to believe everything Geoffrey said. Though she firmly pushed the notion aside, something warm and hopeful settled around her heart, something that wouldn't bear exploring just then.

"Don't let Alma hear you trying to undo all her teaching by filling this boy's head with nonsense. The earth has no edges. You know the Earth is round, don't you, Robbie?"

Robbie nodded.

Geoffrey snorted. "You speak heresy and yet accuse me of spouting nonsense? Everyone knows the Earth is flat, with sea demons abounding near the edges to warn foolhardy sailors away from certain death."

Robbie brightened at the thought of facing sea monsters, and then settled into reluctant denial. "Naw. Miss Harkins says it's round. I guess that means there aren't any sea monsters, huh, Miss Jay?"

The boy's admission of the truth gave Juliette an

idea—maybe she could prompt the return of Geoffrey's memory by asking a few pertinent questions. If she could get him to remember one or two things, everything else would fall into place. "Let's ask Geoffrey. How many sea demons did you see on your way to America?"

"On my way to *where?*" Geoffrey's healthy tan seemed to seep away, leaving him ashen-faced.

"Here. America. Kansas Territory." Juliette encompassed the area with a wave of her hand. "You had to cross the Atlantic Ocean to get here. How many sea demons did you see?"

"This is not China, but 'tis not England either?" If she hadn't been looking straight at him, Juliette would have sworn someone throttled Geoffrey's neck, so garbled did his words sound. "Might the country's name have altered over the intervening years? England has ever been considered a plum ripe for the plucking, and certain conquerors might have impressed their own name upon it."

Her questions only seemed to mire him deeper in his fancies. A very real fear caught Juliette unexpectedly. If she pursued pushing him too hard before he was able to recognize the truth, he might crack beneath the strain. It would be better, for now, to continue as they had been doing, offering little tidbits of knowledge that would draw his far-ranging senses back home.

Besides, something within her would mourn the loss of Geoffrey d'Arbanville, knight. And that was a hard thing to admit.

"If you're interested in a history lesson, ask Alma to explain the American Revolution to you during your picnic." Imagining Geoffrey discoursing on history during the picnic pleased Juliette so much, she offered him what little more she knew about the discovery of her country. "All I can remember is that the country was discovered by someone named Columbus and named after another Italian."

"An Italian!" High color flared in Geoffrey's cheeks. Juliette wondered what he found most disturbing: being reminded that the Earth was round; whether he'd just suddenly realized he wasn't in England; or if some deep antagonism had set him against Italians.

Apparently, none of those matters concerned him.

"Would that more than a token few of those soft-spoken men of the south had ventured along when Edward sought their help during crusade, had they hankered after conquests. Tell me, Juliette, did the Christians wrest the Holy Land away from the godless Saracens?"

"Well, how should I know a thing like that?"

"The Mongol warrior." He looked at her expectantly, as though she should understand, and sighed when her continued silence made it clear that she didn't. "Mongols and Saracens are known allies. I do pray that the presence of that Mongol warrior does not bode ill, for I would hate to think of this place chafing beneath Saracen rule."

"We have Democrats, Republicans, Tories, and Whigs. No Saracens. You'll have to ask Alma about the Holy Land. Now, be off with you before you're late for your picnic." She gently pushed Robbie toward Geoffrey, who stood so stiff and still that he might have been an exceptionally well-made scarecrow. "Robbie, why don't you show Geoffrey the way to your house so he can pick up Miss Harkins."

"I don't know if you ought to let him go off alone with Miss Harkins." Robbie cast a dubious glance from Geoffrey's rigid form to Juliette.

"I know. He's a little confused." It wrenched at

Juliette's heart to turn away when Geoffrey was so obviously in need—but of what? She didn't know how to help him, and she really shouldn't encourage the way he made her feel inside. Reaching out, offering of herself, reveling in dreams and fancies—it would only lead to certain pain.

"I couldn't go on their picnic even if I wanted to," she added. "I'm expecting the Fort Scott advance scouts to arrive tomorrow and I have to get things ready for them."

The boy treated her to a reproachful stare, but took Geoffrey's unresisting hand and urged him into a slow halting walk. Juliette turned away, easily removing them from her line of vision, although she couldn't shake the image of them from her mind. Nor could she dampen the bleak sense that she'd failed them both in some manner.

Geoffrey felt every one of his six-hundred-odd years, meekly reeling along behind Robbie like a bent-boned village grandfather being towed on his daily visit to the cesspit.

God's blood, it was a disheartening state of affairs. Though he sought nothing more than to pass unnoticed, to find a way back to his own time, this century seemed determined to thumb its nose in his face, hurling all manner of shocking discoveries at him. Guns. A round Earth. Kansas Territory. America. *Italian* explorers! Ha!

"She flings her knowledge in my face in such a way that it cannot be denied," he said.

"Aw, Miss Jay bosses everyone around, but she don't mean nothing by it. Miss Harkins says she just acts tough, that a man with smarts would grab her right up before she gets too set in a widow's ways." Robbie's young face pinkened. "I think she's kinda sweet on me. I'm plannin' to ask her to marry me soon's I grow up."

Geoffrey bent a questioning brow to his ten-year-old guide who spoke with a cocky confidence some squires never achieved despite fostering at an indulgent woman's knees. His estimation of the lad rose a notch.

"Miss Jay's the best friend I got, now that pa went and kilt my dog Buster."

"Good as a dog, eh?" Geoffrey marveled, understanding well. He was inordinately fond of canines, himself.

"Maybe better."

They fell into an amiable side-by-side plodding along the dusty path while Geoffrey mulled this bit of news. No doubt the boy misread Juliette's womanish cosseting; still, Robbie's incipient manly pride roused a sharp sense of discovery. He didn't want to squash Robbie's fledgling attempts at claiming a woman's affections, but Geoffrey rather fancied the idea of being the one to penetrate Juliette's protective toughness.

A notion to be squelched immediately.

Unfortunately, naught but his feet obeyed his inward command to put a halt to all untoward reactions caused by the mere thought of claiming Juliette, of saving her from a widow's dreary future. He'd been struggling against his attraction to her almost from the beginning. It was folly to give the matter more than passing consideration. And yet while he stood mired in dust and despair, his heart commenced hammering against his ribs with the authority of an unpaid inkeeper bent upon collecting his rents. His blood rushed through him like the turgid water of the River Thames, with the unfailing commensurate response in his nether reaches. God's blood, he need only permit himself the luxury of thinking of claiming the woman to have his body consider it an imminent occurrence. For naught. For naught.

He'd accepted a bachelor's fate long ago, even reveled in sampling the delights of many while cleaving to none. Doomed to landlessness by being born fourth to a man scarcely capable of settling one son. Knighting during troublous times, when strong arms such as his could be hired for a pittance. Tourneying for silver cups and pretty tokens whilst lending an envious ear to older knights' tales of the vast estates and fortunes once bestowed upon the victorious by kings more generous and wealthy than his own monarch.

Time, he'd always assumed, would eventually diminish his soul-deep longing for lands and a family. Time would see his exploits cheered, his purse fattened, his old age secured.

Time, it now seemed, had been against him from the beginning.

Depressing, to think that he had hurtled through time only to end up in worse straits than before. With Arion lamed, his armor rusting away for want of polish, and with his quest left undone, he had neither time nor energy to spare for seeking out money-making opportunities. Best to harken to his tactical training, which whispered even now that pursuing a lover's course would lead to ruin and heartache. Best to abandon Juliette's affections to his adolescent rival who seemed not at all concerned over his ability to provide for a wife and family.

Perhaps in a world skewed round in which bone-handled snouts spit flame and destruction, a man had different options; a knight ought to probe the secrets held within a ten-year-old mind.

"Supposing you ask Juliette to marry you. How might you provide for her?" He silently congratulated himself for presenting a falsely disinterested mein.

Robbie's fierce frown bespoke his concentration. "Homestead land, of course, providing there's any left by the time I'm old enough to make my claim."

"Ah." Geoffrey commiserated with a sage nod to disguise his complete ignorance. "And how many years hence might that be?"

Robbie's countenance screwed into bewilderment. "Hence? I don't know what that means. A man's got to be twenty-one, and I'm only ten now. 'Less, of course, I get married and can claim my acres as head of household. How old are you, Geoffrey?"

"Nigh onto a score and a half." Noticing Robbie's confusion deepen, Geoffrey shifted for the proper number. "Twenty-nine. Old enough, I daresay, to pursue this homestead course?"

"Heck, you could get your hunnerd sixty acres tomorrow if you're that old." The lad gazed at him with keen disappointment, as if he'd been hoping for a playmate closer to his own age. "How come you ain't staked a claim yet?"

As if he possessed the coin to purchase even such a paltry estate as one hundred sixty acres! Geoffrey shrugged. "Empty purse."

"Homestead land don't cost nothin', at least not right off. My pa's always sayin' that even though the Vegetarian Settlement Company stole all his savings, he still came out owning one of the best stretches of ground this side of the Mississippi."

Geoffrey didn't bother trying to stifle his disbelieving snort. "And what generous benefactor bestows stretches of ground upon men as they enter the prime of their lives? None other than the king could possess such wealth, and I have not found monarchs to be so generous."

"I don't think we got a king. Miss Harkins is always going on about presidents and such. I guess the government parcels out the homesteads. I remember Pa talking about a land office and agent." Now it was Robbie's turn to shrug narrow shoulders, albeit apologetically. "I don't know all that much about it."

"Who would know?" Geoffrey scarcely recognized his own voice, so hoarse and desperate did it sound of a sudden. A hundred sixty acres, scorned in his mind mere moments ago, took on the grand proportions of an entire duchy.

"Anyone around here would know. All the folks in Walburn Ford staked claims." Robbie treated Geoffrey to a sly smile. "Miss Jay would know all about it. Her husband was the first one to settle here. Too bad you went and promised to go picnicking with Miss Harkins before you asked Miss Jay about homesteadin'."

"How else am I to gain the information I need about likely mountain ranges? Juliette refused to enlighten me." Geoffrey scowled at Robbie as a sudden thought struck his mind. "Mayhap Alma told you where a man might find good-sized mountains and you have forgotten your lesson, eh?"

The boy's skin paled with unprovoked fear. "N-no. I promise, we ain't learned about mountains in school. I wouldn't have forgotten. I promise, I pay attention and remember my lessons. I promise."

So affrighted did the lad seem, Geoffrey feared he might keel over onto the dusty path. Robbie's demeanor called to mind the way a cringing puppy flinches where he hears his loud-voiced master, having done nothing to incur the master's wrath and yet certain it was at fault over some trifling matter. Well-treated hounds never behaved in such fawning fashion, only those that were soundly and regularly abused. Geoffrey felt an unaccountable sorrow, bolstered by an urge to protect, and forced a light tone into his words.

"So you see, then, why I must picnic with Alma."

Spoken out loud, though, his reason sounded less than warmhearted, not at all the sort of demeanor appropriate to the instruction of a lad of Robbie's age, particularly one so timid. "A true knight never declines a lady's invitation. Particularly when he finds himself unhorsed and with naught else to occupy his time," he added, prompting a tentative grateful nod from Robbie.

They walked on, Geoffrey's mind aswirl with heady thoughts. Much of Robbie's information struck him as incomprehensible, but Juliette could explain. One hundred sixty acres. Pasture and to spare for Arion and a veritable herd of blooded mares. God's blood, but he'd be content to cast off his knight's status and scrabble about in the dirt and eke out farmer's fare in exchange for the privilege of knowing he owned the ground he worked. A man could feed a family on the bounty produced by one hundred sixty acres, especially verdant virgin acres such as these, fair, flat and lying in full sun.

His limbs quaked with eagerness to rush to this land office Robbie spoke of and stake his claim. Certes, he could meet the age requirement, although he doubted it would be prudent to reveal the full measure of his years.

It smote him full force, then, that this homestead scheme smacked of Satan, although a covert glance toward Robbie revealed no sudden sprouting of horns, tail, or cloven feet. Who else could so clearly discern Geoffrey's unfulfilled dreams, and present him with a solution that would assuage his desires at the cost of forfeiting his honor? For he could not claim acres, save Juliette from sour widowhood, and commence with raising a family in this time without turning his back on all he'd left undone centuries past.

Alma intruded upon his bleak thoughts. Apparently not content to wait for them to reach her lodgings, she ran trippingly toward them, clad in an unbecoming gown of palest rose, a basket slung over one arm, yoo-hooing all the way.

"I hope you have a good time, Geoffrey." Robbie shot him a doubtful glance before bolting back whence they'd come. Juliette's place. Geoffrey longed to take to his heels after him, but instead fixed a chivalrous smile upon his lips and concentrated upon Alma's approach.

Alma would show him the mountains, perhaps lead him to the base of the Eternal Chasm.

Perhaps it was for the best that Alma, and not Juliette, should serve as his guide in this. It would demand a fearsome amount of self-denial to commence the climb honor dictated he make if Juliette stood below, watching him go; he wondered if he could climb, knowing that by leaving her he might be doom-ing her to the lonely existence she seemed bent on achieving. Of course he could. Dozens—nay, scores—well, perhaps closer to one dozen women had waved tearfully at his departing back, and off he'd ridden, knowing a loveless landless life was his destiny.

One would think that such knowledge would grow less burdensome over time.

He broadened his false smile toward Alma and ban-ished all thoughts of Juliette straight from his mind.

9

Juliette made her way through the waist-high grass, wincing when her ankle turned against an unseen tangle of roots. The sun beat hot through the flimsy protection offered by her bonnet. A grasshopper whizzed past her nose, and various unseen crawly things itched against the carefully tied bands at her wrists that denied them entry to her sleeves. A not-so-pleasant walk, if exercise was all she sought. This unkempt section of prairie, neglected by the absentee border ruffian who'd claimed it solely to deny possession to a Free Stater, offered the shortest route between Juliette's boarding house and the secluded cottonwood grove where she knew Alma would lure Geoffrey on their picnic.

Juliette swatted a mosquito away and considered that maybe she should just give herself a good sharp slap across the face. Maybe that would bring her to her senses.

What on earth was she doing, chasing after Geoffrey and Alma with every intention of barging in on their intimate little meal? *I shot the rabbit.* Alma wouldn't have prepared food enough for three. *The only reason she didn't invite me was because she didn't think I would want to join them.* Geoffrey, tying his thick, chestnut-colored hair back in a thong, in the event the afternoon proved physically demanding. *He invited me, too. Sort of.* And she had declined, as she'd turned aside so many offers. Work beckoned, and with Geoffrey off picnicking with Alma and Captain Chaney away on one of his mysterious errands, there was nothing to hold her back from readying her boarding house for the Fort Scott scouts.

So why wasn't she home baking bread and making beds?

Over the past years, Juliette had learned that loneliness grew as comfortable as an old featherbed, rising up and around a person with blissful quiet and isolation, shielding a person from all hurt and pain. Her contentment with that numbing insulation had deserted her now. Instead of relishing her solitude she couldn't abide her house's silence for another minute, couldn't sit at her table and eat her solitary meal without gagging on her stew and biscuits.

God, how she missed her family, and Daniel, and the gentle loving good times they'd shared around the dinner table. What was it about Geoffrey d'Arbanville that so overwhelmed her with his boisterous curious presence? Other men had boarded in her home without rousing such a dreadful ache for companionship.

That's all it was—housing such a large loud stomping male had gotten her to missing her loved ones, that was why she found herself wading through slick sharp-edged prairie grass. The minute she got to easier footing she'd turn right around and head back home and take herself to task in her diary, that's what she would do. It would show resolve, to write a long detailed reminder of how important it was to subdue that frivolous part of her that had caused so much trouble, that even now urged her to forget her respectable ways and go mountain hunting with Geoffrey.

A thorn-tipped vine caught at her waist as if it meant to hold her on track, and with an odd sound, almost like a sob, she jerked it away.

She stumbled as she fought her way free of the clinging grasses onto better tended ground. Her clumsy emergence startled a crow, who flapped skyward cawing its displeasure. It circled overhead, a shimmering blue-black herald pinpointing her presence exactly. Anyone within five miles couldn't help noticing the Widow Walburn standing there in the middle of the prairie with absolutely nothing to do. Too late to go back without offering some sort of excuse for intruding. She pasted a brilliant smile upon her face and strolled over to the couple occupying the nearby cottonwood grove as if she expected to be accorded a welcome.

Geoffrey, lounging incongruously atop a fluffy pink quilt, stared at her in utter surprise. He rose to greet her with an athletic grace that made her want to stand still and admire his movements, and to her horror she found herself doing exactly that.

Alma's complexion mottled a dull red completely discordant with her pink gown and pink bonnet and pink quilt.

"Juliette," Geoffrey's mellifluous murmur gentled some of her quaking nerves. Juliette wildly thought that if she lived to be six hundred, she would never grow blasé over the way his eyes held hers as he inclined his head toward her. At once her determination to stride back home and chastise herself in her diary withered like pea stalks in late June.

"Miss Jay." Alma's greeting bore a decidedly strident edge.

Geoffrey cupped Juliette's elbow and escorted her onto the quilt with all the courtly flair of the knight he claimed to be.

This, she thought, *this is what draws me to him.* All he had to do was touch her, or speak her name, and an ordinary picnic took on overtones of medieval elegance. When looking from Geoffrey's perspective, everything seemed brighter, awe inspiring, capable of sending delight sizzling through a soul that had been buried in dullness and duty for far too long. Oh, God, it felt so good.

Once sitting, she found herself unable to meet either his carefully blank stare or Alma's mutinous expression. She concentrated on the repast prettily spread over the quilt, and felt the dull despair edge back into place. The rabbit, nicely fried; hominy; boiled eggs, two of them; fresh-picked radishes and string beans; a small bowl of sour cherries. Alma had managed well in such a short time, especially considering her status as a boarder in one of her vegetarian student's homes.

Juliette found her gaze riveted upon those two eggs, nestled so cozily against each other, waiting to be peeled. Two eggs, two plates, two forks and knives, Alma and Geoffrey tensely silent as a pair of circling hawks planning a sneak attack on an interloper approaching too near their nest. Two of everything; the Widow Walburn made three.

She shouldn't have come.

She gathered her skirts and began rising to her feet with some sort of excuse when Alma, with a quick sideways look to make certain Geoffrey couldn't see her, screwed her face into a hideous grimace, stuck out her tongue at Juliette, and made furtive shooing motions with her hands.

"Oh!" Disbelief plopped Juliette back onto the quilt. Disbelief, and the sudden irrational childish impulse to fling the rude gestures right back at Alma, an impulse she found exceedingly difficult to stifle. To cover her agitation, she whipped off her bonnet and began fanning herself, uncaring that her hair tumbled free of its hasty pinnings. Her outrage grew with each puff of wind she created. The insult made her realize she'd done the right thing by coming after Geoffrey. Defiantly, she picked up a chunk of fried rabbit and bit into it, meeting Alma's furious glare with imperturbability. She felt protective of Geoffrey, that's what it was, and she certainly didn't want his rough manners further eroded by Alma's rude behavior.

At the moment, however, he seemed utterly without any need of protection. He lounged back on the quilt, his taut length supported on one elbow, seemingly mesmerized by her blowing hair, looking rather like a sleek mountain lion waiting to pounce.

"Hungry, Miss Jay?" Alma asked with deceptive sweetness. "Why, I'd have raided Becky Wilcox's larder more thoroughly had I known you planned to join us. You just go on and have my share. I know how much you love to eat."

Before Juliette could respond to what she felt sure was a slight, Geoffrey spoke up.

"Eating. Now, there is a pastime I relish as well." With none of the heaving grunting noises one might expect from an overly large man hoisting himself out of such a comfortable position, Geoffrey settled next to Juliette. He glanced over the picnic victuals, choosing a portion of rabbit. "I daresay there's food and to spare for three, Alma, particularly since Juliette served such a sumptuous table this morn."

Who was doing the protecting here? Juliette felt a warm glow suffuse her face, certain Geoffrey had meant his comment as a compliment, even though he sent no smile or conspiratorial wink in her direction. If anything, he seemed determined not to look at her at all.

"You shouldn't have come, Miss Jay. You have no idea how you're interfering." Alma's furious whisper was complicated by a half-frightened, half-exasperated expression.

"You have no reason to be jealous, Alma," Juliette whispered back. "I'm not interested in him in that way."

Geoffrey chuckled; Juliette wanted to die.

"Jealous? Who's jealous?" Using a normal voice, Alma sniffed, high spots of color flaring on her cheeks. "Just because you have half the soldiers in Fort Scott panting after you doesn't make me jealous."

"They don't pant—" Juliette began.

"All soldiers pant," Geoffrey interrupted. "'Tis a breath-draining profession, particularly when wearing full armor."

Both women swung glowering looks upon him, which Geoffrey absorbed unperturbed, knowing the sheer power of knightly logic would still their tongues. Women and their spats! God's blood, there was a thing that had gone unchanged for six hundred years.

Let a knight bestow the smallest amount of attention upon a maid and she at once assumed a proprietary air, bristling and sniping at any who dared intervene. Were he to permit Alma to continue her unwarranted attack upon Juliette, both women would read all manner of significance into his silence, when all he sought was information concerning mountain ranges.

Better that he set things straight now, lest he find Alma's pink presence clamped about him like a limpet whene'er he stepped through the door. The very thought roused a shudder. Although the notion of finding Juliette clamped about him . . . nay, best to cast that thought aside.

"Mayhap we might investigate the mountains now," he said, guiding the conversation in the proper direction.

"Geoffrey, I told you there are no mountains in this part of Kansas," Juliette said.

"Not a one." Alma nodded in accord. Her gaze settled upon his hands and she cast him a coy, yet somehow suspicious, glance. "Not real mountains, that is. So why don't you tell us why you're really here, Geoffrey?"

Geoffrey gritted his teeth against his frustration. Hadn't Alma's very own lips promised knowledge of the mountains he sought? Yet now she dithered, teasing prettily, as if false mountains would suit his purpose! Telling the women of the very real chasm he'd descended to arrive here might wipe those puzzled half-sympathetic looks from their faces; unless, of course, it provoked them into hearty peals of laughter.

While he sorted the thoughts in his mind, a low rumbling commenced in the distance. Soon the ominous thundering defined itself into the frantic drumming of swift-running horses. The sound drifted over the prairie, followed a heartbeat later by a flurry of gunshots and the high-pitched shrieks of frightened women and children.

His battle instincts spurred him to his feet even as Juliette cried, "Border ruffians!"

"Oh God, Bean and Josiah were right about him! You're not taking me hostage, Geoffrey d'Arbanville!" Acting before he could twitch a muscle, Alma slapped Geoffrey soundly across the cheek and then, with an ear-piercing shriek, collected the edge of her skirts in pudgy fingers and bolted back across the prairie.

Probably toward the mountains she'd promised to show Geoffrey, when nothing on God's Earth could, at this moment, induce him to follow her. Not with Juliette hovering close.

The devil take Alma, her unprovoked slap, and her boggle-eyed fear of being taken hostage. Much as Arion tested the winds of battle, Geoffrey flung his head back and drew in great draughts of air. Faintly, so faintly, he caught the scent of smoldering straw and a hint of the acrid stench that had surrounded him when Juliette had fired her Colt gun. The scent of devastation wreaked by cheering men who feared no reprisal.

Geoffrey cursed anew the careless lord who left Walburn Ford so ill-defended, wondering whether the noise, the smells, might drift into that undeserving personage's chamber and rouse some modicum of responsibility in time to save the tiny village from total devastation. King Edward's unceasing efforts to stem his own border disputes took on new meaning. If Walburn Ford belonged to Geoffrey d'Arbanville no border ruffians would dare breach its boundaries.

A thought smote him with such suddenness that he nearly reeled from it. Geoffrey's heart raced with battle lust; his flesh yearned for the weight of his armor, his arm for the drag of his shield.

"Juliette—mayhap this is why I have been sent here. Angus Ōg merely shifted me to the wrong border dispute. He is not the One True God, so 'tis not surprising he made such a mistake. However, since I am here and your lord has not seen fit to send his knights to rout these scurvy ruffians, I will fetch my sword and lend it to your cause."

Geoffrey's vow, once spoken, set things to rights within himself. Yes, this was why he had been hurled here. The Celtic god had mistakenly, or mischievously, propelled him forward to help Juliette with these ruffians, rather than into the thick of Edward's border dispute. His inner confidence, sorely faltering since finding himself cast adrift in this future time, surged anew. No man could best him in hand-to-hand combat, and not even a shift in time or locale could alter that fact. He needed but to deprive these ruffians of their guns and commence thrashing them. No longer would his tentative behavior provide fodder for Juliette's amusement. A display of his formidable fighting talents would convince her of the truth of his knightly claims; might even—dare he hope it?—send her swooning into his arms with gratitude when he returned victorious.

Allowing himself the space of a heartbeat to judge how she accepted his protection, he glanced toward Juliette. At once, he forgot his battle lust.

She appeared impossibly delicate, far too slight for the wealth of hair tumbling over her shoulders. Her sun-tinged skin had paled to alabaster unrelieved by the slightest blush, her eyes glowed like the finest pale blue sapphires, glowed because tears shimmered but did not fall. She held her hands in a trembling clasp at her slender waist, the effort of holding them thus evident in the finely etched muscles along her forearm.

"Don't fight, Geoffrey," she whispered.

Her agonized entreaty struck him dumb, held him motionless, despite the sounds of destruction drifting from Walburn Ford.

"'Tis your home at risk, Juliette." Her attitude puzzled him and, truth to tell, set back his attempt to convince her of his prowess. She ought to be shrieking him on, pressing her favor upon his sleeve, exhorting him to slay one of the attackers in her name.

"The soldiers claim that the ruffians won't hurt anyone if there's no resistance. They're really after the big towns, like Lawrence." She laid her hand against his arm, a touch so light it would not forestall a butterfly, yet it anchored him to ground as firmly as a driven post. "Ignore them, Geoffrey. They'll burn a haystack, maybe drive off a few cattle, nothing more."

"Nothing more?" He could barely squeeze the comment from his confusion-clenched throat. How like a woman, to think the burning of a man's fodder, the theft of a man's beasts, did not merit full-blown retaliation. And how like fate, to present this opportunity to impress Juliette only to have her dismiss the destruction of her village like an indulgent mother making light of the neighbor children's pranks. "Juliette, had King Edward turned his back when border lords rioted, all of England would have been rent in half."

"That's what these ruffians want, Geoffrey. They want Kansas to join the Union as a slave state, to strengthen their side. They say war will come and this country will be split apart, brother against brother. If we break out into full-scale war here, we might start the whole conflagration. Our only hope is to minimize the bloodshed."

God's blood, here was a discouraging state of affairs. No full-fledged knight permitted ruffians to frolic unimpeded through his lady's homeland; but what full-fledged knight could do otherwise, when that self-same lady clung to his arm and begged him to keep his sword sheathed? Frustration in the face of his impotence drew a strangled-sounding grunt of acknowledgment from within him.

"Geoffrey?"

Juliette called his name rather timidly. The man looming beside her had altered in some subtle indefinable manner. He stood no taller than before, but seemed larger, more forbidding. She'd always sensed he possessed great strength held in abeyance; now power seemed to emanate from him in invisible waves. The curious, somewhat confused, somehow endearing boarder had vanished, replaced with a tower of masculine confidence that threatened to overwhelm everything he touched.

A knight, ready to lend his sword to his lady's cause.

A sensible woman would react by putting as much distance as possible between such a man and herself; indeed, every one of her scattered wits screamed a warning, urging her to hike up her skirts and run after Alma. Instead, she found herself clinging to his arm, as helpless to disengage herself from his compelling presence as a dandelion puff entangled in a wildcat's whiskers.

For the briefest moment, she imagined Geoffrey clad as she'd found him, in clothes fashioned of metal links; imagined him mounted atop his enormous stallion, brandishing sword and shield. A knight. A class of fighting men who'd never visited this land. And yet that was what he claimed to be and, in this moment, when his eyes narrowed with fury and his powerful body shivered with the effort of staying at her side instead of running off to join the fight, she believed that somehow, in some way, his claim might be true.

Impossible. Geoffrey d'Arbanville was nothing more than a half-crazed penniless actor, fascinated like every man she'd ever known by the promise of adventure, of battle. How could he even think he stood a chance against those well-armed ruffians? He was exactly like her father, like Daniel, like the very border ruffians she sought to protect Geoffrey from, never content with peace, the security of a home, the love of a good woman, and yet achingly vulnerable to the bullets and knives wielded for those very things.

Oh God, where had that thought come from? She didn't love Geoffrey d'Arbanville, didn't entertain the slightest thought of building a home with him. She didn't. Her pounding heart, the melting sensation in her most secret place, must surely be prompted by the sudden danger that had descended upon them, nothing more. Her fingers tightened over Geoffrey's arm, a reflexive gesture, certainly, and wasted—she'd given far more to the other men in her life and been unable to hold them safely at her side. If anything, they'd been punished for being the recipients of her affections.

She forced her fingers away from Geoffrey's arm, but couldn't prevent herself from letting them drift against his sleeve so lightly that she felt certain he wouldn't notice. Another strangled-sounding groan left Geoffrey's throat, and he swooped low to claim her lips with his.

He'd kissed her before, that first night, with the starved desperation of one human reaching out to another, as if to assure himself that he lived. This kiss, so demanding, so confident, confirmed that something about the man had changed.

Or had something about herself changed?

Could this really be the Widow Walburn, tough and independent boardinghouse keeper, determined never again to indulge in sinful passions, clutching tight to a man's shirtfront on the open prairie, drinking in his kiss while border ruffians burned and looted the town she'd vowed to nurture?

"Juliette, lovely Juliette," Geoffrey murmured, neatly banishing penitent Widow Walburn's worries straight from Juliette's mind.

He bent her backwards, shaping her body against his while his lips and tongue ravished her with gentle thoroughness. His scent filled her, vanquishing the lingering odor of smoke from the border ruffians' fires; his heart thundered against hers, drowning out all other sound. It wasn't enough; she tangled slim fingers in his thick curling hair, matching him breath for breath, reveling in the feel of his body tensing and hardening in response.

He swept her off her feet, quite literally, lifted her as easily as she might heft a loaf of bread, but cradled her with an infinite gentleness she found surprisingly stirring. With a motion of his foot, he kicked aside all of Alma's carefully prepared picnic dishes and laid Juliette atop the pink quilt. Though he braced his elbows against the ground, much of his weight still pressed against her and with half-detached amazement she found herself straining against him, craving the pressure.

"Oh, Geoffrey," she whispered when his lips left hers to brush against her chin, to travel along the suddenly excruciatingly sensitive skin of her throat.

He murmured something against her ear, something almost musically rhythmic. The husky timbre of his voice reverberated deep inside her, and when she quivered at the sensation, he trailed possessive fingers from her neck to her knees.

"Vous êtes un ange descendu sur terre."

"What . . . what are you saying?" His kiss, his touch, left her near breathless.

His chuckle, low and supremely masculine, sounded triumphant rather than amused; his lips never left her throat, so she felt his breath hot against her skin, a sensual heat that caused her to shiver.

"Forgive me for confusing you. I spoke to you in French. 'Tis my native tongue, after all, Juliette, and I confess that making the effort to translate into your version of English holds little appeal for me just now."

"But what is it? What did you say?"

She stared up at him, the stormy passion in her glorious eyes reflecting the sky's azure blue with the utmost clarity and, subjected to that penetrating gaze, Geoffrey regained his senses.

You are an angel come to earth, he'd said to the woman who tempted him with the devil's own skill.

God's blood, hadn't he but recently tormented himself with the knowledge that he could never claim this woman? Hadn't he set off a scant hour earlier, a-picnicking with another with the ultimate purpose of locating the mountains that would carry him far away from this time, this place . . . this woman? And the border ruffians—battle madness must have consumed him. He had noted this condition in the past, when the threat of danger and destruction made a man's baser urges all but irresistible, as if to affirm life in the teeth of death. There could be no other explanation for his turning his back on their wanton destruction in favor of dallying with a maid he dare not possess.

"Geoffrey?"

Something about his sudden stillness must have struck a warning chord within Juliette, for wariness had entered her expression. He longed to press her back against Alma's picnic rug, kiss her confusion away, watch her eyelids flutter closed, hear her sigh, and feel her delicate form tremble against his hand, his very own angel come to earth six hundred years beyond the time when a normal woman should have claimed his heart.

It could not be. It could never be.

"Juliette, I . . ." He had to look away from her lest he lose his resolve. "I am sorry. I have behaved in a manner unbecoming to a knight."

It seemed she stopped breathing. Her skin paled, and then reddened with the flush of embarrassment. "What have we done? Oh God. Let me up. Get . . . get away from me, Geoffrey."

It would require but a slight shifting of his weight to set her free, but his muscles ignored his mind's command. Instead, a tiny voice taunted from within: *Release her now, when she feels you have rejected her, and you will regret it for all your life.* But release her he must. Juliette, oblivious to his inner torment, regained her breath in a large rasping gulp. Her hands curved over his biceps and pushed to no avail; she formed tiny fists and hammered them against his chest, and he swallowed hard against the negligible pain, but the ache he felt within had naught to do with any physical distress.

"A knight . . . a *knight* would set a lady free if she didn't want to be held," she sobbed, her futile effort to escape leaving her breathless and exhausted beneath him.

Ha! Now, when he least wanted to be reminded of his status, she would call him a knight. No mortal enemy could fashion a deadlier insult. And how like a woman, to lift a scornful brow at every truth he told, only to fling it in his face when it suited her purpose. Nonetheless, he loosed his hold as if it had been a scalding soup kettle he'd gripped and levered his weight to the side. She rolled away with all the neat skill of a trained tumbler, coming to a halt at the precise spot where he knew his lengthy reach would fall short, much like a falsely nonchalant cat licking its paw two inches beyond the range of a chained hound.

"I can't believe I did this again—" she brought her whisper to a sudden halt, her cheeks flaring red. "You shouldn't have kissed me at a time like this, Geoffrey, not while the town was being attacked. You know that the safety of this town is the most important thing in my life."

He shouldn't have kissed her at all, but it did not seem the proper time to mention that fact, nor to remind her that she'd forbidden him to join the fray to save the town she claimed meant so much to her. A singularly quiet fray; now that his senses remembered their rightful functions, he noticed a distinct lack of battle sounds. A quick glance toward Walburn Ford confirmed that the border ruffians had concluded their sport and spirited themselves away.

"Juliette, I will yet wreak vengeance for you." Geoffrey

closed the gap between them. His thumb brushed against her cheek; he held it aloft, showing her the shimmer of tears he wasn't sure she'd known she'd shed. "Your town is safe. You need not cry."

"I'm not crying." She denied the evidence. "I . . . it's just the smoke making my eyes burn."

"Then take heart, for the smoke shall clear in a moment. What you said earlier is true. Those ruffians seem to have contented themselves with firing but a single haystack. They have fled like the whimpering curs they are." He studied the horizon for a moment and his hand clenched uselessly upon the empty space where his sword should be hanging. "But it seems someone seeks us out."

A small contingent of mounted men approached from the direction Alma had fled, led by a black-haired wraith who looked freshly sprung from the gyves. The men at his back portrayed a decidedly military bearing, although their identical wide-brimmed caps and deep-blue garments carried no trace of chain mail. The coats of arms they bore on their sleeves were singularly bereft of identifying characteristics, consisting only of golden-yellow slashes and curves surrounding a brace of crossed guns.

"You OK, Miss Jay?" called their whip-thin leader as they pulled their mounts to a halt. "Where's Miss Alma?"

"I'm fine, Bean, and Alma ran back to the Wilcox's. Did anyone get hurt?"

"Naw. Lucky for us Lieutenant Jordan and his men got here a day early. The president himself wants an immediate report on the ruckuses going on around Fort Scott. The soldiers rode like hell to bring in some professor from up Boston way to take a firsthand look and make a scholarly report to the president. They was just ridin' in when the ruffians attacked and they scared the no-good bastards off."

"Oh thank God nothing happened this time while I . . ."

A conventlike pallor had drained Juliette's complexion of passion's rosy hue. She gripped her hands in an attitude of prayer, her body swaying with such affrighted relief that Geoffrey would not have been surprised had she sunk to her knees and begun smiting her breast in contrition for submitting to his embrace. It was a sight to dampen any man's ardor, and it roused a fearsome rage within him, that this Bean person should be witness to it.

"Easy there, fella," said one of the blue-clad men when Geoffrey took a threatening step in their direction. "We just want to ask you a few questions afore you decide to run off."

So, they suspected he meant to find mountains and leave. How much more did they know? Geoffrey squared his shoulders, determined to hold his tongue regarding his passage through time, no matter what tortures they devised to break his silence.

They made it easy for him by pursuing a witless line of questioning.

"You been spyin' for them border ruffians?"

"Who's yer leader?"

"Why didn't you get all the women 'n' kids out a' town afore your friends started their trouble?"

Their supposition that a knight would align himself with such cowards as these border ruffians scarcely merited a response. And yet reluctant suspicion dawned in Juliette's eyes; she took an uncertain step back and pressed her knuckled fist against the very lips he had but recently claimed.

This was not to be borne.

"Cease your baseless speculation." His demand did

naught to wipe the disbelieving curl from Bean's lip; a false bravado, considering Geoffrey's unarmed state. Had he been wearing his well-honed sword at his waist, he might ply it about a bit to fortify his words.

"Where'd you come from and why are you here?" the churl taunted him, and Geoffrey stilled, recognizing that at last he faced the threat he'd been expecting since first finding himself in this apparently lordless defenseless place. On foot, without his sword or shield, he stood no chance against these men.

Fate seemed bent upon flinging one confusing dilemma after another at him this day. Very well. Fate had also provided him with an explanation that should satisfy these louts. Admittedly, the explanation had come from the lips of a ten-year-old, but knights who valued their lives learned early on to seize every advantage, no matter its source.

"Why do you think I am here?" Geoffrey challenged. Before any of them could comment, he prayed silently that young Robbie hadn't been bedeviling him with childish fancies. "I am searching for homestead lands, and I heard the lands here represent some of the finest property this side of the Mississippi."

Grudging acceptance lightened the expressions of the men who faced him, including the despicable Bean, but it was Juliette's reaction that held him in thrall. She sagged ever so slightly, as if his words had freed her from an unspoken fear. A tentative radiance illuminated her fine features, piercing him to the core; he'd seen such looks before, bestowed by besotted ladies upon their champions.

A shiver of anticipation coursed through Geoffrey. Robbie had not lied; a man could claim one hundred sixty acres of land, which would ultimately provide him with the means to take a woman like Juliette to wife.

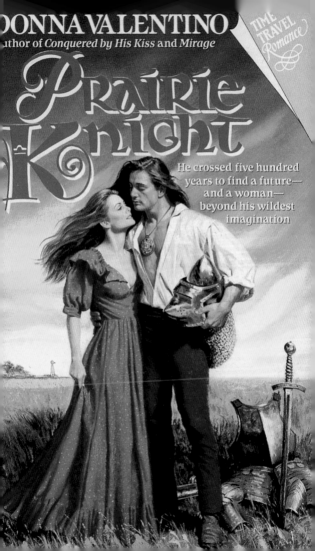

DONNA VALENTINO

author of *Conquered by His Kiss* and *Mirage*

Prairie Knight

He crossed five hundred
years to find a future—
and a woman—
beyond his wildest
imagination

A knight in shining armor...on the Kansas prairie of 1859???

Sir Geoffrey d'Arbanville, a 13th-century mercenary knight, plunges into a chasm, toward certain death, rather than allow a sacred relic to fall into the hands of his king's enemy. But he and his trusty war-horse find themselves very much alive -- in the midst of a buffalo stampede!

Ever since her husband's tragic death, Juliette Walburn has denied her sensuous nature and her dreams of love, struggling to be a prim, practical widow in the eyes of her homesteading neighbors. Certainly the Widow Walburn would never believe that a medieval knight could travel through time to land on her doorstep!

Readers of both time travel and historical romance will enjoy this delightful, humorous tale of timeless love.

He quelled his inner excitement and shifted his eyes away from Juliette. Such dreams were forbidden pleasures. He was sworn to return to his own time and leave this place behind. She was sworn to remain, a widow who so grieved for her dead husband that she meant to devote the rest of her life to his dream.

He knew not whether it would be God or the devil who would exact punishment for the urge he felt to grind honor and duty into the dust.

10

"*So those were 1859 American soldiers.*"

In the stable, with none but Arion to witness, Geoffrey voiced his disdain. "A soft-bellied slouching lot." He ran a practiced hand along Arion's injured foreleg and felt cheered when he measured a slight decrease in the swelling. "Careless of their attire and possessed of revolting personal habits, such as the camellike hawking of vile-colored spittle." Arion tossed his head, as disgusted, no doubt, as Geoffrey himself.

"The one called Lieutenant Jordan dared to invite Juliette to ride astride in front of him." Arion whooshed an amazed-sounding snort. "She declined, of course, as any lady would, and walked back here at my side, whilst the contingent of soldiers surrounded us. Had I possessed the slightest urge to escape, their inattentive ranks could never have reacted quickly enough to contain me." Arion nickered in equine agreement.

Geoffrey gave the steed an affectionate pat and fastened a rope lead to the horse's halter. Arion, ever his boon companion, seemed doubly precious now, with Juliette overly flustered with arranging meals and beds for the soldiers, who had had the poor manners to arrive a day too early. They'd claimed their president's yearning for a report from a stout florid-faced personage called Professor Burns, come from the land of Boston, had hastened their speed.

To be fair, Geoffrey had to admit to arriving unannounced and unexpected on more than one occasion—witness his current situation!—and yet he felt disinclined to absolve the soldiers of blame for ignoring their pre-arranged timetable.

To be fair, Alma's taunt that the soldiers panted over Juliette weighed heavy on his mind. He'd as soon skewer the lot of them on the end of his sword than grant them a favorable thought.

A soft rustling sounded from the far end of the stable, too loud for mice, too quiet for soldier-sized pests. "Young Robbie?" Geoffrey queried without turning around, remembering how fond the lad seemed of lurking about the stable.

"Are you really claimin' a homestead, Geoffrey?" The lad edged out from the shadows.

In truth, Geoffrey held a secret plan for stealing away from this place in the night. Thus might he elude the suspicious soldiers, as well as put behind him Juliette and all the turmoil she roused within his heretofore well-disciplined mind. But it would be best to withhold the knowledge from the boy.

"I had not intended to claim lands, but it seems I must. And I owe you a debt of gratitude for arming me with that bit of knowledge. Well done, boy."

Astonishment greeted his pronouncement, and then such a delighted grin split Robbie's sunburnt face that one might have thought that he'd never received a compliment before. Geoffrey found himself unaccountably wishing he'd waxed more effusive in his praise.

"Arion might benefit from a short walk. Would you like to lead him out to the paddock?" Geoffrey held the rope lead toward Robbie, who snatched at it eagerly.

"I'll make sure he doesn't get hurt while *I'm* with him," the lad stated with puffed-chest importance, not so subtly implying that Geoffrey had been at fault in the laming of Arion. As he had, truth to tell, by ignoring Juliette's warnings over the horse's reaction to hearing gunfire for the first time. Rather daring of the lad to fling that in his face. Fighting the smile threatening to quirk at his lips, Geoffrey followed behind while the slight boy led the massive destrier into the late afternoon sun.

Though lad and horse both seemed to enjoy the exercise, Arion's performance sent Geoffrey's spirits plummeting. There was no mistaking the way the steed hesitated and lurched each time his weight came down on his foreleg. So much for his secret plan. It could well be days or even weeks before Geoffrey dared submit Arion to the full weight of saddle and horse armor, even longer before he added his own chain-mail bulk. Until Arion healed, he was as tightly shackled to this time and place as a priest to his assigned flock—best to remain as celibate as a priest, for the good of his sanity as well as his soul.

As if his thoughts and contrary desires had wafted through the air to summon her, Juliette joined him at the paddock rails. He braced himself for another onslaught of temptations.

"The closest land office is in Fort Scott. Lieutenant Jordan and the soldiers are escorting Professor Burns there first thing tomorrow—they said they'd like it if you went with them to file your homestead claim."

So, he hadn't quite deflected the suspicion cast his

way. It would seem he must needs fulfill this claiming exercise to lend credence to the tale he'd spun. The notion of owning land, which had once gripped him with insatiable longing, rankled sour given these circumstances.

"I suppose that if I refuse to accompany them, your townsmen will assume the worst of me?"

"It's not like that," she said in a rush, though an entrancing hint of color rose in her face to belie her words. "Traveling can be somewhat perilous around here, what with border ruffians and Indians roaming all over. Most folks prefer traveling with a military escort when they have the chance."

He nodded, accepting the good sense of her words, but gestured toward the limping Arion. "Regardless, 'tis evident I am without horse. I would not risk Arion's leg just now."

"You're rather fond of Arion, aren't you?"

"Fond? The emotion a knight holds for his steed delves far deeper than mere fondness." Geoffrey wondered if he could adequately explain something that those in his profession seldom acknowledged, even to one another.

"An extraordinary mental bond sometimes develops between a knight and the proper horse. No human friend can be counted upon to risk life and limb time and again without question. No mere acquaintance possesses such finely tuned senses that a man might fall into sleep confident that his steed would alert him in time to save his skin should danger approach. No manner of friend would expend all strength and yet willingly carry a weary rider to safety although its own knees wobbled and gallant heart pounded fit to burst. Yet a knight's steed asks nothing in return, save an occasional warm stable to shelter from winter's bite, and a measure of oats now and again."

Juliette already thought him a witless fool, so it would cost him nothing to admit the full depth of his feelings for his horse. "Juliette, mine own bones ache with every blow Arion takes, and while his injured foreleg means a delay in carrying out my plans, 'tis not mere frustration that sickens my heart to watch him limp round this paddock."

He glanced at her and drew in a sharp breath. He would never understand women, were he to live another half-millennium. Words which should have dubbed him a sentimental oaf had roused a wobbly tender smile from Juliette. She blinked back a suspicious-looking dampness and laid a gentle hand against his arm, as if he'd pleased her with his confession.

"Few men ever know the privilege of owning a horse like Arion," he concluded.

"The soldiers bought some of Bean Tyler's spare horses. I'm sure they'd let you ride one of them to Fort Scott. I'll take good care of Arion while you're gone."

Bean Tyler, the witness to Juliette's humiliating turn away from his embrace. Given the man's wraithlike appearance, Geoffrey found it hard to credit the suggestion that the man possessed enough coin to send a decent meal into his gullet. "How could one such as he boast a wealth of horses?" Geoffrey asked.

"Oh, he trades with the Indians for some of the larger ponies, and he makes a trip out Texas way once or twice a year to round up some of the wild ones."

He slanted a look to see whether she jested. Horses cavorting about, free for the taking, seemed most unlikely. Surely the king—nay, Robbie had mentioned a president or some such ruler—would be as stingy of wild horses as King Edward was of the deer and pheasants roaming England's forests.

And yet Juliette smiled up at him with pure honesty

shining in her lovely eyes. The tiniest tendril of shimmering brown hair escaped her severe coif, and his fingers twitched with the unseemly urge to pull the thin metal contrivances from her hair so it might tumble all about her shoulders. "Wild," he said, speaking of matters other than horses. "And free."

"Alma says they're descended from horses the Spaniards left behind."

"Ha!" He'd caught her in a lie for certain. "The Spaniards I've known were as mindful of their horses as the royal guard tending the king's firstborn son. Such horses as they might abandon wouldn't be fit for riding."

"Well, wild horses and Indian ponies aren't as fine as Arion," Juliette admitted. "They're very hardy, though, and almost tireless."

"As is Arion," Geoffrey said, refusing to grant any superiority whatever to wild American horseflesh. "I have known kni—others of my profession who swear by heavier steeds, but I find that while they might lend one a slight edge in tourney, they tire too easily and lack the stamina for long marches."

Juliette blinked and said nothing for a long moment. Then she smiled, a wondrous sight. "I've ridden forty miles a day on an Indian pony." She spoke with the haughty air of one who'd taken great pride in the accomplishment.

"And I have slept like a baby whilst Arion carried me one hundred miles each day and more," Geoffrey returned, embellishing the truth ever so slightly—it was true that Arion's strong legs had carried him such distances, but no body could fall into sleep when traveling at such a speed, and even the smartest horse required a bit of guidance over a hundred miles.

"Well, I can't quite believe that riding horseback is

as comfortable as snoozing in a carriage, but I'm glad to hear you remembering *something* from your past."

Encouraged by the merriment dancing in Juliette's eyes as she warmed to the boasting game, he enumerated one or two of his favorite exploits. "Let me tell you some of the things I remember. There was the time we outran a yelping horde of Saracen swordsmen, and everyone knows of their reputation for fine horsemanship. And the time King Edward charged two of us separately with carrying a message to his uncle, and I had the answer back in the king's hands ere my fellow messenger ever reached the uncle. Not to mention Arion's brave stand against Drogo FitzBaldric, and his unhesitating leap into the Eternal Chasm. . . ." Appalled at how easily the urge to prompt more of her rare smiles had lulled him into discussing matters he'd meant to keep to himself, Geoffrey's voice trailed off.

He hadn't stilled his wagging tongue quickly enough. Juliette's expression had shifted from soft delight into something akin to despair. She reached toward him; her slender fingers hovered inches above his arm, but she snatched her hand away and tangled it within a fold of her gown. He ached all out of proportion, against all reason, for the touch she denied him, and fought down the urge to grip her by the shoulders, to talk himself hoarse convincing her that everything he'd told her was God's honest truth. But it was for the best that she think him a horse-besotted madman.

She summoned a deep breath and resumed their earlier conversation, as if they'd never spent a moment discussing horses and kings and exploits of the past. "You haven't had time to look around for a nice claim."

"One gets to choose?"

"Of course. You can't expect a man to build a cabin and pour his sweat into land he doesn't like for five years. That's how long it takes to prove up on your claim."

The only thing Geoffrey intended to prove by staking his claim was that he had no connection with the whoreson border ruffians. "It matters naught, whichever parcel I am allotted. Any acres will do, such as those." He gestured with his chin toward waving grasslands stretching emptily toward the horizon.

"Oh, those acres." Juliette studied the land with a mournful expression. "A Missouri man grabbed that claim, but he's never made any improvements. He won't, either."

"Why did he take it, then?"

"Lots of proslavery men did the same thing. They claim that it gives them the right to vote in Kansas, and it cuts down on the amount of desirable land available to Free Staters who want to move into the Territory. It isn't strictly legal, because whoever claims the land is supposed to live on it and work it for five years."

"Then your president should dislodge him from the claim," said Geoffrey.

"The president doesn't have time to tend to it himself. Somebody could file a preemption claim, but I doubt anyone will." Juliette smiled sadly when Geoffrey cast her a quizzical look. "The preemptor has to file his intention with the land office, and then build a cabin and live on the land for five years, just as if he were the original claimant. Only then can he request an ownership hearing. But if the original filer shows up and makes an objection, there could be a nasty expensive legal fight. The preemptor could lose, which would mean he'd have wasted five years. There's so much land open in the Territory, not many people are willing to risk a preemption."

I would risk it, Geoffrey thought, sensing her unspoken longing for a champion to come and wrest these nearby acres away from the Missouri man. He would risk it, even though affixing his name to property adjoining Juliette's could only torment him beyond endurance, quite like roasting in hell beneath the ordinary sun.

"Look how fine it is," she said, oblivious to his inner turmoil. She shaded her eyes and peered toward the horizon, directing his attention away from Robbie and Arion to overlook vast acres of swaying flower-dotted grassland. "Most of the other folks in town hold claims way out on the prairie. But Daniel was the town's first settler and he claimed the best property. All this is ours—mine now, I guess—between my boarding house and that creek out there. It's never run dry in the years I've been here. That creek is what gives Walburn Ford its name, and it marks the line between my land and the parcel I'm talking about."

Geoffrey tightened his hands round the uppermost paddock rail and welcomed the pain of splinters piercing his skin, glad of anything to distract him from the certainty that he was being bedeviled. A comely woman, with fair well-watered acres, calmly discussing available grounds contiguous to her own. In his time, men plotted to take wives whose holdings would so neatly enhance the value of their own. Seldom did even the most diligent seeker find such a wife with the grace, the spirit, the loveliness possessed by Juliette. If he were a man of this time, innocently arrived for the purpose of claiming lands, how he would revel in the notion of becoming Juliette's closest neighbor.

If he were a man of this time . . . but he was not. And he was done with bemoaning the unfairness of his circumstances, done with wishing things might be different. In truth, it made no matter. Had he lived his years according to schedule, Juliette, being of this time, would still have been denied him.

One thing to say on behalf of traveling through the centuries—it gave a man a philosophical bent.

"I find that land unappealing," he said, and when Juliette flinched as though she'd taken a blow to the belly, he forced his attention back upon Arion where it belonged. "I will ride with the soldiers tomorrow morning and stake my claim on another piece of land, something very very far from here."

"Perhaps that's for the best," she said in a voice scarcely above a whisper. "They're leaving at first light." And then she left him. Her scent lingered, the verdant vista wavered before him—temptations ripe for a man willing to abandon all sense of honor and duty.

The next morning, Juliette cursed herself for failing to remember how starved the Walburn Ford homesteaders were for any sort of entertainment. Though dawn barely lighted the sky, a good number of people had gathered to watch the soldiers depart for Fort Scott. Someone was bound to ask what she was doing, standing next to her saddled mule, obviously intending to accompany the traveling party when it moved off. She had no explanation, not for them, not for herself. For once, she welcomed the sight of Mrs. Abbott bustling toward her. The woman's presence would discourage others from flocking around, asking questions.

Mrs. Abbott fluttered importantly, waving a loose sheaf of letters. "Mind you don't take too long to return, Miss Jay. When the soldiers rode in yesterday, they brought me another letter from Herman. The whole town will be wanting you to organize a social event so I can read it out loud to everyone."

"Naturally, Mrs. Abbott. Walburn Ford thrives on hearing all the latest exploits of the Army Corps of

Topographical Engineers." Juliette knew that her neighbors would pounce on any opportunity for a gathering, even if it meant listening to news from Herman.

Mrs. Abbott rustled the papers right beneath Juliette's nose as if scent alone could impart the news her letter contained. "Herman's passed along such exciting tidbits, about *camels,* of all creatures! He's also quite impressed with his commander, Lieutenant Ives, and tells about a most colorful Lieutenant Beale, who has accomplished great things with those camels in the western wilderness."

"Camels," Geoffrey muttered darkly. "Vile odorous spitting creatures, not unlike some denizens of this land." He cast Juliette an I-told-you-so kind of look, which bounced from her toward the soldiers, and stalked off to mount his borrowed horse.

"Rather surly fellow," Mrs. Abbott remarked before heading back to her house.

Juliette mounted her own mule with ease, blessing her practical Bloomer dress. Every homesteading women she'd ever known could tell a story about ruining a good dress through the hems catching fire while tending outdoor cooking and laundry chores. The Bloomer's short skirt eliminated that hazard. And then there was the almost exhilarating freedom that came from riding astride while retaining some semblance of modesty, though some men were still appalled by the sight.

She'd heard that women back East scorned the Bloomer. So be it. They needn't brave the rigors of frontier living, nor would they be likely to find themselves mounted on top of a mule, determined to ride along with a group of soldiers to make sure a certain muddleheaded stranger came to no harm. Juliette clamped her legs against the mule's sides, just in case any of Lieutenant Jordan's men tried prying her out of her saddle.

Apparently her stance convinced them she was as

stubborn as her mule, for one by one the soldiers mounted up themselves and sat staring at her with rather stoic resignation. All except for Geoffrey, who was studying the machine-stitched edges of his horse's reins with such rapturous delight that he had no attention to spare.

"We mean to ride straight through, Miss Jay. It's a good thirty miles or more." Lieutenant Jordan jerked his thumb toward Geoffrey. "We'll point him in the direction of the land office once we get to town."

"Pointing won't be enough." At the lieutenant's curious expression, Juliette felt compelled to embellish her explanation. "He's a playactor and doesn't know the first thing about homesteading. He hurt his head somehow, and he gets confused every now and again."

"So you're stuck with taking care of him until he gets his wits back?"

"I . . . I wouldn't put it in exactly those words." The trouble was, she *could* put it in exactly those words, and the Widow Walburn would have done so without a moment's hesitation. But something within her rebelled at branding Geoffrey a nuisance, something that didn't bear inspection. "My past travels have left me well accustomed to long rides. And I have my own personal reasons for traveling to Fort Scott." Juliette knew that that would put an end to the questioning; frontier folk were notoriously closemouthed and tended to respect one another's requests for privacy.

But precisely what those personal reasons were she couldn't say, and they became increasingly murky as the day progressed. Geoffrey found the notion of living next to her unappealing, so why should she care if he bungled his homestead application? Land officers wielded a small amount of authority—she didn't know if it extended to the expulsion or incarceration of amnesiac actors. Not that it mattered to her, not a bit.

Still, she didn't regret her decision to keep an eye on him, not even when long-unused muscles began reminding her of their presence, not even when hours passed without Geoffrey so much as saying a word to her. Not that he held his tongue as far as others were concerned; he badgered the soldiers with an incessant variety of questions and demands to identify various objects.

"A curious fellow," remarked Professor Burns, who had spent the greater part of the journey riding alongside her.

"None like him in all of Boston, I'd wager," Juliette said.

"Oh, I wouldn't be so sure about that, Mrs. Walburn."

She listened intently, hoping he might offer some insight into Geoffrey's character. The professor launched into an endless account of the diversity of Boston's population, the cultural wealth boasted by its universities. When it became evident, though, that none of his acquaintances were as . . . colorful as Geoffrey, Juliette paid him scant further attention, barely noting how he droned on, marking the passage of miles.

Lieutenant Jordan had taken her at her word and he'd set a swift and steady pace that found them trotting into Fort Scott at supper time. Or at least she assumed it must be supper time, since the town's street seemed curiously devoid of activity. The unexpected quiet seemed to set Lieutenant Jordan on edge.

"I'm going to take Professor Burns over to headquarters to see what's going on here." He gestured toward the land office. "You two take care of your business."

Geoffrey sighed as if facing an unpleasant task.

Glad as she was to be dismounting at last, Juliette nonetheless knew her legs would shriek in protest the minute she tried swinging across the saddle, and would ache even worse once her feet touched the ground. She removed her bonnet, wincing with dread. But before she could commence the unpleasant task, strong hands gripped her around the waist, hoisted her up, and effortlessly lowered her to the earth, slowly, giving her feet a moment to adjust to the pressure of standing.

Geoffrey. She didn't have to see his face to recognize him; every nerve and fine hair on her body virtually sang his name with silent exultation. Her knight. After ignoring her all day, his first thought was a chivalrous one, to see to her comfort. He hadn't made up his tale about traveling long hours on horseback, because he obviously understood the discomforts a body felt after riding long distances.

"Alma erred," he said. "If these soldiers did pant after you, they would not have left this pleasant task to me."

He stood behind her, his hands lingering in a very forward fashion just at the place where her waist joined her hips. Geoffrey. She had no idea how much space separated them, only that the heat wafted from his body to warm her back. His breath stirred her hair, and she wanted to sink back against him, to luxuriate in the warmth and scent of him.

"This way," she said, wrenching herself loose before she acted out her wanton impulses. She stumbled a little at the wooden walk leading to the land office, but flinched away when Geoffrey offered his arm to hold her steady.

The land officer turned a look of sour disapproval upon them. "Didn't you hear Captain Anderson's proclamation tellin' folks to stay inside today? Damned border ruffians killed two last week, and there's rumor they might attack again tonight."

"We hadn't heard—we just rode in from Walburn Ford." Juliette risked a glance at Geoffrey to see how he was taking the frightening news. He yawned and twisted his torso as if stretching a stiff muscle was his most pressing concern.

The land officer frowned. "Well, hell. I s'pose yer here to make a claim." At Geoffrey's indifferent nod, the officer leaped to his feet. "OK. Face the flag, right hand up to God. Do you swear to tell the truth, the whole truth, and nothing but the truth, so help you God?"

"You are demanding that I speak an oath to tell God's truth?" Geoffrey paled.

"Just say 'I do,'" the land agent whispered, as if he feared being overheard.

"I do."

"All right to go on?" The land officer peered at him, apparently not certain that Geoffrey understood the proceedings.

"I would not condemn my immortal soul by lying, now that I have taken an oath before God."

Juliette closed her eyes and grimaced. With sinking certainty, she knew this oath-taking business would somehow get mixed up with Geoffrey's wrongheaded delusions. She sharpened her hearing, and almost at once was called upon to embellish Geoffrey's "truths."

"Occupation?"

"I must tell the truth?"

"I just swore you to the oath, didn't I?"

Geoffrey drew himself to his full impressive height, and added a proud tilt to his chin. "Then, sir, I have no choice but to admit to you that I am a knight—"

"*Watchman*! Night *watchman*!" Juliette shouted, her words seeming to clang from each wall in the small office. Geoffrey cast her a wounded look. The agent nodded and wrote her answer in the book.

"God's blood," Geoffrey murmured. From the skeptical, yet apprehensive, way he stared at the agent's fountain pen, you'd think he expected it to turn into a rattlesnake.

"Much call for night watchmen up Walburn Ford way?" the land agent asked, continuing his scribbling.

"From what I have seen, 'twould require at least a dozen well trained in *my* profession to hold that town safe," said Geoffrey, tearing his gaze away from the fountain pen to glower at Juliette.

"Mmm." The officer cast a preoccupied glance toward the window and back to the document in front of him. "You got a birth certificate, citizenship papers, suchlike?"

Geoffrey touched his shirtfront. "I have this relic handed straight from Edward, the most royal—"

He possessed nothing, Juliette knew, except for that blasted tarnished pendant, a suit of armor, and a skintight leather shirt. And a big horse. "He, um, lost everything. He had such a rough voyage he doesn't even remember crossing the Atlantic," she told the officer.

Shaking his head sympathetically, the agent swiveled a large ledger in Geoffrey's direction. "Mark down the claim number and sign yer name, then be off wit' ya. I don't s'pose there's any rooms left in town, what with all the soldiers ridin' in and no place for them to stay. Just like the government to sell a fort and wish they had it back a couple years later. 'Less you got friends to hole up with, you'd best head straight back where you come from."

"Claim number?" Geoffrey asked, ignoring everything else.

"From the corner marker." The officer stabbed testily at a column in his book.

"Corner marker?" Geoffrey asked with utter dismay. "Juliette?"

She knew the number of only one parcel besides her own. "I know the marks for the claim we looked at yesterday, Geoffrey."

He shrugged in acceptance, although a shadow

descended over his expression, telling her he scorned the land abutting on her own.

She realized, then, how much she would have liked living close to him, and it hurt, in ways she didn't want to examine, that he was so uninterested.

"One-four-seven-three, Bourbon County," Juliette blurted out before her throat could close, giving Geoffrey the identification for the preempt land parcel.

"Naturally, I am quite proficient at signing my name," Geoffrey said, slanting a smug glance her way that made her wonder if he expected accolades for his ability.

She'd dared to hope that some day a man as devoted to Walburn Ford as she was herself might come along and preempt that parcel, that they might join forces for the good of the town. And now she'd gone and urged the land onto a man who'd already disdained the town and the land, who scarcely knew what year it was.

Why, any time she stood at her kitchen door and looked across her fields she might see Geoffrey working the acres bordering her own. Unbidden, her mind filled with the image of Geoffrey at work, clad in tight homespun and that scandalous leather vest, his mighty, battle-scarred arms bared to the sun . . .

There was still time to call out, to tell him not to sign—she stood still as stone while he marked down the number and signed his name with a flourish, saddling himself with the land he found so unappealing.

Oh God, what had she done?

The officer's grunt brought her out of her unseemly reverie. He swiveled the book so he could enter his own cryptic governmental marks.

"I can answer most of this other stuff my own self. I can tell by the way you talk that yer a Frenchy—"

"Not God's truth. As I tried to tell you, I am a subject of England's good King Edward," said Geoffrey.

Juliette had no idea who the king of England might be, and the land officer didn't seem to care, either.

"Well, hell, it don't matter if he's a good or bad king now that yer here in this country, does it? Nobody pays any attention to the citizenship information on yer paper. Now, let me see what yer claimin'." He swiveled to yet another book and thumbed rapidly through the pages. "Hmm. This here parcel was claimed a couple years back by some fella name of Elias Coates over Missouri way. Goddamn border ruffian, no doubt."

"I was led to believe that taking a claim meant you were not aligned in any way with the border ruffians," said Geoffrey.

"Not always, sir, not always. It's nice to see a Free Stater like you snatch it up from under him. You get that old homestead goin' and come back here in five years and petition the court for preemption." The land officer studied Geoffrey for a moment. "My guess is Mr. Border Ruffian Coates won't make an appearance against you."

"A pity," said Geoffrey in a tone that boded ill should the absentee Mr. Coates make an appearance.

"Now, you folks best be on your way. Here's yer claim voucher. Oh yes, and the United States government thanks you and wishes you well."

The man did everything but apply a broom to sweep them out of his office. Juliette could hear the snap of the lock engaging behind them.

"Well," she said as they stood in the silent sunny dusty street. She wasn't sure what should come next. Her father had acquired and disposed of many properties during their travels, but some amount of excitement had always marked each fresh acquisition, some small family celebration to mark the occasion. Geoffrey betrayed no excitement whatsoever over becoming a

landowner, and his face bore such a glum expression
that the likelihood of a celebration seemed remote.

Lieutenant Jordan's frantic approach reminded her
that she was worrying about the wrong thing. His
mount skidded to a stop before the land office hitching
post, and the lieutenant's shoulders sagged with relief
at the sight of them. "I was ready to storm in there and
bring you out," he said. "I'm right sorry, Miss Jay, but
we're expecting serious trouble."

"I know. The land officer told us."

"Agnes Fowler says she can take you in if you don't
mind doubling up with another lady. D'Arbanville, you
can bunk down in Aggie's barn until we put down this
disturbance. Professor Burns has to hurry to make his
report to the president, so you two just sit tight and you
can ride along when we escort him back."

Lieutenant Jordan, being mounted, sat a head taller
than Geoffrey. Nonetheless, Geoffrey somehow managed to look down his nose at the army officer. "You
would ask one with my prowess to sit idle whilst
defenseless townfolk are besieged?"

Lieutenant Jordan brightened. "You wanna fight?"

"I would not have said so unless it were true. I have,
after all, been but recently placed under oath."

A quizzical frown creased Lieutenant Jordan's forehead. Juliette felt a pang of distress; she'd grown accustomed to Geoffrey's odd remarks, but how would they
sound to someone who didn't know him so well?
Specifically, a trained soldier determined to crush an
insurrection, who didn't know the honor and loyalty
that marked Geoffrey's every action?

If ever there was a timely border ruffian invasion, it
was now, for the lieutenant appeared too preoccupied
with duty to worry about Geoffrey's ramblings.

"We're in pretty good shape here, but I guess we can

always use another man. You know how to handle a gun, don't you?"

Geoffrey fashioned his hand into an imaginary pistol, peered over his extended finger, and made an exploding sound at the back of his throat. Silently telling a lie without verbally breaking his precious oath—how could a man be so peculiarly honest one minute, and so devious the next?

"Of guns, I am most familiar with the Colt," Geoffrey said, entangling himself even further.

"No, you can't do this!" Juliette cried.

The two men, who had only yesterday confronted each other with suspicion, faced her with purposeful solidarity, brothers-in-arms now that mutual danger was to be faced.

Oh God, why had she allowed herself to get caught up in Geoffrey d'Arbanville's chaotic life? She'd come all this way to keep him out of trouble, not to see him ride off with a soldier he didn't know, to arm himself with a weapon he couldn't handle. He could kill himself. He could hurt someone by accident. He was . . . practically helpless. He was . . . the most magnificently awesome man she'd ever beheld.

The sun struck the men from behind, casting shadows to Juliette's feet. Almost equal in length, even though Lieutenant Jordan sat mounted while Geoffrey stood. And a person didn't need a yardstick to measure which man possessed the broader shoulders, which man the brawniest arms. Arms marked with evidence of violence past, the arms of a fighting man; arms that could encircle a woman with infinite gentleness and yet rouse within her the most life-shattering sensations, sensations she'd sworn to obliterate.

Once before, she'd allowed her wayward senses to distract a man from protecting his town. Innocent lives had paid for her indiscretion. Apparently, she'd learned nothing from her past mistakes. Mortification flooded through her—to think that she would be so selfish, so heedless of the needs of others.

"I want to go home," she whispered, soul-numbed. Yes, home—she yearned to close herself within her boarding house and reconstruct the tough uncaring shell she'd so painstakingly crafted for herself. Her knees felt so weak beneath her that she had to hold on to the hitching post for support.

"Darn, Miss Jay." Lieutenant Jordan's eyes darkened with sympathy. "I plumb forgot that you lost your husband and folks like this." He returned his attention to Geoffrey. "Much as I appreciate your offer, I'm pretty sure we got enough men to stand against the bunch headed our way." And then he frowned. "'Course, you'd have to ride like hell to make it back to Walburn Ford before nightfall. Here and back in one day's a hell of a lot of riding for a woman."

"She has boasted more than once of her ability on that score," said Geoffrey. The light smile playing about his lips deflected any insult from the comment.

His teasing barb lent strength to Juliette's spine. So did the realization that Lieutenant Jordan himself had relieved Geoffrey of battle duty—she needn't feel guilty on this account. She lifted her chin, intending to accept Geoffrey's challenge, when his eyes met hers. She realized, then, how infrequently he let that happen, how careful he was to pretend great interest in everyday things rather than meet her scrutiny. Indeed, his gaze skipped past her almost at once, but not before she imagined she read a hopeless longing equal to her own. She found herself gripping the hitching post again.

"We'll be escorting Professor Burns back in a few days.

I'll stop myself to see how you folks fared," said the lieutenant. "You'd best make sure you get her home safe."

"I would die ere letting her come to harm," said Geoffrey.

He spoke this vow with such utter sincerity that she couldn't help believing him. Her heart commenced such a joyful pounding that she could scarcely make out Lieutenant Jordan's words as he tipped his cap and led their tired mounts behind him, promising to send a pair of fresh horses for their trip.

Once they were alone, Geoffrey turned his attention to his claim voucher. Her protector—completely captivated by a scrap of paper. He held it over the back of his left hand, as if measuring the amount of light that penetrated the thin document. Then he lifted it to the sky, squinting against the bright glare, but tracing the writing that showed backwards through the illuminated paper. The position tilted his head back, revealed clearly the strong line of jaw meeting muscled neck, revealed in profile his proud nose, his full lips.

When he finished toying with the paper, he didn't fold it properly; starting at one narrow edge, he rolled it up into a skinny little tube. And then he unrolled it, holding it open like a miniature scroll while he cocked his head and puzzled over the writing thus turned sideways.

He smiled at her then, and she found herself returning it, sharing some small measure of his obvious fascination. How wonderful it must be, to find joy and delight in the most common objects. *I used to feel that way all the time,* she marveled. The sense of something magical waiting to happen. How could she have lost it without putting up a fight?

It seemed as though a knot inside her loosened ever so slightly, a knot that held together the mantle of obligation and practicality that weighed so heavy upon her.

She had tied that knot herself and shouldn't let it unravel . . . but when she fought to retie it in its old comfortable position, the knot didn't hold quite so well.

She found herself smiling up at the sky with her eyes closed, enjoying the feel of the sun and wind against her skin.

"'Tis an incomparably wonderful day, is it not, Juliette?"

"Yes," she whispered.

Juliette fought down the urge to call Lieutenant Jordan back and beg him to take her to Agnes Fowler's. Cowering beneath a blanket while border ruffians attacked suddenly seemed less threatening to her peace of mind than traveling thirty miles or more alone with Geoffrey d'Arbanville.

11

Josiah paused in his plowing to wipe the sweat from his forehead. He squinted across the field toward the cabin, but he was too far away to make out if anyone was using the front porch.

He always arranged the porch chairs to place Rebecca in front of the kitchen window. Sometimes she sat out there to do her sewing, and then he could stand inside the kitchen and watch her without her knowing. Or when they sat there together in the dark to catch the cool evening breeze, he would make some excuse to go into the kitchen and light a candle. Its soft golden glow would spill onto the porch, illuminating her lovely features while keeping his own in darkness. On the best nights, the boy joined them, and Josiah could drink in the sight of them both without ever once letting on how he reveled in their presence.

Boarding that pesky schoolmarm helped some, too. Rebecca seemed to relish having a lady friend; her rare laughter rang out and her musical voice chattered like

a squirrel's whenever she thought she was alone with
Alma. He enjoyed working in the barn at some quiet
chore, like polishing his harness, while the happy feminine sounds drifted across the yard. He knew that the
minute his lanky frame darkened the cabin doorway
the merriment would cease, the familiar pale desperation would replace Becky's animation, the schoolmarm's smile lines would twist into a frown, as if she
was disappointed that he wouldn't say, "You gals just
keep on with your funnin'."

It wouldn't do, it would never do, for them to read the
constant hunger that consumed him. The never-ending
dread that one day the man Rebecca had loved, Robbie's
real father, would come to take them away from him.
And they would go, he just knew they would go.

Who could blame them, considering what a failure
Josiah Wilcox had turned out to be?

"Hup!" He shook the reins across the mule's back,
and shoved his strength into the plow, knowing he was
still hours away from achieving the blessed exhaustion
that would numb his sense of failure.

He wasn't nearly tired enough when Robbie greeted
him at the end of a furrow.

"Ma . . . Ma says it's late. Miss Harkins is hungry.
You should come in for supper."

Late, yes, but on these summer evenings it took forever to get dark. And Josiah couldn't abide walking
alongside the child when sunlight illuminated Robbie's
white-faced disdain, couldn't abide sitting across from
the boy when he wasn't tired enough to remain unaffected. Times like this, when his arms still had strength
to raise themselves, he longed to gather Robbie into his
arms and give him a big hug instead of forever pushing
him away.

"You go on and eat with the women. I'll be in when

I'm ready." As always, after a day of working in silence, his voice sounded rough as a saw hasping away on a chunk of cottonwood.

He turned the mule and reset the plow to commence the next furrow. All the while he felt Robbie staring at him, yet saying nothing; Josiah felt certain that the boy must be comparing him unfavorably to the real father he'd never known, a man of wealth and substance against a dirt-poor homesteader who couldn't even afford to buy his wife a Bloomer dress.

"What're you still doing here?" The question couldn't have sounded any meaner coming from a gut-shot bear. And yet Robbie didn't back away. Could it be that the boy craved his company? The very thought sent a rush of warmth flooding through Josiah, which he did his best to cool down before he did something foolish. It would be easy enough to demand an explanation for the boy's hesitation. "Why ain't you off pesterin' your friend Miss Jay and that new boarder of hers, that Geoffrey?"

"They . . . they . . ." Robbie blinked rapidly, swallowing so hard Josiah could see his immature Adam's apple bobbing in his tender throat. "They went off to Fort Scott with the soldiers so Geoffrey could file a claim."

Disappointment knifed through Josiah, a sensation so sharp that he pressed his aching muscles into the plow handles to give himself something else to think about. What had he expected? That the boy would willingly choose to spend time with him if his latest hero had been available?

That Geoffrey—it still rankled, remembering how the huge stranger, with no weapons but a commanding voice and haughty stare, had sent the bunch of them cowering against Miss Jay's kitchen wall. Thank God Becky hadn't been there to witness that humiliation. But the boy had seen, and now Robbie dogged after the so-called knight like a faithful puppy, and some uncontrollable impulse within Josiah Wilcox struck out against the pain.

"Well, how would you feel about your hero if the soldiers lock him up once they get there? There's something funny about him, and I for one ain't gonna rest until I find out what it is."

Robbie stifled a cry. He retreated a few steps, as if he feared turning his back with his stepfather in striking range, and then darted away toward the cabin.

Josiah sighed, aware of a hollow feeling that threatened to overwhelm him. There was something funny about d'Arbanville and it wasn't so different from what ailed Josiah himself. They both had addled minds, but Josiah didn't have the excuse of a blow to the head or a mind filled with memorized lines from stage plays to blame his own delusions on.

He took off his hat and wiped a grimy hand over his sweating forehead. Talking to the boy had worn him out even more than the plowing had done, especially since everything he'd said had come out all wrong. He ought to go after Robbie, apologize, but there was no point in doing so. If he coaxed an unwilling smile from the child, it would only come back to haunt him, to taunt him, when mother and child left him.

He judged himself: Legs not yet trembling, stomach not too sore, shoulders not too stiff, back of the neck burnt like it always got, no matter how many days he spent in the sun. Nope, not nearly uncomfortable enough to go home. Maybe another two hours.

He got the mule going again, although the beast sent him a baleful stare over its shoulder before setting its weight against the harness. "Don't go glarin' at me like that," Josiah muttered. "Your kind's neuter from birth. You don't know the agonies a man feels when he's promised not to let himself . . ."

Admitting his weakness to a mule! His face flamed, probably as red as his sunburnt neck, even though it was well shaded by his hat brim. Thank God a sterile sexless mule was the only witness to his outburst. Must be the goddamned hot weather causing all sorts of sap to rise. Hell, who was he kidding? His own sap hadn't settled for years now, and each passing year saw his risabilities grow more excited rather than less. And the way his life was turning out, he wouldn't earn the privilege of relieving the pressure any time soon.

He tried to concentrate on the unfolding furrow before him, but now that he'd let his mind wander, Rebecca's image kept intruding. Beautiful Becky. Sweet Becky. He'd made her so many promises and failed to keep every blessed one of them. The punishment he'd devised for himself was fitting, oh, so fitting; unfortunately, the malicious God who'd done so much to torment Josiah Wilcox seemed determined to destroy Becky and Robbie right along with him.

It wasn't fair. The only thing that would save them was to send them away, and that was the one step Josiah wasn't strong enough to take, though he did everything in his power to force her to make that decision for herself.

"Damnation!" He swore aloud, and then mentally tested his strength once again, and condemned himself to yet another extra hour at the plow.

Geoffrey's instincts shouted a silent warning.

The horses maintained their long-legged strides with no pricking of the ears, no flaring of the nostrils, to indicate that they sensed approaching danger. Juliette, far more familiar with these environs than he, held to her saddle in a slumped huddle that bespoke an utter lack of concern—or exhaustion. He had no way of knowing how she fared since she had discouraged all attempts at conversation.

And yet he felt certain that something approached. Although no evidence supported it, his battle-honed wits sensed a shift in the air, fancied the ground rang with more than their own borrowed animals' hoofbeats.

Lieutenant Jordan had provided him with his very own snout-nosed bone-handled Colt to belt at his waist. Better the officer had loaned Geoffrey the slim rapier gracing his side. If true danger lay ahead, only Juliette knew the first thing about employing the Colt. And Sir Geoffrey d'Arbanville would rather hide like a coward until this threat passed them by than sit idly whilst a lady defended a full-fledged knight.

This Kansas terrain offered precious little in the way of concealment. His practiced eye raked the surrounding countryside, spotting a low prairie swell to the east, a small copse of trees to the west. Trees promised water, making their shelter a poor place to hide in these dry climes, should the oncoming peril approach with thirst searing its vitals. Now, how to coax Juliette away from the road without rousing her fears?

"Juliette, we have traveled enough. Let us stop and rest."

"I'm not tired. I told you I'm used to long trips."

He tried again. "Then let us venture across the prairie."

His suggestion roused a small shudder from her. "Oh Geoffrey, this road's bad enough. Prairie riding's so hard on the horses. They slip on the grass and twist their forelegs between the tufts if they try going too fast."

"You need not remind me of that," he said, knowing only too well how quickly Arion had gone lame. He abandoned his pretense that nothing was amiss.

"Nonetheless, you should indulge me and bide a while beyond yon prairie swell. I fear we face an enemy."

"Ruffians. Or Indians." For the first time since this return journey commenced, she looked at him. Apprehension darkened her eyes and lent an unaccustomed pallor to her skin, and he cursed his swordless person, knowing he possessed no means to protect her or dispel her fear. She wasted no time on womanly hysterics, but nudged her mount toward their hiding place.

Lieutenant Jordan had packed their saddlebags with blankets and food for the journey. Geoffrey made full use of these scanty comforts to settle woman and beasts behind the swell and then traversed the area on foot in a great sweeping arc, assuring himself that from all points she was safely invisible in her hiding place. As he was completing his swing, his apprehension was rewarded. A cloud of dust marred the horizon. He crouched low in the grass, watching, until he could discern what approached.

He could make no sense of it. He watched as long as he dared, fighting the urge to stand tall and afford himself a better view. Juliette might know what it all meant. Holding himself low to the ground, he rejoined her behind the prairie swell. She sat with her back up against the low-rising ground, and he was glad to see that she'd shed the unattractive headgear so favored by these American women, and that a goodly portion of her hair had escaped those infernal pins she kept stabbing into her head.

"A caravan approaches." The sight of her gentle features softened even more by the wealth of hair spilling down around her shoulders left him somewhat breathless. Fortunately, his brief sojourn handed him a ready explanation: This prairie indeed made traveling more difficult than its flat-looking appearance indicated.

When she didn't question his physical state, he continued. "A horde of tall well-featured Mongols with flowing black hair has overtaken the road. Horses, children, and dogs—all traveling silent as nuns caught between chapel and cloister. There seems no sinister purpose in their quiet approach, but also no minstrels or heralds to announce their presence. They look to be transporting a great deal of goods, but with nary a single camel or elephant, so that even the women must needs tow bundles on contrivances dragging behind them."

"Indians." Such a dejected slump curved her shoulders that he did not bother to correct her miscalling of the Mongols. "They've been moving south for the past couple of years, ever since the government decreed that they had to move out of Kansas."

"Aha. Your president." Geoffrey silently admitted a new respect for the ruler of this land. "Presidents must be more powerful than kings, if they possess the authority to order such masses of people about against their will."

"I guess." Color returned to her features, although it seemed to be embarrassment rather than relief that prompted it. "I don't want you to think I'm tired or anything, but I'd just as soon stay here until the Indians pass us by. I'm not real proud of the way my government treated them."

"Flogging? Torture? Hanging from the gyves with no support for the feet?" Geoffrey offered, curious. Knowing what lengths this president would go to achieve his means might prove valuable, should he find himself facing that man someday.

A weak smile tilted Juliette's lips. "No, Geoffrey. Paper and promises. We defeated them with paper and promises."

"How so?"

"Well, the way I understand it, the government promised them that Kansas would be theirs forever.

And then a few years back, the army came out and surveyed the land into individual claims."

"Aha," he said again, recalling the pompous old crone who continually boasted of her son. "Mrs. Abbott's son Herman and the Army Corps of Topographical Engineers."

- "Not quite. Mrs. Abbott's son is surveying somewhere out West—a new government discovery, she says. I'm not sure which engineers did this work, only that the government passed a law that opened Kansas Territory for settlement. White settlement, I mean. They paid the Indians a little money and told them the treaties were no good, that they had to move south. Now they say that the new Indian Territory will be theirs forever, but I don't know."

"This land I claimed today, it once belonged to those Mong . . . Indians?"

Juliette nodded and leaned back against the blanket, as though the admission had exhausted her.

Geoffrey drew out his claim voucher, appalled to think that he had, however briefly, benefited from such a humiliating exercise. As if a knight could profit from a broken treaty and still hold his head high!

He unrolled the voucher, for once regretting his inability to read. It might have been nice to harken back and recall that he'd once held proof of a dream come to life: "These lands belong to Geoffrey d'Arbanville." His own name, written in his own hand, was clear enough; likewise the number one sixty which he knew defined the number of acres he'd been accorded. The rest, written in the land agent's hand, was as indecipherable as the exotic markings he'd once seen etched into a Persian brass vase. And yet this wondrously thin crackling scrap of paper conveyed to Geoffrey the one thing he'd always craved. Soured, though, by the knowledge of how it had come about.

Perhaps God had cast his favorable eye back upon him, by making it so easy for him to turn his back on this overwhelming temptation. He ran his finger over the inked lines, marveling for the space of a heartbeat at what he held in his grasp, and then rolled it back into shape. He tucked it into Juliette's hand.

"You may give this back to the Indians, Juliette, and explain to them all about preempting. I shall not be here long enough to enforce my claim."

"Why not?"

The question burst forth before Juliette could place trembling fingers over her lips, and seemed to hover as if the low-rising prairie swell prevented them from dissipating. And so the words mocked her, ringing as they did with poignant desperation, as if it mattered one whit that he meant to leave soon, this man who raved of camels and elephants and minstrels and barbaric torture methods.

He knelt before her, sinking to his knees with supple-limbed grace. The shadow of an incipient beard darkened his cheeks, though not thickly enough to disguise the faint marks attesting to his clumsiness with a razor. Odd, that a man his age, clean shaven by choice, should nick himself with the frequency of an adolescent secretly using his father's razor to scrape off the first hairs over his lip. She couldn't understand why a clunk to the head had robbed him of his ability to shave. The sight provoked in her an almost irresistible urge to touch him and soothe any lingering pain.

And yet despite his flights of fancy and lack of shaving skills, there was nothing remotely boyish in the man who knelt before her. His hardened muscles strained the seams of Captain Chaney's borrowed clothing from ankles to shoulders; the sleeves, too short, bared inches of flesh scarred in yet another manner; the column of

Geoffrey's neck bulged so strong and sturdy that he hadn't been able to button the shirt to his throat. The dull gleam of his pendant rested against crisp curling hair, the sight more spellbinding than any of the disks and twirling devices Dr. Mesmer used to hypnotize his subjects.

Geoffrey, wallowing in fantasy; Juliette, never indulging in a frivolous thought. Together, they might balance each other out. . . . The outrageous impossible wanderings of her thoughts caused her to gasp aloud. "What kind of actor are you?" she demanded. "Why . . . why have you come here to torment me? I was doing so well . . ."

"I am only a man, Juliette." He spoke with a quiet dignity. "I know not why or how I have come here. I know only that I have sworn to find my way back and complete my quest, no matter if it means I must deny myself the delights I have found here. And as God is my witness, I vow I would carve out mine own heart ere cause you a moment's torment."

His deep-set gaze met hers unflinchingly. The rich hazel of his eyes smoldered, tempting and sinful as warm honey, while at the same time glowing with purity of purpose—whatever his purpose—that dared anyone to challenge his vow.

Vows. Quests. The stuff of knights. God. Witness. The stuff of oaths. Oh Lord, Geoffrey still believed himself to be bound by the oath he'd taken at the land office!

Which meant he would tell her the truth, the whole truth, and nothing but the truth, no matter how bold or intrusive her questions. Maybe they'd all spent too much time tiptoeing around his amnesia. Maybe, by asking the right questions, she could work her way beyond his delusions of knighthood and learn the truth about Geoffrey d'Arbanville.

The wind drifted over them, heavy with the sounds

of the journeying Indians, the tired sounds of plodding hooves, dust-caked feet thudding against the hard-packed road, the dragging weight of travois scratching tracks destined for obliteration by the next rainfall. Soon there would be nothing left in Kansas of these people who'd roamed the prairies for centuries beyond remembrance; fitting, then, that the sounds of their passage should serve as the backdrop for her interview of a man who claimed he'd come from centuries past, and who would soon depart, leaving no trace of his brief presence in her life.

"Geoffrey," she said, "tell me the truth. The whole truth and nothing but the truth, so help you God. About everything."

12

Juliette almost withdrew her demand when it roused the sharp hiss of an indrawn breath from him.

"You did not want to hear the truth from me when I tried speaking it before."

Something made her persist. "I didn't want to rush you into an explanation if your head hadn't cleared. But I don't want to wait anymore. I want to hear it now."

He studied her with brooding assessment. "You might wrongly believe that what I say smacks of witchcraft. You might even . . . laugh at me." Geoffrey's expression shifted into a scowl.

"I swear I won't laugh," she promised, even though his obvious preference for being accused of witchcraft rather than serving as a source of amusement prompted the most unseemly urge to giggle.

"Very well." Slowly, never releasing her from his troubled stare, he rose to his full height. "Stands before you Geoffrey Charles Walter FitzHugh d'Arbanville, fourthborn son to the Honorable Edward Montcrief

FitzHugh d'Arbanville, and knighted in the year of our Lord 1271, upon the battlefield in defense of the Holy Land by the man who would soon thereafter become His Royal Highness, King Edward of England."

His utter sincerity sucked her amusement dry.

He dropped back to his knees and studied her with an intentness that defied her to refute his claims, while at the same time piercing her soul. *I would not dare lie to this man,* she thought. And it seemed completely unfair, since despite her hopes that he might tell her the truth, he seemed so determined to spin tales for her.

But he believed himself to be under oath. Could this outrageous story possibly contain the seeds of truth?

Juliette's common sense scoffed at every claim he made, while her heart urged her to believe. She squared her shoulders, and the movement sent a rush of blood through her veins, until she fancied she could hear her heart imploring her to believe, just for a little while.

"This pendant serves as proof of what I say," Geoffrey said, urgently, as if he sensed her inner wavering. He pulled the leather string over his head and pressed the pendant into her hand. It had looked so small set against the broadness of his chest. Juliette was surprised to find it as big as her palm, where it lay heavy with the warmth absorbed from his skin. She rubbed the leather strand between her fingers, raising an elusive whiff of his scent.

"What about the pendant?" she asked, eager for any explanation that would tear her mind away from wondering what it might feel like, to rest so intimately against Geoffrey's skin, to absorb his essence, as this leather had done.

"Its deliverance is my quest. It is a token representing true love between a man and a woman. When I hand it to the golden-haired Demeter, she will rejoice in knowing she is the most beloved of women."

"The most beloved of women." She could picture it in her mind: a laughing delighted Geoffrey cradling a petite golden-haired lady in his arms while she draped the pendant over his head, roping him like a wild stallion and branding him as hers, all with one gesture.

"Demeter." Gentleness, and regret, settled over Geoffrey. "I wonder . . . I wonder how she fared."

"You left her alone?"

He drew back, looking as shocked as if she'd accused him of treason. "Not by choice, I assure you. No man could have strived more diligently, or sacrificed more, to reach her side and kneel before her to proffer this gift."

Juliette didn't care at all for *that* mental image, of Geoffrey kneeling with bent head before the golden-haired Demeter.

"Edward must think I have failed." A quivering breath shuddered through him. "He cannot know my determination to return at all cost."

"Edward? He? What does Edward have to do with this lady Demeter that you . . . that you love, Geoffrey?" Oh God, she found the words so hard to form.

"Love Demeter? God's blood, Juliette—you have not understood a thing I have told you." He caught her face between his hands and tilted it up. She found herself breathless before the golden glow lighting his eyes, and her lips trembled as if only the pressure of his touching hers could still them. He stroked the line of her chin without giving her the kiss she silently craved.

"Demeter is no beloved of mine. She is John of Rowanwood's loyal lady wife. The two of them have long conspired against King Edward, conducting raids and suchlike from their border stronghold. A fellow knight captured John and after languishing for a bit in Edward's dungeon he agreed to put an end to his rebellion. 'Twas my task to carry this relic to Demeter from her imprisoned husband and thus effect a reconciliation between Rowanwood and Edward—King Edward, who I am certain must have died cursing me as a cowardly failure."

"Nonsense." Juliette found herself defending the king, driven by an inner impulse that told her it would be one sure way to comfort Geoffrey—and by the singing in her heart, to know that he didn't love another woman. "The king chose you, I'm sure, because of your, er, knightly bravery."

A wry smile crossed Geoffrey's features. "My fame has ever preceded me. And yet, there were others eager for the work. Edward chose me because of my horse."

"Arion?"

"Aye." He tilted his head, as if the sight of her perplexity amused him. "Do you not remember your Greek mythology, Juliette? The goddess Demeter, who disguised herself as a mare to disport with the god Poseidon and bore the wild stallion Arion as a result of that union?"

"Oh, that Greek mythology." Juliette swallowed. "It slipped my mind for a moment."

What had really slipped her mind was common sense. So much for following her heart. How could she have believed, even for a moment, a man spouting nonsense about princesses and quests and mythological Greek high jinks of a sexual nature?

You promised to believe, for a little while, whispered her conscience.

"It must be fearsome dull to rule as king of England. Edward is ever seeking diversion. It amused him to entrust this task to the knight possessing a horse bearing a name from the Greek myth."

"Oh sure, I can see that." Juliette nodded as if everything he'd said made perfect sense. "What I don't understand is why you leaped almost six hundred years to bring the pendant to Kansas."

He leaned forward, his features earnest and relieved, as if he appreciated this chance to expound his nonsense. "Not by intention, I assure you. Once Drogo FitzBaldric employed his cowardly back-stabbing strategy, I had no choice but to take shelter within the sacred oak grove, and no choice again but to leap into the Eternal Chasm, a rent in the earth so deep no man has seen what lies at the bottom."

"So you never did fix things between the king and Rowanwood," Juliette said.

"Nay." He stared past her shoulder, a frown creasing his forehead. "Angus Ōg saved me, but mayhap he misunderstood my quest. That Celtic god sent me to right a border dispute, but chose the wrong one. Ah, but I wonder, Juliette, if you have forgotten your Greek mythology, perhaps you are not well versed in Celtic lore, either?"

She shook her head, anxious now only to put an end to her disappointment. She hadn't solved anything by believing him. Celtic gods sending him to solve border disputes throughout history, leaping into bottomless chasms, indeed! "I must have missed that Celtic lore session."

"Angus Ōg, the restorer of life to those who relinquished their last breath in the cause of love," he prompted, not noticing how her attitude had shifted.

"Oh, that Angus Ōg." She closed her eyes, filled with leaden discouragement. The prairie wind blew quietly now; the Indians must have completely passed them by. They could recommence their return to Walburn Ford, and she could resume her healthy skepticism.

Exhaustion gripped her, an aching inner tiredness that had nothing to do with the sore bottom or overtaxed muscles that accompanied too many hours in the saddle.

She felt a stabbing sensation in her fist, and realized that she'd clutched the pendant so tightly that some of the ancient Celtic swirls had embossed a matching pattern in her skin. *See, I have engraved you on the palms of my hand.* Not Greek or Celtic, but Christian "mythology," from the Book of Isaiah.

A curious feeling overcame her. According to Geoffrey, star-crossed lovers and the king of England himself might have centuries ago gripped the relic in this very same way. Impossible. There was no such thing as Celtic magic.

She rubbed a surreptitious finger over her patterned flesh, and a tingling sensation shot straight into her heart. She would welcome the return of her common sense—but not just yet. She rose and held the pendant before her.

"Sir Geoffrey," she intoned in her most serious voice, "take charge once again of your quest."

She knew a moment's doubt. Maybe *this* was the tack she should have pursued all along. Maybe he would laugh, now that she'd caved in and was playing his silly game along with him, and tell her it had all been a wild far-fetched scheme to lure her out of her carefully constructed conservatism.

Geoffrey flashed her a blindingly brilliant smile. His eyes darkened with satisfaction, his entire demeanor aligned itself into a proud stance as he lowered his head. The very image of giving homage that she'd driven from her mind, and yet there wasn't any hint of humility or obsequiousness in his manner.

She lifted the leather strand over his head, but since he wore his hair long and loose, the strand didn't fall against his skin where it belonged. She lifted the springy wealth of his hair and slid her finger between coarse leather and warm skin, to make sure the supple strand could lie against his neck. She found herself standing there stupidly, listening to the suddenly harsh cadence of his breathing, feeling his suddenly hot breath searing right through the waistband of her skirt.

Her fingers curled over the hard ridges of muscle joining his neck to shoulders, and she didn't see how she could ever let him go.

"God's blood, Juliette."

Moving with infinitesimal slowness, he brought his forehead to rest against the softness of her belly, taking a scandalously intimate liberty that she lacked the fortitude to deny. He flouted decency even more, settling one huge hand over each of her hips, his fingers resting wonderfully heavy against her waist, his thumbs just brushing the nubs of her pelvic bones, which she hadn't, until this very moment, realized were so excruciatingly sensitive.

"When you touch me, when I touch you, I forget that I should by rights be naught but a six-hundred-year-old pile of dust and moldering bones."

His pulse thrummed against her fingers, his flesh pressed firm and resilient against her own. He claimed he should be dead, but he felt more vibrantly alive than anything she'd ever encountered. His voice, low and husky with passion, seemed to pass right through her skin to resonate against a wonderfully sensitive place she hadn't even known she possessed.

"Geoffrey," she whispered, thinking that if anyone's bones moldered or turned to dust, they were her own— her knees, she noted with surprised detachment, seemed to have lost their ability to support her weight, and she swayed against her kneeling prairie knight.

He drew a ragged breath and brought her toward the blanket with exquisite tenderness. He somehow lowered her within his mighty arms so that he had time to trail a path of kisses she could feel right through her gown against her belly, through the valley of her breasts, until his lips rested warm against the base of her throat. His hand, impossibly gentle, glided from waist to breast, drawing a soft whimper from within her.

Some spark of consciousness calling itself the Widow Walburn mentally chided her with wagging finger. Instead of moaning with pleasure, scolded the nagging spark, she should be denying his familiarity, should put an immediate halt to this wanton behavior. She'd spent years—*years*—heeding such inner warnings, but she doused the spark now with only the tiniest flicker of regret for all the time she'd spent nurturing it.

She had more important matters to consider—such as giving thanks that Geoffrey had mastered the art of unfastening buttons.

Her buttons popped free for him with the ease of fresh peas exiting the pod beneath a determined sheller's thumb. Despite his self-professed ignorance of modern-day fashions, he had them both divested of their clothes in less time than it had taken him to shuck his chain-mail shirt the first day she'd met him.

She had never completely bared herself to another, not even to Daniel. She might have been embarrassed to do so now, so exposed were they beneath the waning sunlight and the wide-open prairie, except that Geoffrey saw to it that she didn't remain uncovered for long. His lips, his hands, his heated flesh lying belly-to-belly with her own, cradled her within a shell of sensation that excluded everything save her awareness of the man teaching her what it meant to live, and to love.

"Juliette."

His fevered whisper reverberated deep inside her, rousing an unquenchable thirst to see whether his passions matched her own. She stole a glance at him through slitted eyelids to find his smoldering gaze kindle into a supremely male satisfaction. And then his lashes swept low, long and dark in comparison to the rough beard stubble shading his cheeks. He captured her nipples between gentle teeth and questing tongue, and gave a low groan of triumph when he roused a shuddering gasp from her.

His shoulders strained, each fine-honed muscle outlined and quivering as he employed them to spare her his weight. His battle scars lent him a savage perfection; she raised trembling fingers to touch one of the faint white lines crossing his skin, and couldn't hold in a shuddering breath to feel his flesh so hot and supple above her own. The setting sun teased golden shimmers from his hair, the sky framed him with melting orange and red. A jagged streak of gun-metal gray shafted through the warm color . . . like the fracture that had ripped the sky that day he'd stormed into her life. . . .

His flesh parted hers, consuming her, claiming her, and no rift in sky or time could have shattered her more thoroughly.

She had given her maidenhead to Daniel so long ago, and ever after regretted the sacrifice. It seemed a trifling loss now. In Geoffrey's arms she felt virgin again, for never had she been so thoroughly possessed. He surged within her, compelling her body to match his thrusts. His kisses stole her breath until her breathing adjusted to his. Her skin chilled everywhere he didn't touch her, burned wherever he did, yearned for his return whenever his movements altered his position. With hard prairie beneath her and hard man above and within her, she felt as though her very essence had been compressed into a soft weightless mass of sensation, building to an unbearable crescendo, until she found herself crying her ecstasy to the heavens, and reveled in the sound of his shouts joining hers.

For one breathless minute she found herself believing implicitly in everything he'd told her, for such love-making could only occur once in a millennium.

An eternity, or maybe only a heartbeat later, he drew her back against his chest, nestling her intimately against those parts of him that stirred and hardened against her still-quivering flesh. His hair fell over them and entwined with her own, chestnut mingling with brown, until the strands were indistinguishable from one another, as if they belonged to one person. A slight flutter of panic rose within her, to realize how easily she'd cast aside her hard-won aloofness. She pushed against his arms, suddenly frightened of her vulnerability.

His arms enfolded her, his heart thundered against her ear, and all urge to escape dissipated like raindrops soaking into sun-seared earth. He must have felt her capitulation; his fingers brushed against the tips of her breasts, his leg crossed over hers and drew her still more tightly against him. He bent low to place a kiss against her collarbone, and then drew a moist trail with his tongue along her jawline to her ear. His whisper, low and rumbling and filled with wicked confidence, resounded deep within her.

"If it please you, my lady, I would have you stay. I have not yet done with you."

A real lady would not have spent the past hour or so rolling over the prairie with an actor who couldn't seem to find his way out of a stage play, nor would a real lady find herself longing to say, "By all means, continue having your way with me, sir knight." A real lady would certainly never have uttered the scandalous gasp of anticipatory delight that was the only reaction Juliette found herself capable of making; nor would she have twisted about to force an even more intimate contact with the bold smiling man who pressed her back against the blanket before doing the most shockingly pleasurable things to her with his lips and his tongue and his hands.

The prairie lay bathed in moonlight, and her bones were as insubstantial as the waving grass before Geoffrey d'Arbanville had done with her.

And she, with him.

Geoffrey kept watch throughout the long night, propped in a reclining position against the prairie swell whilst Juliette slumbered against his chest. A poor job he was making of this surveillance, permitting his glance repeatedly to drift away from studying the horizon toward the woman in his arms.

All in all, it was the most pleasant sentry duty of his life.

He'd covered them both to the hips with their discarded clothing. Her hair fanned across her bare back and over his chest in a soft scented curtain, revealing naught but the curve of her cheek and the crest of one pink-tipped breast peeking through the curling strands.

Mine. The proprietary notion was as humbling as it was exhilarating.

For whatever reason, he'd come hurtling through time straight to this woman's side. His half-hearted attempts to resist her had come to naught, and upon reconsideration, he could see he'd been a fool even to try deflecting the intentions of fate. Forces beyond his understanding had chosen his insignificant soul from

among the countless hordes of humanity and brought
him together with Juliette. He'd entrusted her with the
truth, and she'd not laughed, nor called him a liar, but
turned to him with a gentle passion he'd be best served
to forget just now, while she slept.

Mine.

Perhaps Rowanwood's Celtic god had not acted so
capriciously as Geoffrey had thought. He could imagine no time or place more in need of his skills. Perhaps
he had been hurled forward to settle these border skirmishes as practice before returning to face his more
determined foes.

It was a notion that demanded exploration but, for
now, his mind was of a decidedly nonmilitary bent. He
tightened his embrace slightly, calling up a soft sleepy
sigh from Juliette.

"Dawn approaches, my lady," he whispered, not
particularly eager to wake her.

"Dawn." Her slumberous murmur escalated into a
small wide-awake squeal. "Dawn!"

She scrambled free—not without some playful effort,
since Geoffrey felt disinclined to let her loose. She turned
away from him, fumbling with her pale blue cotton gown,
obviously in an agony of embarrassment. As he pulled
on his borrowed chausses, he could only imagine the
rosy hue tinting her skin, and heartily wished he'd
waited a few moments longer ere waking her, but even
in the predawn gloom she seemed to glimmer with an
ethereal beauty. He strove to find words that would tell
her how her inner light captivated his heart.

"I am not facing east, else I would think fair Juliette
is the sun."

His compliment resulted in the sound of tearing
cloth. She had all but ripped her sleeve straight from
her bodice.

"What did you say?"

He could not fathom the reason behind her ruining her garment or her sudden hoarseness of voice, but did not care for the subtle distance it placed between them. He stood next to her, intending to catch her again in his arms. "I said, 'I am not facing east, else I would think fair Juliette is—'"

With an outraged shriek, his half-naked lady walloped him in the jaw.

"You . . . you big fat liar! You had me halfway believing your wild tales about coming from the past, and then you prove you're nothing but an actor, taunting me with mangled Shakespeare!"

Geoffrey had thought his compliment particularly well fashioned; her rejection of it stung worse than the blow to the chin. "You speak nonsense, woman. I carry no spear, mangled or otherwise, to shake at you. And," he added, with a significant glance at his flat belly, "I am neither fat, nor an actor, though you persist in calling me such."

"Ha!" She insulted him yet again, though she flung the word with a curious trembling, as if he were wounding her, instead of the other way round. She yanked her gown's sleeves into place, but as she had torn the one so badly, the blue fabric fell away from her neck to reveal her left breast. She seemed unaware of the tempting nature of the display. "You tell me, Mr. So-Called Knight from the year of our Lord 1283, how anyone besides an actor would sort of know a piece that wasn't written until three hundred years after you claim you lived? I never imagined I'd be grateful that my father's obsession stuck me with such a . . . a romantic name."

Truly, it was difficult to concentrate on her senseless diatribe with her breast peeking out at him like an impudent invitation. "The name? What's in a name?"

"You're making it worse." Improbably, tears welled in her eyes. "Next thing I know, you're going to forget all that knight nonsense and claim to be Romeo Montague. Let me put the rest of the words into your mouth: 'What's in a name? That which we call a rose, by any other name would smell as sweet.'"

He reached for her, but she slapped his hands away. He longed to gather her into his embrace, felt a desperate need to hold her close. "Why are you accusing me of impersonating an Italian and renaming flowers?" It boded a perilous shift in her attitude toward him. "I cannot understand your distress, Juliette. You speak, and yet you say nothing."

"Stop it!" The rising sun sent tentative shafts of light toward them, illuminating the angry tears that swam within, but did not fall from her eyes. "My father named me after the girl in that play. He just spelled my name a little differently, is all. When I was little, he read the words to me over and over again until I knew every speech by heart."

To his amazement, she clapped one hand over her heart and lifted the other imploringly toward the sky. " 'But, soft! what light through yonder window breaks? It is the east, and Juliet is the sun!'" She scowled at him whilst he gazed openmouthed upon her, and then shifted into another graceful, if impractical, pose, this time with one palm draped over her forehead. "'What's in a name?' I already quoted the rose part that follows *that* one." She lifted an imperious brow, and continued in the face of his silence. "'She speaks, yet she says nothing.' You might as well have brought your stage copy of *Romeo and Juliet* and read it straight to me instead of twisting Shakespeare's words around and pretending you didn't know what you were saying. You're a liar, Geoffrey d'Arbanville, and a seducer of women who were perfectly content with things the way they were, and . . . *you're just plain mean for making me want to believe you!*"

He felt utterly helpless to counter the pain and embarrassment he read in her expression. "Juliette— your words are like blows . . ."

"Stop it! Just stop it!" With that, she burst into tears and stumbled away from him, over the prairie.

Better to be dead than endure the knowledge that smote him with the force of a battering ram: She didn't believe him. She had never believed him. Love and trust had had nothing to do with the flaming of her innocent passions.

She thought him mean. Geoffrey d'Arbanville, knight. She thought him mean. And an . . . actor. Certes, death would be preferable to this shame.

And yet he could not lift the Colt so fortuitously provided by Lieutenant Jordan and plug himself in the head, not with his lady staggering bare-bosomed over the brightening prairie, thinking him a mean-spirited liar. He spared no time to don his boots against sharp-edged grasses, and regretted it not, for he felt so numbed by her repudiation of all that he was that his feet and limbs might have been forged from lead.

Even so, he ran her down with ease.

She sobbed as he came up behind her and she collapsed into a dejected heap of wind-fluttered blue cotton. Her hair, tangled from his touch, shielded her face from him. Geoffrey crouched next to her and tilted her chin, dreading the sight of tears as any knight would, but knowing their presence would mean she shared some part of his inner agony.

She glared back at him dry-eyed, her expression stony, condemning him silently for a betrayal he'd committed only in her mind.

He didn't understand. Perhaps, neither did she. He

wished he'd spent more time constructing his thoughts and less time admiring her in her sleeping innocence, but it was too late for such regrets. He must present his theories half-formed, else lose her forever.

"Juliette, everything has come clear to me."

"Enlighten me. But spare me the Shakespeare."

"The border disputes, Juliette. I was engaged in resolving such forays between Welsh and Englishmen when I suddenly found myself diverted here. I assure you, border lords such as Rowanwood fought with stouter heart than your own border ruffians."

She glared at him, granting him no quarter.

"There is your own situation, not unlike that of Demeter's. She was sworn to hold Rowanwood castle, and thus sealed herself within its walls, intending to defend it against any who dared besiege her, friend or foe. Like yourself, Juliette. Young Robbie has said 'tis common knowledge, round about here, that you are determined to consign yourself to a sour widow's future." He ignored her gasp of outrage. "There are no knights here, you say, and thus none to save you from this loveless course. The gods must needs have sent a man like myself to accomplish the purpose."

"To save me."

"Aye." He raised a forestalling hand when she cast him a disgusted look and made as if to rise. "And mayhap far more is at stake. King Edward has charged me with a vital quest. Its failure could well alter the course of history. My sword arm must strike truer than ever before. My shield must stand strong against every vicious thrust. The gods must believe I face overwhelming odds. And so I have been sent here, to gain practice against border ruffians. To save you, to save us both, by falling in love."

"Oh, of course." She pushed his hand away and stood over him, slim and supple, her face a careful

mask that hid all emotions. She'd become aware of her
torn gown, because she clutched the ruined cloth over
her breast as if she meant to conceal every part of herself, body and soul, from his sight.

But she didn't run. Perhaps his tentative explanations weren't as far-fetched as they sounded.

"Aye. Of course. Everyone knows a knight taps his
most formidable bravery when he finds his true love, as
I dare to hope I may have found with you."

A barely perceptible shudder caused the folds of her
skirt to tremble.

"True love gives the knight his courage," Geoffrey
whispered. "Before God I pledge all I ever was and ever
will be to you—my lady, my love. Were you to offer the
same in return, no foe, no obstacle, could stop me from
doing what I must."

"From finding a big mountain to climb so you can
get back to the year 1283."

"And you have told me there are no mountains.
Mayhap I needs must instead find a great chasm to leap
into, as this was the method of my arrival here." He
frowned, embarrassed that he had not sooner considered this other option. "You have said the Earth is
round, but I assure you 'twas flat when last I left it.
There must be a passage from one side to the other."

"And of course, as true lovers, we would leap
together, from one flat side to the other. Then when
you've taken care of that Drogo Fitzsomething and
saved the world, I suppose we could just leap back here
and prove up on your homestead claim."

"My lady, 'tis more than I dared hope for in all my
life." He bowed his head, awed by her offer, his heart
racketing against his chest.

She said nothing for so long that he felt certain
he'd find love-light in her eyes, her trembling smile of

acceptance when he looked up. Instead there were now her tears streaking silvery along her cheeks.

"You have me confused with that other Juliet. The one in the play. The one who ignored every warning and risked everything . . . for a love that was *never meant to be*."

It was humiliating, that he swayed on his knees while she laughed, a bitter derisive sound that made a mockery of everything he had to offer. It was humiliating, that despite her rejection, he couldn't prevent himself from reaching out to her.

She spurned his hand; she spurned him.

"There is no such thing as magic or a love that transcends time. I don't believe in happily ever after. Maybe you should try getting that sort of nonsense out of your head so a little reality can get back in."

13

Juliette wondered if she'd somehow betrayed the inner shivering shame that gripped her after her outburst. Never before had she fashioned a verbal barb with such utter certainty of wounding her mark. It gave her pause, to wonder at this new and admittedly troubling aspect of her personality. And to wonder at Geoffrey's susceptibility, at her unerring instinct, almost as if the two of them possessed a heightened sensitivity toward each other, a sensitivity that had no place in the casual relationship that was all they could share.

Geoffrey rose without comment and draped his shirt over her shoulders. He busied himself with saddling the horses while the rough homespun grazed the side of her breast, reminding her she still clutched the edges of her ruined shirtwaist, as if such flimsy cover could shield her against her memories.

Her once-disciplined mind delighted in replaying the sensation of beard-stubbled cheek brushing against tender skin, of warm gentle lips teasing the most astounding sensations from that very same bare breast. Her trembling fingers weren't doing a very good job of holding her torn seam together; in fact, she fought the unseemly urge to let it gape open and see if the sight of her breast could rekindle the desire, rather than betrayal, that had filled Geoffrey's eyes when she'd rejected his plea.

Come to think of it, her whole carefully constructed life seemed to be unraveling around her since meeting Geoffrey.

"You must understand." His silence unnerved her, forcing her to speak. "I blame myself completely for what happened between us."

A faint smile curved his lips. "I daresay I had a hand in the matter."

"No. I mean yes. I mean no—it was all my fault." Her heart simply wouldn't stop knocking against her chest. "I used to be a bit . . . wayward. I'm not like that anymore, not really. Ask anyone in town, they'll tell you. I'm a hardheaded practical business woman. My sole concern is the welfare of Walburn Ford."

"Ah yes, the vow wrung from you by your husband."

"He didn't wring it from me. I . . . I love this place. Nothing would make me happier than to live out my days building up Walburn Ford."

But what had happened to those vows, that firm resolve? She couldn't seem to spend more than two minutes on the prairie with Geoffrey without ending up flat on her back with his lips against hers. Against every part of her, last night. And, Lord help her, but she craved his touch again . . . Oh, God . . .

"You need not make excuses, Juliette. The devil himself understands how carnal temptation can temporarily distract one from honoring a vow."

His words should have absolved her of guilt; instead, she wanted to shout aloud that he was—that he *could* be—so much more than a carnal distraction. But he couldn't be.

"I'm glad you understand." Her voice shook, and so she spoke softly. "You didn't ask me to turn my back on my business and tag along while you filed your claim. And I alone have to bear responsibility for . . . for lingering when we should have been riding straight through to Walburn Ford to warn the settlers that Fort Scott faced a border ruffian attack. The town should prepare. The town must survive."

"I think this husband placed an overly heavy burden upon your shoulders, Juliette. Have you ever considered that this promise he extracted from you might have been inspired by fevered ravings? That, had he not been consumed by pain and agonies of the gut, he might not have spoken so? A man come face-to-face with death oft times makes one last desperate plea for immortality."

She flinched, a physical reaction to his observation. She couldn't even dare let herself think along those lines for one moment, she couldn't, not unless she wanted to brand the last four years of her life as wasted.

She felt almost numb as she rose to Daniel's defense. "Daniel believed in me. And I believe he asked for my vow with the best of intentions. That's why I must apologize for my behavior. I've . . . I've acted like a senseless wanton who doesn't give a snap for propriety. I can't blame you at all for thinking I might be willing to find a big hole and jump into it with you. I am sorry I misled you."

"And I am sorry for a man who died with the name of a town, rather than the name of the woman he loved, upon his lips. If I am granted the choice, I would prefer that my woman nurture love in her heart as my memorial rather than see to the welfare of a town called after me."

She gathered Geoffrey's shirt together at her neck,

and wished there truly was a big hole around for her to sink into. Geoffrey barely knew her, and yet he'd divined that she'd buried Daniel with guilt rather than love in her heart. And now, with talk of her dead husband swirling about her, all she could concentrate on was the way her motion released a faint trace of Geoffrey's scent from his shirt, and her traitorous body burned with remembered passion.

And she'd called *him* crazy.

He turned away from her to finish tending the horses, working with a jerking precision that conveyed impatience. She couldn't help staring. Captain Chaney's borrowed britches rode low over his hips. He'd left his borrowed belt unfastened; it hung loose around the solid muscled column of his waist. His torso widened into a set of shoulders she felt sure was unmatched in the Territory.

He'd used a leather thong to tie back his hair, the hair that had entwined so well with hers last night, so that it curled in a thick tail against his spine, drawing her gaze over his sun-bronzed skin. Not so many scars on his back as those that crisscrossed his arms and chest, almost as though he'd endured his wounds at the hands of men equally boggle-minded as himself, knights obsessed with the notion of playing fair. Unlike herself, who'd pretended to indulge him before calling him a liar to his face.

Where, she wondered, and how, did a man acquire so many wounds, of such depth and severity that they would leave uncountable scars? "Why do you bear so many scars?" she asked.

"I have done with furnishing explanations that you refuse to believe. Think what you will."

A knight might accumulate so many scars, she thought. Certainly not an actor.

She thinned her lips, angry at herself for sliding once again toward believing him. She'd spent far too long a time developing her hard-won practicality to let her woman's heart overrule it. What did he expect of her? Supposing, just supposing, she caved in to the urge to believe Geoffrey's far-fetched stories—he'd have her racketing off to a frontier never even imagined by her footloose father, abandoning the promise she'd made to her dying husband, all for the sake of some tarnished, crudely fashioned pendant Geoffrey intended to give to another woman.

Believe him anyway, taunted that annoying little voice.

She shook her head no. Believing in Geoffrey meant abandoning her cherished ideals regarding stability, responsibility, independence.

But what if Geoffrey was the magical thing she'd always dreamed might happen? Her cherished ideals hadn't offered much company during last winter's big blizzard.

Loneliness had weighed heavy upon her, and still she'd spent next to no time mourning the man who'd shackled her to Walburn Ford. Maybe Geoffrey was right. Maybe Daniel really wouldn't have wanted it this way.

She shook her head again, wishing she had a mirror so she could see her own sensible gesture and let it sink into her bedazzled head. She couldn't do it, not without destroying the creature she'd fashioned herself, the Widow Walburn . . . and so she'd destroyed Geoffrey d'Arbanville instead. The wounds she'd inflicted would leave no scars for others to see.

"I'm sorry, Geoffrey," she whispered.

He glanced over his shoulder, an ordinary movement any man might make, and yet the play of muscles in his neck and shoulders sent her blood surging. He met her glance for only a moment before turning away again, yanking so hard on a belly strap that the horse snorted in protest.

He seemed determined to deliberately misunderstand her apology. "I'll not miss the shirt. 'Tis not overcold, and your need of it is greater."

"I'm not apologizing for borrowing your shirt."

He shrugged, as if he had no interest in anything she might say. "If it please you . . ."

He paused, and a tiny voice in her mind provided the missing courteous address: *My lady.*

"We might stop at an outlying cottage so you might mend your garment ere riding into the village. You would not want your Mrs. Abbott to send word of your predicament to her son Herman in the Army Corps of Topographical Engineers."

Everyone joked about Mrs. Abbott's obsessive pride in her son, and she dared hope that Geoffrey's comment hinted at a thawing in his attitude. But a quick glance at his rigid jaw, his carefully blank expression, told her he'd spoken in deadly earnest. She forced herself to speak sensibly.

"The Wilcox place is on our way, though it might not be a good idea to stop there. But I want to—"

Again he interrupted her apology. "Do you fear that sour-tempered churl might accuse me of rending your garment asunder?"

"No, I meant—" Whatever rash confession she'd meant to make died unsaid when he whirled about.

Her tender, teasing, tempting Geoffrey of the night before had vanished, leaving in his stead this stern-visaged cold-eyed stranger assessing her as if she were his worst enemy. Juliette took an involuntary step back, driven by a force that radiated so palpably from him that he might have had an invisible cowcatcher clearing his way.

Or an invisible suit of armor shielding him within, isolating her without.

"It maddens me that you keep attempting to soothe my pride. I would have you forget my witless meanderings of these past days . . . Miss Jay."

Her throat closed around her protests so they echoed only in her own mind. *Juliette,* she grieved, aching for the sound of his voice calling her name. *My lady.*

My lady, my love, he'd called her. A witless meandering he meant for her to forget. The Widow Walburn could point to that as proof that he couldn't be believed, about anything. Juliette could grieve, knowing she'd hurt him, and that he retaliated at the blow to his heart and his pride.

No. She'd never asked for the endearment in the first place. His rejection of her apology actually made it easier to gather the remnants of respectability about her. She stiffened her shoulders, accepting the weight.

"Well, I'm pleased you've finally gotten around to calling me Miss Jay, as I prefer." She pasted a false smile on her lips. "Since we're going to be neighbors, I'd appreciate it if you would continue addressing me that way."

The faint humorless smile returned to curl his lips. "No worry there. It will not be hard for me to remember, Miss Jay. I will not be here long enough to call you anything else. Now I shall escort you to the Wilcox place."

Rebecca had to strain to hear Alma's low whisper over Robbie's one-sided jabbering with their silent guest.

"What did you say?"

"I said, if we run short of matches, we'll just borrow Geoffrey from Miss Jay and point him toward the fireplace."

"Whatever are you talking about?" Rebecca asked,

even as she stole a sideways glance at the glowering bare-chested Geoffrey d'Arbanville.

"He's so mad about something I expect fire to shoot through his nostrils at any minute." Alma tittered. "I'll bet touching his skin would be like poking at a hot stovepipe. Sssst!" She paused. "Of course, a girl might feel a tingle even if he wasn't so upset."

"Alma!" A respectable matron like herself should set a good example for a flighty single girl, so Rebecca compressed her lips against the laughter that wanted to burst free. Still . . . Josiah had no doubt seen Miss Jay and this fellow ride into the yard, and was probably even now racing in from his plowing. If she wanted to get a good look at this newcomer to Walburn Ford, this tale-spinning actor who held Robbie so fascinated, she'd have to take it now.

Coffee. A good hostess would offer refreshments to her guest, even if he was half-naked. Josiah couldn't take exception if he found her facing Geoffrey with a pot of coffee in her hand. She wound a section of apron around her hand to guard against the hot handle, nearly dissolving into laughter when Alma outright giggled, and hissed, "Ssst."

"Coffee, Mr. d'Arbanville?" Rebecca turned to face him, and found a familiar sadness welling within her. She'd lived with a tormented soul for so many years that it was easy to recognize another when she saw one.

There's something about this place that destroys a man, and we women don't have a clue how to mend them, she thought while somehow managing to retain a polite smile, to hold her hand steady while she poured.

Miss Jay had retreated into the bedroom to repair her dress. Geoffrey had taken a braced-leg stand in front of the closed door, his crossed arms and flexed muscles posing a more formidable barricade than any barred plank or latch string. Just like Josiah, creating barriers where none were needed. Just like Josiah, so rigid and unyielding, so determined to deflect pain that he abraded it into life. Rebecca wondered if Miss Jay understood Geoffrey any better than she understood Josiah.

Miss Jay opened the bedroom door; Robbie's excited prattle ended in a squeak. Wariness radiated from Geoffrey and Miss Jay, casting them all into an agony of embarrassment, even though no words were being spoken.

"My God," Rebecca whispered, appalled. The uncomfortable silence held an unwelcome familiarity—the mistrust raging from Josiah to herself often similarly stifled a roomful of chattering folks. Rebecca had always taken refuge in the belief that so long as she kept her misery to herself, no one would suspect the depths of her despair. "We've never kept our problems a secret at all."

She remembered Alma saying that she and Miss Jay were a lot alike, and she wished she had the courage then and there to take Miss Jay aside and tell her to straighten matters out between herself and Geoffrey before they festered beyond salvation.

A heavy footstep thumped against the porch floorboards, followed so quickly by Josiah's lean frame darkening the doorway that Rebecca knew her husband hadn't stopped by the boot scraper to spare her kitchen floor. His haste portended the worst.

"What the hell's going on here?" Despite his healthy sunburn and a morning's worth of plowing dust layering his skin, his complexion turned a sickly white as he took in the sight of Geoffrey standing shirtless before the bedroom door.

Rebecca thought she would die of the shame when

Josiah's suspicious gaze swung immediately toward her, as if he expected to find her in a similar state of undress.

And mortification threatened to send her swooning when Miss Jay offered an explanation for the question that would never have been asked by a man who trusted his wife. "Your wife graciously loaned me the use of her needle. Just as Mr. d'Arbanville loaned me his shirt when I carelessly tore my dress." Miss Jay handed Geoffrey's shirt to him, and he shrugged it into place.

"So *you* say." Josiah's challenge was offered with a sneer.

Not even politeness could still the gasps of outrage coming from Miss Jay and Alma.

Not even a lifetime of churchgoing could prevent Rebecca from suddenly breaking a goodly number of God's commandments—at least in her heart. She yearned to trade her soul to the devil or any deity that could promise an end to this constant mental battering. She wanted to kill her husband. She wished she had committed adultery so that Josiah would have some reason for his unfounded jealousy. She coveted the decent, loving husbands of every woman she'd ever met, not for any physical or economic reason, but for the sheer pleasure of loving someone without so much heartache involved.

"I care not for your viper-tongued outbursts, Wilcox," Geoffrey said. "You have insulted your lady and mi—Miss Jay. Did danger not hover so near, enhancing the value of every defender's life, I would sever your tongue from its root and leave your silent bleeding carcass for the crows to pick and caw over."

"What danger are you talking about?" Josiah didn't back away from his belligerent stance, though a dull flush rose from his neck. Whether from embarrassment over the belated realization of his boorish behavior, or a reaction to Geoffrey's quiet threat, Rebecca couldn't tell.

"There's rumor of a border ruffian attack heading for Fort Scott," Miss Jay said.

"So you ran back to Walburn Ford with your tail between your legs. Did you hear that, Robbie—your hero ain't nothing but a yellow-bellied coward."

"Don't you call Geoffrey no coward!" With a choked sob, Robbie flung himself at Josiah, his small fists pummeling him about the waist. A disbelieving numbness rooted Rebecca in place as Josiah lifted her flailing son by the collar. He cocked his elbow, looking for all the world as if he meant to fling Robbie against the far cabin wall. Maternal instinct wrenched her free of her paralysis, and she curved her fingers into talons, ready to claw Josiah into shreds before he could harm her child.

Geoffrey, moving with blinding speed, ripped Robbie free of Josiah's clutching hand. The child ran to her, wrapping his arms around her knees, and Rebecca sank to the floor, gathering him within her shaking arms. Relief, and pain, locked her throat, so she couldn't sob her anguish aloud. She felt her silent tears drip down her cheeks, and watched them fall into her precious son's golden hair.

"You and I seem destined to cross swords." Geoffrey glared at Josiah, who'd gone white-faced and trembling, staring openmouthed at his empty hand, as if only now realizing how close he'd come to causing Robbie physical harm.

Geoffrey crouched at Rebecca's side, and tipped up Robbie's tear-streaked face with one finger. "You displayed stout-hearted bravery in coming to my defense, young Robbie. Should you seek to learn the squirely arts, I would ask your mother's permission to send you fostering with me, now that I have a homestead of my own." He cast a disparaging look toward Josiah. "Though 'tis evident the knightly code does not prevail in this realm, 'twould not be amiss to train you to protect yourself and those you love."

Rebecca drew a shuddering breath. This was wrong, all wrong. She'd accepted Josiah's irrational behavior for far too long, always hoping against hope that one day he'd realize her love was honest and true. But now he'd endangered her son, and it had been a virtual stranger, not his own mother, who'd stepped in before any serious physical damage had been done. She pressed Robbie's head tight against her heart, noticing for the first time that it was no longer the tender, tiny skull of an infant, but the maturing head of a young man she cradled. It could only get worse between Robbie and Josiah as the boy grew, as Robbie's masculine traits developed, as he took offense at the treatment they both endured in the face of Josiah's unfounded jealousies.

Miss Jay and Alma had managed to find each other during the uproar, and they stood together, staring at her with wide sympathetic eyes. Though Miss Jay was no tongue-wagger, Alma would no doubt spread word of this confrontation throughout town before nightfall. Rebecca could just imagine the shaking heads, the sorrowful expressions, the muttered comments: "Well, she obviously doesn't mind, been putting up with his nonsense all these years. Too bad about the boy, though. He didn't ask to be born into this."

Her memory flew back to the day when she and Alma had talked about baking cakes. You had to break a few eggs, she'd told Alma. You had to stir things up sometimes if you wanted them to turn out right. Robbie, more precious and fragile than any egg, could not be risked. And yet stir things up she must, for she could no longer endure the constant suspicion, the endless unsuccessful placating, the aching loneliness that only a true husband could ease. Maybe if she sent Robbie away for a brief time, if it were just she and Josiah for a few days, alone as they'd never been in all their married years, it would give Josiah one last chance to resolve his inner torment.

If it didn't turn out right, she would reclaim her son and leave.

"This has to stop," she said, rising to her feet. Geoffrey and Robbie peered up at her questioningly. "This fostering, Mr. d'Arbanville. What exactly does it entail?" Her question ended in something quite like a sob, when pure joy shafted through Robbie's expression and told her how eagerly he would go off with Geoffrey if she gave the word.

"Fostering is common where I come from," Geoffrey said, and launched into an explanation.

"Male offspring must not be coddled, lest they fail to develop strength of body and will. Mothers are forever weeping over a child's hurts, whether real or imaginary. And fathers sometimes take false pride in a lad's accomplishments, even though the lad's skills prove lacking when compared to others of his age. And so loving parents send their boy child to a household where he becomes the foster son of the lord and lady in residence, so the lad might learn to fight and fend for himself beneath a fond yet critical eye."

"How long does this take?" Rebecca asked.

"'Tis a lengthy process," Geoffrey admitted. "For myself, I began fostering at the age of seven. My foster father taught me the use of arms, and to acquire a graceful habit with ladies." He cast a derisive glance toward Josiah. "After a mere seven years, I joined the best lads and commenced training as a squire."

"Seven years?" She couldn't keep the dismay from her voice. She nearly relented in her decision to send

Robbie away, when a realization struck her. Without doing some serious stirring up, the next seven years would be a replay of the past; could be even worse, if Josiah lost his tenuous control over his emotions. She had to bring matters to a head once and for all.

"Young Robbie might compress his learning into a shorter period." Geoffrey seemed to sense her inner turmoil. His solemn gaze met hers, warm with a depth of understanding that reassured her. Improbably, she found herself trusting him, this stranger who'd had the entire town gossiping for days.

"Then take him," Rebecca said, silently resolving that Robbie would spend no more than seven *days* away from her. "I give my permission."

"Thank you, Mama! Oh, thank you!"

She really felt she might die when Robbie leaped up and spun around in an ecstasy of excitement before clamping his arms around her waist.

"I forbid it, missus," Josiah thundered, his voice faltering. "You . . . you ain't letting m . . . my . . . you ain't letting that boy go off—"

Rebecca let her fingers entwine in Robbie's hair, still damp from her tears, taking strength from feeling him whole and healthy, remembering how unreservedly he'd flown to Geoffrey's defense. She could do no less for her son. For the first time in their marriage, Rebecca defied her husband, and she didn't care that everyone present learned her shameful secret at last.

"You've spent the past ten years telling me in a thousand ways that Robbie isn't your boy. Well, you're right, mister, you didn't father him." Alma gasped, but Rebecca continued. "And your treatment of him denies you any right to have a say in what I tell him he can do."

She caught her son beneath the arms and lifted him, amazed at his weight, his very bulk and solidity reassuring her that she'd done the right thing. She hugged him, hard, hard as she could, before setting him back on his feet next to Geoffrey. "Off with you now," *before I change my mind,* she added silently. "And Miss Jay—do you think you could board Alma for a few days? My husband and I have some things to discuss that are best worked out in private."

Miss Jay sent her an encouraging smile and gripped a protesting Alma around the upper arm, hauling her toward the door. "We'll leave right now, Rebecca. I'll ask Captain Chaney to stop by later for Alma's things."

And then they were gone, and all Rebecca's bravery deserted her like shriveled leaves torn from their branches by winter's cruel winds.

She stood in her place. Josiah stood in his place. She couldn't look at him. The silence made her teeth ache; her heart pounded so, and still she swore she could hear the tick of her parlor clock clear into the kitchen. She'd lost count of the ticks before Josiah spoke.

She'd expected anger, a fury that might be dangerous, maybe even a physical manifestation of the anger he'd held in check for so many years. She set herself to absorb a blow should one be forthcoming. Instead she found herself bludgeoned by a wave of raw aching pain that poured from Josiah and matched her own.

Strange, to think that such agony could form the basis for a new beginning. She reached toward him. "Josiah—"

He turned on his heel, rejecting her tentative supplication. "I always knew it would happen, missus. I always knew you'd take my son away from me."

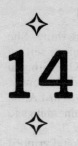

14

Beds. Riding from the Wilcox place toward her boarding house, Juliette couldn't drive the thought of beds from her mind.

Fluffy feather-filled mattresses. Crude-cobbled rope-strung wooden bedsteads. Pillows plump with goose down; colorful quilts waiting to be folded back to reveal warm woolen blankets. A lantern burning low, casting a golden glow over soft, rainwater-washed sheets.

Her responsibilities as a boardinghouse keeper no doubt paraded these images through her mind, presented as she was with the dilemma of Alma and Robbie to house in addition to Geoffrey and Captain Chaney, along with the contingent Lieutenant Jordan had promised from Fort Scott within a few days.

Yes, if she spent a minute or two thinking about it, she would realize it was the challenge of her work, and not the presence of Geoffrey d'Arbanville, riding rigid and silent ahead of her, that created this untoward preoccupation with beds. Heavens, she'd never even seen him lying on a bed.

The scent of crushed grass mingling with sun-warmed male skin. Horse blankets coarse and yet cloud-soft against her bare back. The feel of scar-sculpted sinewy flesh beneath her fingers, the taste of salt and passion upon her lips, the sound of ragged breathing and courtly endearments against her ears. All stirring into life feelings and emotions she'd thought so safely buried that she'd lashed out against them. And then the flare of hurt betrayal in proud deep-set eyes, the vanishing of all expression from a face grown impossibly, improbably dear . . .

Oh God. Beds and betrayal, so indelibly intertwined that she couldn't even convince herself that it didn't matter that Geoffrey had scarcely cast her a glance, that he hadn't spoken a word to her, from the moment other people surrounded them.

If he would just look at her—but he seemed completely absorbed in Robbie's boyish exuberance. If he would just utter one of his peculiar observations—but he seemed intent on listening rather than speaking. She'd never realized how pervasive Geoffrey's good humor had been until it had gone, never realized how she'd been cheered by his self-assured smile until his lips settled into the grim unreadable line of a stranger.

Nothing in her carefully constructed life was working out the way she'd planned. And she didn't quite know what to do about it.

Alma broke into her thoughts. "I'm sure glad Rebecca finally worked up the gumption to take a stand against Josiah."

"She's proven herself to be a very brave woman," Juliette agreed, her attention never deviating from Geoffrey's broad back. She couldn't help muttering her next thought aloud. "I just wish she'd waited another day or two."

"What's that?"

"Nothing." Juliette didn't feel up to confessing that she had some man mending of her own to do, a task that would surely be less daunting without Alma and Robbie underfoot. On the other hand, maybe the presence of other people would ease some of the tension between them, give her some time to think things through.

"I have to confess," said Alma, "after seeing how kindly Geoffrey treats Robbie, I'm feeling a little guilty now about the way I tried to trick him the other day." Juliette stared at her in puzzlement, and Alma continued. "The picnic. Josiah Wilcox talked me into it, said he suspected Geoffrey might be a spy, and wanted me to pry his secrets out of him."

"That's ridiculous."

"Well you have to admit that those blasted border ruffians have been rampaging more than usual ever since he got here." Alma sent her a sidelong glance. "It wasn't just Josiah who was suspicious. Practically the whole town was in on it. Josiah thought it best you didn't know, in case you and Geoffrey were in cahoots."

Juliette couldn't tell which stunned her more—the remembrance of the jealousy that had burned within her at seeing Geoffrey walk off to picnic with Alma, or the information that the people in Daniel's town, *her* town, had concocted a secret plot without including her, actually distrusting her, in general acting as if they didn't need her at all. A tiny worm of disillusion lodged itself in her heart.

"So you've all overcome your suspicions?" She didn't bother trying to keep the resentful edge from her question.

Alma had the decency to blush. "I reminded them myself that you wouldn't have anything to do with a border ruffian. As for Geoffrey, everyone feels that the soldiers would have kept him back in Fort Scott if they thought he was a troublemaker."

"He's no troublemaker." It shouldn't have been so easy for her to defend a man she'd called crazy, but it was—the words fell from her lips as if she'd been rehearsing them for days, imbued with the same sense of certainty regarding his motives that she'd found so disquieting earlier. "If anything, we should be grateful he's here. He'd protect this place with his life." Like the knight he claimed to be, defending the realm, but she couldn't say that. "For as long as he's here."

"Is he planning to leave? I thought he went to Fort Scott to claim a homestead."

"I . . ." Juliette stopped herself before admitting aloud that she dreaded Geoffrey's leaving more than the overflying of geese that heralded the approach of winter; either event meant frigid, desolate isolation. The knowledge struck her too fresh and raw to share with another. She felt a resurgence of her determination to set things to rights with him, and took some small comfort in knowing circumstances bound him close, almost forcing him to listen to her, no matter if listening to her apologies maddened him.

"He can't leave. His horse has a bad leg."

Alma grunted noncommittally, but a tiny worry line puckered between her brows.

They clattered into the barnyard. Usually, the sight of her house, her barn, her fences, fostered a sense of rightness within Juliette, an assurance that her hard work and dedication were bringing Daniel's dream to fruition. Today the structures appeared distressingly crude, haphazardly designed buildings fashioned of dull gray weather-beaten planks, sagging where her woman's strength hadn't been enough to ensure tight joints and seamless fittings. Her mind played tricks, teasing her with the image of how bleak and dismal these rough structures would seem without Geoffrey's huge horse overwhelming the barn, without Geoffrey himself striding purposefully about the yard, without the sound of his deep voice resonating through the air.

Geoffrey dismounted with fluid ease and turned at once to Alma. "Your servant, lady." He helped the schoolteacher from her saddle, and then stood facing the barn, as if debating the choice of checking his ailing horse versus attending to his chivalrous duties by aiding Juliette next.

Disappointment whisked through her, and then she stiffened her spine. It wasn't as if she hadn't spent her whole life clambering up and down horses' backs without any man's assistance—except that one time, in Fort Scott, when Geoffrey had gripped her around the waist. Juliette's legs clamped viselike around her poor horse's ribs. She gripped the reins more tightly than any nun clutched her rosary beads, knowing the leather would leave red welts in her skin, while she prayed that he'd help her next, embarrassed that she craved it so.

Her embarrassment lengthened into mortification as endless minutes passed. He prolonged his dallying even further by removing his saddlebags, the very saddlebags that held the blanket upon which they'd loved, and then slung them over his shoulder, all without him turning to her. Hens, heedless of the silent drama, strutted into the barnyard, their red eyes watching her humiliation with curious caution. Juliette's horse tossed its head, snorting, obviously put out over still bearing a rider when the other beasts had been relieved of their burdens.

"Forgive me, Miss Jay. I have been remiss in coming to your assistance." Geoffrey swung about at last, apparently prompted by the restive horse. He extended his forearm, no doubt disdaining to offer her his hand. She stared at the saddlebags covering his heart, thinking things weren't looking so good for the meeting of the minds she'd planned between them. Very well. There was bound to be a moment later, when Alma and Robbie were settled, when she could get Geoffrey alone. She wouldn't provoke another disaster by forcing him to listen to her while his pride was still smarting. Her pride was doing a fair job of raising its own hackles.

"I don't need your help." With her chin tilted high, she dismounted on the wrong side, causing her mount to sidle nervously right into Geoffrey. He staggered, but did not fall, and it occurred to her that they both seemed particularly adept at maintaining their balance no matter the blow.

She rubbed her hands against her skirt, wishing that she didn't miss the feel of Geoffrey's firm handclasp. "Now as far as sleeping arrangements go, it would save some work if you'd share my room, Alma. I'm not sure when the soldiers will return from Fort Scott, so we can put Robbie on a cot in Geoffrey's room—"

"The boy and I will not be sleeping in your house," Geoffrey stated.

Juliette blinked back her surprise. "Well I'll admit I might have to ask you to move into the barn once the soldiers arrive, but there's no reason why you can't stay in your room for the time being."

"'Tis not a room—'tis a shrine, and I scorn sharing space with the ungallant spirit haunting it."

Alma let out a little shriek of alarm. "Is your house haunted, Miss Jay?"

"Oh, for heaven's sake, of course it's not haunted."

Juliette fumed, watching helplessly while Geoffrey stalked into the barn, as he'd obviously been itching to do from the minute they rode onto her property, Robbie close at his heels. A joyous whinny greeted Geoffrey's entrance into the barn, and Juliette flushed, just imagining Geoffrey's deft hands fondling his stallion's ears, caressing Arion's silky neck.

"You don't need to get all red-faced over it, Miss Jay. I can't blame you for not wanting anyone to know. Goodness—a haunted boarding house!" Alma edged back toward her mount. "I could go back to the Wilcox place. I'm sure Rebecca wouldn't mind too much, once I explained. Or the Thatchers. They'd take me in, I'm sure of it."

"My house isn't haunted," Juliette cried, just as Geoffrey reemerged from the barn with Arion's massive saddle perched on one shoulder, the saddlebags still draped over the other, the unequally balanced weights parting his shirt at the neck to reveal the golden-haired Demeter's Celtic pendant. He clutched his spear in his hand. He cocked a disbelieving brow in her direction, accompanied by an amused tilt to his jaw that silently cast doubt upon her declaration.

Robbie followed in his footsteps, his own narrow shoulder encumbered with the blue hawk-emblazoned tunics Geoffrey and Arion had worn, while he clutched Arion's lead in his free hand. Geoffrey's shield and suit of armor, its silvery glitter dulled and stained here and there with brownish orange speckles, lay spread over the stallion's broad back.

"We bid you adieu, Alma." Geoffrey inclined his head toward each woman in turn. "We shall proceed at once to my homestead."

"Goodness, he *is* leaving!" Alma wrung her hands, her head swiveling rapidly between Geoffrey and

Juliette. "I have to say, Geoffrey, I'm not at all sure Rebecca Wilcox had this in mind when she let you take Robbie. Wouldn't you agree, Miss Jay?"

"You can't go." Though Alma had posed the question, it was to Geoffrey that Juliette directed her outcry. Little more than a harsh whisper, the words sounded torn from her throat.

"And why is that?" He, too, ignored Alma.

"You just can't, that's all."

Oh, God, how she cursed these past years of constant vigilance over her emotions, of ceaseless preoccupation with presenting a tough impervious demeanor to the outside world. With Geoffrey alone, she might, *might,* be able to beg him to stay, might be able to carry out her plan of setting things to rights between them. Alone, she could bask in the cautious hope that she read in his eyes, feel her inner numbness dissipate if that hope kindled into something warmer, something . . . eternal. But her too-carefully cultivated reserve made it impossible for her to reveal her turmoil in front of Alma and Robbie.

She pasted a cajoling smile over her features. "Alma's right. I'm sure Rebecca expected you to keep Robbie here with me. You can't take up residence on your homestead, Geoffrey. You don't have any food or shelter over there."

Though the sun blazed high overhead, she'd never felt so cold as she did at that moment, watching the hope fade from Geoffrey's eyes until they glinted like polished topaz. His voice sounded as frozen as she felt.

"Lady Wilcox shan't worry with Robbie and I a mere hundred sixty acres away." He hitched his shoulder, settling the saddle more solidly in place. "The foraging of food and construction of shelter from native materials are amongst the squirely arts I mean to teach young Robbie."

"Geoffrey." She couldn't help whispering a plea, despite Alma's glittery-eyed speculation swinging between them. "Please don't go."

He flinched, his jaw jutting skyward as if he'd absorbed a roundhouse punch. He tightened his hand around his spear shaft and jammed it into the ground. "You are ever expecting the impossible of me," he rasped through gritted teeth. "You ask me not to fight, and yet you claim to treasure the welfare of this town above all else. You ask me to stay, when 'tis plain you will never think me better than a lack-witted oaf bent upon playacting." He wrenched his spear from the ground and shook it at her. "A rose by any other name would smell as sweet. The Widow Walburn by any other name wallows in insurmountable guilt and encases her heart in a shield of ice no mortal man can melt."

"Not even a knight?" She didn't know how she managed to speak the challenge; it seemed that the ice he spoke of was even now crushing her within its grip, that unless she goaded him into staying, the ice would prevail and seal the real Juliette away forever, leaving only the cold, empty husk of the Widow Walburn. "I thought . . . I thought you were sent here to save me."

His spear clattered to the ground. The saddle slid from his shoulder and landed upon the ground with a solid thump. He extended his hand to her; she couldn't tear her gaze away from his curving callused fingers. A tremor shook her hand, as if unseen forces tugged it between them, one straining to join her hand to Geoffrey's, one exerting a supernatural pressure to keep her hand at her side.

A similar quivering rattled Geoffrey's breathing. His assessing gaze swept her from head to toe, and she knew he could sense her inner struggle. His long strides narrowed the distance between them, and she could hear the swish of the air as he jabbed his proffered palm toward her once more.

"Five steps, Juliette, no more. Take them. Put your hand in mine, and we will leave this place and save each other."

The low rich timbre of his voice vibrated within her, weakening her knees at the same time her long-cherished responsibility weighted her legs, effectively rooting them to the ground. Misery choked her so, she wasn't certain he'd be able to hear the words that sounded deadened and dull to her own ears. "I can't go. Not just like that."

His fist snapped closed, crushing the chance he'd offered her the way she might squash a mosquito. "I can." Proving his point, he swiveled on a booted heel and abandoned his saddle and spear to the dust.

Before Juliette could stir herself, his lengthy strides had put an insurmountable distance between them. She heard him call over the prairie, "To me, Robbie. To d'Arbanville." The chill that had settled around her bones deepened even more, to realize that his thoughts were no longer upon her.

"We're comin', Geoffrey." The boy shrugged toward the abandoned saddle and spear and shot her an apologetic smile. "I guess he'll send me back later for that other stuff." Robbie tugged Arion into a slow trot and set out after Geoffrey.

"Goodness," Alma murmured, bobbing on tiptoe to watch their progress. "What's so all-fired important that you couldn't go with him? He probably just wants to show off his new homestead."

Juliette folded her arms over her waist, shivering. She couldn't manage to tell Alma that Geoffrey wanted her to leap off the edge of the Earth with him. "The town. I promised Daniel. We still need a general store, and a livery, maybe even a newspaper. And the name, Walburn Ford, it has to show up on all the maps once Kansas achieves statehood."

She didn't realize she'd spoken aloud her secretly nurtured promises until Alma gave an incredulous sniff. "Why on earth are you worrying your head over those things, Miss Jay? Nobody could expect one puny little woman to do it alone. We're all working together to make this town succeed. Geoffrey must want those things, too—he's homesteading here, after all."

No humpbacked old woman could have had a harder time shaking her head. "Whatever Geoffrey wants lies elsewhere. He feels he must prove something. . . ."

Alma's expression softened, just shy of pity. She gave Juliette a sisterly pat. "Men are always bumbling around trying to prove things. They come to their senses sooner or later."

Juliette attempted an unconcerned smile, something she would have found effortlessly simple just a day or two earlier. Now, watching Geoffrey's huge frame dwindle with each step he took away from her, it seemed almost impossible to tip the edges of her lips into some semblance of nonchalance.

Nonetheless she forced herself to smile, and stiffened her backbone. A practical woman like herself could divine a good purpose behind this sudden rift in their relationship. Better a clean break now, when Alma's presence deterred her from racing after him and agreeing to go along with every one of his insane plans. Who knew what might happen if she allowed her heart and mind to become hopelessly entangled, only to have him make good on his vow to depart for the thirteenth century?

"I'm glad you're here, Alma," she said impulsively.

"You don't look so happy to me."

"Oh, but I am." She turned her back on Geoffrey d'Arbanville, and blinked back the sudden moisture that sprang to her eyes, no doubt resulting from her quick twirling about into the teeth of the prairie breeze. "You're right, we all have to work together for the good of this town. Sometimes a person needs reminding of what's really important in this life."

"Maybe." Alma bent a brow wrinkled with concern at her. "But I'm still going to stay with the Thatchers tonight. I don't guess Daniel is haunting your house, but his memory might be spooking other things. Looks to me like you need some time alone to think things through."

15

A man accustomed to the rigors of knightly travel should find the traversing of a woman's one hundred sixty acres a trifling bit of exercise. Particularly when the land lying at the edge awaited the very first impression of its new master's footprint. Particularly when that new master had coveted land almost from the time he could toddle about on chubby legs, legs that should now be stalking manfully strong, but instead gradually degenerated into a short-strided stagger such that an observer could be excused for thinking Africa's sucking mud dragged at Geoffrey's boots.

Young Robbie caught up, then matched Geoffrey's step, and then forged ahead, whilst Geoffrey wrenched one pace and then another from his balking limbs. If he dared curse a god, he would rail at Angus Ög now with marked venom. Celtic gods must be as hard-pressed as King Edward for entertainment, if it gave them pleasure to catapult a man six hundred years into the future only to entice him to fall in love with a woman commanded

by the shade of her dead husband, forcing him to pro-
cure lands he could not hold, and then dooming him to
spend the better part of all this wasted time plodding in
a ten-year-old's wake.

"Geoffrey!"

Robbie's eager shout roused Geoffrey from his
gloom. The boy stood near a crooked stake jammed
into the ground, and waved his hand high over his head
while Arion turned a curious muzzle toward the stick.
"Here's your marker, Geoffrey."

"Ha." He could scarcely summon the energy to spit
forth the oath. He glared at the marker, fancying an
invisible line stretched from it to mark the boundary
separating him from Juliette. A certainty possessed
him, that once crossed, that invisible line would prove
less easily breached than the Eternal Chasm that had
brought him to her side.

Though he had sworn to himself that he would not
do so, he looked back over his shoulder, gripping the
shoulder-slung saddlebags to prevent them from
falling. From such a distance, he could barely discern
the separations between Juliette's buildings; they
appeared no more than a nondescript gray huddle
between prairie and sky. Against such a backdrop he
could have seen if a blue-gowned woman stood staring
after him, regretting her scorning of his hand.

No splash of color relieved the sun-bleached gray.

He swiveled back toward Robbie, idly amazed that
this barely perceptible pause in his journey had so suddenly robbed him of breath. He drew in a huge rasping
gulp of air lest he suffocate in the midst of swirling
summer breezes. It seemed the air settled his boggled
mind; his conscience found its silent voice, whispering,
*Praise God she released you from temptation ere you
compromised your very soul.*

The inward chiding whipped his black-biled spirit into fighting form. Duty and honor—those concepts were important, not the nigh irresistible lure of passion-glittered blue eyes peering at him through a tangle of sun-gilded hair that went on to curl over proud upthrusting breasts. Angus Ōg had truly erred in sending him here. A knight's oath to a sorely beset king held sway over a sadly besotted man's drive to free a self-styled contented widow from a ridiculous pledge. He inhaled another great chestful of air and held it for a moment, relishing the expansion of his chest and flexing his muscles, the reminder that his strength and power had met more formidable challenges and prevailed.

Five paces ahead the boundary marker poked up from the ground. Five paces—exactly the ground span *she* had refused to cross at his request. So be it. Geoffrey bounded across the distance, leaped over the invisible barrier with a springy bounciness any gazelle might envy. "Ha!" he shouted, with vigor to spare, when his skidding heels plowed deep furrows into his very own soil.

And then he proved himself a failure at this business of casting off his desires by glancing once more over his shoulder, yearning for a glimpse of fluttering blue cotton.

Robbie poked him hard in the midsection. "I'm hungry," the lad announced.

Geoffrey grunted, glad of the flesh stabbing that reminded him he had a fosterling to tutor.

"Shelter first," he decreed. He raked his gaze over the terrain, startled that while no flash of blue greeted his eyes, color nonetheless smote his senses with the golden green of late-summer grasses, the verdant emerald leaves shimmering atop every tree twig, the crystal clarity of creek water burbling round worn brown stones.

Mine. He exulted in the notion for the space of a heartbeat—before remembering the last time he'd felt such proprietary pleasure, staring down at a slumbering soundly ravished Juliette curled soft against his breast.

"Geoffrey." Robbie called him back from his reverie by once again applying his finger to Geoffrey's midsection with the intensity of a woodworm boring augerlike into a freshly hewn chunk of oak.

"Shelter," Geoffrey repeated, indicating the cottonwood copse with a thrust of his chin to cover the wince prompted by Robbie's diligent drilling. He slapped a palm over the saddlebags. "We shall spread the blankets contained herein upon the ground, and tie my colors amidst the branches to guard against rain and falling debris."

"It'd be a lot easier if we just stayed in Miss Jay's barn," Robbie said, squinting back toward Walburn Ford with a doubtful expression.

"A squire never questions his lord's decisions." Geoffrey passed along his first bit of instruction. Within moments he'd employed his greater height to fasten his tunic and the matching cover for Arion's horse armor high in the branches. The boy sighed but fell in willingly enough, taking charge of spreading the blankets Geoffrey wasn't at all sure he could bear lying upon, considering who had last shared them with him.

Robbie also arranged the saddlebags' hidden treasures in a neat row: a packet of dried meat strips, one of which the lad immediately filched and commenced chewing on; a round container sloshing with water; and a flatter receptacle, curved to fit a man's hand and filled with an amber liquid that stung Geoffrey's nostrils when he took a wary whiff.

"Whiskey," said Robbie.

" 'Tis meant to slake thirst?" Geoffrey asked, thinking a man must needs be parched upon the desert ere willingly quaffing this vile fluid.

"Naw. It's meant to get ya drunk."

"Drunken!" Geoffrey looked at the flask with new respect. By his reckoning, he'd not taken wine or ale for well over half a millennium, a stretch of abstinence unmatched by even the most devout Saracen. The notion of drinking himself into a stupor held considerable appeal just now. Alas, although the flask brimmed nearly full, the liquid it held would barely fill a single ale mug. As a survival measure Geoffrey had, with great skill and determination, acquired the ability to swallow the contents of a dozen or more mugs without dulling his senses. It would seem he'd find no oblivion by downing such a small portion of whiskey.

"What the hell," he muttered, borrowing a phrase he'd learned from the soldiers, and took a hearty swallow.

He fought the near-instant urge to spew the whiskey back out, and prudently swallowed the liquid down instead, remembering the scanty quantity the flask held. It commenced scraping raw the passage from mouth to gullet and set up a burning knot of hellfire in his stomach so hot it sprung tears from his eyes.

Robbie settled cross-legged before him, expectancy lighting his thin features. Ready for his first lesson in the squirely arts, no doubt, and all Geoffrey could summon forth was a thready gasp.

"The Injuns call it fire water," the lad offered helpfully.

"Aha." Geoffrey clutched the flask tighter, but felt no warmth emanating from within. He took another less fulsome swallow, which traversed his throat with greater ease, but added to the heated cauldron in his belly. By the time he took a third sip, the whiskey had ignited a lively boiling of his blood that cooked his wits.

Or perhaps sharpened them, for he found himself gripped by a maudlin awareness of his glaring faults. If he sought to train Robbie well, he must needs whip himself into order first. Juliette had claimed no knowledge of courtly behavior, but all knights knew women possessed depths of deviousness unplumbed by mortal man.

"It occurs to me, young Robbie, that yon Juliette has treated me with the disdain common to noblewomen who demand unwavering loyalty from their knights. Mayhap 'twas a test."

"Huh," Robbie said.

"A test I may have failed." It seemed only fair to warn his fosterling that his lord possessed one or two faults. He sipped some more whiskey. "I, Geoffrey d'Arbanville, allowed her barbs to veer me off course." Small wonder she had scorned his bumbling vows of love, when her first test had provoked from him bristling pride rather than a lover's humility.

God's blood, but this whiskey was a fine drink, shedding all manner of light upon what had been a dark mystery.

"A knight," he intoned, feeling unexpectedly wise, "finds himself both cursed and blessed in the pursuit of perfect love."

Robbie blinked, but leaned forward, displaying a willing attitude Geoffrey felt sure would cheer any foster father's heart. The roiling in his belly settled into a pleasant warm simmer.

"How could I have forgotten that a knight must expect his lady love to test his steadfastness at every turn?" He touched the whiskey flask to his lips. "A knight can never be certain that his lady holds love for him in her heart, or whether she holds another in higher regard. Thus, the knight must accept any slur to his bravery, absorb any disparaging remark toward his character, until he proves himself upon any battlefield that his lady has devised, be it a tourney or a more subtle quest, such as the saving of a small town."

Young Robbie hid a yawn behind his fist, and fidgeted into a new position.

"God endowed women with soft curves and gentle manners capable of ensnaring a man's soul without a word. And women alone can smile and say one thing with their lips, but they are ever testing a man's—"

"I thought you were going to teach me how to forage for food and build shelter with native materials," Robbie burst out.

A shocking lapse of squirely courtesy, that, but Geoffrey felt uncommonly forgiving. He tipped the flask again and swallowed as he inclined his head first toward the saddlebags and then to his colors tied amongst the trees. "Already the shadows lengthen. We have food and shelter for this night. Now, as I was saying about women—"

The boy interrupted again. "I thought you were going to teach me how to hunt with a spear and build a sod house."

"A sod house?"

"You know, where you plow up big chunks of prairie turf and stack 'em up to make a house. Everybody's doing it in Kansas. My pa says if he'd a' known about sod houses before he spent the last of his money on planks for our cabin, we'd a' had a nicer place to live. I thought that maybe if you taught me about sod houses, I could sorta like help my pa, and he might . . ." Robbie's shoulders drooped as his words trailed away.

"Naturally, we shall build a sod house. In due time." Geoffrey tossed back another mouthful of whiskey, wishing now that his wits weren't quite so pleasantly dulled. This sod-house building sounded an enticing prospect, but he lacked the clearheadedness to think it through just now.

"Rance Cutler helped his pa build a soddie." Robbie's shoulder blades all but stuck forth like wings, so dejected was his posture. "I'll bet he'd help us. Heck, I'll bet all the fellas around here'd help us, if you was to teach us all to be knights." He treated Geoffrey to a glum look. "I don't expect anyone would stick around long enough, though, if all's you're gonna do is talk about girls."

"Robbie! No knight can be brave lest he loves—" Geoffrey stilled his tongue in concert with Robbie's resigned sigh. Perhaps he had erred in first broaching the most sacred of the knightly attributes to an unschooled lad. Especially if by slightly altering the superb training he offered he could entice more youths to lend their backs to building a shelter upon his land. Although a soft buzzing had commenced between his ears, his thoughts seemed sharper than ever. "There is no end to the interesting things I might share with you and your friends."

"Such as what?" Robbie challenged.

"Well, there is The Boasting of Glorious Deeds Past."

That prompted a huge smile from the boy, and a straightening of his backbone, but Geoffrey shook his head, deciding almost at once that this particular lesson must needs wait. Half the fun in boasting was in attempting to best the other knights' recountings, and it seemed unfair to pit his own vast successes against anything young Robbie might have accomplished in his short life.

"Better yet," Geoffrey substituted one of his favorites, "is The Assumption of a Fearsome Countenance."

Robbie's perplexed aspect struck anything besides fearsome, so Geoffrey demonstrated. He pulled his facial features into a mask of violent intent, one he'd practiced endlessly in front of a polished bit of silver, so horrific that young Robbie whimpered and pulled back in fright.

Geoffrey relaxed his countenance and nodded with satisfaction. "There, you see. Knights need not battle physically for every victory. At times, 'tis enough to strike such fear in your quarry's heart that they fall prostrate before your greater strength without loss of blood."

Robbie scowled, squinched his nose, pursed his lips in a manner Geoffrey found more comical than frightening, although he would not betray his amusement to the lad. "The skill demands much practice," he said, hiding his smile behind another uptilt of the whiskey flask. This fostering was not so difficult a task as he'd feared.

"Then, too, there is The Summoning Forth of a Terrifying Noise, which ofttimes prevails when the knight's frightening aspect alone does not provoke surrender. Of course, this tactic works best when several knights are on hand to lend their voices. Hold your ears, young Robbie." The boy obligingly clapped hands over his head while Geoffrey dragged in a great draught of air, held it for a moment, and then expelled it in a roar last uttered during crusade. Arion blew a surprised snort in his direction. The Terrifying Noise seemed to undulate endlessly over the prairie, although Geoffrey could well see that the terrain was not conducive to such a throwback of his voice; then again, quite a few of the words he said had seemed to echo in his head since consuming most of the whiskey.

Robbie's childish shout joined Geoffrey's stout bellow, and then the lad shrugged. "I guess that needs some practice, too."

"You have time," Geoffrey said, feeling quite benevolent toward the lad. "At your age, I, too, despaired over mine own shrill timbre, but matters improved once hair sprouted in my armpits."

"Teach me some more."

Geoffrey cast a weather eye skyward, and shook his

head in denial. "Nay. Dusk is well on its way, and as a new squire you must ponder ere going to sleep."

"I'll go, er, ponder by the creek," Robbie said. "Do you have to ponder, too?"

"Nay. My course is clear." Geoffrey glanced back toward Juliette's homestead. A haze seemed to soften the intervening space; perhaps it was the whiskey that made the distance seem less daunting, or perhaps twilight beckoned, promising to conceal his passage beneath the cover of night. "I must leave you for a short while. I shall picket Arion near your blanket. He will watch over you whilst I am gone."

Geoffrey felt a surge of pride when Robbie betrayed no fear at being left alone. Already his wise counsel was stiffening the lad's backbone.

"You goin' back to Miss Jay's?"

"Only long enough to tell her that I understand why she pretended to disbelieve in me. And to tell her that if my word of honor had not been given ere meeting her, nothing would tear me from her side now. I daresay she will be gracious once she realizes I have divined her motives."

Robbie cast him an admiring glance. "Knights must be awful smart about women. My ma and Alma are always whispering that men don't know the first thing about the way a woman thinks."

The whiskey's warm glow settled like a balm over Geoffrey's heart. "Knights are not the same as other men, as you shall learn, young Robbie."

An Army doctor from Fort Scott had given Juliette a bottle of laudanum to ease Daniel's last days once it had become evident that his belly wound wasn't going to heal. Although she hadn't looked at the bottle once during the intervening years, she knew a mouthful or two remained. The bottle would have been empty, if she had heeded the doctor's advice to swallow some of the tincture of opium herself.

"It'll dim your feelings until they get bearable again. It's tough on a woman, losing her husband." The medical man's hooded eyes had kindled with sympathy. Juliette remembered nodding, pretending agreement. She couldn't tell the doctor that the drug wouldn't be necessary to ease her through her bereavement, because then she'd have to admit out loud that the gnawing ache inside her had more to do with guilt than the loss of love.

Juliette fished the bottle from its hiding place, holding it toward the setting sun, watching the liquid swirl in response to the mock salute she made toward heaven. "I'm doing my best, Daniel," she whispered. "The house is three times bigger than it was when you died. You never met half the folks who call Walburn Ford home today. We . . . we even hired a schoolteacher . . ."

Her one-sided conversation drifted away. She stared skyward through the green glass bottle, but the murky liquid seemed to reflect the blurred image of her dead husband before shifting into the finely chiseled features of her addled prairie knight. Oh God, she hadn't even taken a sip and she fancied she watched Geoffrey's deep-set eyes blaze with resolve, his firm generous lips speak with utmost sincerity: "I would prefer my woman nurture love in her heart as my memorial rather than see to the welfare of a town called after me."

Two men. Two chances. And she'd failed them both.

The bottle weighed heavy. She studied it, remembering how administering too large a dose had sent Daniel into a nightmare-plagued state that could not be called sleep, while a more temperate dose simply dulled the edges of his agony without granting him blessed oblivion. She took what she hoped would blunt the pain sawing at her heart and measured the level of remaining liquid. Excellent. After this dose, there would be enough to lull her through two more nights. And by then she would surely have her wayward emotions well in hand once more.

By then, Geoffrey might be gone.

She went about her bedroom, wastefully lighting every single candle against the darkness. She settled onto her bed and drew the cotton coverlet clear up to her chin, and welcomed the languor that gradually melted into numbness.

"My lady."

Geoffrey's whisper drove her even deeper into dreams. Odd, that a person could realize she was dreaming *while* she was dreaming, but there could be no other explanation. He had, after all, taken to calling her Miss Jay, as if he were an ordinary person like anyone else in Walburn Ford.

"My lady." More urgently, accompanied by a gentle pressure against her shoulder.

Odd, how getting caught in a dream made it so difficult to see. A giggle threatened to erupt when all her eye-opening effort resulted only in certain proof that indeed she did dream. She distinctly remembered lighting a good dozen candles, and now only one flickered uncertainly, framing Geoffrey d'Arbanville with a golden glow as he knelt next to her bed.

"I once thought you looked like a guardian angel," she murmured. How obliging of her dream, to enhance that image. He looked so impossibly handsome, all masculine lines and clean strength, his hair a thick riotous tangle hanging to his shoulders, his eyes darkened by dream-spun concern.

"Mayhap I am, since yon candles threatened to set this house ablaze, had I not arrived so fortuitously."

His fingers tightened over her shoulder, a protective grip, as if he feared she might slip away from him. Well, there was the benefit of possessing such heavy eyelids—their weight made it exceedingly simple to tilt her head until it rested against his hand, catching him between her cheek and shoulder. "There, I have trapped you," she said with some satisfaction.

"Ah lady, but you did that when first we met." He made no effort to extricate his hand, although she felt it tremble against her skin.

"Then kiss me," she demanded. This dreaming was certainly a pleasant business, and she meant to wallow in it to the fullest.

For the briefest moment, she thought he meant to refuse. But it was her dream, after all, and soon she felt the brush of his lips against her own. Unsatisfying. Surely he should kiss her with enough fervor to press her deep into the featherbed. "More," she ordered.

"God's blood, Juliette, do not test my forbearance now. I am half besotted with whiskey." He leaned close, studying her. "Might you have tippled that devil's brew as well?"

"Ladies don't drink whiskey!" The giggling urge gripped her again, and she indulged it. Lifting one finger, she haphazardly waved it toward her bedside table. "Ladies drink laudanum."

He caught up the bottle with his free hand and thumbed the cork loose. He took a wary sniff and then returned the bottle to the table, turning a disapproving glare upon her. "Opium. We must be closer to China than you led me to believe."

She wanted to wave away this boring aspect of her dream as easily as she might swat a fly, but her durned arms wouldn't obey her. Instead, she caught Geoffrey's hand with her own and tugged it downward until his strong fingers gently cupped her breast. My, but she relished his inward whoosh of breath. It took scarcely no effort at all, in a dream, to sigh with contentment, and arch her back, and wish out loud that he'd untie the ribbon at her throat.

"This is how you are determined to test me now, lady?"

"Geoffrey." She loved the way his name sounded, so she said it again. "Geoffrey. Sometimes you talk too much. Shut up, or you're going to fail your test."

She smelled the sun in his hair when his lips trailed over her neck, and down. The seams of her nightgown parted with dreamlike ease, exposing the softness of her breasts.

"Love me, Geoffrey. Love me."

The bed ropes creaked when his weight joined hers. Cool prairie wind drifted through the open window to caress her skin; how nice that in dreams one's garments simply melted away. Odd, and yet thrilling, the many textures of a man: firm lips, moist questing tongue, beard-roughened skin, callused fingers. She clung to his broad shoulders while he caught first one nipple and then another between his teeth. She cried her pleasure aloud when he traced circles over her belly, and then lower, and lower still, and settled upon her woman's core with a mastery that melted the reserve that haunted her waking hours.

"Love me!" she cried, she begged, until rippling waves of ecstasy undulated through her, choking off her ability to speak.

"I will pleasure you, lady," he whispered a long moment later. The rasping edge to his voice revealed

the tenuous hold he exerted over his will, rousing shivers from her. "But I will not claim you in this bed, nor
will I claim you when your senses are flown. I will not
claim you as a man claims his woman, until you come
to me with no doubt and no regrets in your heart."

"I don't want to doubt you." A shaky tremor passed
through her. "If anything, it frightens me that I believe
so much of what you say."

His hand halted its delightful travels. "How much
do you believe, Juliette?"

For the first time, she articulated the confusions that
had swirled around her ever since meeting this man. "I
believe you sincerely mean every word you say, especially about being a knight. I accept that you believe
with all your heart and soul that you long-ago made an
oath to a king, that you swore to complete your quest
by finding a . . . chasm to leap into, or a mountain to
climb." Gracious, but the laudanum had loosened her
tongue. "I just wished I could believe it all to be true."

"And what stifles your belief?"

At the moment, she couldn't think of a single stifling
thing. "You're an actor," she said at length. "It's an
actor's job to convince people into believing. You're . . .
you're awfully convincing, Geoffrey."

"How long might a particularly skilled actor succeed
in fostering this temporary belief?"

"For as long as the play goes on, I suppose."

"Ah, Juliette. Then let us play for a lifetime."

Still, he would not claim her. But he whispered nonsense of quests and duty and words of honor while his
weight pressed her deep into scented cotton sheets and
proved without claiming that she could belong to no
other man. She felt him hard and urgent against her,
she traced the outline of his manhood through britches
that threatened to burst, felt the taut outlines of rigid

muscle, the heat of his skin that threatened to burn away the clothes he refused to remove. He brought her again and again to soul-shattering fulfillment while denying his own pleasure.

A dream come true for women who decried intimacy, no doubt, but one that left her feeling aching and deprived despite the rapture, until it stole all her strength and drove her into a deeper, dreamless sleep.

Juliette awoke to brilliant sunlight. Her coverlet was tucked snugly across her chest and under her arms, her nightgown tied firmly beneath her chin. The dull throb of an incipient headache made her wince. She raised shaking fingers and raked her tangled hair away from her forehead. The pillow next to her lay plump and pristine, the coverlet stretched taut over that part of the mattress.

She realized, as her fingers tested the knot at her throat, that she was looking for evidence to prove that her dream was . . . not a dream.

But the knot had been tied in her usual way. The bottle of laudanum sat just where she'd placed it. If a man had trekked across the prairie to visit her in the night, surely there would be a muddy footprint, a loose tuft of grass, something, *anything,* to mark his presence. But she spotted nothing. Only a curious, heavy sensation lying below her belly, an unusual tenderness in her breasts, as if they pined for her dream lover's caress.

She laughed, a shaky sound in complete accordance with the blush she felt raging over her cheeks. Surely it had all been a dream; no decent widow would really writhe so shamelessly beneath a man's sensual touch. And if it wasn't a dream—why, she could never face him again! While she'd melted into an incoherent mass wallowing in sensation, he'd remained cool and detached, in perfect control. An actor, holding her in thrall while he spun out the play. She hadn't affected him at all. Her cheeks burst into fire from remembering the liberties she'd granted and he'd taken, from the humiliation of having him leave her before dawn.

She prayed it had been a dream.

She prayed it wasn't a dream.

She grabbed the laudanum bottle and ran to the window, where she poured the remaining few swallows outside. And then she stared across her acres. A bay smudge moved against the horizon. Arion. Geoffrey would be somewhere close by his precious stallion. She slammed the window shut and drew the curtains, locking herself away like some fairy-tale princess sealing herself inside her castle.

Her refuge seemed so terribly quiet, like the inside of the shrine Geoffrey had called it. Lonely. Familiar.

"There." She gave a curt nod of satisfaction, and brushed her hands together with brisk dismissal, gestures often practiced by the Widow Walburn.

Her house closed in around her, silent, dull, stifling, a premonition of what the rest of her life would be like, without Geoffrey there, urging her to play.

But what would happen if she remained silent when doubts leaped to the forefront of her mind? What if she stifled her questions and fears? It wouldn't hurt, it couldn't hurt, to let silence and stifling work on her behalf for once, not if it let her believe in him a little while longer.

And then Juliette spun about. She tore the curtains open, and flung the window wide, silencing and stifling the Widow Walburn into temporary oblivion.

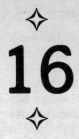

16

Geoffrey led Arion to the creek for a midmorning drink and found the tightly packed food basket set atop a rock. He knew what it meant—Miss Jay, the Widow Walburn, not trusting that Geoffrey d'Arbanville could ensure that her town's young resident did not starve past usefulness.

He rummaged through the contents, recognizing the carved pattern gracing the forks, the color of what Captain Chaney had called Juliette's everyday dishes. Fierce hunger held him in its grip, but it was not food that could slake his appetites. He could not manage to swallow a bite of the foodstuffs she had sent his way.

"Miss Jay'll be powerful worried if you don't eat," Robbie noted, chomping happily at his own portion, no doubt delighted to be feeding from the basket rather than foraging for wild fare. "She sort a' watches over everyone. She'll think you're sick."

"Mayhap I am."

"Don't tell her. She'll make you take medicine."

Would that there were a tincture to cure the illness ravaging his spirit. Not despair—something worse, and far more dangerous, for it was within his own power to end his misery. Juliette belonged to him. He need only cross the prairie and burst through her door, need only gather her into his arms and the passions that seared them both would meld them into one being. Geoffrey knew, with a certainty seldom granted him, that his kisses could stifle her doubts, his arms could hold her against his heart until she recognized it beat for her, only for her, and she would forget about the promises and obligations wavering between them.

The trouble was, the same could be said the other way round.

Her smile lit his spirits, her voice soothed his lonely soul, her wondrous body cleaved to his with a completeness he'd never found with another. She need only say, "Geoffrey, stay with me," and he might not be able to resist the urge to cast aside the vows and obligations that ordained he must leave her. Were he to turn his back on his word, he would not only lose all pride—he would no longer be the man he wanted her to love.

And so he must stay away from her, building a house he could not keep, fostering a boy he could not adequately train, yearning with all his heart to remain in this place but knowing he must go. It was a devil-devised torment burning hotter than scorching hellfire. The pain could not grow worse.

But it did.

She came to him that night, when the moon hid its all-seeing eye behind late-summer clouds and young Robbie slept in the safe oblivion only children could find. Geoffrey had been lying sleepless in the dark, and his keen night eyes had no trouble seeing her when she slipped to his side. She held out her hand in a wordless request, and he joined his hand to hers.

Geoffrey asked no questions.

Juliette offered no explanations.

He gained his feet and they stood quietly for a moment, measuring Robbie's even breathing to assure themselves he still slept. Juliette tugged at his hand and led him away, and she was the one who caught the edge of his blanket and dragged it along behind them.

"I know you're not planning to stay. But if you were, where would you build your house?" she whispered.

"There." He indicated a low prairie swell.

She spread the blanket over the highest ground, kneeling to smooth the edges flat. A curve of moon escaped its cloudy prison and illuminated her when she finished. She sat back on her heels, her hands gripped together in her lap, her bosom rising with light, quick breaths as though she'd labored at a task far more oner-ous. "Will you sit with me?"

"Aye."

Without consciously aligning himself, he found his greater length somehow wrapped around her until she nestled against the curve of his shoulder, her limbs pressed to his own.

"If I could, Juliette, I would hold you thusly and never let you go."

"You could, if you wanted to. You could build the house and hold me forever."

He groaned, feeling the walls of his self-control crumbling like the ancient mortar holding together the shreds of a castle erected in William the Conqueror's days. "Juliette, I cannot—"

"Sssh." She pressed gentle fingers against his lips. "I'm just teasing. I didn't come here for explanations.

In fact, I've sort of taken a vow of silence. I came . . . I came to see my knight in shining armor."

"What?"

"Look, Geoffrey." She lifted a graceful arm and twisted it so that moonlight silvered every smooth line. "Almost as good as your chain-mail costume, and not a speck of rust."

She slanted him a glance of such wanton anticipation that he sucked in his breath, and it burst forth in delighted laughter, until she pressed her own smiling lips against his. He imagined the two of them lying naked on the space where a man who meant to stay might fashion a bedchamber, with moonlight casting its silver glow over their entwined limbs. His manhood threatened to explode the front of his chausses. It was the most difficult chore of his life, to wrench his thoughts away from moonspun magic toward righteous knightly behavior.

"Juliette, there is much we must discuss—"

Again she stilled his lips with her own. "Silence. I don't want to discuss anything. I want . . . I want to play."

Odd, that a man's heart might break and rejoice at the same time. "For how long, my lady?"

"For as long as we can hold reality at bay."

There was but one reality that would part them—the moment when he returned to his own time, never to see her again. Would that he could postpone that moment for a lifetime. No man could, no matter how firm his intent. But perhaps he could delay it for a few days, by building the house he'd always wanted, and loving the lady he never thought to find.

Surely the gods would not punish him for claiming such a small amount of pleasure, particularly when he would spend eternity pining for all that might have been.

"A knight never denies his lady's request," Geoffrey said as he pressed Juliette back against the blanket.

*   *   *

Over the next days, the rising of the sun marked the beginning of a ragtag and bobtail parade, as Walburn Ford youths darted across Juliette's land. Surging with youthful exuberance, they forged toward Geoffrey's claim, eager to commence squirely lessons. Eager to learn to become knights.

Soon half the women and girls of Walburn Ford joined Juliette in watching Geoffrey coach the town's young men. Some of the women maintained disapproving frowns; others, like herself and Rebecca Wilcox, did their best to stifle giggles behind their fists. They needn't have bothered trying to conceal their amusement. So much commotion raged over Geoffrey's land that Juliette doubted that the swarming males would have noticed a buffalo herd stampeding through their midst.

"Geoffrey should be chastising those boys for making those God-awful noises at one another," Mrs. Abbott said, virtue all but dripping from her voice. "And those horrible faces—why, when my son Herman was a child, I warned him against making faces for fear his expression could freeze that way. As you might imagine, such a disfigurement could have kept him out of the Army Corps of Topographical Engineers."

"Robbie doesn't want to be an engineer," said Rebecca.

"Neither do I. I sure do wish they'd let me play, too," a little girl sighed wistfully.

"Heavens, Mary Sue, your *pa* would give anything to join in with them," said her mother. "He's just afraid the other menfolk'd make fun of him."

"You get your man out here and mine'd be the next to follow," said Verdie Cutler. "As it is, Mr. Cutler has Rance show him everything he's learned the minute Rance gets home to help with the milking."

Mrs. Abbott sniffed.

"They're just having fun, Mrs. Abbott," Juliette said, amazed by the soft indulgence she felt. Fun. They were all having fun.

Geoffrey, brandishing his spear, towered over the motley collection of males. He seemed delighted with the constant din of bloodcurdling shrieks and adolescent bellowing. While the wind whipped his dark hair, he contorted his handsome features into gruesome grimaces and lent his deep-chested roar to the cacophony.

He'd discarded Captain Chaney's borrowed shirt in favor of his tight leather vest, and his biceps bulged and flexed with every skyward thrust of his spear. The boys hacked and clacked at one another with whittled cottonwood limbs, parroting Geoffrey's smooth-muscled lunges and jabs.

And from time to time he would look her way, and send her a slow heavy-lidded smile that made her blush and tremble in broad daylight, calling to mind every detail of the moonlit nights they continued to share.

"Oh look, Miss Jay." Rebecca pointed over the prairie toward Juliette's yard, where a brown horse-sized smudge topped with blue circled in confusion. "It looks like a soldier's in your barnyard. He probably knocked at your door and didn't get an answer, with you being here and all."

"Good. Maybe he'll go away."

"Miss Jay!"

Rebecca stared at her with wide-eyed astonishment, and Juliette recognized an awakening sense of dread. She clapped a hand over her mouth, scarcely able to believe that she'd forgotten all about soldiers, and the attack on Fort Scott, and border ruffian threats, so immersed was she in the world Geoffrey d'Arbanville had spun around her. *For as long as we can hold reality at bay,* she'd told Geoffrey, and they'd had nearly a week of pure fantastic delight. She felt reality encroaching, tearing with determined fingers at her dreamlike state.

"Just ignore me, Becky. I . . . I haven't been at all myself lately."

Rebecca sent her a warm smile. "Well, neither have I Miss Jay, neither have I. And I'd say that it's all to the good."

The soldier must have spotted them, or been drawn to the cacophony, for the horse now headed in their direction. Deciding to ignore the soldier for as long as she could, Juliette instead studied Rebecca, marveling at the inner radiance that seemed to illuminate her. Until that day when Juliette had stopped to sew her torn dress, Rebecca Wilcox had moved through town as if she'd feared being noticed, keeping her head lowered, and speaking only when pressed. "Yes, you certainly have changed, Becky. Would I be getting too bold to ask what's brought it about?"

"Can't you feel the magic in the air, Miss Jay? I've decided to take a chance on it. And it feels purely good."

There was no time to pursue Rebecca's statement. The soldier rode up and aimed for her when Juliette sent him a halfhearted wave. He tipped his cap and reined in his mount. "Miz Walburn?"

Widow Walburn. The rising dread seemed to crush Juliette's heart in its grip. She'd never felt less like acknowledging her name, but she had no choice but to nod and pretend an interest in matters that had once consumed her. "How did the fighting go at Fort Scott, private?"

"Nothin' to it, ma'am. We routed them ruffians before they could spit, pardon my language, ma'am. Lieutenant Jordan sent me on ahead to give you notice that he'll be arriving tomorrow or the day after with Professor Burns."

And then Geoffrey was there. Juliette hadn't noticed any appreciable reduction in the din surrounding them, so she imagined he must have urged the boys to continue their shouting to mask his approach. He didn't speak, but placed himself just to the side, between her and the soldier. His arms crossed at his waist with deceptive nonchalance. Deceptive, because her intimate knowledge of his body noted the tensed bunching of his muscles and told her that he held himself ready to strike if the soldier made any untoward motions. Her protector. Her champion.

She rested her fingertips against his forearm, a scandalous intimacy in broad daylight, before witnesses, but she felt the desperate need to touch him. The warmth of his skin, his pulse beating against her own, banished a bit of the dread.

But not all of it. She felt it settle in, biding its time, and she shook her head, determined to ignore it for as long as she could.

"I'll fix you a hot meal, private," Juliette said.

"I'd sure appreciate that, ma'am. If you don't mind, I'll get my horse settled. We rode straight in from Fort Scott."

She nodded her permission, and Geoffrey covered her hand with his when the soldier returned to her barn.

"Your boardinghouse duties will now keep you at home nights, Juliette."

"Yes."

Though they both whispered so softly nobody could hear, Juliette knew that the raptly watching women were putting the correct interpretation on their touch and the blush she felt stealing over her face. "You . . . you could come to me, Geoffrey."

His fingers tightened over hers. "Never there. Only here."

"Yes."

He stepped away from her. His lips quirked in a rueful grin, and she ached to feel them brush her skin with tender possession, yearned for the touch of his tongue.

His voice boomed with a cheerfulness completely at odds with the regret she saw lighting his eyes. "So then, Juliette, yon Chester Thatcher tells me yesterday's rain makes this the perfect time to commence cutting turf for my sod house. Might we borrow your mules whilst the soldiers are garrisoned in your boarding house?"

She wondered, while her heart commenced a fearful pounding, if he had forgotten that he'd told her he was sworn to leave Walburn Ford. He must have forgotten, or he wouldn't be building a house. But a sod house, so maybe he wasn't breaking his vow after all. More folks were building soddies, with Kansas gaining settlers so fast that the sparse forest growth couldn't keep pace with the demand for lumber. Everyone said the turf structures wouldn't last long against the capricious prairie weather.

But a sod house could always be rebuilt, if a person stayed longer than originally expected.

"You want to borrow my mules? Chester suggested it?"

Chester Thatcher proved he was one of the town's more promising young men by running up at the sound of his name. "Just for a couple days, Miss Jay, while we do all this important stuff with Geoffrey."

"Important stuff?" Hearing he actually meant to build the house must have sapped her wits, for she seemed incapable of anything other than echoing phrases tossed at her. "Like what?"

"Aw, Miss Jay." Chester scowled down at his boots.

Juliette feared he might turn one of those hideous grimaces upon her, but he merely shrugged and shuffled his feet. Juliette realized he expected her to behave in a sterner fashion.

"The most important thing you can do is look after your family and your home, Chester."

"Well, we mean to, Miss Jay. That's why Geoffrey's teaching us all these, er, *manly* things."

She swayed, her body thrumming to life with the reminder of the manly skills Geoffrey possessed. She stole a glance at Geoffrey, who nodded approvingly at Chester, seemingly completely unaware of her inner turmoil. Somehow Juliette doubted that Geoffrey could impart to a lesser male his ability to transform a respectable widow into a passion-crazed hoyden.

"So can we borrow them, Miss Jay? The mules?"

"You know I never turn down a request to borrow my mule team, Chester. And I suppose poor Arion's leg hasn't healed yet."

Both Geoffrey and Chester stiffened into towers of masculine outrage.

"Geoffrey says it would be an insult to ask Arion to pull a plow," said Chester.

It was exactly what Juliette needed to hear at that moment, this reminder of Geoffrey's inordinate fondness for his knightly steed. Reality wasn't quite having its way, not yet.

"We certainly don't want to offend Arion's dignity," she said. "You can walk over to my house with me, Chester, and fetch the team."

"Thank you, my lady," Geoffrey whispered, sending her on her way with a heart so light, she barely noticed the dread that continued to crouch deep within.

*   *   *

Rebecca knew a man couldn't lose half his weight in only a few days, even if he spent every mealtime pushing his food around his plate instead of shoveling it into his mouth as he usually did. Still, Josiah's frame seemed to shrink each day, as if Robbie's absence were sucking him dry, one ounce at a time.

Paradoxically, even though she managed to visit Robbie every day, she missed her son with an ache that weighed her down, so that she could barely heave herself out of bed in the morning, could scarcely manage the few steps between cookstove and kitchen table. Josiah's behavior threw her off balance even more. She wouldn't have been at all surprised if he'd displayed a gleeful satisfaction, a hand-rubbing triumph that he'd finally rid himself of the child whose presence irritated him so. She'd never expected this almost-palpable grief, as if he harbored a secret affection for Robbie that he'd never let show.

"Verdie Cutler says her husband planted an extra acre in pumpkins this year," she said, poking halfheartedly at a mound of mashed potatoes.

Josiah gripped his fork so tight she feared he might bend the metal. "Cutler's got four strapping boys to help him in the fields. That's five sets of eyes keepin' watch during the night so's the Injuns don't pick him clean once harvest time comes. You can't compare my workload with Cutler's, missus."

"Oh, Josiah." She sighed, and set her fork alongside her barely touched plate. She gripped her hands together in her lap, praying for strength as she stared down at them. "All's I did was tell you an interesting bit of news. You're the one comparing workloads. In fact, you've done nothing but compare yourself against other men since the day we got married, and I'm plain sick and tired of it."

He must have lost his hold on his fork. She heard the dull thump of metal against the oak tabletop, and then the clatter as the fork fell to the floor. *Just like all my hopes,* she thought. Despite her brave words to Miss Jay, she might as well admit that life with Josiah was a complete failure. If she had only herself to worry about, she could become resigned to sitting across the table from him, measuring every word, absorbing the instant ridicule and twisted intent he was so adept at fashioning to everything she said.

But she wasn't alone. She had Robbie. The minute she cleaned up these supper dishes, she'd march over to Geoffrey's and demand the return of her son, and then they'd go . . . well she didn't know exactly where they'd go, but they'd find someplace. Glad for something that would divert her from the ache clogging her throat, she leaped from her chair and snatched the fallen utensil up off the floor.

And it was as though the fork served as a magical conduit sending strength surging straight into Rebecca's soul. She found herself pointing the fork at Josiah, looking for all the world as if she meant to stab a big hole right in the middle of his forehead so some sense could soak in.

"The Cutlers held on to most of their pumpkins because they bartered like gentlemen with the Indians, not because they watched over their fields. And don't you go tormenting me, mister, about the Cutlers having four sons. In case you haven't been paying attention in church, I'm telling you right now that the last Immaculate Conception happened close to two thousand years ago."

Josiah sucked in his breath, and narrowed his gaze into warning slits as he made to rise from his chair. "Missus—"

"Don't you 'missus' me any more, either. We might've spoken the words in church, but we've *never* been man and wife." To her dismay, Rebecca found some of her strength deserting her, evidenced by an alarming wobble in her voice. Needing to grip onto something, she reached for the nearest solid object, which happened to be Josiah's shoulder. So surprised was she by the physical contact that she snatched her hand away almost at once, while he collapsed right back into his chair.

"Eat your potatoes!" she shouted, slamming the fork onto the table, not even bothering to see whether it had picked up any dirt from its brief stint on the floor.

"You ain't never touched me before, mis . . ." Josiah's voice sounded no steadier than her own.

"It's not a woman's place to be the one to . . ." She gulped, so flooded by embarrassment that she couldn't continue for a moment. "Especially when the man makes it clear he doesn't want to . . ."

She was beginning to doubt whether either of them would ever again complete a sentence when Josiah gripped the blasted fork and got himself all riled up in turn.

"How could I touch you, or expect you to want to touch me?" he challenged, stabbing the fork into the air for emphasis. "You know the promise I made when we got married."

"You promised to make a new life, *for the three of us,* in Kansas."

"I promised to make you a *better* life," he corrected. "I swore to God that if you became my wife, I would deny myself everything until I proved myself a better man than that rakehell who made you all those sly promises and left you holding a fatherless baby."

"There you go, comparing again! You're ten times the man he was, you self-denying blatherskite!"

They were standing toe to toe, nose to nose, shrieking at one another like crows flapping for mastery over a ripe rabbit carcass.

"A God-fearing wife shouldn't dare taunt her husband . . ."

"Blatherskite! Blatherskite! Blatherskite!"

A few days ago, fearing that Robbie might bear the brunt of Josiah's anger, Rebecca would have cowered away rather than further inflame the red surging across her husband's cheeks. Today, she felt shockingly invigorated by their venomous exchange, even though one final "Blatherskite!" squeaked out rather less forcefully than she would have liked.

"Why don't you say what you really mean, Rebecca—Failure! Failure! Failure!"

"Josiah, why on earth would I want to call you a failure?"

Her puzzlement over his outburst caused her to back up a step; a similar confusion clouded Josiah's features. He lowered himself back into his chair, shakily, as if something had melted his leg bones and he feared the rest of his skeleton would soon follow suit.

"You want me to set out my failings point by point, missus, I'll do it for you. First off, I invested every cent I'd ever saved into that Vegetarian Settlement Company, and it went bust before we got so much as one good night's sleep in Octagon City."

"Dozens of folks lost everything when the company failed." Rebecca found her own bones seeming to desert her as she settled into her chair across from Josiah. "Nobody could fault you for believing that Octagon City might prove to be a paradise on earth. Don't forget that I believed it, too, Josiah."

A shudder coursed through her husband's lean frame. She felt the table quiver from the force of it. "Then I got the summer complaint and couldn't leave when the rest of the settlers went on North. We might've had ourselves a good place up Wisconsin way."

"We have ourselves a good place here in Walburn Ford." Rebecca laughed, even though she'd never felt less mirthful. "You read Birdie Slocum's letter. She said they about starved to death in your precious Wisconsin, spent all winter snowed under. They're worse off than ever and heading back to her folks in Ohio. And don't forget that note from Miriam Davis telling us how her husband and boy both died after leaving Kansas, how she wishes they'd stayed and got over their illness and fought to keep their land. Why, she's even written a book on it, so's folks back East will think twice about coming to Kansas. Seems to me we're doing right well in comparison."

Rebecca felt a sudden awareness of her heart beating, as if she'd spent so long steeling it against her husband's wrath that it hadn't dared remind her of its presence until now. Josiah's expression gentled, calling to mind the traits that she'd fallen in love with: Hope. Pride. Integrity. The brief glimpse of the man who'd held her illegitimate son to his breast and swore he'd never fling her past indiscretions in her face sent longing coursing through her, almost like staring at the photograph of a loved one who's died.

"I was so disappointed, on our wedding night, when you said you didn't want to . . . to touch me," she said. "But then you explained, and I found myself thinking it was actually quite romantic. Do you remember what you promised me, Josiah?"

She knew her own face reflected fiery red from discussing such matters aloud. Josiah had gone deathly pale.

"Josiah?"

His voice was little more than a thready whisper. "I

told you I'd give you a paradise on earth before you ever had to give me a thing."

But their arrival in the vegetarian settlement at Octagon City had turned up nothing more than a hastily constructed shanty where would-be settlers crowded every inch of dry space, affording no privacy, mere survival such a struggle that there had been no chance for a newly wedded couple to learn each other's ways. He'd refused to touch her when it became apparent that the promised sawmill, granary, and school would never be built, when the bulk of the settlers abandoned their dreams and deserted the struggling settlement. He'd refused to touch her when mosquitoes and snakes and starving Indians overtook the few acres they'd managed to clear and they'd retreated toward the closest settlement, Walburn Ford. In time, her yearnings had soured into resentment; longing for his touch had melted into resigned acceptance that she'd made a bad bargain.

She knew that a good woman, a *decent* woman, would praise God nightly for granting her a marriage without the necessity of enduring a man's conjugal demands. Like Josiah, she'd been caught in a trap of her own making. She'd sworn upon her marriage that she would become a good woman, a decent woman. So how could she have told Josiah that she'd never quite dispelled her unladylike desires, that she ached for his embrace, when his stalwart adherence to *his* vow kept him away from her?

Vows and promises. How did any couple ever manage to find happiness when pride and honor kept getting in the way?

She inched her hand toward his, stopping just shy of brushing her fingertips over his work-roughed skin. It sickened her now to realize how many years they had spent with barely perceptible physical distance yawning like an open chasm between them: lying abed, listening to each other's breathing, being careful not to move; at mealtime, like now, guarding against any accidental touch. This stirring-up business, hard as it was on a woman's nerves, should have come about long ago.

"Don't you see, Josiah, that I never felt I *had* to give you anything? I felt honored and blessed that you wanted me to be your wife."

His hand twitched, and her heart leaped, anticipating that at last he meant to breach the infinitesimal gap separating them.

"It's that stranger, he got you all flustered." His tone, flat and suspicious, sliced her barely sprouted hopes away from their roots. "First you give him the boy. Now you're thinking of . . . of matters that ain't ever been discussed between us. I got two eyes in my head, missus. I see how women flock around him. Ain't no woman in Walburn Ford what gave him what you did, though."

"You're wrong, Josiah. You're so wrong." She pulled her hand back. It seemed to take an eternity to drag it across the worn oak tabletop, probably because it felt numb and so heavy, as if each fraction of an inch she moved it widened the rift between them.

Josiah lurched to his feet, bracing his fists against the tabletop, swaying a little as he leaned toward her. Rebecca felt another tendril of hope when she saw the agony etched into her husband's features, and she despised herself for it when his mouth settled into its familiar suspicious scowl.

"Yessir, I've been expecting for a long time to see that look in your eyes, missus. You ain't never sassed me before, or got to talkin' in broad daylight about subjects that ain't proper between a God-fearing man and wife. I'm warning you—I mean to find out what's behind this sudden change in attitude."

A tiny sob escaped from her throat, the sole remnant of the high hopes she'd brought to this confrontation.

"Alma was wrong. I'm not strong like Miss Jay. So do whatever you like, Josiah. I'm . . . I'm too worn out to care anymore." She pushed herself away from the table and headed for the sanctuary of her bedroom. The supper dishes lay congealing all over the kitchen, not so different from the impervious shield she formed to protect her battered spirit.

It would take her a few days to prepare, no more. She'd fetch Robbie and warn Geoffrey to watch his back as far as Josiah was concerned, though she'd never known Josiah to wreak physical violence. He'd never had to, with her—he'd proven time and again that he could destroy her with a few well-chosen words.

Even now she heard him mumbling.

"What are you saying, mister?" Habit forced her to stop at the bedroom door and ask.

He sat scowling down at the tabletop, his hands gripped in an attitude of prayer. "I said you got no call to be saying other women are better than you. You're the best there is."

Either he moved faster than she believed him capable of, or his backhanded compliment had frozen her in place, she didn't know. But scant heartbeats later his chair was empty, and she was still staring open-mouthed where he'd sat, wondering what on earth she should do next.

17

Professor Burns muffled a belch behind his fist. "Excellent supper, Mrs. Walburn. I must confess the folks back in Boston scoff to think one might enjoy the culinary experience afforded by the common prairie dog. I shall set them straight on the matter."

"Right good, Miss Jay." Captain Chaney echoed the sentiment to a chorus of agreement from the sated soldiers sitting around Juliette's dinner table.

Juliette sent the captain a distracted smile, wishing they'd all clear out of her kitchen. She'd endured her fill of burping, coughing, scratching men, and couldn't clear her mind of Geoffrey's comment comparing camels to U.S. Army soldiers.

She couldn't clear her mind of Geoffrey; two nights without sleep, aching for the feel of his arms around her, the wonder of his body joining hers, had robbed her of the ability to think of anything else.

Not so very long ago, she'd anticipated a lifetime of catering to these selfsame soldiers, knowing that Daniel would have been so proud to see how she honored his dream. Now she didn't see how she could tolerate her guests' presence for more than ten minutes at a time.

She quelled the surge of revulsion that rose at thinking of endless days spent cooking up boardinghouse fare, endless afternoons washing bedding slept in by another, endless nights listening to strange footsteps violating the privacy of her home. It was hard to believe now that it had taken the arrival of an amnesiac actor to make her ask, "What about the things *you* want from life, Juliette?"

"Got an assignment for you, Chaney," Lieutenant Jordan said as he leaned back, accompanied by a sound and smell no polite company would ever acknowledge.

Juliette wondered how the retired soldier would accept this officious-sounding demand. To her surprise, Captain Chaney straightened in his seat, almost as if he snapped to attention while sitting. "Ruffians rampaging?" he questioned. "Time for me to go into action?"

Lieutenant Jordan nodded, and cast Juliette an apologetic glance. "Don't get scared, Miss Jay. You're in no immediate danger. The ruffians have always been more interested in Lawrence and Fort Scott than these small settlements. Even so, the president himself placed Captain Chaney here to keep an eye on the town. He's been filing regular reports. It's thanks to him that we garrisoned Fort Scott before the ruffians could mount a disastrous attack. I'm a little worried that they might try attacking someplace that's not so well defended. We're reactivating your commission, Chaney, so you can get these men ready in case something happens."

"I don't understand." Juliette turned toward Captain Chaney. "All this time, you've been a spy, sort of?"

"Yup." If the captain wore suspenders, no doubt he would have snapped them proudly. "For the good guys."

"Oh." Juliette slumped in her seat, remembering how Alma had been engaged to determine if Geoffrey was a spy. Juliette had scarcely given a thought in her entire life to the matter of spying, and not only had there been an undercurrent of suspicion swirling around Walburn Ford all this time, but she'd been sheltering an army spy under her own roof for months. It seemed she didn't know a single thing about the goings-on in the town she'd committed the rest of her life to building.

"Fooled you good, didn't I?"

"Well, I guess calling yourself a *retired* soldier was sort of like a disguise," she admitted, though it seemed a pretty flimsy cover, now that she thought on it.

"Thought so." Captain Chaney nodded. "The folks in town respect my experience, which'll make it easier now that I'll be mustering the men and passing out army weapons for militia duty."

"Er." Lieutenant Jordan seemed to choke, though he hadn't swallowed any more food.

"Guess I'll be wantin' your soldiers to fan out tonight to notify the town's menfolk, so we can commence drilling and target practice tomorrow at first light."

"Chaney." Lieutenant Jordan gulped hard. "We want you to muster and drill but, fact is, we don't have any weapons for you. It's all we can do to arm the garrisons in the bigger towns. Border ruffians captured the last two loads we tried shipping into Kansas. The president put a stop to arms shipments, said it didn't make sense to supply the enemy." He sneaked a furtive glance toward the captain. "Sorry."

To a man, the soldiers hunched forward, as if they meant to shelter their own firearms from possible confiscation.

"The hell you say!" Juliette feared for Captain

Chaney's health when his skin mottled with fury. "There ain't more 'n four decent guns in this whole town. How the hell am I supposed to organize a bunch of farmers into a fighting force without a supply of Sharps rifles?"

"Geoffrey would help you," Juliette found herself saying. "He knows a lot about fighting without guns."

She could see him in her mind's eye, his muscled arm lifted toward the sky, hefting a six-foot-long spear with such skill that he might have been born holding it. Her ears roared with the remembered sound of boys engaged in mock battle, the strangely disciplined disorder which had them all standing taller and prouder. Knights, skirmishing on the Kansas frontier.

The slumbering dread stirred. It insinuated itself between her mind and her heart; her mind, which told her she must at all costs protect the town, and her heart, which cried against her return to reality.

"Huh." Captain Chaney's eyes narrowed upon her with speculation. "You might have somethin' there, Miss Jay."

Recognition, and relief, dawned over Lieutenant Jordan's features. "Yes, that big d'Arbanville fellow. He seemed anxious to pitch in down at Fort Scott. He'd probably help if you asked, Miss Jay."

Juliette knew she could never pose the question to Geoffrey herself. If anything, she wanted to race across the prairie and fling herself into his arms, beg him to run away with her and leave all this behind them. A strange sound escaped her tightly clenched throat—laughter, the humorless variety. Something had inexplicably shifted. She might be tempted to abandon everything in order to continue her impossible love affair, but she knew Geoffrey d'Arbanville, with all his muddleheaded notions of honor and duty, never would.

"Geoffrey relishes fighting. You won't need me to

come along when you ask him. Captain Chaney knows the way to his homestead."

"I see," said Lieutenant Jordan, though the puzzlement in his eyes didn't match his words. "Well, if Chaney means to begin drills in the morning, we'd best be going. Leave the back door unlatched for us if you would, Miss Jay, so we needn't disturb you if we come back late."

Juliette nodded, and found herself inordinately interested in clearing the supper dishes while the soldiers clomped out of her kitchen. Performing these normal everyday activities dulled the edge of the pain sweeping through her. Everything was coming to an end, she just knew it, and there was nothing she could do to prolong the joy. She prayed that the false numbness would last until she found herself alone in the sanctuary of her bedroom. She was bending over the swill bucket, scraping the supper leavings for the Thatchers' pigs, when the scrape of a chair startled a small yelp from her.

"Professor Burns!" She clapped a hand over her rapidly racing heart. "I didn't realize you'd stayed behind."

The professor gave her a benign smile around his pipe stem, all his concentration seemingly centered on lighting his tobacco. "All this soldiering isn't quite my forte, Mrs. Walburn. I'm more the scholarly type, as you can imagine. I'll take books over bullets, research over rioting, any day."

"So would I." Juliette turned back to her chore, and then a sudden thought struck her. How could she be so convinced of Geoffrey's honorable nature without believing, even a little bit, that there might be a shred of truth in his outlandish stories? What if . . . what if it were true, and Geoffrey d'Arbanville really was a mercenary knight somehow transplanted from the thirteenth century?

Oh, God, if only it could be true.

"Research, Professor Burns? Would it be possible

for someone in your position to verify the names of some people who might have lived a long time ago? A *very* long time ago?"

"My dear, the Harvard research libraries are second to none, second to none." He seemed so puffed up with self-importance that he might have stocked the libraries himself. "How far back and where does your interest lie?"

"The year of our Lord 1283, northwest England," she whispered. "A border lord named John of Rowanwood and his wife, Demeter. An outlaw named Drogo FitzBaldric. And a knight, a mercenary knight, named . . ." She closed her eyes and willed herself to continue, afraid of what the professor's reaction would be once she listed the final name. "Geoffrey d'Arbanville."

"Ah, an ancestor of the young fellow the soldiers have gone to see."

Juliette prayed that the cloud of pipe smoke wafting around his face would shield her sudden slumping relief at hearing the professor provide such an excellent excuse for her inexplicable interest. Maybe not. Through the smoky haze she could clearly see the professor's forehead crease into a frown. Her agitation could be no less evident.

"Late thirteenth century. Hmm. I'll have a go at it, but I'll have to admit right up front that even Harvard's facilities might prove a bit deficient. Tumultuous times back there, my dear, tumultuous times. Welsh upstarts calling themselves kings and princesses and whatnot, tormenting Good King Edward to death. The written record is by no means complete."

"And don't forget the Celtic gods," Juliette added. "They were very important—or so I hear."

"Oh my, yes." The professor patted his pocket and withdrew a small notebook. "A pen, if you please, my dear. I doubt I'll remember those names unless I write them down at once. So much on the mind, as you can imagine."

Juliette brought him a quill pen and pot of ink, and watched with her breath held while he scratched the names onto the paper. There was no reason why this simple exercise should leave her feeling nervous, and yet it did. She wasn't sure what would be worse: learning Geoffrey was nothing more than an amnesiac actor, or learning that he really was a time-traveling knight sent here by some ancient Celtic god to put an end to the border dispute and save her from sour widowhood. And she couldn't help wondering what Geoffrey would say when he found out what she'd done.

The professor mumbled as he wrote. "Demeter. A good Celtic name. Holding a castle, you say? Can't say I recall a female called Demeter in the Plantagenet line. Sounds like one of those upstarts I mentioned. Drogo Fitz—what?"

"Baldric."

"Yes, of course. And Geoffrey d'Arbanville." He ended the writing of Geoffrey's name with a small flourish, and blew over the ink to dry it before snapping the notebook shut and returning it to his pocket. "I'll tend to it straightaway, upon completing my report for the president, of course."

"Of course."

"Providing I make the same excellent train connections I enjoyed on my way down here, there's every chance I could get an answer back to you within the fortnight, Mrs. Walburn."

"So fast?" The tiny leap of excitement she felt within took her by surprise. "I hope . . . I hope I'm not asking you to inconvenience yourself, professor."

"The miracles of modern transportation, my dear. And don't trouble yourself over asking such a small favor. Why, it's the least I can do to repay your excellent hospitality, which I fear shall not be equalled in many of the other establishments I will patronize along the way home."

The professor heaved himself from his chair and lumbered out of the room. Juliette braced her back against the wall, suddenly weak-kneed to realize what she'd done.

She hadn't asked the professor to inquire after the existence of a Shakespearean actor named Geoffrey d'Arbanville.

She wanted Geoffrey's story to be true.

It had been well over a week since Captain Chaney had departed their bargaining session with a decided air of stunned confusion, Geoffrey remembered. As usual knightly logic had prevailed. Work on his sod house in exchange for military training had seemed a fair trade to him, and one eagerly taken up by the men of the town. With the exception of Josiah Wilcox, who had glowered at him with an anger bordering on hatred, the men of Walburn Ford had thus been working and training beneath Geoffrey's critical eye, and though he was proprietorially pleased with the results, he found the need for constant supervision while they built the sod house somewhat puzzling.

"You would think," Geoffrey grumbled, "that the building of a simple motte and bailey keep has become a lost art."

"Well, I doubt anyone in these parts has seen anything like this before," Captain Chaney said.

" 'Tis not so different from other sod structures."

"I ain't never seen a round soddie surrounded by a moat. Can't even imagine what Mrs. Abbott's son in the Army Corps of Topographical Engineers would have to say about it."

"Mayhap you have struck on one of this land's defensive liabilities, then, if your president's foremost troops cannot fashion such an impregnable dwelling."

Geoffrey stared with pride at his small but stout-looking keep. All of England had been littered with the foundations of similarly shaped stone structures dating back to the glorious era of William the Conqueror. He and his band of would-be squires had plowed the sod bricks from a large circle of land surrounding the only slight rise on his homestead claim. The bargain with Captain Chaney had come just in time to enlist the full-grown men in digging. Whilst they shoveled and heaved dirt from the ditch, the boys had tamped the excess soil atop the prairie rise, creating a small hill surrounded by an empty moat—a very small moat, to be sure, considering the sluggish nature of the creek that must struggle to fill it.

Geoffrey's house was rising from the top of the hill, featureless and squat and unattractive in a way that endowed his modest home with the aspect of a somewhat grassy medieval castle, providing he squinted and turned his head just so when viewing it. Nothing at all like his ancestral home. But although he'd oft yearned to possess his father's manor, the sight of it had never provoked one shred of the satisfaction his land-starved soul found in this dirt hovel, temporary as his ownership of it might be.

"Have to admit," Captain Chaney said, "that eliminating the corners made the work go easier. And those, whatchamacallit, arrow slits, won't weaken the roof into sagging as much as regular windows do. Fact is, the whole town's excited about finishing it today."

"As well they should be. Is it so unusual for towns-people of this time, er, this place to gather for communal festivities?"

"Not much to celebrate on the frontier, Geoffrey. Folks don't have much wealth or energy to spare out here."

"Nor did they in my . . . where I hail from. And yet people did not isolate themselves as they do here, with sometimes only one or two people to a hut. Why, I haven't seen a single minstrel or tumbler since my arrival. Simple pleasures, such as the sharing of a meal, singing, listening to tales—I miss them sore. I must admit there were times when I thought I would have been willing to sell my soul for a moment's privacy. No more. 'Tis fearsome lonely on this prairie."

He had taken to making statements like this, for the good of his soul. Aye, it was lonely here, especially with Juliette bound to her duties. But it was not so lonely here that he wouldn't relish staying, amidst the farmer friends whose male camaraderie he found so appealing. Were his honor not sworn, he'd revel in living out his days on land he could call his own, sharing his sturdy new dwelling with Juliette.

For the good of his soul, he must needs begin acting, as Juliette always accused him of doing. Far too many days had passed without his seeking a way back to his own time. Everyday, he told himself, "I will see her once more, and then I will go." But their daylight visits, while eminently respectable, did nothing to assuage the desires ever raging through him. And so each time he resolved to leave, after seeing her once more. He should be seeking mountains or chasms, not building sod houses and moats. He should be striving to reach the lady Demeter, not yearning for Juliette.

He should begin acting more like a knight, and less like a man in love.

Each night, stretched upon his sleeping pallet with the weight of physical exhaustion hard upon him, his mind bedeviled him, denying him sleep. Juliette, pressing his hand to her silken-soft breast. Juliette, breathlessly begging him to love her. Juliette, her wondrous eyes clouded with desire and confusion, holding to her promise to play so long as reality stood at bay, but silently fearing he would leave her to her solitary respectable responsibility.

As he must. Two days, no more, and he must go. And he would ask her to come with him.

But would she? Would she turn her back on all that she held dear, for the sake of a man who could offer her nothing once he reached his destination?

Lest his inner turmoil be remarked, Geoffrey turned his attention once more to the building of his keep.

Men and boys alike were now engaged in stacking the final sod blocks according to Geoffrey's instructions. Pigs borrowed from the Thatchers' sty rooted in the ditch, their questing snouts and sharp cloven hooves packing the soil hard. By the end of the day, men, boys, and pigs would have finished their work. Geoffrey himself would breach the two feet of earth separating the creek from the moat, letting the water trickle through.

Everyone had welcomed Geoffrey's suggestion to conduct a celebration accompanying the filling of the moat. The town's womenfolk had promised to arrive with baskets packed with every available delicacy. After feasting, the men and boys would display their newly acquired skills in a mock tourney. Geoffrey, of course, intended to hold himself aloof from the competition. Although he'd done his best in the brief space of time allotted him, none of the men he'd trained could match his skill, and it would be shockingly unsporting to flaunt his superior abilities.

He watched young Chester Thatcher struggle with a

turf clod too heavy for his half-grown strength. There, it seemed, lay a way to sap the clamoring potency that urged him to cross the prairie and claim Juliette, declaring his intention to stay by her side forever.

"I shall lend my back to the hoisting of the last row of sod." Without waiting to hear anything Captain Chaney had to say in response, Geoffrey sprinted across the ground, leaped his inadequate moat, and turned his strength to something he could understand, something he could conquer.

Something he could hold between his two hands and call his own, if only for another day.

18

Juliette was bent low over her weeding when she heard the excited babble of approaching women: soft feminine laughter, an occasional sharp-edged retort, all accompanied by the creak of what sounded like an inordinate number of feed buckets. They carried celebration fare, as they crossed her land to get to Geoffrey's.

"Miss Jay! Whatever are you doing in your garden? Don't you realize how late it is? We promised the men we'd be there at half past five, sharp." Alma's classroom voice blared across the dusty yard, prompting a chorus of assenting murmurs.

Juliette wiped her sleeve over her forehead; she could tell by the gritty sensation that she'd smeared mud over her skin. "It's barely noon, Alma."

Actually, she'd spent most of the morning in a frenzy, primping her hair and trying on each of her four dresses, finding satisfaction with none. The soldiers had left after an early breakfast, leaving her once again free to make her moonlit walk across the prairie. Somehow she had to make it through the day, and the scheduled celebration, with Geoffrey full in her sight but untouchable. The unpleasant task of weeding promised to wear off the edges of her excitement, but hadn't done much so far to blunt her inappropriate thoughts.

Mrs. Abbott frowned at Alma and Juliette in turn. "I'm purely amazed that this whole town's going along with this nonsense. You can't seriously believe that Geoffrey d'Arbanville's going to turn all those men into knights."

"Well, we know that, but so what?" Alma dug her elbow into Verdie Cutler's side, and they all began giggling. "Them men're having the time of their lives, and it sure is fun to watch them carry on."

Juliette settled back onto her heels, doing her best not to laugh at Mrs. Abbott's expense when Verdie Cutler said, "If you're so all-fired against it, why're you going early with us, Mrs. Abbott?"

"We have to get there early," Alma explained to Juliette. "You have to judge the contest, Miss Jay."

"Yes, ma'am, you're always in charge of anything important," said Verdie.

"Contest?" Juliette wondered who'd squeaked the response, and then realized she'd done it herself.

Rosie Thatcher hustled forward, a rough, oak-plank bucket clasped tight to her generous bosom. She thrust the bucket toward Juliette, revealing two small holes hacked midway up the bucket, and a wide slit gouged near the brim. She displayed it proudly, as if delighted that she'd transformed a feed bucket into something resembling a nondestructible jack-o'-lantern.

"We secretly made helmets for our menfolk, Miss Jay, like Geoffrey's. They'll surely be surprised."

"You held a helmet-making contest?" Juliette spirits

sank to think of so much valuable homesteading equipment sacrificed to such nonsense.

"Gracious, no. Rosie's just showing off her bucket because she has no talent for the needle. We held a *sewing* contest to work up a coat of arms for Walburn Ford." Alma pulled a length of yellow cotton from her apron and flapped it free of its folds. But before Juliette could decipher the intricate embroidery decorating the material, Mrs. Abbott snatched the cloth away.

"No fair! Miss Jay looks at all our coats a' arms or she don't look at any. If my son Herman, from the Army Corps of Topographical Engineers were here, he'd say you're trying to influence the judge, Alma Harkins."

"Don't get all het up, Mrs. Abbott. And no need to sic Herman and the engineers on me. I'm just trying to explain things to Miss Jay."

Alma recaptured her cloth from Mrs. Abbott and made an ostentatious show of folding it in such a way that Juliette couldn't catch a glimpse of it even if she tried. "We wanted to make them blue, like Geoffrey's coat of arms, but nobody had enough blue material to give everyone an equal chance. I had this yellow stuff ordered in for a school project, but I figured this would count just as well, since the whole town's in on it." Alma continued once her cloth was safely concealed in her apron pocket. "Soon as you decide which design wins, we'll get busy sewing an identical tunic for each of the men."

Most in the crowd nodded vigorously, though Verdie Cutler's lips trembled despondently. "My man says he won't wear nothin' with flowers or birds on it."

Verdie's comment unleashed a torrent.

"Geoffrey's tunic has a hawk. Your husband wouldn't mind that, Verdie—just so long's it ain't a dumb bird, like that chicken on Louella's."

"It's a rooster, not a chicken, and everyone knows how mean-spirited a rooster can be."

"A *rose* wouldn't look unmanly if we sewed big thorns on the stem."

"No fair sneakin' your ideas in on Miss Jay!"

"Oh hush, Mrs. Abbott."

"*My* man said he won't wear nothin' that'd make the border ruffians laugh themselves sick."

"If only those goldurned ruffians *would* laugh themselves sick, our men wouldn't need these helmets for protection."

"They don't need much protection anyway, hard as their heads is. Besides, them ruffians ain't used to our men fightin' back. They'll probably hightail it back to Missouri at the first sign of fighting."

Juliette rocked back on her heels. The women's excited chatter continued but struck her ears with less intensity, as if an invisible barrier had slammed down between them and her.

The people of Walburn Ford, with no assistance whatsoever from her, had pulled together in a project igniting community spirit in a way even Daniel could never have foreseen. Juliette closed her eyes, swaying, imagining work-worn farmers discussing coats of arms over the supper table with their wives. Harried women taking precious time away from children and chores to secretly gouge holes in feed buckets. Boys and men and even the Thatchers' pigs pitching in to build a sod house for a muddleheaded stranger who didn't intend to live in it for long, trusting him to prepare them for a battle that could cost them their lives.

And now everyone intended to celebrate their efforts. With or without the Widow Walburn's approval.

She waited for resentment to seep through her, some perfectly reasonable outrage at finding that her authority had been so neatly usurped. Instead, anticipation surged through her. They were truly becoming a town. She could join them all . . . and have fun.

Thank you, Geoffrey, she said to herself.

"You go on and change your dress, Miss Jay. We'll try to hold off the contest until after dinner."

Alma's strident voice sounded even more distant, and for good reason; when Juliette opened her eyes, the cluster of women had left her yard to scamper with unseemly haste over the prairie. Toward Geoffrey, as she'd ached to do for all these wasted nights.

My lady, he called her when they were alone. He never asked for a bit of credit for strengthening her town and its people until all responsibility had been shifted from her shoulders to his. She longed to hear it again. *My lady.* The endearment played endlessly in her dreams. Even now, when prairie wind and whispering grass were the only sounds, she shivered at the memory of his passion-roughened voice rumbling from his chest as he'd cradled her against his heart. Free and joyful in a way she'd never thought to be again.

She tilted her head skyward and felt the midday sun dry the mud smearing her forehead. Her cheeks prickled as the sun did its work, too, on the moist tracks streaking from her eyes. She knew what she had to do—she would wash away the dirt and the tears, don her best dress, and join the rest of Walburn Ford, now. She would bask in the welcome she was sure to receive from her townsfolk.

"Miss Jay!" they would call.

"Miss Jay," Geoffrey would say in front of other people, and she would smile, pretending it was exactly what she wanted to hear from his lips.

If she'd gone off with Geoffrey when he'd first asked, jumping into holes and doing all manner of the unladylike things he tempted her into doing, all this house building and coat of arms designing would never have taken place. Geoffrey's stubborn adherence to his own vows took on new meaning. Daniel's town, her town, had certainly benefited from a bit of self-denial on her part. What might she and Geoffrey accomplish if they pursued *his* vows together?

Once she had thought shouldering responsibility meant a life doomed to loneliness. She couldn't wait to see Geoffrey and tell him that now she knew better.

Rebecca looked so beautiful that Josiah had to sit on his hands to keep from pulling her into his arms. To even consider that he might one day do so seemed more remote than ever, considering how she'd taken to stealing away from the house while he worked.

"That's your best dress," he said, trying to avoid looking at the way the much-washed calico settled over the soft swell of her hips.

"It's a special day, Josiah."

"We ain't going to the moat-fillin' tournament."

She made no response, merely hefted a packed dinner pail in slender fingers. He could tell by the way its weight dragged against her shoulder that she'd filled it with a substantial meal. "Here's your supper, mister."

"My supper?" The sun slanted through the open cabin door, burnishing the soft wings of golden hair that framed her forehead. Her wide brown eyes sparkled with an excitement he hadn't seen since they'd first headed toward Kansas. Her vibrancy roused a yearning ache from within, something he knew he had to tamp down immediately. "You had no business packing my supper, missus. I told you we ain't going to celebrate with that no-account Geoffrey."

"Oh I knew you wouldn't want to go to the moat filling." She spoke lightly and swung the pail to rest at his feet. "But don't I pack you a supper most nights, mister? You are going back out to work in a few more hours of weed plowing before nightfall, aren't you?"

He couldn't keep the source of his pain to himself any longer. "You're planning to sneak over there the minute I'm back in the fields."

She lifted her chin, and there was an honest-to-God smirk tilting her lips, as if she welcomed his accusation. "What's so unusual about that? I've been doing it every day for the past week." She narrowed her eyes, and curved her lips with supreme satisfaction. "Sometimes I've been over there twice a day. As well you know, Josiah Wilcox, considering you've followed me each and every time I *sneak* over there . . . to see Geoffrey."

"No!" Something happened to his innards; he slumped in his chair, as if to protect himself from an invisible blow. "I watched every move you made. You ain't scarcely said ten words to that Geoffrey."

"Oh really? Then why do I continue to sneak over there, do you think?"

"You go to see the boy, like any woman missing her child. I watched you."

"Every minute?"

He'd never heard such coy amusement from his Rebecca; he jolted upright. "Yes, goddamn it, every minute."

"Well, then, I guess you're getting slack with your suspicions, Josiah." She turned toward her stove, and *sashayed,* there was no other description for it, over to its cast-iron hulk. She cast him a secretive glance over her shoulder. "I distinctly remember spending twenty minutes all by my lonesome with Geoffrey, where he gave me some very, um, personal specialized . . . instruction."

"He showed you how to tie some knots in a big hunk of rope!" Listening to his wife cast aspersions upon her own innocent behavior yanked him right out of his chair; it clattered behind him, as chairs had been doing all along for the troublemaker Geoffrey d'Arbanville. "There ain't nothing wrong with visiting your boy. Hell, I miss him myself. And knowing how to tie knots is a handy skill for a farm wife."

"Trying to convince *me*, Josiah, or trying to convince *yourself*?"

An awful feeling welled up inside him, a mixture of shame and dread and embarrassment. She was right; it seemed like two Josiah Wilcoxes wrestled within, one protesting her innocence, another screaming her guilt. The latter voice had won out for so many years that it had grown uncomfortably comfortable to doubt her, twisting every one of her innocent actions. He couldn't dare listen to that other voice, the one that urged him to trust her, because it would mean he'd been wrong, that he'd wasted far too many years of the heaven on Earth that he'd promised this suddenly confident woman.

"Goddamn it, Becky, you ain't sassed me so much in ten years as you have this past week."

"You'd best get used to it, then. It feels so good, I wish I'd started sassing you years ago."

She seemed determined to lure him into an argument. He couldn't indulge her, even though that long-stifled part of him urged him to roar out each and every one of the regrets he held deep inside. He pointed a threatening, albeit shaking, finger at her. "You stay in this house tonight, you hear? You ain't going nowhere. I swear I'll drag you right back if you even try."

She sent him a mocking smile, with her eyes half-closed, that made him want to scream. "We'll see who goes anywhere, mister."

He turned on his heel and stormed over to the door. He heard the soft scurry of her footsteps following. He took two steps onto the porch, and heard her give a little grunt, as if she'd tugged at something that offered more resistance than she'd expected.

A limp, heavy, dusty-smelling weight fell from the porch ceiling, harmlessly knocking him off his feet.

"What the *hell!*" He thrashed, succeeding only in entangling himself amidst strands of close-knotted twine. He kicked. He punched the air. The twine wound around his limbs. "It's a goddamn *net!*"

"Aha!" Rebecca crowed. She drew his surprised oof as she hurled herself atop him. She straddled his chest and pinned his heaving shoulders to the porch floor. "Try running away now, Josiah."

He bucked his weight a few times without accomplishing much of anything. Rebecca clung with all the skill of a broncobuster, grinning all the while as if enjoying herself immensely while he exhausted his strength.

"What in tarnation do you think you're doing, woman? And where the hell did you get this net?"

"Geoffrey showed me how to make it. I tied every single knot myself. Now, you just stop blaspheming, and give up struggling, too, Josiah. It'll just tighten up on you if you don't lay still."

He glared at her, gulping some air into his spent lungs while she sat on him, looking as comfortable and contented as if she rocked on her porch chair.

"I know how to fix things between us now, Josiah."

"Fix what? There ain't nothing wrong."

"Josiah." She treated him to a stare filled with sad reproach, and he could feel himself blushing, could feel the two arguing voices inside him fighting for mastery. She poked a finger into the muscles banding his heart;

he fancied she skewered the mean-spirited voice upon the tip of her fingernail. "Geoffrey said you have a jealous demon lodged inside you, Josiah Wilcox. He told me that this special net would let the demon escape, while it trapped you inside. People use nets all the time where he comes from, to get rid of witches and suchlike."

His pride churned, to think that she'd discussed their marital discord with a stranger. "Geoffrey, Geoffrey, Geoffrey. Netting witches and demons. Sounds like everything he says—like a pack of superstitious nonsense that sensible folks stopped believing a thousand years ago."

"Maybe you're right. It sure seems like a thousand years since we did anything like this." She bent, parted the knotted twine covering his face, and planted a light kiss on his lips.

Such an innocent kiss; real married folks would bestow one just like it without thinking, to greet the morning, to mark the end of a meal. Rebecca's kiss sizzled through Josiah like a bolt of lightning, leaving him quaking and excruciatingly conscious of her warm weight pressing so intimately against his belly, her strong legs gripping his sides, her sun-scented hair falling in a silken skein against his cheek.

"So tell me what you have to say about that, mister."

Astonishingly enough, he found himself spouting out the very words he'd struggled so long to contain. "I want to hold you. I've wanted to touch you for so long, and look—I still can't do it." He made an ineffectual struggle against the net, which bound his arms physically; for too many years, his arms had been bound mentally, and he was suddenly possessed of the need to break free. "I don't know if I can do this, Becky."

"You can. You can." She whispered the phrase again and again as she peeled the net away, planting kisses in its wake, setting him free inch by inch until she lay flat on top of him and his arms encircled her in an embrace he would never have even dared himself to dream. "We got rid of that demon, Josiah. We did it."

He shuddered, pleasure and pain and a long-dormant hope shaking him in equal measures. And maybe crazy Geoffrey's nonsensical superstitions were proving true—Josiah felt remarkably clearheaded, in control of the swirling emotions that usually clouded his thoughts.

He loved his wife with an all-consuming intensity that had nearly destroyed them both. Becky stared into his eyes, her own expression awash with the same yearning and fears that he felt. Now more than ever, when it looked like they might have some small chance, he had to admit the truth.

"I don't deserve you, Becky. In my heart, I'll never be good enough for you."

"Josiah, no—"

"Let me finish. Please." He drew a quivering breath. "There's nothing in this world that can ever change my mind about that. So what I'm saying is, right now, we might've gotten rid of that demon temporarily. But he'll be back, Becky, he'll be back. I won't want to do it, but I'll suspicion something, or you'll say something completely innocent and I'll fly into a jealous fit. I'll cause you a power of hurt and pain, and I won't be able to stop myself. I just know it."

Tears brimmed in her eyes, maybe in his, too, because she touched his face with a gentle finger, and it came up wet.

"You won't always have a special net, either, to keep me behind while that jealous demon slinks away."

"But I'll have these." She wrapped her arms around his shoulders, rested her cheek against his. "Maybe when that old demon rears his head, I'll just hang on tight and hope you'll stay here, with me."

"You'd . . . you'd be willing to put up with my nonsense?"

"Long as you admit every once in a while that it *is* nonsense—and long as you don't complain about getting sassed when you deserve it."

A funny noise came from his throat. It took a minute for him to recognize his own laughter, it'd been so long since he'd made a joyful sound. It'd been so long since he'd done many of the things that gave pleasure to ordinary human beings. He'd have to make a point of doing just that, on those occasions when the demon deserted him and left him in control of his senses. He made a stab at trying.

"You want to go to that moat fillin', Becky? I swear I might even be able to be polite to that Geoffrey today, considering."

She eased away from him, leaving him bereft and aching to draw her back, but she slanted a look along his lean frame that suddenly made her withdrawal endurable. "You know, Josiah, it strikes me that our boy won't be home tonight."

"We'll fetch him right off, if that's what you want." He spoke around the dryness in his throat.

"Oh, I want him back, all right, but he'd purely hate it if we came after him now. The way Robbie tells me, there's some kind of secret ceremony going to tie up the menfolk all night after the tournament."

"The whole town will be at Geoffrey's all night?"

"Um hum."

"I never did like crowds."

"Maybe that's why we all suffer so when that demon's rampaging inside you."

Someone listening in might have thought they were

bantering. Josiah studied the seriousness in his wife's expression, and though the years hadn't granted them much intimacy, he could sense her trepidation despite her brave assurances. He sat up and took her hands within his, holding them tight so that their mutual trembling stilled. "I'll try to keep him . . . I'll try to keep *myself* under control, Becky."

"It's a beginning." She smiled, and disengaged one hand to brush her thumb over his lips. "But you can start controlling yourself tomorrow, husband. I think I'd like to become acquainted with your wild side tonight."

Geoffrey watched the roistering townsfolk greet Juliette's tardy arrival with joyous abandon. Tired boys stood taller, hefting their mock spears with little skill but ferocious pride. Dust-grimed men gestured toward the newly reared sod keep, their teeth flashing white as satisfaction in their accomplishment coaxed grins from faces creased with exhaustion. The women fluttered, waving tempting morsels of their feasting fare beneath Juliette's nose, seeking her approval. Juliette walked amongst them and smiled; nodding, she graciously acknowledged every visual and physical offering with a noble dignity any highborn lady might envy.

Realization smote Geoffrey with such force that he staggered, as if Drogo FitzBaldric's sword hilt had descended to bash the knowledge into his thick head. Juliette Walburn was lady of this place, its life force bound to her own, its demeanor reflecting her own brave spirit and fierce determination. Tearing her away from the town, as he yearned to do, would be akin to ripping the heart from Walburn Ford—providing Juliette herself could survive the amputation.

It might have begun with her holding fast to her husband's deathbed rantings. But it was her own stubborn pride that had prevailed, carrying them all through the lean times he'd been told about; it was Juliette's unfailing optimism that had helped them weather a host of scourges biblical peoples might have quailed before. He couldn't help wonder, as he watched her move among her people, whether Juliette's long-dead husband could have succeeded half so well as she in inspiring this motley collection of dirt-poor, ill-equipped homesteaders to carve a thriving community from such an obstacle-ridden wilderness.

She had told him, time and again, that she was content with things as they were.

Every knight dreamed that such a lady might grace his hall, guard after his wealth whilst he tended to business, mourn him upon his death. Small wonder that he had been drawn to her from the first, that he found himself powerless to turn away from her now, despite the inner voice that mocked him, taunted him, dared him to measure his scanty offerings against what she possessed.

What did he have to offer? An admittedly risky foray back through time. Love and a strong sword arm, nothing more. No manor, no wealth, set against the respect and independence she had wrought here with her own indomitable spirit.

He could not ask it of her, not if he loved her.

"Geoffrey." She came to him at last, although several young ones hovered near, obviously waiting for her attention. Firelight flickered behind her, casting a rosy glow about her well-shaped head and slender form. She had gathered her hair into a loose ball at the back of her neck, an austere style that nonetheless suited her fine-boned features. She smiled, but he could not find it within himself to send her one in return.

"Geoffrey?" He heard her puzzlement, but still he could not respond. Her smile took the pasted-on quality of a noblewoman charged with judging the tourney attire of an entire contingent of knights when all in the stands knew she must needs grant the award to her overlord.

"You seem somewhat fatigued, my la . . . Miss Jay."

Her smile stretched wider, but lost some of its honesty for its increase. "You must be the tired one. Even though I . . . haven't been present, I hear you've been working without sleep for days on end."

"Aye. Work has been my refuge these past lonely nights."

"Mine, too."

Her lips moved to speak again, but the waiting children interrupted her. "Miss Jay! Come see what we've done." She sent them an encouraging smile, and lifted one finger to indicate it would be but a short wait until she joined them.

"Geoffrey, something's wrong, isn't it?"

She whispered, but he heard her clearly over the clamoring crowd. Something primitive, possessive, stirred inside him, remembering the last time her whisper had caressed his ear, the last time her attention had been devoted to him alone. Oh yes, something was indeed wrong, and he had been a blind man not to see it before. He curled his fists, lest he indulge his desire to free her hair of its loose bond and set things to rights.

"Nay, Miss Jay. I would say that for the first time matters have presented themselves to me in their true light."

Her confusion manifested itself with trembling lips, a pale cast to her sun-kissed skin. "Please don't talk this way. I wanted to tell you . . . I want matters between us to stay just as they are."

" 'Tis too late, Juliette. 'Twas ever too late for us."

He'd dealt many a deathblow in his day, and sometimes regretted doing so. But never had his heart felt so skewered as it did now, witnessing the blanching of Juliette's features as her demeanor shifted from joy to despair.

"Geoffrey, listen to me." She shot him a tremulous smile, one that would have made him call back his hurtful words, if he hadn't loved her so. "Some of the things you've told me started to make a strange kind of sense. I asked Professor Burns to check his history books when he went back to Harvard, to see whether he could prove your story. He promised to send a letter within a couple of weeks. I should be hearing from him any time now."

Moments ago, before realizing he could not take her away with him, he might have reveled in knowing his claims would all be proven. Now, it would be easy to twist her innocent action to suit his purposes, to pretend it provoked a bitter rage that only he knew stemmed from inner pain. There were times, it seemed, when the defeat of a man's deepest desires outweighed his sense of fair play.

"You stand looking at me for all the world as if expecting I would take pleasure in this insult. I would rather you had called me a liar straight out than stand there admitting you have charged another with verifying my claims."

"Geoffrey?"

He thought he might relent, were she to whisper his name once more. He strived to gather even more hurtful words, hoping to goad her into anger of her own so she could look back someday and remember she had stood strong against his irrational behavior. He could not bear hurting her without granting her some pride.

"I see how it is with you. You will ever doubt me but take as God's own truth the writings of a stranger who has not even dedicated himself to the churchly life of a monk."

Uncertainty dawned in her eyes, coupled with the red flush of embarrassment. "No! I mean, yes, I will believe Professor Burns. I know he's not a monk, but don't you see, he's a scholar. He can prove what you say."

"By thumbing through books any enemy of mine could have written? You are forgetting that I know something of scribes. Despite their pious demeanors, their work often smacks of bribery and favoritism, and their parchments can be scraped clean and written afresh should a new lord so demand." A sudden sense of inadequacy gripped him. He had knighted, crusaded, protected his liege, and honored his word—nothing so magnificent that it would deserve chronicling. There might well be no scribbling for the professor to find.

But he could not voice this inner dread, and Juliette's countenance took on a stony cast that told him he'd succeeded in strengthening her mind against him. A victory he would take no pleasure in having achieved.

"Everytime I'm with you, you try convincing me you've come from the past. And now that I found the means to prove it, you turn it against me."

He felt suddenly weary, as if the past week and more of hard labor at last drew its toll from his bones. "To what end do you seek this knowledge, Juliette? I mean to find a chasm to traverse, regardless of what your professor learns from his dusty writings. Nothing can hold me here, no matter the pleasant diversions you have granted me. It matters naught that you have finally decided to grant me some small bit of your faith."

She bent her head, but not before he'd seen the

shimmer of tears filling her eyes. "You've done so much, rallying the men, training the boys, joking with the women until they're all half in love with you, even building a house."

"I would not have done so. I would have been gone long ere this, if I had found the means for returning to my own . . . place. But then Captain Chaney asked for my assistance and swore there was some urgency. And it pleased me at the time to help you in your own charge." Also his feelings for her anchored him to this place—but he would die ere admitting it to her now.

She nodded, inclined her head, accepting this gift that was as like to tear out his soul from him as lightly as she'd acknowledged young Robbie's ten-foot toss of his cottonwood spear. "I was hoping all this meant you were thinking of staying."

He thought of little else. "I cannot stay, Miss Jay."

She flinched everytime he called her by the harsh-sounding name, but he felt no satisfaction when it happened again at his deliberate use. She plucked at the folds of her skirt, and then caught the cloth up well off the ground to make walking easier. "I think I'll go home," she said.

"No." He stopped, all but breathless, because a leaden heaviness filled his heart space, robbing his lungs of air. He had never wavered so in his life. "Stay. Please stay."

"Do you want me to stay, Geoffrey? Or should I stay for them, to judge their contest and watch their tournament?"

For me, he longed to say. Instead Geoffrey studied his charges, who were milling about, bursting with excitement over displaying their new skills. Considering the constraints of time and material, he'd done his best. It was enough—if the ruffians were the drunken and disorganized cowards everyone said they were, and if these homesteaders fought with stout hearts.

"Stay for them. They are ill-equipped and but sketchily trained. Captain Chaney tells me there is no more time to spare in making them ready, so they must needs be filled with confidence over their ability. It would give them pause, and diminish their pleasure in their accomplishments, if you were to leave now. They seek always to impress you."

"And what about you, Geoffrey? What do you seek?"

He betrayed his heart's desire with a sweeping gesture, encompassing his sod keep, his acres, men he might call friends, the woman standing tearfully defiant before him. He betrayed himself, but with God's grace not so much that she would recognize that he could quest through eternity and find nothing that suited him better. To claim it he would have to abandon his honor and forsake all pride, and that he could never do.

He turned, so that the motion of his hand seemed no more than a waving toward the people awaiting their presence.

"I told you a scant heartbeat ago what means more to me than anything. A chasm."

"Geoffrey—"

He interrupted, not able to bear hearing the pain in her voice. He could think of only one verbal barb that might harden her heart even more.

"Perhaps 'tis fitting that you cannot believe finding a chasm is so important to me. It seems I must needs hurtle back in time where there are women aplenty who can believe anything I say without first seeking corroboration from a stranger."

19

"Laissez aller!"

Juliette didn't understand the words Geoffrey shouted, his voice booming like cannon shot over the prairie. His powerful form stood silhouetted against the red-streaked sky, his proud head tilted back, his long hair blowing in the breeze.

She knew that once he was gone, she would never again take pleasure in a glorious sunset. She would never watch the sun dip below the horizon without feeling something was missing.

"Laissez aller!" The air vibrated again with his cry.

"What does it mean?" Juliette asked Alma, dully amazed that she could speak as normally as though her heart hadn't been shattered.

"I think it means 'let it begin.' The menfolk seem to think so, anyway."

Let it begin. Odd, that such words should mark the end of Juliette's brief . . . flirtation.

And it had ended, there could be no doubt. Once she

had thought that a lifetime of practicality and responsibility had dissolved all the whimsy from her soul. But she'd overcome her own inner resistance, and begun to believe in him, only to have him lash out at her in a way that proved he didn't care for her at all. A pleasant diversion, he'd called her, when she'd been ready to turn her back on everything important, for him.

"Everyone's having so much fun," Alma said, brimming with enthusiasm. "I never expected this kind of excitement when I came to Walburn Ford."

"Neither did anyone else, I'd wager."

Juliette set aside her painful thoughts. The sidelong glances sent her way, the nervous flushes she caught on her neighbors' faces, told her that Geoffrey had spoken the truth when he'd said her support was important to the townspeople. So she admired the skill of the men as they pummeled one another, and she judged the women's hastily sewn tunics, choosing Verdie Cutler's as the winner, to roars of approval. She applauded and cheered and pretended to revel in the merriment when all she wanted to do was return to her lonely bed, curl into a ball, and cry.

She wondered if she'd ever again look over the prairie's broad grassy expanse without hearing the echoes of cottonwood spears clashing against bucket helmets, the rowdy voices of her friends and neighbors raised in mock battle cries, the boisterous cheering and celebrating that forged a new impregnable foundation for Walburn Ford.

Geoffrey held himself apart from the competitions, an observer like herself. She found herself glancing his way more often than she liked. She didn't know what had come over her. A woman who had been all but scorned, who had exchanged tempestuous words with a man, shouldn't find herself surreptitiously studying the swell of his muscles, or comparing his taut fitness against that of other men. But she couldn't seem to stop looking, or regretting that he didn't take part in the games. Appalled, she realized she would have loved to watch him in action.

"Time for you ladies to leave," Robbie announced importantly when the contests were concluded and everyone had eaten their fill. "Us men have to conduct a knightly vigil."

A tide of objections greeted his news, although Juliette welcomed the chance to escape.

"'Twould be boring for you to stay on," Geoffrey said. His gaze flickered briefly over Juliette, and she knew that she'd never find a minute in his presence boring, although he seemed determined to convince them all. "We must all cleanse ourselves in the creek, since the moat is not yet filled. Then we will don our coats of arms and pray the night long, striving for the state of grace that will prepare us for knighthood."

Just like that, he changed the objections to approval. And not one of the careworn homesteaders laughed, or argued over the waste of time; nobody seemed at all opposed to carrying out the elaborate whims of a man who thought himself to be a time-traveling mercenary knight.

"I'm just purely curious about all this, from a teacher's standpoint, of course," Alma whispered as they joined the other women heading home. "What do you say, Miss Jay—do you want to sneak back later and watch?"

She couldn't imagine why Alma would think for a minute that the Widow Walburn would be interested in participating in what sounded like an episode that would appeal to giggling schoolgirls. She couldn't imagine why she would want to go back, when he'd made it so perfectly clear that he wanted no parts of her.

"Yes, I'll come back with you," said Juliette. "For . . . for education purposes, of course."

*   *   *

They met at the stable and stole across the still-dark prairie.

"We're probably breaking some kind of unwritten rule from his knightly code of honor," Juliette murmured.

"So what?" said Alma. "Nobody really believes it anyway."

It should have cheered her to know she wasn't the only one with a skeptical attitude. Instead she felt a sense of betrayal on Geoffrey's behalf. "Then why is everyone going along?"

"Well, it's no more ridiculous than having Captain Chaney parade them around and tell them they're bona fide militia. Our men are ignorant as day-old puppies when it comes to anything besides farming, and some of them aren't even very good at that. I think they would have gone along with anyone who took the trouble to show them a thing or two about fighting."

They paused well away from Geoffrey's house. Its unfinished doorway afforded them a view of the tableau within. Candles, dozens of candles, flickered from holders rammed into the walls. The men of Walburn Ford kneeled facing away from them, and it was evident that they'd been kneeling all night long. Some swayed with exhaustion, others arched with the bent shoulders marking them as farmers accustomed to hunching over a plow. Geoffrey knelt at the front of them all, his wide shoulders uncompromisingly straight, his head high, his hair a river of chestnut tamed into a queue curling down his back.

"Oh my." Alma's whisper sounded dismayed. "It looks kind of *holy*, doesn't it, Miss Jay?"

Juliette couldn't answer.

A slanting sun ray penetrated the doorway. It was as though the men had been waiting for this first sign of daybreak. A masculine murmur drifted through the air, drawing them closer. Even before she got close enough to decipher the words, Juliette knew it was Geoffrey who spoke; no other man's voice could rouse such tremors from within her.

"We beseech thee, O Lord, to bless these men with the right hand of thy majesty. That they may defend thy churches, widows, orphans, and all thy servants against the scourge of the pagans and blatherskite ruffians, that these men may be the terror and dread of other evildoers, and that they may be ever just in both attack and defense."

A ragged chorus of "amens" marked the end of his prayer.

He rose, betraying no trace of exhaustion despite his night-long vigil. Juliette cringed back, fearful that he might catch sight of her. But all his attention seemed riveted upon the solemn men kneeling before him.

"Had we enough spurs, they would be fastened now upon your heels. And could we boast a sufficient number of swords, we would brandish them about three times ere girding them on. Without such essential accoutrements, we must needs do the best we can with mine own spurs and sword."

The men rose and shuffled into a line that pressed close, with only Geoffrey's exceptional height letting her keep him within view. She caught the flash of candle-light against metal as he raised his sword and brought it down smartly upon Bean Tyler's right shoulder.

"Be thou a knight, Sir Bean," Geoffrey intoned. "And swear to protect and defend Walburn Ford to your dying breath."

"Er, I do." Bean's proud response echoed over the prairie.

"Oh my," Alma said again, very faintly.

Each man who earned a wallop of the sword managed to stand taller, and strode away from Geoffrey with a purposeful determination that boded ill for any border ruffian who dared attempt attacking the town. Juliette's heart swelled, with pride, with gratitude, with regret, humbled before the dignified majesty of this simple ceremony, the ancient sacred words so inextricably wound through the common terms of the day.

Geoffrey's gaze skipped away from the homesteader he was dubbing a knight and met hers across the distance.

She felt his power jolt through her like lightning surging through a metal wire. A madman? Maybe so. Only someone with his otherworldly strength of will could imbue a whole town with a sense of community and confidence that would assure its survival long after they all were gone.

Only a madman would have braved the thick layers of resignation and practicality with which she had wrapped her heart and dared her to love him in return.

And she did. Oh God, she did. The man she loved wouldn't have hardened his heart against her unless he thought he had good reason. She couldn't let him walk out of her life without finding out why.

His gaze flicked away from her. She didn't know if it was the sudden withdrawal from their tenuous connection or the weighty realization of her love for him that sent her sinking to her knees, her hands clutched in an attitude of prayer.

"*L'ordene de chevalerie.*" His thunderous announcement pierced the hushed stillness as he lifted his sword high in benediction, and the men knelt once more. "A knight should never give false judgment."

"Amen."

"Your word of honor is your most solemn oath."

"Amen."

"A knight's word, once given, can never be retracted unless his liege absolve him from such oaths."

"Amen."

Without her being conscious of a shift in his position, she found him staring straight at her. "A knight must prefer death to shame."

"Amen."

"Arise, fellow knights, and shoulder your responsibilities, knowing the grace of God will lend strength to your sword arms."

The men nodded to Alma and her as they filed past, some looking abashed at the realization they had witnessed the ceremony, others grinning with a somewhat stunned delight. Juliette had no idea as to what expression had fixed itself to her own features, but she must have projected some sense of normalcy, for none of them questioned her presence or the state of her mind.

Alma rose without comment when Bean Tyler approached and linked her arm with his as he paraded them both away from Geoffrey's soddie.

It seemed to Juliette that she waited an eternity before she felt a hint of coolness brush her skin where Geoffrey's shadow shaded her from the rising sun.

"I almost didn't come," she said. "I don't know if I did the right thing."

"Nor do I, Juliette. I only know that I am not strong enough to continue pretending that your presence does not fill me with delight."

She almost couldn't speak. Joy suffused her, tempered by a wistful awareness of the truth. "Something happened to change you. I've hurt you by not completely believing—"

"Juliette, not even an angel come to earth could absorb my cruel jibes with saintly acceptance. Will you accept that I hurled hurtful words at you with naught but good intent, and forgive me?"

He extended his hand to her and she stared at it for long minutes, afraid that once she enmeshed her fingers with his she would never let him go. And yet she had to let him go, to pursue his quest. Terror, pure and lethal, lanced through her, giving her a glimpse of the pain she would feel when he left her for good. Still, she slipped her hand into his.

His fingers closed around hers, banishing the terror by lending his warm steady pulse to strengthen hers. She thought he would pull her up to stand next to him, but he crouched beside her, resting their joined hands atop his knee. "What becomes of us now, Juliette?" His words confirmed that there could be no future for the two of them.

"I don't know." She used her free hand to trace the ropy veins marking the back of his hand, letting her finger drift higher to stroke gently over the barely perceptible mark at his hairline, where he'd been wounded. All healed. There was no reason to believe he suffered any lingering effects. "I heard what you told those men. *L'ordene de chevalerie.* You really believe it, don't you, all that stuff about words of honor and oaths."

"'Tis my life, and ever shall be."

"And so you must go."

"I must go."

"Without me."

"Without you."

As always, the husky timbre of his voice vibrated deep within her, but this time there was an edge of resigned sorrow that found a matching well within her, and it pooled deep until she felt she might drown in it.

"Can you understand that it frightens me beyond speech to think of you leaping into a chasm with good intentions but ending up dead? That I find myself sinfully jealous and resentful of an oath you might or might not have made? That I . . . that I love you, Geoffrey, but I'm frightened, so very frightened, because once you jump over a cliff, it won't be playacting anymore."

"I can understand. And that is part of why I cannot ask you to come with me."

It could not be the shine of tears glistening in his eyes; he believed himself a knight, and she knew with bone-deep certainty that a knight would never cry. Even so, his tone carried an extra layer of huskiness.

"Reality, Juliette. We have failed to hold it at bay. Do you think we might pretend for just a little longer? One more day. Leave off worrying over whatever might happen on the morrow and believe me when I say that I love you right now."

She seized on the chance to cling tight to him, to prolong the magic. "Yes. Please. One more day."

His eyelids fluttered down, as if he sought to shield his emotions from her. His lashes spiked low, pointing out dark bruiselike half circles of exhaustion beneath his eyes. But he pulled her into his arms and lifted them both with one easy fluid motion, cradling her hard against his chest. She rested her hand against his shoulder for support, reveling in the play of his muscles beneath her skin, sensing no tiredness in him whatsoever as he splashed through the puddles of his damp moat and carried her into the new house he meant to leave at the first opportunity.

They had told him that folks in Kansas called a straw-stuffed pallet a prairie feather mattress. It might have been an oaken plank or a sultan's silken divan for all Geoffrey cared at this moment.

"Maybe you should rest first," Juliette whispered a protest as he set her down atop the bedding. "You must be worn out, especially after the vigil last night."

"I would not have you challenge my stamina just now, Juliette."

He could not take the time to express the bittersweet craving that gripped him. It was more than just knowing he would soon leave her. A voiceless foreboding whispered in his mind that he must claim her now, now, that all of the hundreds of years his life had spanned narrowed into this one precious day. They would have no more.

He meant to be gentle, meant to hold his heart aloof, but once his flesh melded with hers all such vows deserted him like tail-tucked hounds fleeing before a slavering boar. "*Mine.*" He said it aloud, his utterance a feral proprietary growl, claiming her, claiming this place, this time, for this one day. And she maddened him into further insensibility, lifting her slim hips to meet his every thrust, clutching at his shoulders and taunting his nipples with her own when he sought to hold himself above her and spare her his weight.

"You do love me today, Geoffrey."

"I will love you for longer than you can believe, my lady."

"Ah!" Her gasp of pleasure at the endearment, more rapturous than his honest declaration merited, robbed him of still more control. He plunged into her again and again and again until her shuddering spasms against his belly prompted his own release and his cries joined hers, circling endlessly along the round walls of his sod keep.

And once their heartbeats subsided he began it all afresh, lest she raise questions once more over his stamina.

And then he did it again, taking longer than any

dream could ever last, making sure the memory of it
would endure through eternity.

After all, if a man is to be granted only one perfect
day in his life, he must needs make the most of it.

"Perfect timing," Juliette whispered, much later, when
the raucous clanging of a dinner bell drifted over the
prairie. She wondered if whoever it was announcing
their mealtime might have a bite or two to spare.
Actually it sounded like her own dinner gong, but as
she was here and had been engaged in decidedly non-
culinary activities all morning long, that didn't seem
possible. She hid her contented yawn and the rumblings of her neglected stomach with a head-to-toe
stretch. Amazing that these muscles of hers could tense
like steel and melt like warm taffy and then settle back
into their normal function with no outward sign that
they'd been so thoroughly, delightfully tested.

Clang. Clang. Clang.

Her movements, or the dinner gong, or both, woke
Geoffrey. She forgot to breathe momentarily when his
arms tightened around her and he swept his gaze along
her naked length before coming to rest upon her face.
His eyes glittered through the chestnut forest of his
lashes, potent, supremely male, possessive, setting her
heart hammering. Like a dinner bell.

Clang. Clang. Clang.

And then his hold upon her altered, his expression
froze, his body hardened in a way alien to the tensile
tautness she'd become so accustomed to, so addicted
to, over the past hours.

"God's blood—'tis perfect timing indeed. It has
begun already. I will have the chance to see it through."

He bounded from the bed and had his britches on,

his sword gripped in his hand, before she could make a protest. He shoved his passion-tangled hair behind his neck with an impatient gesture, and the movement caused his muscles to ripple and flex, throwing into excruciating detail the myriad scars marring his masculine perfection. Barefoot, with only a worn pair of homespun trousers covering his vulnerable skin, he projected such an aura of awesome devastating intent that she found herself cringing away from the human fighting machine that he'd become.

"Geoffrey?"

He cast her a hooded stare that held no hint of recognition, no acknowledgement of the hours they'd just spent wrapped in each other's arms.

"'Tis Chaney's signal. The border ruffians are on their way and we must needs hurry to arrange an ambush." For a too-brief moment, *her* Geoffrey returned, grinning ruefully. "'Twould seem they are descended straight from Drogo FitzBaldric. So skilled are they at turning up when I least want to face them, they might have spent the past six centuries planning this intrusion."

Her fingers trembled against the light blanket she held over her breasts.

"Go into town at once, Juliette. Gather the women and children and bring them back here. 'Tis the best fortified and most easily defended of all the buildings in town."

"You can't fight!"

He lifted his jaw with a scornful wordless repudiation of her protest, and she struggled to explain. She gestured toward the space next to her on the rumpled bed, hot with embarrassment, partly over speaking of such matters out loud, but mostly because he meant to fight on her behalf, knowing her faith in him was less than rock solid.

"You've barely slept. And this isn't your fight, Geoffrey. You've done enough."

"I will finish what I started. I am certain Angus Ōg sent me here for this very purpose. Now, do not tarry. Lives may depend on how quickly you bring them all to safety." He snatched his shirt from the floor and shrugged it on as he strode to the doorway.

"No!" He couldn't go off to fight what should be her battle, not just like that, leaving her naked and warm from his loving. She knew then that the doubts plaguing her were far more lethal to her own confidence than they were to his.

"Geoffrey—what if . . . what if you don't come back?"

If she possessed the artistic skill of a Michelangelo, she couldn't capture the fleeting regret, the soft longing, the responsible acceptance that settled over his features as he paused, looking back at her over his shoulder.

"Juliette, the hour looms when I must be gone. But for now, I would have you remember your promise."

"My promise?"

"You promised to believe in me. If only for today."

20

Arion snorted and issued a few bone-jarring bucks. Geoffrey reined him in, sensing the horse's trepidation, and understanding it well.

He bent low in the saddle to disguise the fact that he meant to speak to his steed—should these people share Juliette's lack of faith in his abilities, they might take to their heels rather than follow him into battle.

"Men, like any others," he whispered.

Arion's ear flicked, as if to point out that these men wore no armor, and though outwardly brave, the random nervous twitch betrayed a tentative demeanor.

"Boys, like squires in our own day."

Arion pawed equine displeasure, all but enumerating the youths' deficiencies in size and experience.

"Admittedly, those few mules are not the equal of a fine destrier like you, but there are weapons . . ."

Here Geoffrey trailed away, dismayed at the crude protection promised by buffalo-hide shields, rough-hewn spears. Difficult to cast such in a good light, even to a horse.

"Native weapons. Not to mention four wondrous guns."

Arion stretched his neck and shook it wildly, sending his mane flying, his reins jingling, as the stallion neighed all the screaming frustration Geoffrey knew he couldn't utter himself.

"Let us at 'em!" One voice, and then another, took up the shout, and sent Geoffrey sitting upright with new heart. Confidence, he knew, could win the day against a superior enemy, so he must needs guard against revealing any doubt in his men's presence.

"Men, like any others," he repeated, this time for the benefit of his own ears. The unknown border ruffians they faced might be no better equipped, no better prepared. Farmers fighting farmers. But these defenders of Walburn Ford would battle knowing their wives and children and lands awaited the victors. So would he fight, considering that for this one day, everything he wanted belonged to him.

"Ha!" he shouted, making a rude gesture he'd learned from the Italians toward the far-off still-unseen enemy, and feeling better for doing it.

He wheeled Arion about only to yank him to a plunging halt when he found Juliette standing there, with the town's innocents clustered about her. With soft dust-choked movements, the women and children surrounded him.

"We're ready to go to your house, Geoffrey," Juliette said.

Many of them carried foodstuffs, some no doubt left over from the previous night's feasting, when all the jousting and listing had seemed little more than sport. The women's eyes glittered with tears held stoically unshed. Tight-pursed mouths could not disguise their trembling fear for their men and half-grown boys, but their shoulders were squared with faith and determination.

All in all, well worth fighting for.

Juliette studied him; there could be no other word for the careful scrutiny she accorded him from boots to pendant, as if she meant to burn his every line and feature upon her memory. These silent visual leave-takings had ever marked the prebattle separation between knight and lady. Geoffrey had never thought to find himself blessed by such, and common sense scolded him to cease his unseemly reveling in it now. This separation would be a trifling time spent apart, considering that he meant to leave for good on the morrow.

"You're not wearing your armor," Juliette said.

"Yon Robbie carries my helm."

Understanding kindled in her expression. "You won't wear your body armor because the other men don't have any."

No sense in embellishing upon God's truth. He sought to divert her to more important matters. "Should the children grow restless, hold them within the walls of the keep."

"Don't you worry none about that, Geoffrey." Mrs. Abbott reached into her pocket and flapped a much-handled missive beneath his nose. "I'll keep them entertained by reading them this here letter from my son Herman in the Army Corps of Topographical Engineers. Talks about camels and such wonders as you can't imagine. And he drew a map. Everyone knows kids just gobble up stuff like maps." Her aged face sagged; her chin quivered as she looked out over the assembled men. "I've been meaning to read it to all of you."

"You may read it to us all when we return from this day's work. For myself, I would be particularly interested in viewing your son's map ere you feed it to a young goat." Mrs. Abbott first smiled, then frowned, bedazzled as many women are by a knight's interest, but he had no more time to bestow upon her. "Now, get you all to safety."

They backed away and with the herding instinct all women seemed to possess gathered their roving children into a protective huddle as they struck out across the prairie. He watched for longer than he could spare, his attention riveted upon one slim, hip-swaying, blue-clad form, wishing with all his heart that their final words could have concerned other than the welfare of this town; wishing, too, that her proper ugly bonnet didn't conceal the hair he could remember entwining about his limbs. Arion's annoyed snort shook him from his unseemly reverie, and Geoffrey gave him a grateful pat on the neck. Better that he concentrate upon making mayhem than making love.

"*Laissez aller,*" he muttered, turning Arion about.

"Geoffrey!" Juliette halted him with but one calling of his name, though she gasped it again and again as she ran back to him. And when she reached his side, he saw how his fleeting wish had been indulged. Her bonnet had slipped from her head and curling tendrils had escaped her careful combing. She gazed up at him, breathless as he'd left her time and again throught their morning lovemaking, but with a half-embarrassed pleading that was new.

"I . . . I don't know much about knights." She paused, her breath still eluding her. "Isn't there something, though, about ladies giving something when their men—when their *knights*—go into battle?"

"You would give me your favor to wear, my lady?"

"Yes, I would, Sir Geoffrey."

God's blood, when would the gods cease testing his honor? Incapable of speaking around the fullness welling up in his throat, he released his lance from Arion's saddle. There should have been hornsmen blaring a fanfare, giggling ladies showering them with rose blossoms, as he held his lance toward her, tip first.

She stared at it with blank incomprehension.

He found his voice. "A bit of cloth from your gown, Juliette. Or a flower that you are particularly fond of carrying. Something that will immediately call you to mind when I see your favor gracing my weapon." As if he needed any provocation.

She tested his forbearance by frantically patting herself from neck to waist, an exercise he urgently ached to help her accomplish. She sighed with relief when her hands settled over her belt, which she untied with nimble fingers. He held the spear steady while she tied it in a somewhat festive bow that would have been hooted down by his fellow knights, had they seen it. No matter. It seemed the mere act of her affixing the belt marked his battle shaft as well as his man shaft as belonging to her, at least for this day, and he couldn't suppress his delight at the notion.

"You'd better come back to me," she said as she stepped away. She scowled at the ground, as if hoping to see sprouting there some reason for her declaration. "I . . . I need that belt."

"Mmm." He frowned, pretending concentration. "I swear to return your belt. Is that the only reason you would welcome my return?"

"Oh no, though that is quite important." She glanced away, all atremble, and he loved her stammering shyness. "Mrs. Abbott would hound us all to death if you broke your promise to listen to her read that letter from her son Herman."

"Aha. A tiresome situation to be avoided at all costs. Now I understand why you want me to return, to deflect some of the boredom."

"Geoffrey." She almost visibly groped for words, and all semblance of lighthearted bantering faded. "How do ladies endure sending their knights off to battle?"

"They trust us, Juliette. Our abilities, and our promises to return."

"But you cannot always promise to return."

"Nay. On those occasions when a knight senses he will not see his lady again, he merely leaves without making any promises at all."

She sent him a wobbly smile and touched his hand where it gripped the spear. She looked up at the sun and it seemed that its golden warmth flowed through her into him, that it melted her lighthearted veneer to reveal the true woman lying within.

It seemed the gods were not yet through having their sport with him.

"There are a lot of hours left in this day, Geoffrey," she said. "To use your turn of phrase, I would have you promise to hurry home."

He let his spear slip through his hand until his skin rested against her favor. "I will see you again ere the night is flown, my lady."

Josiah hadn't anticipated that Robbie would gain so much confidence during their brief time apart, or that he would turn on him with so much pent-up fury.

"You can't fight with us. You didn't come to the training lessons, and you didn't help Geoffrey build his keep." Robbie fixed his gaze upon Josiah's yellow coat of arms and stiffened with rigid rage. "I can't believe Ma made you that tunic and helmet. You don't have the right to wear them."

"I know. I'm sorry."

Robbie's startled gasp blended into the trudging sound

their feet made as they headed toward the small growth
of trees where Captain Chaney had suggested they lay an
ambush. Josiah pounced at the opportunity to explain.

"I'm sorry for so many things, Robbie. Your ma and
me—well, we're going to try to make things better for
the three of us. I guess my being here now is my way of
getting started. I talked it over with Geoffrey, and he
agreed to give me a chance. Would you take a chance,
too . . . son?"

He nearly staggered away from the stark hope flooding Robbie's face. He clasped the boy's shoulder for
reassurance and found it lent him support, as well, this
gentle physical touch between father and son.

"Sometimes you're just so *mean,* 'specially to Ma,"
Robbie whispered, once again the confused little boy.
"Are you gonna stop bein' so mean?"

"I'm going to try," Josiah whispered back. "Trouble
is, I got this jealous demon living in my head. Just ask
Geoffrey. I'm going to have a hell of a time beating it
down."

"Huh." Robbie frowned with youthful concentration. He darted Josiah a fearful look, but more as
though afraid of Josiah's reaction than Josiah's presence. "Geoffrey taught me a lot about fighting. Maybe I
can help you whup it."

"Maybe you can." Josiah might have said more, but a
sudden blinding pain cracked him in the forehead. He
touched the source of the stinging, and swallowed hard
to avoid screaming in front of the boy when he drew
away his hand, covered with his own blood. Muffled
laughter came from the trees.

Someone, it seemed, had beat them to the ambush.

"Some shit head border ruffian hit my pa with a
rock!" Robbie shrieked. "We're bein' attacked—and
there's Injuns with them!"

"Rocks and engines?" Geoffrey pounded toward them, bent so low over his mount's neck that it was hard to differentiate man from horse. Woozily, Josiah thought the odd sounds Geoffrey made might be chokes of rage, until he got close enough and Josiah could see d'Arbanville was laughing. *Laughing*, while stones and arrows and an occasional bullet whizzed over their heads.

"Don your helms, men! Young Robbie, you wear mine. If these shit head ruffians seek to dent heads with these cowards' weapons, 'twill not be our skulls that bear the wounds."

The man could lead a battle, Josiah noted with the part of his mind that wasn't frantic to protect his son. Although Geoffrey moved among them, exhorting them to assume their fearsome countenances, to utter their terrifying sounds, he also surreptitiously dispatched those owning guns to provide cover.

His horse screamed once, when an arrow grazed its foreleg, and then Geoffrey leaned low, deflecting another barrage of arrows with his shield as easily as if he could see each arrow's approach. He led the charge while the rest of them surged toward the ruffians. Geoffrey's lance, flying true, buried itself up to its peculiar ribbon in the chest of a shotgun-aiming ruffian who dared abandon the sparse protection of the trees. Geoffrey's sword, swinging with practiced might, lopped the head from a luckless ruffian who dared risk a shot at closer range, and he never gave the decapitated ruffian a second look. His deadly, determined precision drew cries of fear, and a visible retreat by a significant number of the attackers.

Geoffrey swiveled in his saddle, and brandished his sword, apparently heedless of the bullet crease in his shoulder that sent blood trickling to his elbow.

"Swarm, knights!" he called. "This enemy's bravery is nonexistent, and their weapons are useless close to."

Josiah pulled his bucket over his head and joined his neighbors as they swarmed, for the glory of Walburn Ford.

A woman didn't need to watch a clock to note the passage of hours. One by one the women surrounding Juliette fell silent, the children stopped bickering and playing, until nothing was heard except for Mrs. Abbott's droning voice, endlessly rereading her son Herman's letter. She might have been reciting the entire Constitution of the United States for all the attention Juliette paid to her words.

She couldn't pay any heed to anything, not with dread clogging her mind and her heart pounding an ominous warning. But her sense of foreboding had little to do with the honest trepidation that marked the other women's expressions. *They* had sent their men off with love and trust acknowledged between them. *She* had sent Geoffrey away exhausted from hours of illicit lovemaking, with her confession of not believing completely in his story no doubt still ringing in his ears. She wished with all her heart that she'd never told him, especially since she longed to believe him with every ounce of her being.

Someone squeezed her shoulder, and with her skirts quietly rustling, Rebecca Wilcox settled down next to her.

"Don't worry, Miss Jay. He'll bring them all back."

"I know." She pressed back against the sod wall, taking unwarranted comfort in its solidity when it truly served as a reminder of Geoffrey's outrageous claims. Who'd ever heard of building a round house surrounded by a moat? Then again, who'd ever heard of convincing a bunch of homesteaders that they were knights? And yet he'd built his house and trained the men, and leaning against his wall, Juliette felt unutterably certain that they'd all be trooping back home soon, tired and triumphant. "I was happy to see Josiah join the other men, Becky. I didn't think he approved of . . . well, of all these goings-on."

"He didn't." A secretive smile tugged at Rebecca's lips. "I convinced him."

Juliette couldn't prevent her brows from lifting, and Rebecca giggled, the thrilled giddy sound of a woman sharing the secret that she'd fallen in love.

"I know Josiah and I haven't been the best of neighbors. I don't know if you realized we were having serious problems."

Juliette welcomed Rebecca's confidence; it felt familiar and comfortable, to shoulder the concerns of one of her townspeople. "I figured your marriage wasn't as happy as most."

Rebecca flushed with embarrassment. "Until just recently, I thought we were doing a fine job of hiding it. And then when you came to our house with Geoffrey, I saw how the two of you—" She clapped a hand over her mouth, flushing a deep red. "I'm sorry, Miss Jay. I'm sure you've worked things out."

Juliette shook her head. "No apologies necessary. Besides, you and Josiah are married. Geoffrey and I aren't, and never will be. There's too much . . . too many things separating us to ever work things out."

"I thought the same thing myself, just a couple of days ago." Rebecca found Juliette's hand and gave her a reassuring squeeze. "I was going to run off with Robbie, I swear I was, but Geoffrey convinced me to give Josiah one last chance. A leap of faith, he said."

"Oh, he's a great one for leaping," Juliette murmured.

"I can see where a woman might have a bit of trouble accepting some of Geoffrey's ideas. Maybe you need to make a little leap of faith, too."

Juliette disengaged her hand, suddenly uncomfortable with Rebecca's offer of friendship, now that she'd accompanied it with the same advice her own heart had been urging for days. "I'm glad you and Josiah have settled your differences. You can't compare trusting someone like Geoffrey to a . . . a regular person, like Josiah. You two believe in each other. You don't have a million doubts and crazy ideas swirling around in your heads."

"You're wrong, so wrong." Rebecca's eyes glittered with unshed tears. "Josiah's going to have to struggle constantly with believing in me, no matter how well or how often I prove that he can trust in me. And I'm going to have to do a lot of pretending and smoothing things over if I want us to succeed. I suspect we won't be successful half as often as I'd like."

"Will it be worth it?"

"I love him. And he loves me. If that's not worth fighting for, I purely can't see what is."

Nor could Juliette. Rebecca's brave acceptance and willingness to challenge her husband's faults showed her how she'd failed Geoffrey. With but the slightest effort, she could imagine herself and Geoffrey sharing the Wilcoxes' fate. She, Juliette, struggling but often failing to believe. Geoffrey holding steadfast against the blows to his pride, pretending it didn't matter. The heartbreak of their failures, but the sweet successes of days like this, when she set aside her doubts and he set aside his pain. Until the magical day when it didn't matter anymore. Yes, it would be worth it.

She had to tell him. And the chance presented itself

at once, almost as though his meddling Celtic god had once again arranged for him to be in the right place at the right time. A distant commotion announced the return of Walburn Ford's defenders. It roused the children from their lethargy, and they surged around the doorway, shouting descriptions of the approaching contingent until the adults gained their feet and crowded them all outside, running, running to welcome their men back home.

Juliette held back, craning her neck to see him, and felt a tremor of fear threaten to explode when she spotted Arion among the mules, riderless. Geoffrey was so tall—if he were walking, he would stand head and shoulders above the rest. She pressed trembling fingers over her lips to avoid screaming her anguish, and then nearly fainted with relief when the throng parted and she saw him striding alongside Arion.

His head was bent attentively toward a companion, which was why she hadn't seen him at first. He seemed, amazingly, to be engaged in serious conversation with an Indian, something no resident of Walburn Ford had ever managed to do.

She didn't call his name aloud, but it echoed joyously through her heart, and somehow he heard. His head snapped up and his gaze swung unerringly straight to where she stood. A smile of such radiance lit his face that she felt its glow bathe her across the distance, and then she was running, running to welcome her man back home.

21

"*It seems an eternity* since I enjoyed such grand sport!" Geoffrey exulted as she ran into his arms.

She wanted nothing more than to inspect him from head to toe, to ask a million questions about the skirmish that had left him so exhilarated. She didn't have a chance. He caught her against his chest and ravaged her with a kiss of such immoderate thoroughness that his Indian companion grunted a protest. And then he simply scooped her up, with one arm curving around her shoulders and beneath her knees, so that her thighs met her breasts and her bottom bumped against his hip.

Juliette had bedded him, tasted him, studied each line of his body until she knew it more thoroughly than she knew her own, but she had never realized the extent of Geoffrey's strength.

She knew she weighed more than a good-sized bale of hay, but he carried her as effortlessly as one might a single straw wisp. She wrapped both arms around his neck, telling herself it was the better to distribute her weight, but she gloried in the heat of his skin penetrating her sleeves, and the strong steady thud of his heartbeat pounding against her breast as they moved along with the crowd toward his soddie.

He seemed in fine fettle. Nonetheless she vowed to conduct a thorough inspection of his anatomy later, and to do her best to verify that all was in good working order.

The Indian said a few words and, after a slight pause, Geoffrey answered him. They spoke what she assumed must be the Indian's tongue. Its cadence struck harsher than the French words Geoffrey had once spoken to her, but sounded almost mystically musical.

Geoffrey tilted his head back and laughed.

It amazed her that he could act so carefree, as if he were well accustomed to riding out to battle and returning victorious. She felt the familiar pull, torn between wanting to believe everything he'd told her and knowing his claims were too outlandish to be true.

What about the leap of faith Rebecca had urged upon her? A nervous tremor skittered through her, telling her she wasn't quite ready to make such a leap. But she had promised, for this day, to put her doubts aside, and so she would match Geoffrey's lighthearted attitude. "What's so funny?"

She felt his cheek graze her hair and, she wasn't certain, but she thought he might have planted a light kiss on the top of her head.

" 'Tis not a matter for a lady's ears."

"How do you know what he's saying? The soldiers told us that it's impossible to learn to speak their language."

He sighed, as if deeply disappointed in her. "I have spent the better part of four hours in this man's company, Juliette. Do you not remember what I told you about my gift for learning tongues?"

"Handed straight from God." She hid her smile

against his shoulder when he tightened his grip about her, conveying approval.

"Aye. Though I must admit I am as yet unclear as to how this fellow is called. I shall ask him again." There occurred between Geoffrey and the Indian another rapid-fire exchange of clicking guttural sounds, followed by a half-muffled snort of laughter from Geoffrey.

"God's blood, but he owns such a fine wit, and yet cracks nary a smile. Mayhap 'tis as I think—he is called Limp-Waddling Duck. I know 'twould doom me to a permanently glum countenance did my father saddle me with such a name."

Juliette stole a peek at Limp-Waddling Duck, who did indeed stare forward with no emotion whatsoever. She had often wished for an opportunity to speak to an Indian, but even with her resolution to act lighthearted, the chance could have come at a better time. "He wasn't with you when you set out earlier today. Where did he come from, Geoffrey?"

"He is my prisoner, captured in the heat of battle. Now there is a thought—mayhap he hesitates to smile given his circumstances. But he knows I mean to ransom him. There seems precious little opportunity for one of my profession to earn money in this town, despite what I told that land officer under oath."

He spoke with such matter-of-fact casualness that it took a moment for her brain to sort out the implications of what he'd said. A battle had raged, Indians fighting alongside border ruffians against her townsmen. A sober practical woman like the Widow Walburn should launch an immediate barrage of questions, demand explanations. Instead Juliette considered the fact that Geoffrey had nowhere besides his soddie to house a prisoner, and asked, "Does that mean we can't be alone tonight?"

"Not for hours, at least," Geoffrey answered. He heaved a sigh laden with regret, but anticipation glittered in his eyes. "There is the boasting to attend to, after all."

It did take hours for every participant to stand and brag about his exploits during the brief skirmish with the ruffians. Women exclaimed over every wound, from Geoffrey's bullet crease to Josiah Wilcox's stone-cut forehead to the splinter Chester Thatcher's spear had driven into his own finger.

Juliette sat next to Geoffrey on the floor, their backs pressed up against his round wall. She gazed about at the animated townsfolk, her heart filled with an emotion she found difficult to express. They seemed so happy, so united. And she felt safe and secure in a way that had nothing to do with the day's driving away of the ruffians, and everything to do with the presence of the man beside her.

She slipped her hand into his.

She sensed his exhaustion in his light grip, in the barely perceptible lowering of his proud head, but he made no motion to conclude the boasting. If anything, he seemed determined to prolong it, reminding one man or another of a forgotten exploit, a particularly valiant deed—almost as if he didn't want the day to end.

Nor, it seemed, did the people of Walburn Ford. But first the babies drifted into sleep, and then the younger children ceased acting out the glorious deeds they heard described. Even the youths who'd fought man-to-man alongside their fathers curled tiredly against their mothers' sides, and men who normally spent their days plowing lonely furrows, their voices rough from unaccustomed amounts of talking, gradually stilled. Geoffrey's eyelids fluttered down, his long lashes spiking against his cheeks.

Juliette gathered herself to rise and order everyone home, but settled back when Mrs. Abbott strode into the middle of the room, waving her son Herman's letter. Guilt stabbed at her. Reading the letter to the town's children obviously hadn't been enough for Mrs. Abbott. With all the townsfolk together, it might be a good time to get it over with. She'd even force herself to pay a little attention, considering she hadn't heard one word of the letter despite Mrs. Abbott reading it aloud all day.

But that would mean setting aside for a minute or two her preoccupation with working out a way to be alone with Geoffrey without completely ruining her reputation, and she didn't fancy the thought of meeting while he held a prisoner on the premises. She certainly couldn't stay here when everyone trooped away. Even if she could convince him to abandon his scruples and come to her house this once, he seemed so tired that she hated to think of him making the lone walk across the prairie after everyone had gone. She hated even more to think of spending this night—any night ever again—apart from him.

Mrs. Abbott cleared her throat. "Here's your chance folks. Won't take five minutes to read, now that you're all here."

There were a few groans, but since everyone seemed disinclined to disband, nobody moved to silence the proud mother. She shook the letter open and began reading.

"'Dear Ma, Hope this letter finds you well,' et cetera, et cetera—" She stopped to peer over the letter. "I'm just gonna read the parts that ain't personal between mama and son, if you don't mind. Ahem. 'Lieutenant Ives has been writing a history of our explorations, which will surely astound the world upon its publication. I asked his permission to share some of the information in advance with my dearest mama, and of course he agreed.'" Blushing, Mrs. Abbott glanced around, as if to make certain everyone noticed her son's endearment.

"'Our land party, led by the Mojave Indian Iritaba, availed ourselves of Mr. Beale's new wagon road to reach these stupendous canyons. You will recall my earlier letter where I explained to you how Mr. Beale combined his engineering chores with an experiment using camels as beasts of burden in the southwest. Regular search parties continue to comb the desert in search of some few camels that managed to escape. But I digress.

"'To give you an idea of the awesomeness of the chasms we are charting, I can only tell you of our recent effort.'"

"Chasms?" Geoffrey whispered, sitting bolt upright.

Chasms? An awful sensation settled in the pit of Juliette's stomach. Angus Ōg and his mischievous sense of timing appeared to be rewarding Geoffrey.

Mrs. Abbott cast Geoffrey a quelling glare.

"I'll read on if some of us can keep our mouths closed. 'We attempted to descend to the Havasu Canyon floor, but could find only one trail wending down the mountain, and that measured less than a foot wide. Bravely, we men of the Army Corps of Topographical Engineers proceeded. Men and mules were stretched out along the steep path tentative as a row of bats clinging to a rotted roof beam. Even the most surefooted of the mules balked at descending all the way to the bottom. I tell you, Mama, retracing our dizzying way to the top is not an experience I would care to repeat. As we were descending, I would swear we couldn't see the bottom. And as we ascended, it seemed a lifetime before we could see our way clear to the top. It is a grand canyon, indeed.'"

Geoffrey sat rigid. His hand had tightened painfully around Juliette's, but the sensation was as nothing compared to the terror filling her soul as she heard

Mrs. Abbott describe the very death trap Geoffrey had been seeking.

"'My respected Lieutenant Ives commands the language so well. Again, with his permission, I will share with you the words he uses to describe these canyons so picturesquely: gigantic chasms, vast ruins, and fissures so profound that the eye cannot penetrate their depths.'"

Geoffrey disengaged his hand from hers; she watched, spellbound, sick at heart, while he bent his elbow and gripped his Celtic pendant with shaking fingers.

She had lost him.

She knew it with a certainty that had struck her but rarely in her lifetime: when she'd witnessed a newborn foal struggle to its spindly legs and knew there had to be a God; when she'd felt Daniel's heartbeat still beneath her hand and she knew he was dead; when she'd watched Geoffrey d'Arbanville knight her townspeople and knew that she loved him.

Already he seemed more distant, determined, a man with a mission to complete. No more playing at knighthood and homesteading. Yes, she had lost him, and she thought she might die from the agony of it.

"You said you have a picture, Lady Abbott. And a map."

Juliette wanted to erase the strained eagerness of his remarks, the taut tensing as he gathered himself, almost as if he meant to leap up and grab Mrs. Abbott's papers.

"You didn't let me finish, Geoffrey." Mrs. Abbott cast him a reproachful frown. "But since you're so all-fired anxious, yes, Herman sent me what he called a preliminary sketch by some famous person, Heinrich Möllhausen, or some such. Have a look."

She shuffled her papers and removed an ink drawing, which she held just beyond Geoffrey's reach. Grotesque mountain peaks pierced the clouds, and the artist's skill was so profound that a person could almost feel herself falling from the cliffs into the seemingly bottomless black pit welling at the bottom.

To Juliette's eyes, the drawing portrayed the essence of death, the vision of hell.

"And a map?" Geoffrey persisted.

"Yes, a map."

"I must have that map."

"No you must not!" Mrs. Abbott flared bright red. "I won't give up one single thing my son Herman sends me. But I'll let Bean Tyler draw you a true copy. He has a fine hand for art."

"'Tis most generous of you, Lady Abbott. Might I see it for a moment, though? I have a fair head for memorizing terrain."

He left his position next to Juliette without sparing her a glance. Her side, accustomed to his warmth, grew chill, and the coldness swiftly seeped into her middle.

He carried the map to a candle and crouched down to take full advantage of the flickering light. He raked an impatient hand through his hair, tucking it behind his ear, so that she could see the dark circles beneath his eyes, the brooding intensity with which he studied the map.

He made an imperious motion with his hand and barked some words she couldn't understand, and Limp-Waddling Duck hurried to his side. Together, they pored over the map, first one man and then the other pointing directionally. She could tell by Geoffrey's excited shifting and Limp-Waddling Duck's affirmative grunts that they understood the mysteries the map contained.

Geoffrey turned to look at her then, and she added one more certainty to her list: She had never seen anyone, man or woman, betray such unutterable sadness with their eyes.

"Don't go," she whispered.

He might not have heard; she would never know, for just then Rebecca Wilcox exclaimed, "My land, it's midnight! We'd best be getting home, Josiah, Robbie."

Midnight. Geoffrey had found what he was seeking at the very moment she was released from her promise to believe in him.

He continued staring at her, one hand gripping the map, the other holding tight to his Celtic pendant. She knew he could read her fear and despair. Like echoes from the past, she heard the sacred words he'd quoted in the knighthood ceremony swirling through her mind. *L'ordene de chevalerie.* A knight must prefer death to shame. A knight's word, once given, can never be retracted.

He had vowed to go back in time, to deliver his pendant and right a wrong long done, even if it meant dying in the process. To leap into a chasm where sure-footed mules feared to descend, where full-grown military men felt like bats clinging to an insubstantial beam.

"Don't go," she repeated, hating to beg but unable to refrain. He tore his gaze away from her and focused on the pendant, as if drawing strength from its crude design.

She didn't remember making the conscious effort to stand and join the departing crowd. If only he would make some sign that he wanted her to stay. If . . . if he would just ask her, she would somehow overcome her almost paralyzing fear and go with him.

He didn't even send another glance in her direction.

She found herself grateful for the close straining bodies carrying her along as they surged through Geoffrey's door.

*   *   *

Juliette knew that Geoffrey had no supplies. Even one endowed with his formidable strength would require a little sleep after the physical demands he'd placed upon himself during the past days. She had sensed his exhaustion and knew how powerless it left a body; he'd no doubt crawled into bed the minute the crowd had left his soddie.

Or maybe he'd spent this night like herself, falling repeatedly into fitful slumber while declarations and denials whirled through her head.

He couldn't leave without talking to her first. He wouldn't. A knight never departed without first taking leave of his lady . . . unless he didn't expect to see her again.

She drove the thought from her mind each of the dozen times she slipped from her bed to stare back to his soddie through the unrevealing darkness.

At the first hint of dawn, she pulled her blue gown into place, not paying much attention to the way she buttoned it. She knew it was a good omen when she couldn't find her belt and remembered that she'd given it to Geoffrey. He had sworn to return it; he wouldn't leave without making sure she got her belt back. She tugged her brush through her hair until she could gather it into some semblance of order. She'd yanked one shoe onto her foot and was bending to tend to the other when she heard Arion's distinctive whinny in her barnyard.

"Thank God," she whispered. She swayed in her awkward position; now that Geoffrey was here, she could admit to herself how terrified she'd been that she would never see him again.

She knew that she must look a sight, bursting through her kitchen door into the yard with one shoe on, the other gripped in her hand, her dress as badly buttoned as the mess Geoffrey had made of his shirt that first night. She didn't care. If she had her way, all of her buttons would soon be unfastened.

"Geoffrey?" She called his name and shielded her eyes against the rising sun, looking for him. "Geoffrey?"

Arion snorted and pawed the ground. She saw, then, that the stallion wore no saddle. No bridle, either—just a simple rope halter, and her bloodstained blue belt braided into his mane.

"Geoffrey." His name left her lips like steam escaping from a kettle; her strength deserted her in the same way, and she settled into an inelegant heap on the hardpacked barnyard dirt.

"He's gone, Miss Jay."

The words struck like blows against her chest, confirming the leaden premonition that had haunted her all night.

She hadn't spotted Robbie Wilcox leaning against a corral post—her eyes had been searching for a taller, broader frame. Robbie came to her, his feet scraping light furrows in the dirt, and sat down alongside her as if her heartbroken position were the most perfectly natural thing in the world.

"Him and that Injun prisoner of his stopped by our house after we was in bed. Pa got real mad, and Ma said something about sassin' him if he didn't behave. Can you credit it, Miss Jay—my Pa laughed."

"What did he say, Robbie? What did Geoffrey say?"

"Huh. I knew you were gonna ask me that." Robbie wrapped his thin arms around his calves and rested his chin atop his knees. "Something about how I should learn my lessons well, because, um, there are times when a man regrets he cannot read or write. I disremember the exact words. You know how Geoffrey talks sometimes."

"Yes." She would give anything to hear Geoffrey's occasionally torturous phrasing now. "Please, Robbie.

Think carefully. Are you one hundred percent certain that he's gone? I can't believe he'd leave without taking Arion."

Robbie cast her an insulted glare she knew he could only have learned from aping Geoffrey.

"A man never gives false counsel to a lady," he said, and her heart ached, hearing Geoffrey's honorable fancies echoed in every word Robbie said.

Robbie scowled and shook his head with boyish embarrassment. "Durn, I wish he would have told all this stuff straight to you. I tried to memorize it as best I could. Geoffrey said vows and pendants command a man's honor, but gifts from the heart span eternity. Arion belongs to you now, Miss Jay. Geoffrey said you would understand no knight could give his lady more."

She remembered Geoffrey telling her about the mental bond forged between knight and horse, remembered him telling her how his bones ached with every blow Arion took. No gift could have cost him more than leaving her his extraordinary horse, who could carry a person a hundred miles a day or more without tiring.

"Robbie—did he say anything about coming back?"

"Geez, Miss Jay, if he'd of said he was coming back I would've told you straight off not to worry so much. Now, um, he said ol' Limp-Waddling Duck would guide him to the canyon in exchange for his freedom. Geoffrey said you would understand that he doesn't want you to come after him. Your, uh, destiny lies here. He said I was to be, um, most forceful in that regard, because belief in himself is all he has left, and he cannot risk being dis . . . dissuaded?"

Juliette felt the wet trickle of tears trail down her cheeks, and watched unblinking while they disappeared into the dust. She looked up when Arion neighed, a drawn-out sad trumpeting which seemed to reverberate endlessly. The stallion had been well tended very recently; his coat gleamed from the sort of currying only a man's strong arms could deliver. She pictured Geoffrey denying himself sleep and delaying his departure just long enough to brush his beloved horse one last time, to braid her belt into Arion's mane. Arion neighed again, his well-bred head pointed unerringly toward the West, where Geoffrey intended to leap into a grand canyon rifting Arizona.

Where she could follow him. Except that he had forbidden her to come after him, and he had not promised to return, which meant he never intended to see her again. And she had no clue as to whether he feared dying during his leap or whether he simply wanted to disappear before reality ended all the magic.

"Miss Jay, is he really going to jump into that big canyon Mrs. Abbott told us about?"

She sensed the inner struggle prompting Robbie's question: heartfelt apprehension for a misguided friend balanced against dread that she might ridicule his concern. Now that the magic had gone from her life, shades of the Widow Walburn returned. The Widow Walburn could easily tell Robbie that Geoffrey was probably no more than a failed actor who'd taken to his heels before his deceptions came to light. Nobody would be crazy enough to travel halfway across the continent in order to leap into a bottomless chasm; it was an elaborate hoax, nothing more.

Juliette wished she could believe it was a hoax.

She thought of the descriptions that had so captivated Geoffrey: fissures so profound that the human eye could not penetrate their depths, walls so steep a mule refused to scale them. No human could fall so far without ending up crumpled and eternally still upon a canyon floor. He had been right to tell her to stay behind. It would take a stronger woman than herself to ride along and watch him leap to his doom.

"I'm afraid he will jump, Robbie."

"Somebody should have tried to stop him."

"I should have stayed with him last night." Her pride had forced her to walk away. Why had she been so determined that he ask her to stay? Despite all her good intentions, she'd failed to make even that small leap of faith. No wonder he'd set off without her and never wanted to see her again.

"He won't . . . he won't get hurt, will he?"

"He says he's done it before."

"Why?"

"I'm not sure. It's all tied up in his mind with honor and knightly duty, and a promise he made a long, long time ago."

"Oh, he had to go, then, if he gave his word." Relief washed over Robbie's face. "It's all right."

Arion whinnied again, a wistful sound, as if he knew, like Juliette, that nothing would ever be quite right, ever again.

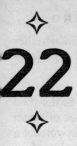

22

Soldiers came through Walburn Ford that day, carrying supplies, bringing mail from the States, stunned to learn that a battle had raged and that Walburn Ford had emerged virtually unscathed. Juliette watched the usual crowd welcome the soldiers. Men, women, and children clustered around them; despite the recent excitement, they were as eager as ever for any break in the daily tedium of homesteading life.

"There's one for you today, Miss Jay," said a smiling sergeant who would be boarding with her that night.

"Thank you," she said, her heart lurching when she read the elegant writing scrawled over the sealed flap. "Professor Willard T. Burns, Harvard University, Boston."

She stared at the letter for what seemed like hours, turning it in her hand, tracing the blob of sealing wax protecting its contents. She even smelled it and imagined she caught the scent of dust and incense, imagined a curved-back monk scribbling Geoffrey's name for Professor Burns to verify and report. All she had to do was to open the letter and she would know whether anything Geoffrey had told her had held a grain of truth.

She couldn't do it.

Had his outrage over learning that she'd asked Professor Burns truly been the honest reaction of a man insulted to think that she would believe the word of a stranger over his own? Or the conniving ploy of an actor eager to avoid being caught out? She couldn't let the letter prove or disprove the life of Geoffrey d'Arbanville, couldn't take the risk that opening it and reading its contents might effectively eradicate all trace of the man she loved against all reason.

All around her, those lucky enough to receive letters from back East tore open their missives, reading aloud, laughing and crying over news from their loved ones. Juliette pushed Professor Burns's letter deep into her pocket unopened.

Later, when the boarders were fed and snoring in their assigned beds, she sat the letter atop her dresser. She stared at the small folded oblong while she brushed her hair and made ready for the night. When she closed her eyes, the image of the letter hovered as a background for the presence filling her mind. Geoffrey. His thick chestnut hair whipping in the wind, his eyes scanning the horizon for enemies, his teeth flashing white with one of his many smiles. She remembered everything, his scent, the texture of his skin, the way his chest hair tickled her breasts. The rumble of his voice calling her *my lady*.

She couldn't sleep, so she stole over to his round, moated soddie during the cover of darkness. Nothing remained of Geoffrey; he'd taken his rusting armor, his tunics, his gear. If not for Arion's pining presence in her corral, she could question whether he'd ever existed at all. She lay on the straw-stuffed mattress remembering, and returned home just before dawn.

Walburn Ford, and Juliette's responsibilities to it, had always anchored her in place. With Geoffrey's departure, she felt like an abandoned plague ship, moored in place but deserted, sails whipped into tatters, the relentless waves battering her lifeless hulk into splinters.

Firm anchorage, she learned, wasn't necessarily a haven.

She wondered how long it would be before the townsfolk stopped mentioning Geoffrey's name. Soon, she knew, thrifty homesteaders would fashion the yellow coats of arms into new kitchen curtains, and someone would try to seal his bucket-helmet's eyeholes with carefully whittled cottonwood plugs.

"I guess Geoffrey wasn't meant to settle down. Lucky thing he moved on before things got too serious between you two," Alma said the next morning when she stopped to borrow Juliette's team.

"I thought *you* had a sweet spot for him. I know Bean Tyler was looking mighty worried any time he heard you and Geoffrey mentioned in the same breath." Juliette managed a nonchalant tone, seeking only to deflect Alma from the truth.

"Oh, that Bean!" Alma smiled, blushing prettily in her delight. "Besides, Geoffrey wasn't here long enough to compromise any decent woman." Juliette watched her drive the team away and prayed that nobody in the town imagined that the staid, proper Widow Walburn had indeed been well and truly compromised.

Juliette ignored her chores and spent the day in the pasture with Arion, standing with her arms wrapped around the horse's sleek neck, the both of them staring West.

"You thought any about chasin' after him?" Captain Chaney asked that night over supper.

She had thought of little else. "I can't leave this town." She wondered if she sought to convince the captain or herself.

"Seems to me that part of you's already gone, if you'll pardon my sayin' so, Miss Jay."

She stabbed a potato chunk. "Geoffrey said I wasn't to follow him. He ordered me to stay here."

"When did you start listening to orders?"

Her fork mashed the mealy potato with more success than she'd had in squashing her doubts that she'd been foolish to accept Robbie's word for everything. But even if the boy had mixed up his messages, there was no arguing her way around several important points. She enumerated them aloud, telling herself it was for the captain's benefit, but needing to say them.

"Geoffrey would have asked me to go with him if he wanted me. Or if he wanted me to follow him, he wouldn't have stolen away in the middle of the night. He . . . he worried too much about my safety to expect me to track him on my own."

"Well, could be you hit on something there, Miss Jay." The captain nodded. "What if he is one of those actor fellows after all, worked himself into a part and couldn't see his way clear without up and disappearing? Maybe he don't have no more intentions than you of jumping into that canyon and couldn't face up to admitting the truth."

"No." She couldn't explain her certainty, and couldn't withhold a shaky laugh to realize that now, when he was gone, she found herself believing so implicitly in Geoffrey's honor. Ironic, too, to realize that she could never prove this to Geoffrey, even as he'd found himself unable to prove any of his innermost beliefs to her. "Besides, it's too late. He's been gone since the day before yesterday. I could never catch up with him in time to stop him." Unspoken between them was the surety that once Geoffrey leaped into the canyon, it would be too late.

"I'd say that horse he left you could catch up with any mule or Indian pony he finds himself riding. Could be he's hoping you might prove something by coming after him."

Juliette's fork clattered to the table.

"Fact is, I asked those soldiers about that trip he set out on." Captain Chaney settled back; it was almost as though he'd been wary of divulging this information and felt relieved to get it out in the open. "There's all kinds of ways to get out there. For instance, some fellow named Aubry, F. X. Aubry, rode a hundred fifty miles a day and made the trip between Independence and Santa Fe in five days and sixteen hours. Wouldn't take no time at all to get from Santa Fe to that canyon in Arizona."

"Geoffrey once told me Arion could travel more than a hundred miles in a day." Again, there was that warring of emotion that accompanied so many circumstances surrounding Geoffrey. Had he told her this information and left her his magnificent horse so that she would be equipped to follow him? Or was he exactly what he claimed, a knight leaving his most precious possession to the woman he loved and never expected to see again?

"There's the overland mail stages, too, Miss Jay. They run regular out of Westport, Missouri, cost a hunnerd twenty dollars to hitch along. They take a sight longer, considering you have to stop at all the post offices along the way. And there's always soldiers gettin' transferred between forts. 'Course, it could take upwards of a month for a party of soldiers to get to that site sketched out on Mrs. Abbott's map."

"A month?"

"Probably longer, considering some soldiers hoof it on their own feet. I think it'd be fair to say two men riding light, like Geoffrey and that Indian, could travel some faster than soldiers and mail stages, but not so quick as that Aubry fellow. *So . . . ,*" Captain Chaney paused to take a fortifying slug of coffee. "You might have to put your faith in an old washed-up Army spy if you really want to catch up with him in time."

"You, Captain Chaney? You'd help me find him?"

"Long's you hold up and don't get all womanish on me, I'd say we have a fair chance of catching him," Captain Chaney said.

"I'm well accustomed to long trips," Juliette whispered. "I could ask Bean Tyler to make us a copy of the map."

"Already done that." Captain Chaney patted his breast pocket. "I gotta warn you, though. It's big country out there, Miss Jay. Even if he aims directly for that spot on the map, there's a good chance we could go all that way and not find him. Or get there too late."

Gratitude, and hope, robbed her of speech for a heartbeat. She caught the captain's gnarled hands between her own. "If the Geoffrey d'Arbanville I love is out there, I'll find him."

"Might be you'll not be able to change his mind," the captain warned.

"Might be I'll change *my* mind," Juliette said, "and go right along with him."

The captain studied her for a moment, and then gave her a sad, yet approving, nod. "Sounds like you already have."

"You know, considering everything, maybe it's time you called me by my given name. Juliette."

She could tell her offer pleased him, and she wondered

why it had taken her so long to make an overture of friendship. He gave her a shy smile. "Juliette. Like that gal in the Shakespeare play."

"Just like her, Captain Chaney. I didn't want to be, but I found that I am."

"Well, I hope not exactly like her. Seems like I recollect a sad ending to that story."

"Not as sad as it could have been," Juliette said. "I always thought she did the wrong thing by giving up everything for the man she loved. Now I know she would have been doomed if she'd done anything less."

They set out at dawn. Juliette wore her Bloomer dress and, like Captain Chaney, carried only one change of clothes and a food supply in her saddlebags so they wouldn't have to waste time hunting or foraging.

She pinned Professor Burns's unopened letter on the inside of her dress, so that it rested against her heart for every minute of the next seemingly endless weeks, over every exhausting, exhilarating mile they traveled.

Geoffrey sat his horse, marveling that the flat expanse they stood upon should end in the far-off fissures twisting into the earth. Even from his self-imposed distance of half a mile, he felt overawed and humbled by the majesty of the red rock clefts yawning before him.

Limp-Waddling Duck cast him a brooding scowl as he reined his mount next to him. Geoffrey knew this might be their final exchange in the magical tongue that so suited this terrain.

"You mean to do this foolish thing now."

"Aye."

"Before my very eyes."

"I swear you are the poorest excuse for a prisoner I have ever had the misfortune of capturing," Geoffrey said with false lightness. "You bungled a thousand chances to escape, so cast me no blame that you find yourself still lurking here, taking offense at my intentions."

"Ah, but without my gifted tongue to immortalize your deeds, who would ever believe one such as you ever rode these plains?"

It eased something in Geoffrey's soul to know that he would be remembered by a fellow warrior, and not merely some book-boggled professor. Perhaps one day Juliette would hear Limp-Waddling Duck's song, and believe, no matter what her illustrious Professor Burns reported. "Thank you, my friend."

They sat for long moments, lost in silent camaraderie.

"You should look over the edge first, Geoffrey, as I did. What you see might change your mind."

"My mind cannot be changed."

He touched the pendant for reassurance. It seemed to throb against his fingers, holding him still well past the time when he had intended to nudge his horse into a full gallop.

And then his companion and both horses all swiveled their heads. A scant heartbeat later his own inferior hearing caught the sound of approaching hoofbeats.

Limp-Waddling Duck smiled.

Geoffrey could not tell which startled him the more: the sight of his implacable friend's stern lips tilted upward for the first time since he'd known him or the approaching clouds of dust. They gradually sorted themselves out—Captain Chaney urging his tiring mount on, but lagging behind a smooth-running bay steed, a wild-haired woman, aimed straight for him.

A witch, he'd thought her, the first time he'd seen her. And so she'd proven herself to be, casting a spell over his heart, stealing his wits and enrapturing his senses. He had no more eliminated his yearning for her than he could stop the steady pounding of his pulse. After all, succeeding in either endeavor would doom him to death. Even now, when he knew her presence could represent nothing more than an attempt to distract him from his purpose, he exulted at the sight of her.

He held his position, though every ounce of his being urged him to kick his horse into motion so he could meet her halfway. He doubted he possessed the strength of will just then to hold to his course if he took a single step away from it. He waited.

Arion whickered an excited greeting and nearly sent him tumbling from his saddle with a welcoming nudge. He rested a palm against the steed's silken muzzle, feeling the warm whoosh of Arion's breath against his hand. He wished it were softer skin he caressed, sweeter breathing that tickled his flesh, but it was difficult to maneuver close to Juliette with more than a half-ton of horseflesh squirming for position with the abandon of an overeager puppy.

"God's blood, Juliette, we must dismount ere Arion crushes our limbs between himself and this other."

And then he was standing one good stride away from her, inwardly cursing the rusted armor he wore. Were he to pull her against him as he longed to do, he'd feel nothing, and it seemed a devil-devised torment. Or perhaps it was exactly otherwise. To feel her yielding against him, after these endless weeks of craving, might distract his all-too-human heart away from what he must do.

Dust caked her from the tips of her boots to the tangles of her hair. All of her glorious coloring was thus masked in dull brown-gray, save her eyes, and the fist-sized circles showing where she'd rubbed away tears. Were he to live another six hundred years, he knew he would never see another woman more beautiful than she looked to him at that moment.

Limp-Waddling Duck and Captain Chaney might have themselves leaped into the chasm for all the notice he spared them now.

"Why did you come, Juliette?"

"Because this is where I could find you. You were right, Geoffrey. Augus Ōg sends you exactly where you need to be. I had to follow you to some dangerous frightening place . . . I had to leave Walburn Ford to find my love, my life."

She came into his arms then, and he had been wrong to think he wouldn't feel anything. Her weight pressed the rusted links through gambeson into his flesh, a thousand prickling reminders of the ache that had stabbed his heart ever since leaving her. Her warmth flowed through the metal, her very essence permeating straight through to his soul, which would always and forever belong to her.

And *she* wore no armor, which made it a highly pleasant exercise to trace his lips along the curve of her chin, to taste the heated skin at her neck.

"What is this?" he murmured upon finding a stiff paper oblong pinned beneath the cloth over her bosom.

"The letter I was expecting from Professor Burns."

His passion cooled liked forge-reddened iron plunged into freshly drawn well water. "You cannot put all your faith in words written by a stranger."

She slanted a coy smile at him. "You're right. Mrs. Abbott's son Herman wrote all about escaped camels, and I haven't seen a single one, have you?"

He ignored her mischievous diversion and jutted his jaw at Professor Burns's letter. "Mayhap he corroborated what I told you and you have come to apologize."

"No."

So his worst fears had come to life. He could have endured leaving her, if she remembered him as a hero who had sacrificed their love for a worthy cause. "He called me a liar, then, and you believe him, and have come to taunt me over it."

"No." She released the letter with graceful movements. "Look. I never opened it."

Beneath a mass of scribbling, an unbroken wax seal held the letter folded shut.

She stuffed the letter back into place and pressed against him once more. "I don't care what it says. I love the man you are right now. I can't promise that I'll never experience any doubts, but I will always love you." Her fingers traced the leather thong encircling his neck, rousing shivers all along his frame when the pendant seemed to throb in approval. "Let's go now, before I lose my nerve. Let's deliver this pendant to wherever it belongs. I'm as tired of sharing you with a long-dead king as you were of sharing me with poor Daniel's memory."

"You . . . you would leap with me? And your town, Juliette? You are turning your back on it?"

"I doubt the entire U.S. Army could rout those settlers out now, thanks to you. Walburn Ford will still be there, no matter how long it takes us to get back."

"So for now you believe in all I have told you."

Her wondrous glow dimmed like a fine summer's day melding with the night, but she smiled, and rested her hand over his heart. "Oh Geoffrey, this will surely be one of the world's all-time leaps of faith."

Arion sidled away when Geoffrey attempted to lift Juliette onto his back, so he settled her on the horse he had been riding. Perhaps it was for the best, for he knew Arion would jump without hesitation, drawing the lesser animal in his wake. They would have need of the second horse once they returned to his own time.

She was coming with him. He could scarcely think, such was the joy pounding through him.

He drew a deep breath and looked toward her, his heart lurching to find her sitting with corpselike rigidity in her seat, not even her coating of dust able to disguise her pallor.

"You are frightened, my lady."

"When you call me your lady, I can do anything. But . . ."

"But?"

"What if we don't make . . . what if we find ourselves in a completely different time or place than what you're expecting?"

The pendant seemed to vibrate against his chest. "Fear not—Angus Ōg will set me down exactly where I need to be. You have said so yourself. And we shall be together, Juliette."

She placed her hand in his and, after gulping a huge measure of air, nudged her horse into a slow walk. He gripped hard, wishing he could infuse some of his heat into her ice-cold skin.

"What should I expect, Geoffrey?"

Pride surged through him; a valiant lady, she was, careful as any knight to seek the advantage of knowledge.

"The leap itself will seem at once endless and yet elusive as a cricket's chirp. Followed by a pervasive weakness, and a most unfortunate urge to retch." He pulled on the reins, slowing their already sluggish progress. "When we arrive, pretend you are mute, and I would have you sit in a huddle until I can find a cloak to cover your garments. The people where I come from would not be so accepting of a stranger like yourself suddenly appearing in their midst."

He felt her anxious shudder clear into his bones, and

tamped down his far-flying hopes. "Juliette, were you to tell me that you are too frightened to proceed, I would not ask you to come. I vow to return to you. You need not do this, my lady. 'Twas enough of a gift that you came here—"

She muffled his noble objections by leaning over and stilling his protest with a kiss.

"Geoffrey, sometimes you talk too much."

With that, she pressed her heels into her horse's flank, sending it plunging ahead, whilst she held onto his hand, nearly wrenching his arm from its socket.

He wouldn't have thought it an easy matter to race side by side whilst remaining hand in hand, but Arion seemed to sense his need to hold onto Juliette and altered his pace to the other animal's. Two running horses can cross a half-mile in no time; still, there was time enough for her to change her mind. When they were but ten strides from the canyon edge, he heard her give something like a sob and felt his spirits plummet, certain she meant to wrench her horse's head in another direction.

She didn't.

"Don't let me go!" she cried as they plunged in unison over the embankment.

"Never, my lady."

But though he'd never spoken a vow with firmer intent, God's own forces conspired against him. He outweighed her, doubly so with full armor, and Arion was half again the horse that she rode. He fell faster than she did, there was no stopping it.

"Geoffrey!" He heard the edge of panic in her voice when his handhold slipped to encompass only the tips of her fingers.

Would that he had held her before him, but Arion had refused to accept her, and he had been so bedazzled by her presence that he'd given the matter no thought. He felt the almost unbearable drag between them and he swore, knowing he lacked the time and leverage to pull her onto Arion. He knew he must needs let her go, or risk wrenching her from her saddle and dropping her into the endless abyss.

"Geoffrey! Promise me I'll see you again."

Her cry echoed from the canyon walls, muffled now that mists enveloped them, and he could not bear the sense of isolation.

"Take heart, Juliette!" he bellowed. "We shall be together for eternity. I swear it."

23

Juliette's head ached.

Her tongue felt swollen to twice its normal size, and her facial skin prickled with the warning that she'd spent too much time in the sun, promising added misery. She passed in and out of consciousness, listening to her discomfort roar with audible mind-numbing intensity, before realizing that it was water, enormous quantities of water, rushing past her that made the sound. She licked her lips, suddenly desperate for a drink.

She lurched to her knees and nearly swooned from the effort it took, and pressed a hand against her lips to still the sudden nausea that slammed into her belly. Oh God, some awful ailment must have laid her low—cholera, summer complaint, any one of the endless illnesses that struck homesteaders. . . .

A choking wheeze drew her attention to the horse. It swayed on splayed feet, its muzzle brushing the ground without making any effort to graze. She'd seen a horse

in such straits once before. Arion. The first time she'd
seen Geoffrey.

"Geoffrey." She meant to shout his name, but it
passed through her parched lips as a croaking whisper,
so faint it didn't even bother a curious bird hopping
nearby. Geoffrey had warned her about the weakness,
the unsettled stomach, but she hadn't realized how
intense the sensations would be. Even so slight an
effort as whispering his name heightened the pounding
in her skull. She wanted nothing more than to curl into
a tight ball against the harsh sun, but her craving for
water would not let her, her craving for the sight of
Geoffrey threatened to drive her mad.

Or maybe she'd already lost her senses. She studied
every inch of her surroundings, swept her gaze along the
racing river, peered upward until she lost sight of the
cliffs in the mist, and found no sign that any human
besides herself had ever violated the canyon's pristine
beauty. This had to be the base of the Eternal Chasm he'd
spoken about. England, in the year of our Lord 1283.

"Geoffrey." She would find him; she had to find him.
Her limbs would not obey her, so she crawled and
gained the river, took several fortifying sips of its ice-
cold bounty. It strengthened her enough to enable her to
struggle to her feet, but she couldn't manage more than
a few steps without tiring. "Geoffrey." Calling his name,
weakly as she did it, sapped what little strength she'd
mustered and she crumpled into a dust-puffing heap.

She felt a pinching near her shoulder. Professor
Burns's letter, reminding her that she'd stuffed it into her
bodice without taking the time to pin it properly. She
could read it now that she'd proven her faith in Geoffrey
by jumping with him into the chasm. She pulled it free
and cracked the seal with her thumbnail. How he would
laugh when she found him and told him she'd opened it

because she was so desperate to see him, so happy that they'd made this leap and survived that she'd settled for seeing his name scrawled on a piece of paper.

It took enormous concentration to focus on the writing, considering how the paper seemed to advance and recede, even though she would have sworn she held it steady. She squinted, and that improved matters somewhat. The very quiet surrounding her seemed to demand that she read the letter aloud, so she did.

"'My Dear Mrs. Walburn, I approached your assignment with great zeal, aided by my most thorough research assistant. I regret to say that neither of us was able to uncover a single reference to a John or Demeter of Rowanwood or a Drogo FitzBaldric. While there were d'Arbanvilles aplenty, there is no record of a knight errant calling himself Geoffrey. I shall take up the search as a hobby, and pursue it during my travels throughout this country and overseas, although I caution you I may meet with no better success. . . .'"

Pain shafted through her head straight to her heart. Awareness of her solitude settled about her like the burlap sack she used to quiet chickens before readying them for the stewpot.

She balled the letter and threw it into the river where it bobbed for mere seconds before being sucked under. "No." She staggered once more to her feet. "No." Only birdsong, and flowing water, and the belabored breathing of her horse answered her denial. "No." The canyon, exactly as described in Herman Abbott's letter to his mother. She hadn't traveled back through time at all. She'd somehow landed safely at the base of the canyon, but she was alone. Utterly alone. No warhorse named Arion. No rusty-armored knight who'd sworn they'd be together through eternity.

An anguished wail howled through the canyon. It

might be a wolf mourning the loss of its mate, and she didn't question why the sound dried *her* throat or increased the pounding in *her* head.

Oh God, if she could only think straight. Maybe . . . maybe she'd done it wrong.

She'd jumped without truly believing. That was it. That was why it hadn't worked. Sobbing, she kneeled to gulp more water, and then crawled toward the canyon wall, heedless of the slivers of shale cutting her hands and knees. She would do it again. Climb back to the top and do it again. Her pulse raced its approval, sending energy surging through her limbs. She grabbed at protruding rocks for hand- and footholds, and made it at least two feet off the ground when she heard the sound of hoofbeats louder than the roaring river, louder than the pounding of her heart, louder than the pebbles dislodged by her climbing.

"Geoffrey." She closed her eyes, praying her thanks, not caring when she slid down and lost every inch she'd gained or that the sharp stones cut her Bloomer dress and scratched her skin.

But when she opened her eyes, two weather-creased faces, neither of them Geoffrey's, peered anxiously at her.

"I told you that bellerin' wasn't no runaway camel."

"Holy shit. It's a woman. A white woman."

They were clad in army blue, and their shoulders bore an insignia that any acquaintance of Mrs. Abbott's would recognize as belonging to the Army Corps of Topographical Engineers.

"What the hell are you doin' out here, ma'am?" The older of the two caught her hand in his callused grip and hauled her to her feet. "Were you held captive by Indians?"

"We'll get you back to camp, get you cleaned up," said his companion. "You're safe now."

Disappointment had held her silent; when the soldiers began guiding her solicitously toward their horses, she dug in her heels, fighting the dizziness that urged her to let them take care of her. "I'm sorry, gentlemen. I can't go with you. I have to go back and try again."

"Go back where, ma'am, and try what again?"

She waved toward the invisible crest of the chasm, feeling panic well up within her when she realized how daunting her task would be. She had to get started at once. "Up there. I didn't do it right the first time."

They squinted upward, frowning, as if they could make no sense of what she said. "Are you tryin' to tell us you climbed down the cliff, ma'am?"

"No, we didn't climb down. We jumped. Geoffrey and I . . ." She snapped her teeth shut. Good God, they were gaping at her as if she'd lost her mind. She had no time, no breath to spare, to convince them of the truth. She had to get back to the top and jump again before too much time had passed, before her waning strength flagged, so that Geoffrey wouldn't worry too much over her prolonged absence. She jerked her arm free and bolted for the wall, dismayed that her progress was so erratic, so slow.

They caught her before she reached the first handhold and stood over her with the wary superior confidence of coyotes circling a wounded antelope.

"There, there, ma'am," said the older one, treating her shoulder to a tentative pat like one might risk when daring to touch a caged lioness.

"You didn't jump off that cliff, ma'am, now did you?" said the younger, as if coaxing a child into admitting the truth. "Why, anything falling from such a height would be splattered from here to the Rio Grande."

"Geoffrey," she whispered, sinking back against the wall. "We jumped together. I must find Geoffrey."

The soldiers exchanged glances, telling her without words that they disbelieved her story, that they doubted Geoffrey's very existence.

"There, there," repeated the older one, patting her furiously now, looking almost as distressed as she felt herself.

"We'll look for, er, Geoffrey," said the young one. "It'll be a nice change from huntin' camels. In the meantime, we'll be gettin' you back to camp. Our lieutenant'll be mighty curious to hear what you have to say."

She shook her head, knowing she had to clear the confusion from her mind, had to stop making incautious remarks that made them doubt her sanity. Geoffrey could be lying injured somewhere, needing medical attention. She had to find someone who would help her. "Herman," she said. "Herman Abbott. He serves with the Army Corps of Topographical Engineers."

"Why, yes ma'am, he does. He's one of Lieutenant Ives's right-hand men."

"You must take me to him at once."

This bit of lucidity seemed to cheer them, and they spoke kindly, encouragingly, as they guided her around sharp-spined shrubs and protruding rocks. They settled her on a horse; she noticed they were careful to keep the reins out of her hands and under their control.

They headed downriver. "What do you make of this, Marty?" muttered the young one, barely loud enough for her to hear.

"Beats hell out of me," said the older one.

Geoffrey clutched the pendant while his will struggled with his impulses. He wanted nothing more than to tear it from his neck and fling it into the Eternal Chasm, cursing Angus Ōg, reviling the Celtic god's name, consigning his wretched pendant to oblivion. Spiteful, vengeful, mean-spirited god, to promise the restoration of life to those who gave their last breath for the cause of love . . . for though Juliette had leaped with him, her beloved presence did not grace this sacred oak grove. He knew, for he'd scoured every inch of it, forging through his weakness and nausea, and lending an aching throat to his woes, so ceaselessly had he shouted her name. Stirring no response.

He was alone. Utterly alone.

Save for Arion, of course, who wheezed and coughed amidst reproachful glances in his direction. This chasm leaping took a fearsome toll upon a horse, it seemed.

"We must needs brave it but once more," Geoffrey promised, laying a soothing hand along Arion's shuddering neck. "Once more, when our work here is done, and then never again."

He pushed through the spreading oaks, and the eerie silence of the sacred grove gave way to the muted din that accompanied the movement of an army: thousands of feet, human and equine, plodding across turf; the creaking of overladen wagons; the jingling of chain mail and harness, all wrapped around the low rumble of men's voices. From Londontown direction, aiming straight for the rebellious Demeter's keep, waving pennants telling anyone who bothered to look that the King of England marched against his enemies. Just as he'd told Juliette, Angus Ōg had set him down exactly where he was needed.

His hopes dove to his toes. If King Edward were marching on this Welsh border upstart, her husband John might already be dead, and Geoffrey d'Arbanville marked in the king's mind as a failure. Moreover the king would strike Demeter's hold without mercy, thinking she'd spurned his negotiations, not knowing that his knight had failed to deliver the pendant and his ultimatum. Worse, the king might well stumble into Drogo FitzBaldric's trap.

Well, he had not traversed through time and back to let matters come to this pass.

Geoffrey d'Arbanville had developed, by necessity, the knightly knack for disengaging his mind from all save the task at hand. It did not always weigh easy on a man's soul, fighting for gold and glory. A man could grow mad, were he to permit his thoughts to dwell on what might have befallen those who'd been innocently caught up in his struggles. Lest he wanted to wallow in impotent despair, he could not indulge his gut-twisting worry over Juliette, could not torment himself with the image of her lying helpless and broken at the base of the canyon, her voice echoing from the walls as she begged him to come to her side.

He had vowed to return and spend eternity with her. And so he would, or die trying. For now, although his heart screamed in protest, he must put thoughts of her aside, placing his faith in Celtic and Christian gods alike, that they would hold her safe while he tended to the things he was sworn to do.

"Follow when you are able," he advised Arion, trusting that the loyal stallion would mark his progress and seek him out. And then he struck out toward the advancing army, nearly gaining the rearmost laggards before any of the witless churls thought to fling him a challenge.

"State your purpose, *sir*," sneered a squire, and Geoffrey quelled the pain shafting through his heart at remembering the last time he'd heard those very same words, in a different tongue, in his lady Juliette's warm kitchen.

"I must see the king at once. Privately."

"And I would relish a personal benediction from the pope. Get you gone." The squire turned away.

Astonishment caused Geoffrey to lose a step. "How dare you let me walk away without raising the hue and cry! Who is your master, you baseborn lout? Did he not teach you the constant vigilance a warrior must exercise to ensure his sovereign's safety? And do not attempt to pretend you recognized me for an ally, for you certainly did not employ a respectful turn of phrase when addressing me."

The squire glowered but had the good sense to look abashed.

A knight, to Geoffrey's mind far too belatedly catching sight of their minor confrontation, disengaged himself from his traveling companions and cantered back toward them. "Peasants accosting our rear, Beauregard?" he called to the squire as he drew closer, and then leaned forward to squint between his mount's ears. "What, ho—d'Arbanville?"

"Mountford," Geoffrey said, acknowledging his fellow knight. He gestured toward the now-fawning squire. "I hope 'tis not your lackey."

"Nay. Mine is even less adept. Squires are not what they were when we served as such, as the state of your armor shows, eh, d'Arbanville?"

"A bit of rust, I will admit."

"A bit? It looks to me like you might have spent the past month swimming the channel whilst wearing your chain mail. Mayhap 'tis why the king's countryside search failed to turn up your pitiable hide."

Geoffrey sighed. Edward turned closed-minded when enraged; it would be difficult enough to convince the king of the danger presented by Drogo FitzBaldric without expecting his liege to credit that Geoffrey had been detained six hundred years in the future. "I have news for the king's ears."

"Whether you do or no, I daresay he has a blistering in mind for yours." Mountford gestured toward the luckless Beauregard. "Give over your horse for Sir Geoffrey."

"And you," Geoffrey informed Beauregard as he gained the saddle, "keep watch for my steed. And once Arion is stabled, you will polish this rust away from my armor, whilst contemplating the sad consequences that befall one with a slothful nature."

"Aye sir," said the squire.

"I do not think Edward will absolve you so easily," Mountford said as they spurred their horses into motion.

But Edward, showing little appetite for routing a female from her border stronghold, accepted Geoffrey's homage and warnings without delving too deeply into Geoffrey's mysterious temporary disappearance.

"Fortune smiles. I have not yet rid the earth of Rowanwood's presence, nor have we stumbled into FitzBaldric's trap. We will discuss this at length later, d'Arbanville. For now, you can redeem yourself by bringing me FitzBaldric's head." The king waved Geoffrey into the night. "I would have this matter come to an end. I think one man, working alone, would stand the best chance of taking him by surprise."

Geoffrey inclined his head in acceptance, understanding, then, the depths of Edward's kingly displeasure.

Sending him alone into an armed enemy camp smacked of a royal death sentence.

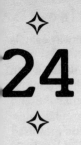

24

"*Here you go, Miss Jay.*"

Herman Abbott hunkered down next to Juliette's cot and handed her a mug of steaming coffee. She took a sip, but even its scalding progress into her belly did nothing to warm the pervasive chill that had gripped her since losing Geoffrey.

"The search patrol rode in about fifteen minutes ago."

"Any sign today?" she asked, although Herman's failure to meet her eyes had already answered the question for her.

"Naw." From somewhere Herman produced a stick, and traced meaningless lines in the dirt. "They've been out six times over the past three days. I wouldn't be surprised if Lieutenant Ives calls off the search, considering there hasn't been any sign of a man or horse."

"No camels, either, but I'll bet you're not going to stop looking for them." Her hand shook violently; she set the mug on a flat rock, afraid that she'd spill its contents all over herself.

"Well we know for a fact there are runaway camels out there, Miss Jay."

"And you're not so sure I'm telling the truth that a man was with me when I jumped off the edge of the precipice."

Herman pressed so hard in the dirt that the end snapped off his stick and, his eyes darting around, whispered, as if he feared being overheard. "You promised you wouldn't say that again. Now look, Miss Jay, I feel downright responsible for your . . . for your misery. I never should have sent that map and information back to my mother, but I never imagined anyone would take it into her—excuse me, into *their*—heads to come out here for a personal inspection. It's a hell of a rough trip, especially for a woman, and you got to consider that it might have taken a toll on your sensibilities."

She closed her eyes to hold back the helpless rage that made her want to leap up and scream the truth again and again at these bone-headed military men. They'd held her a virtual prisoner in the medical tent while she wavered between wanting to rush back to Kansas and searching the canyon, knowing that Geoffrey would be found in one place or the other. Geoffrey had said the Celtic god would send him to where he was needed most—and she needed him now, desperately. Faced with the soldiers' ever-present skepticism, a less strong-willed person might easily begin to believe she'd imagined everything. She had to remember her namesake, the Juliet from the Shakespeare play. If Juliet had held despair at bay, she would have been joined with her beloved on Earth as well as in heaven.

"I'll begin my own search tomorrow, Herman. I'm feeling quite restored."

"We can't let you do that, Miss Jay." He stood and brushed nonexistent dust from his uniform. "Our survey's almost complete. Except for a few men who'll stay behind to finish some minor mapping, we're pulling out tomorrow evening. We'll escort you to Fort Defiance, and from there you can return to Kansas with the next batch that heads back East."

"And you'll see that I comply, whether I want to or not."

"Yes ma'am, I'm afraid that's true." Though subdued, there was no mistaking Herman's determination. "It's an important part of a soldier's job, to protect women."

"So I've been told," Juliette said. She settled back on her cot and closed her eyes, putting a halt to the unpleasant interview. Geoffrey would find her.

He had promised.

Drogo had devised his ambush with exceptional cunning.

It had taken Geoffrey three full days of studying the cleverly designed death trap before he found the one weak point common to armies throughout history—a dozing guard. But only one. The other sentinels appeared discouragingly vigilant.

He felt an odd rifting in his heart. He had been right to return and warn Edward; had the king blundered incautiously into Drogo's stronghold, the blood toll could have cost England its ruler. It was a wondrous moment, for a knight to realize that he might well have saved the realm from disaster. It was a sobering moment, to regret the personal cost of it all and to find oneself in such a fever to end it and be gone that it seemed a chore rather than the achievement of a long-cherished dream.

The moon floated high, bathing the deadly countryside in silver light. Not the best of circumstances for a stealthy approach, were one to employ the usual method of dressing in black and darting from one dark spot to another. But on this night, Geoffrey had wet himself down and then powdered his person from head to toe with the royal baker's best white flour, and he welcomed the added pallor cast upon him by the moon.

"Juliette." He whispered her name in lieu of a battle cry. He tied Arion to a tree and cautioned him against betraying his presence, and then stole on silent feet and soundlessly slit the throat of the snoring sentinel, breaching Drogo's lair.

"Ha!" he cried when he flung aside Drogo's tent flap and let the moon illuminate his pale presence.

Drogo's display of spineless cowardice surpassed anything Geoffrey had hoped for whilst disguising himself as his own ghost. Drogo pizzled in his chausses, adding the acrid stench of fear to the terrified trembling that shook his sleeping rug off the pallet. "You . . . you . . . you . . . you are dead. I saw you fall straight through the Earth."

Geoffrey bared his teeth without humor. "The Earth is round, you incontinent worm, round as the tonsure encircling a scribbling monk's head."

"Heresy! You are truly sprung from the devil. Get you back to hell, shade!"

"Not without sending you first."

Awareness dawned then in Drogo's eyes, too late. Geoffrey's disguise had earned him the hairbreadth advantage he'd sought.

As often as he'd imagined their final confrontation, he found surprisingly little pleasure in dispatching this man who'd plagued him over the years, who'd dared envision the enslavement of a woman and the defeat of a monarchy to achieve his own greedy ends. He would not, he knew, boast much over this deed.

Geoffrey's sword swung swift and true. And it seemed the Celtic god eased his path that night. None of Drogo's tardily awakened henchmen made any effort to stop him when he left their camp, his fingers wound through the hair, his arm weighted down with the head, of their slain leader.

It took him most of the next day to scrape off the dried flour paste that clung to his skin like the clay-based mud peasants used to coat the walls of their huts.

"I would have a word with you, liege," Geoffrey said when he was clean enough to play servant, handing his king a tankard of ale.

"So I expected. A happy ending for all, eh, d'Arbanville?" Edward smiled, obviously gratified at receiving homage not only from Demeter, but from her neighboring dissidents as well. He gestured toward the rear of the hall, where Demeter and her John shared a joyous reunion beneath Drogo FitzBaldric's pike-spitted head. "All is well in the land, thanks in no small part to you, Sir Geoffrey. Before you make your plea, I would tell you I know of your hankering for property. It so happens I have a barony in mind for you, land and lady to suit."

"My . . . my liege—no." Geoffrey swallowed, appalled that frugal Edward's generosity should manifest itself now, after years of fruitless longing. How the gods must be chortling, to present him with his heart's desire for the second time, knowing circumstances made it impossible for him to accept.

"No?" Edward's amiability shifted into implacable royal displeasure. "You have grown too bigheaded to accept a mere barony as my boon?"

"Never, sire. 'Tis higher than I ever dared dream. I would be content with a worthless token and your word on three matters."

Edward subsided in his chair, glowering at the rejection of his beneficence but ruled, as ever, by the limits of his purse. "Such as?"

"Such as that Celtic pendant I have worn round my neck. I know 'twas Rowanwood's, but I miss it sore." Geoffrey prayed Angus Ōg would forgive his previous urge to fling the pendant into oblivion. He knew only that the pendant had somehow served to carry him through time, and he prayed it would do so again.

"Rowanwood owns nothing that is not mine as his liege. Done." Edward's word was little more than a grunt. He summoned a page and instructed him to fetch the pendant before returning his attention to Geoffrey.

"And a release from my vow, liege. I would have you free me from my knightly obligations."

The king studied him with narrowed eyes. "'Tis no small matter, this. I do not enjoy such an overabundance of knights that I can release them without counting the consequences."

"The consequence of denying me saddles you with a knight who has lost his taste for battle, sire."

Edward frowned. "You are behaving in a most willful manner, so I know you have not turned coward. You have dedicated your life to knighting, d'Arbanville. How would you earn your bread, were I to grant you this?"

"I had thought to take up farming, liege."

Edward burst into laughter. "The very notion amuses me into granting this. Done, but not without some reluctance."

"My family, sire. Send word to them that I am hale and hearty and happier than I have ever been. And although I might not see them again, they will always be in my thoughts and prayers."

"Done, although I doubt your father would pine for

the presence of a farmer, d'Arbanville. And your final matter?"

"That you assign a scribe, sire, to make a full accounting of this day, making certain that my name, that of John and Demeter of Rowanwood, and that of Drogo FitzBaldric all appear in the writing."

"Did FitzBaldric strike a wit-stealing blow to your head ere falling to your sword?"

"No, sire."

"Then certainly you must understand that if you want your name entered in the books, you must needs only accept the barony I offered you and continue lending your sword arm for the glory of England. The duties would not be so burdensome that you could not find time to indulge your farming urges. It rankles me, to think of glorifying a border upstart by writing of him."

Geoffrey stood firm before the king. "I would have you grant these boons as I have asked, my liege."

"A farmer who has displeased his king would deserve no more than one very small mention in a most obscure book."

"'Twould serve me well enough. There are not so many books in this world that the information could not be found, did someone of determination seek it out."

"Oh, very well. Done," Edward conceded with a show of petulance.

The page returned with the pendant, and Geoffrey caught it in his hand, unable to restrain a growl of triumph when he felt its familiar design press into his flesh, throbbing as if pleased to find him again. He owned the pendant, and he owed allegiance to no man. Juliette awaited, and he could return to her unencumbered by oaths and obligations. Joy suffused him, and an uncontrollable impatience; without taking his final leave of his king, he turned and bolted for the Eternal Chasm.

*   *   *

Arion refused to jump.

He skidded to a stamping halt well before the edge of the Chasm, shaking his mighty head and neighing his objection.

"God's *blood,* Arion!" Geoffrey cursed and urged the horse to circle round, and made the approach again, with no better results.

He tried a blindfold.

And an oak switch, and for the first and only time marred the stallion's silken bay hide outside of battle. Or perhaps not outside of battle, for it was certainly a clash of wills that left them both gasping for breath but no closer to leaping.

Geoffrey had always treasured Arion's intelligence, had profited from it time and again, by merely paying attention when his steed's superior senses urged caution. It probably made excellent sense, from a horse's view, to avoid a repetition of the debilitating weakness and gut-churning agony that followed each jump. Pray God that it wasn't some innate horsely instinct warning Arion that one more leap would be pressing too far. Geoffrey drove the fleeting doubt from his mind. To indulge it, even for a heartbeat, might invite failure.

He walked toward the Chasm and hauled with all his strength against the bridle. Arion wedged his hooves into the dirt and settled back on his haunches, his massive weight too much to drag, even for one as determined as Geoffrey.

Gripped by frustration, Geoffrey dropped the reins and stalked toward the Chasm. Mists roiled like bubbling witch's brew spewing from its cauldron. A distant roaring dulled his ears. Dizziness washed over him and

stole the sense from his head; he was left with naught
but doubts and fears.

The Celtic god might have deserted them entirely,
now that noble causes were served and naught but the
heart's desire of one common man, one ordinary
woman, hung in the balance.

Juliette had worn no pendant, and he had failed to
hold her tight. She might be dead.

He might leap and find himself in some entirely different place, some never-imagined time.

He might leap—and die.

An inborn instinct for survival sent him sprawling
back toward Arion. A memory reverberated through
his mind: Limp-Waddling Duck urging him to look
over the edge, warning that what he saw might lead
him to change his mind. His friend had not mentioned
that the frightening visions might exist only in his
mind. Geoffrey clung to Arion's mane, shivering,
appalled at his momentary lapse in determination, and
whispered, "No, no, no."

He could waste no more time soothing Arion's fears,
lest the delay provide demons of doubt with fresh-
plowed ground to plant their perfidious notions.

Geoffrey's teeth clenched so hard that pain shafted
through his jaw while he stripped the saddle and bridle
from his steed. Arion might wander for days, forever,
before someone discovered him. Geoffrey couldn't bear
to think of him starving or dying of thirst through getting his gear caught in a low-hanging branch or entangling shrub. He flung the stuff over the edge.

Long moments later, when he found himself gasping
for air, he realized he'd been waiting with bated breath
to hear the sound of it landing. He'd heard nothing.

"You know how to follow, should you work up the
courage," he said to his horse, who watched with flaring

nostrils and pricked ears, as if unable to credit his master's behavior.

And then, holding tight to the pendant, Geoffrey commenced a dead run a good hundred feet from the edge. He summoned his fiercest battle cry and leaped, poised as a lance, hurtling through mists that suffocated all sound and sensation save for the pounding of his heart, yearning for Juliette.

25

Since discovering her in the canyon, Sergeant Marty Cronin had developed a paternal attitude toward her that Juliette neither resented nor appreciated.

Half the soldiers thought Geoffrey was a figment of her imagination. The other half was divided even more. The U.S. mail traveled two ways, and Herman Abbott seemed as intent as his mother in sharing his letters. Mrs. Abbott had sent him news of the actor Geoffrey d'Arbanville who'd settled in Walburn Ford. Some of those who believed in Geoffrey's existence thought he had deserted her—actors, it seemed, were notorious for such behavior. A few, like Sergeant Cronin, believed that Geoffrey had died and that she'd developed this elaborate story to avoid reality.

No matter which version they believed, everyone attributed her almost inhuman calm to grief-induced lassitude. They cast her sympathetic glances and whispered about her when they thought she couldn't see or hear. She understood.

Death had robbed her of loved ones—her parents, Daniel—while leaving her with some outlet for mourning—nursing, laying out, burying—all the final loving chores that brought sympathetic friends together for comfort, for prayers, and granted her some opportunity to say good-bye, to honor cherished memories by laying flowers before a crude wooden cross.

Not at all like Geoffrey's disappearance, so thorough that he'd left no physical trace behind. Nothing. To those who believed he'd existed, it seemed she mourned a drifter who'd accepted what she'd offered and then disappeared when he'd tired of her. She knew the sympathy she received was for forgetting her pride and chasing after a consummately skilled actor. She was the only one who knew for certain that she'd fallen in love with a sometimes muddleheaded, time-traveling knight who'd meant it when he called her *my lady*.

Who'd meant it when he said they would spend eternity together.

So it helped to have someone like Sergeant Cronin look after her, especially through the tedious process of mobilizing an army corps for travel. She would have to think of some way to repay him when Geoffrey returned and she was herself again.

"We're settin' off now, Miss Jay. A small advance party, so we don't have to eat the caravan's dust clear into Fort Defiance. The travelin' will be easier after that." Sergeant Cronin gave her saddle straps a final inspection. "Don't you be afraid to call out if we go too fast, or if you need to stop for . . . well, if you need to stop."

"I'll be fine, Marty," she said, drawing his approving nod.

They'd ridden in companionable silence for quite a few miles when ear-splitting thunder boomed despite the cloudless sky. It seemed the very earth trembled.

The horses plunged and reared, snorting their fear, while fast-rolling clouds darkened the sky.

Nature's unexpected violence provoked a matching thunder in Juliette's breast, a swift racing of her blood that surged and retreated in concert with the weather. The rifting of the sky was followed a moment later by the clouds dissipating as quickly as they'd come. The sun shone again, even brighter than before.

"We have to go back," Juliette said, so amazingly calm that she knew she'd never doubted his promise. "Geoffrey's here."

Marty shook his head and caught her reins away from her. "We can't go back, Miss Jay. Looks like that cloudburst hit over the canyon. Lucky thing we left when we did."

Juliette settled into her saddle, waiting. They'd covered too much distance for her to run back on foot. Her eerie calm soothed her. He would find her.

Hours passed before Marty twisted in his saddle, squinting back toward one lingering wisp of cloud. "If that don't beat all," he muttered.

"What?" She tried looking, but her civilian's eyes couldn't make out whatever it was the experienced soldier had spotted, even when she pushed her bonnet off her head to widen her range of vision.

"It looks like a goddamned camel. Running straight at us like it can't wait to be caught. And us chasing them all over these hills for six months and more." He put two fingers between his teeth and uttered a shrill whistle that roused a startled snort from his mount. "Get on over here, Carville, and tell me if that don't look like a goddamned camel," he bellowed toward the young soldier who'd accompanied him the day they'd found her.

Carville cantered up, reined his mount to a halt, and lifted his spyglass to follow the direction of Marty's gaze. "Holy shit. 'Scuse the language, Miss Jay. You're right, Marty, it's a camel."

"Hump looks odd."

"That's 'cause someone's ridin' it. And there's a big old bay stallion chasing after them. Never saw a horse staggerin' around like it's gonna fall flat on its muzzle."

Juliette clutched Carville's sleeve, wishing she could yank the spyglass out of his hand and look for herself, but the way she was shaking, she'd probably just drop it in the dust. "The rider—he's wearing armor, isn't he?"

"Huh?"

"Armor. Chain mail. Shiny, like silver. Or maybe a little bit rusty."

"Naw. He's just got on britches and a funny leather vest. Got a passel of hair, though, and looks like he's swearin' up a storm at that damn camel. . . ."

Carville continued offering a description, but she didn't hear any of it. She shrieked "Ha!" at him and yanked her reins free, and then couldn't hear anything over the drumming of her horse's hooves and her own voice screaming Geoffrey's name as she raced to meet him.

Too much space separated them when her horse skidded to a stop from aversion to the camel. The camel stopped from what looked like pure cussedness. Juliette felt frozen in place herself, unable to move for fear that the man facing her would dissipate like a dream at dawn.

"Juliette." Geoffrey's voice broke. She could see the smooth column of his throat work, framed as it was by the leather thong holding his Celtic pendant. When he drew a deep breath, she did, too.

"Hold well away from this vile, spitting beast."

It seemed important that she joke with him as she dismounted; otherwise, she might just burst into sobbing incoherence and fling herself at him, knocking him from his unsteady perch. "Which do you mean, Geoffrey—the camel, or American soldiers?"

He smiled then, a glorious sight that seemed to lend added radiance to the sun-washed day, as she knew he would for all her days.

"It seems I must needs change my opinion of American soldiers, they have done such a fine job of holding you safe for me."

He pummeled the camel's hump with his heels while shouting something exotically incomprehensible. To her amazement, the camel pitched facefirst to its knees, and then lowered its rear haunches—but Geoffrey reached her side before the camel uttered a final, baleful sigh and set about waiting, chewing its cud.

Geoffrey enveloped her, his arms wound tight, his lips warm and urgent against hers while his hands pressed her close. Her skin would bear the pendant's imprint, but she didn't care. He had promised he would hold her and never let her go. He rocked slightly and shivered, as she realized with stunned amazement that her own faith had been greater than his own. But it didn't matter. He had promised they would spend eternity together, and they would.

"That camel understood you." She reveled in his possessive clasp, and wished she could burrow right into his skin.

"Saracen commands. Lent me many advantages during the camel races over those who scorned to learn the infidel's tongue."

"Camel races?"

"To relieve the boredom during crusade. Besieging is a tiresome business. I relish knowing I've seen the last of it."

His embrace remained constant. There was only one position which might have brought them closer, and

Juliette knew they would find it when soldiers and camels weren't watching their every movement. But for now it felt beyond wonderful to have him simply hold her, to feel his heart pounding against her breast and know he found himself as unwilling as she to put so much as a hairbreadth of space between them.

He lifted her and crossed the few steps to the camel's far side. He leaned back against the animal's hump, sliding down until his back rested against the patient beast, without ever once relaxing his embrace. They were effectively shielded from prying eyes, which was a very good thing, considering the shocking intimacy of their position. She felt his body harden, but he made no effort to kiss or touch her. He just kept holding her, holding her, and Juliette knew she had never felt so thoroughly loved in all her life.

"Angus Ōg missed the mark by setting you down so far away. We left that canyon days ago."

"And forged a trail any half-blind Navajo could follow. Limp-Waddling Duck taught me the most amazing skills whilst guiding me to the chasm."

"You're not wearing your armor."

"I gave it away, to one who will appreciate it well when 'tis worth wearing again. I will need it no longer."

"How can a knight give away his armor?"

If he had not held her so tightly, she might not have noticed the spasm coursing through his limbs. He stilled, by accident or force of will, she could not tell.

"I am no longer a knight. I am a common farmer."

He spoke with such deliberate casualness that she knew it had to cover soul-deep pain. Her own emotions warred within her. This was what she'd thought she'd wanted, to hear him abandon his wild fantasies. So why did she want to cry a protest at hearing him call himself a common farmer?

Because he's not, her mind whispered.

He was her very own champion, his proud head filled with foreign languages and camel races and chivalrous notions of honor and duty; his strong body tempered with scars he didn't care to explain and dedicated to protecting what he loved and held dear.

She wanted desperately to hold on to him, exactly as he was, which meant exploring his sudden spurning of the past.

"Geoffrey, what happened while you were gone?"

His sigh tickled her scalp. "Everything. And nothing, since you were not there. My mind was so beset with worry and longing for you that I moved about as though in a horrific dream. I know who I am and what I have done, and yet . . . even now I am torn between wonder and disbelief to realize that matters which once loomed large in my thoughts are so diminished that they might have belonged to another man."

"Tell me."

"I will say this once, and then nevermore speak of it, Juliette. I accomplished all that I was sworn to do. In reward, my liege relieved me of my oath to him. So it is done, and we need never refer to my past again."

Tears pricked her eyes; she wasn't sure why. "You'll have to do a better job of explaining than that."

It took so long for him to respond that she thought he might refuse altogether, but eventually he spoke.

"Very well, although I seem to have lost my taste for boasting. I shall reserve the gruesome portions of the accounting, as such is not fit for ladies' ears. Suffice it to say that my return to the year of our Lord 1283 brought about the resolution of a number of border disputes. I also saved King Edward from certain death, thus ensuring the future of England."

Reality—or foggy dream-spun delusions? She clung

tight to him, remembering how she'd prayed, how she'd dreamed of his return, knowing her world would never be safe and whole without him in it. Considering the odds against it happening, who was to say his dream was any more outrageous than her own?

"The king himself promised that my exploits would be chronicled in a book. I daresay you will have read all about it, if you have opened that letter sent by your Professor Burns."

"Oh, that letter. I lost it." She swallowed against the ache in her throat.

He was silent for a moment, and then he laughed, a self-deprecating sound one might make at finding himself the butt of a practical joke.

Or at finding himself unexpectedly relieved of continuing an elaborate lie.

She resolved never to let such doubt enter her mind, ever again.

"If you love me, Juliette, you will join me in turning my back on the past. No more tales of knights and quests and traveling across the centuries. I mean to make my mark as Geoffrey d'Arbanville, farmer. With Juliette, my lady wife."

"Oh, Geoffrey." She pushed her face against his shoulder, and knew that tears soaked through to his skin. "I feel like you're giving up things that are so important to you, and I don't know if it's right."

"I will tell you these most important things about myself. You should know that I love children, and am overfond of dogs and high-spirited horses, and would delight in filling our home with dozens of each."

He caught her chin in his fingers and tipped her face up to his. His gaze smoldered—with passion, with understanding, with absolute honor and integrity that promised a safe haven for her love, starting at that very moment.

"I will love and cherish you, my lady, for as long as there is breath in our bodies, or room in heaven for our souls."

"And I, you." She pressed even closer, so close that she knew there was no room for doubt between them. "But Geoffrey—*dozens* of dogs and horses?"

"And children. Which means we must needs shed ourselves of that soldierly presence and begin at once, as the human female body is notoriously slow in doing its part to produce offspring."

"While the male body is regrettably quick?"

"At times, Juliette." He slanted her a wicked grin. "Though there is something to be said for a man waiting nearly six hundred years to achieve his heart's desire. It teaches him a thing or two about taking his time to savor his pleasures."

Epilogue

September 1860

    Juliette balanced baby Geoffrey on one hip and the tray of coffee mugs against the other, all the while doing her best to avoid tripping over the eager puppy tugging at her skirts.

    "Recess, you two," she called to Alma and Geoffrey.

    "My land, look at the time!" Alma blinked her surprise after glancing at the mantel clock. She stuffed her teaching materials into her satchel. "It purely is a pleasure tutoring such an avid student. If you keep up this pace, Geoffrey, you'll be calculating geometry even faster than you learned to read and write. But I'm afraid I'll have to turn down that coffee today, Juliette. Bean and I promised to have dinner with the Wilcoxes. Robbie's real anxious to introduce us to his new baby sister."

    Juliette didn't pay much attention to Alma's departure. She watched her husband ease his book closed and lean back in his chair until it tipped onto its rear legs.

She doubted she'd ever still the impulse to reach out and steady him for fear he'd send the chair toppling.

She knew she would *never* get over the blushing delight she felt every time he swept her with his bold, possessive glance.

"What does the babe chew upon?" Geoffrey asked when Alma had left and they sat across the table from each other, he sipping his coffee, Juliette unable to swallow.

"It's a letter. From Professor Burns. It appears he sent it from London, England."

On that day when they'd leaped the canyon, she had warned him that doubts might occasionally plague her. None had, until this letter came bearing the word *London,* calling to mind thoughts of universities . . . and theaters. A professor could research history in Oxford's hallowed halls, or he could discover the truth about a man who might have spent the better part of his life acting on the stage.

Geoffrey would notice her preoccupation; he noticed everything.

"Aha. It took him a full year and a trip round the world to find me out."

A tide of dread swept through her, tightening around her throat so she couldn't speak, couldn't demand an explanation of Geoffrey's enigmatic statement.

He took more coffee, and with the utter absorption that marked nearly everything he did, he studied the baby's toothless gnawing. "I would have you take it from him, Juliette, lest it is your intention that he gum it to a pulp."

From silence she burst into babbling. "It won't hurt him. My mama always said it's good for teething. I used to chew paper all the time when I was a little girl." But she disengaged the letter from the baby's grip, and felt like joining him when he wailed a protest. She wouldn't mind, not a bit, if he mangled the letter beyond recognition. She should have given it to one of the puppies, or tossed it into the paddock, so Arion's mares and foals could have churned it into the mud.

"You have not opened your letter."

"No."

"Aha." He tipped the chair again and studied her with brooding intensity, and she wished she'd just crumpled the stupid letter into a ball and burned it in the stove.

"I love you, Geoffrey." She sensed a desperate edge to her voice, and a brief flicker of his eyes told her he noticed it. "I've never felt more alive, more in love, than I have during this past year. You have cherished me, and proven yourself trustworthy in every way. You have protected this town and earned the affection of our neighbors without resenting or dishonoring the memory of my first husband. You are my very own prairie knight, and I couldn't bear it if some . . . some reminder of your past put a chink in your armor. It doesn't matter what the letter says. It doesn't matter at all."

"It matters to me, beloved."

She cradled their child against her heart while Geoffrey broke the wax seal, and she watched in vain for any sign of emotion, anything to betray his reaction to the information the letter contained.

"Professor Burns lacks skill with words," he said eventually.

He shook his head before pushing the letter toward her and turning it so she could read it from the tabletop. Tears blurred her vision, so that she saw only half of the words.

"In London for a working vacation . . . international

symposium on the rule of Edward the First . . . tiny volume, concealed within another in the king's personal library . . . your Geoffrey's ancestor . . . an unexplained absence . . . single-handedly defused an insurrection . . . saved the king's life . . . changed the course of history . . . a discovery of great historical significance . . . requires further study. . . ."

She hadn't realized he'd moved, but Geoffrey was standing there to pull her and his son into his arms when she tore her dazed attention away from the letter.

"You're right," she whispered, leaning into his warmth, her lips a breath away from a leather thong that held the Celtic pendant he never removed. "Professor Burns lacks skill with words, but that could stem from lack of information. I think you should write to him with a full firsthand accounting."

"Later, lady wife." He claimed her lips with his kiss, a kiss that ended in muffled laughter from them both when baby Geoffrey howled his outrage at being squashed between them. "Just now I would demonstrate to you my skill for altering the course of history. I have an endeavor in mind which I predict will affect the lives of everyone in this household nine months hence. I love you, my lady."

Juliette shivered with pleasurable anticipation. "That is the one matter I would have you prove to me again and again, Sir Geoffrey."

Glory in the Splendor of Summer with
101 Days of Romance

BUY 3 BOOKS —
GET 1 FREE!

Take a book to the beach, relax by the pool, or read in the most quiet and romantic spot in your home. You can live through love all summer long when you redeem this exciting offer from HarperMonogram.

Buy any three HarperMonogram romances in June, July, or August, and get a fourth book sent to you FREE!

Look for details of this exciting promotion in the back of each HarperMonogram published from June through August—and fall in love again and again this summer!

Say You Love Me by Patricia Hagan

Beautiful Iris Sammons always turned heads and was doted upon by her parents, whereas her fraternal twin sister Violet was the quiet one. An attack on their caravan by Comanche separated them irrevocably, but their legacies were forever entwined through their children, and through the love that ultimately bound them.

Promises to Keep by Liz Osborne

Cassie McMahon had always dreamed of a reunion with the father she hadn't seen since she was a child. When her hopes were dashed by his distant manner, she found consolation in the arms of a mysterious but seductive stranger. But Alec Stevens was a man with a secret mission. Could he trust his heart to this irresistible woman?

Cooking Up Trouble by Joanne Pence

In their third outrageous outing, professional cook Angelina Amalfi and San Francisco police inspector Paavo Smith team up at the soon-to-be-opened Hill Haven Inn. Soon they encounter mischief in the form of murders and strange, ghostly events, convincing Angie that the only recipe in this inn's kitchen is the one for disaster.

Sweet Deceiver by Angie Ray

Playing a risky game by spying for English and French intelligence at the same time, Hester Tredwell would do anything to keep her struggling family out of a debtor's prison. Her inventive duplicity was no match, however, for the boldly seductive maneuvers of handsome Nicholas, Marquess of Dartford.

Lucky by Sharon Sala

If Lucky Houston knows anything, it's dealing cards. So when she and her two sisters split up, the gambler's youngest daughter heads for Las Vegas. She is determined to make it on her own in that legendary city of tawdry glitter, but then she meets Nick Chenault, a handsome club owner with problems of his own.

Prairie Knight by Donna Valentino

A knight in shining armor suddenly appeared on the Kansas prairie in 1859! The last thing practical and hardworking Juliette needed was to fall in love with an armor-clad stranger claiming to be a thirteenth-century mercenary knight. Though his knight's honor and duty demanded that he return to his own era, Juliette and Geoffrey learned that true love transcends the bounds of time.

COMING SOON

Someday Soon by **Debbie Macomber**

A beautiful widow unwillingly falls for the worst possible new suitor: a man with a dangerous mission that he must complete—even if it means putting love on hold. Another heartwarming tale from bestselling author Debbie Macomber.

The Bride Wore Spurs by **Sharon Ihle**

When Lacey O'Carroll arrives in Wyoming as a mail-order bride for the unsettlingly handsome John Winterhawke, she is in for a surprise: he doesn't want a wife. But once the determined Lacey senses his rough kindness and simmering hunger for her, she challenges Hawke with a dark passion of her own.

Legacy of Dreams by **Martha Johnson**

Gillian Lang arrives at Lake House, a Victorian resort hotel in upstate New York, determined to get answers to questions about the past that have haunted her. As she is drawn to the hotel's owner Matt O'Donnell, her search for the truth unfolds a thirty-year-old tragedy involving both their families and ignites a dangerous passion that could lead to heartbreak.

Bridge to Yesterday by **Stephanie Mittman**

After falling from a bridge in Arizona, investigator Mary Grace O'Reilly is stunned to find she has been transported one hundred years into the past to help hell-raising cowboy Sloan Westin free his son from an outlaw gang. They face a perilous mission ahead, but no amount of danger will stop them from defying fate for the love of a lifetime.

Fool of Hearts by **Terri Lynn Wilhelm**

Upon the untimely death of her father, Lady Gillian finds herself at the mercy of her mysterious new guardian Calum, Marquess of Iolar. While each attempts to outwit the other to become sole heir to her father's fortune, they cannot resist the undeniable desire blazing between them. A witty and romantic novel.

The Lady and the Lawman by **Betty Winslow**

Amanda is ready to do whatever it takes to uncover the mystery behind her father's death—even live in a brothel in a rugged backwater town in Texas. More disturbing than her new lodgings is the undercover Texas Ranger assigned to help her, with his daring and hungry kisses proving to be the most dangerous obstacle of all.

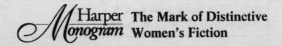